BIG BEN

TIM BRADY & MELANIE WILLEMS

BIG BEN

First published in Great Britain 2011

Copyright © 2011 Tim Brady and Melanie Willems

Published by Tim Brady and Melanie Willems

Paperback ISBN 978-0-9567919-0-0

1 3 5 7 9 10 8 6 4 2

Printed in Great Britain by CPI Mackays Ltd

Typeset by Alison Padley

www.melandtimbooks.com

"Home is heaven, and orgies are vile
But you need an orgy, once in a while"

Ogden Nash

1

Welcome to London

"Move on, girl! You might have been hot 30 pounds ago, but you are one overweight overeater – and he is so over you!"

Crystal chuckled as she remembered her remark, ignoring what a poor show it was to laugh at one's own jokes.

She had walked into the Ministry of Sound on Kerwin's arm the night before. It had been a great entrance. She *had* stopped traffic. She had somehow managed – for once – to take full advantage of her height and her natural flamboyance. She had looked, or perhaps only felt, like an African goddess. The short white dress glittered, the lights caught on her discus earrings, and she did not fall over on her Eiffel tower heels. For a precious, privileged moment, it had been all about her. Eyes followed her like predators looking for supper.

Her retort had been the end of a girls' spat. Over Kerwin, no less. The satisfaction of finally slapping down that Amber Bluett (who, when she was thin, used to look like a short Elle McPherson), was just too good. Amber had thought she could outshine Crystal Smith. *As if!* That

Essex tart in last year's shoes walking the path to plus size had lost her man, and Crystal had won.

Of course Crystal had had to then apologise to Amber for her javelin remark. That was the way these things went. Crystal *had* to be Amber's friend. Amber got on all the best guest lists – somehow. Crystal had therefore long followed where Amber led. But it went without saying that the foundation of their friendship was less than sturdy.

It wasn't all bad. Both women enjoyed genuine moments of shared fun and laughter – usually at someone else's expense. However, the convenience of having a friend to share shopping and clubbing cohabited with jealousy, resentment and out-and-out rivalry. This led, via the spat over Kerwin, to the retort. The retort which could not be unsaid. But could perhaps be concealed under a thick layer of kiss and makeup.

That's why Crystal had been out tonight. After yesterday's bitch fest, she'd made the long call to Amber (*"I didn't know what I was saying! I'm sorry, hon. You know I'd had a few."*). They had arranged to meet, said sorry again in several saccharine ways, hugged and wiped away the tears, before the other girls had thankfully arrived.

Their gaggle of blonde friends seemed so sweet and tinsely at first. But they weren't. They were sharp-edged baubles, getting smashed. The attractiveness of the group was a mirage. It evaporated in short order as you approached the palm trees. Half a dozen bottles of Lambrini came and went. Before long the girls were screeching and caterwauling. A posse of yowling territorial cats would, in complete feline unanimity, abandon the territory to them.

The rest of the bar was glad and relieved when the group decided it was time to go home.

The fun was over. Now there was the long and rather dark, cold walk home to contend with.

The silence and cool air in the back streets felt strange after the fuggy atmosphere of a drinking den. Surrounded by concrete and inadequate street lighting, the rare passers-by scurried past, eyes averted.

Hurrying down the alley towards her flat, Crystal heard footsteps behind her.

She was still nervous when walking on her own in the dark in London. The pavements were uneven and treacherous for a woman in full nightclub gear. One obvious danger lay in her shoes. The leather fiends were a challenge, some way ahead of any threat posed by an actual physical aggressor. These shoes were not made for walking, still less for any panicked, flailing run. Crystal dismissed her creeping fears by picturing herself wielding her fake Jimmy Choos like a twenty-first century heroine would, hardily impaling her attacker with a stiletto. If only. *If only you could get one off in time*. There would be the straps to contend with first. Difficult, and fiddly, after all that Lambrini.

The footsteps were gaining on her. "Stop being stupid", she thought. Surely they could see her Fendi bag wasn't real. But then, neither were her breasts, and she had noticed many a covetous look aimed in their direction.

"Excuse me. Have you got a light?"

As Crystal turned round, someone pushed her hard and she fell to the ground. Someone hit her, hard. She started screaming as the fake Fendi was ripped from her arm.

Blows rained. Then, as the muggers ran off, she fainted.

"Ladies and gentlemen, welcome to London. We have now landed at Heathrow Airport."

Ben Barlettano couldn't quite believe it. There, at last.

He was not quite sure he could uncurl from his economy seat. He felt as if he had set like a giant Jello, and that he would have to remain in this awkward bent shape for ever. But on the plus side, he was now in London. All the way from New York, and not so much as a rosebud in his black hair.

He stared through the small window at the vast expanse of aviation kingdom stretching out before him. The skies were battleship grey – soon to be black as a goth's wardrobe.

Of course he'd been to London before. The first time, he was sixteen. Although he'd tried to absorb the atmosphere, he had been rather more absorbed in Claire Mendez. Obsessed, in fact. You never forget your first obsession. Most of the boys at school shared his painful enthusiasm. Her Majesty's city was a mere backdrop to Ben's teenage libido.

What an excitement it had all been. Everything had been twisted into sexual innuendo, with Her Majesty Queen Claire at its heart. He thought at the time that he wouldn't mind being her Beefeater. Happy days. There was no mad cow disease around then. Where was Claire now, he wondered.

On Ben's next visit, three years later, he had vowed he would take in the sights. But he was with the guys. The football guys. Who knew there were so many pubs in London? He liked that it was easier for a nineteen year old to get a drink than a gun.

He sighed. Time had flown between nineteen and twenty-six. Third time lucky?

When Ben found out that he had got the secondment from New York to the London office of international law firm SKB, his mother Claudia naturally did what all good Italian mothers would. Upon hearing his wonderful news, she beamed from ear to ear, soaking up the reflected glory of her son's success. Then, after patting his cheeks and smoothing his hair, she burst into tears.

The time was ripe for a spot of old-fashioned emotional blackmail.

Claudia moved with a theatrical flourish to the window. "Cosa faccio da sola?" she moaned dramatically.

As if Claudia would ever be alone, between her art exhibitions, lunch parties and of course her tennis lessons with Cody, an awesome jock from Orange County with abs as hard as his calculating little eyes. *As if!* Cody was waiting for Mrs Barlettano even as they spoke. Ben had timed his career revelation carefully, as he thought this would limit the opportunity for the emotional discussion to develop into a full-blown act.

Ben adored his mother and knew the score for the opera scenes, too. This was his cue to go to her, hug her and start crying with her, telling her that the Atlantic between them would do nothing to change how much he loved his Mamma. But then again, it was so much less embarrassing to stay calm, and keep a safe distance. He made placatory noises, advising her to get out there and focus on her serve, giving Cody a nice big tip, in the hopes of Cody reciprocating with his nice big tip. Claudia Barlettano would probably benefit from a few "extras" now and again. Ones that didn't involve shopping, flower arranging or criticising ex-husbands over a charity lunch.

Ben could not remember how he had extricated himself from the scene, but he had survived the operatic adieux and made good his escape. Leaving might have been hard if it did not seem to offer so much in exchange. Freedom. Travel. Change. A whole new world of women to discover. It is not only the preserve of politicians to trip on these.

He stepped up to Heathrow's passport control desk with butterflies in his stomach. *Yes I am legitimate but oh, you make me feel like such a miscreant.* Glancing around he wondered, not for the first time, how anybody illegal ever made it through any border these days. Clearly they did. So what were the stats? Did they come legally, and disappear? Did they creep over the bits of border unmanned by mannish ladies? Did they hide? All three, no doubt.

"What is the purpose of your trip to the UK?"

"A work secondment."

The joy of immigration. The woman on the next desk along looked kindly and greeted everyone with a smile. His woman had perfected the art of the forbidding scowl. It seemed unnecessary. His visa was in order.

He wondered what would happen if he casually asked her why she was being such a bitch. Did she hate men? Or just human beings in general? Had she had her heart broken? Maybe she had simply been born with the gift of making her interlocutors feel like cockroaches partying on a favourite cake. He thought of letting her know that she made him feel like going back to the US.

Finally, she stamped his passport. Not a moment too soon: Ben felt as he if had been growing roots. Time to scarper, as they said over here. Before she could open her mouth again, he moved quickly on.

She leaned after him:

"Excuse me, sir?"

The harpy wasn't done yet. This time he was ready. He swivelled with a face like Mount Rushmore in winter.

She gave him a kindly smile:

"I think you've dropped something."

His headphones were lying on the floor behind him. He hadn't noticed he'd lost them. He thanked the ex-harpy, who actually nodded at him, and said she hoped he had a lovely time living in London. He smiled back guiltily. She wasn't so bad after all. Books. Covers. Hmmmm. Maybe he did sometimes rush to judge people too quickly.

After the usual wait during which the passenger idly imagines the contents of his bags spread like roadkill all over the runway, Ben's suitcases appeared from the mouth of the baggage carousel. They were among the first to appear, largely intact, only a little bashed up. An unexpected pleasure, a rare feature of travel, and a good sign. Why such random matters lift spirits the way they do is anyone's guess, but Ben felt that some non-existent God was at least not flicking grape pips his way. Yet.

He eyed a coffee bar on the way out but decided to get going.

He left the warmth of the airport cocoon. It was now quite late and night had fallen. Lights twinkled all around him. The cool air caught at his cheeks. The taxi queue was not too long – another nice surprise. It gave the illusion of control. Ben had no idea how extraordinarily expensive a London cab from the airport is. A beginner's mistake.

"Can I go to The Castle Lofts, SE1 please? It's on the – er – Fernberry Road."

The Castle Lofts. He'd forgotten to Google Earth the building before he left. A castle. He'd heard the expression "an Englishman's home is his castle", but he hadn't expected to be living in one himself. How... *posh*. He would need to get used to that word too, apparently. He was going to be living just one mile from Big Ben. Ben didn't know SE1, but he loved SW1 and couldn't wait to feast his eyes on all those marvellous Georgian terraces. And, according to the itinerary provided by the firm, there was supposed to be a welcoming committee of the existing trainee solicitors who lived in the Lofts. He wouldn't want to show it to his new colleagues, but it made him feel special.

"Which castle is it in SE1?"

He didn't catch the driver's reply in full. He could not really understand the driver at all – but reasoned that, as he knew the address, the rest did not matter. It sounded as if he had said something about an elephant and then started to snigger. Maybe it was better to wait for the surprise, and just enjoy his trip into town.

By the time he'd reached anything looking like a London dwelling, Ben was staring guiltily at the taxi meter. *This could be claimed on the firm.*

He'd asked the driver to go through the West End. He couldn't wait to see Piccadilly Circus again – especially on a Friday evening.

It hadn't changed. The neon lights still flickered in their own commercial rave. As ever there seemed to be two tribes present – the tourists and the Londoners. The out-of-towners wandered aimlessly, blocking pavements, photographing Eros, and thoroughly enjoying just being there – a flock of contented sheep, visiting and re-visiting a familiar field. Then there were the Londoners, intent on their destination (mostly alcohol-related) and good-naturedly cursing the sheep blocking their paths. The energy was palpable through the cab windows.

The cab reached Trafalgar Square. Ben craned his neck to stare up at the statue of Nelson. *"That is an honour,"* he thought, *"to be placed so far above the most important square in the most important city in one of the most important countries of the day, looking down, surveying all beneath you."* An edifying thought. But that was the 1800s. In the twenty-first century, reality was defecating pigeons and most people thinking your surname was Mandela.

Big Ben and Parliament Square were followed by the thrill of crossing the Thames. Not that he particularly liked Baroness Thatcher, but he did enjoy her joke of finally acquiescing to a tunnel linking her beloved island nation to the old enemy, yet ensuring that the train from Paris should arrive at Waterloo. Things must have been so much more fun when the French were regularly getting assaulted by "la dame de fer" with that handbag.

As he approached Waterloo, Ben felt the excitement

getting to him. The cabbie mumbled something about *not far now, guv*. The lights of London on the Thames were beautiful. It could not be more different from New York. It seemed almost another form of society, where tradition and custom mattered more. He loved the history of Europe, and could not believe he'd be living in the midst of it. In a castle.

It's funny how feelings can change.

South of the river, there was a great deal of concrete to contend with.

There was no castle in these parts.

Reality bit, hard. It was·sudden, and unexpected. Things felt as if they were rather crashing down around Ben's ears. His mood swung low like a corpse on a gibbet. After some inoffensive, if somewhat nondescript buildings, there followed what could only be described – charitably – as blocks produced by architects who must have had way too much fun in the sixties. Maybe concrete and pebbledash looked really cool on LSD? It was really rather ugly around these parts.

The taxi drew to a stop, chugging away diesel-ly to itself like a large exhausted donkey.

"Here you go, mate."

Where was the castle? The driver had pulled up in front of a dully lit, large, drab concrete box. He must have seen Ben's look of bemusement, as he then explained again, more slowly and deliberately this time, that the castle referred to the Elephant & Castle, the name of this area of London. Far from being a real castle, it was a bright red shopping centre stuck between two large roundabouts.

The only Beefeater to be seen was a picture on a rather awful looking restaurant with photographs of the food on a plastic menu outside.

He paid the cab (*"How much? Oh, well – I'll expense it."*) and made his way to the unappealing entrance.

Two police cars were parked outside the grey box. As Ben walked towards the front door, a rather stern-looking policeman stormed past him followed by a female officer whose face indicated a largely citrus-based diet. What had happened to the friendly British Bobby?

Ben followed them through the revolving door. There was some blood on the glass. Not a mood enhancer, blood on glass. In fact, a veritable shaker of faith. What was he doing in this god-forsaken town? The place was fast losing its shimmer. He wondered if he had made the right decision in coming to England.

An older, still handsome and distinguished man stepped towards him.

"Welcome to London, Mr Barlettano."

Arthur Bilks had seen a lot of eager young Americans arrive. Little legal juniors, all keen as mustard, and green as grass. But he didn't normally have to explain that a woman had just been mugged outside the building and that the welcome party was comforting the victim. For a big lad this one looked pretty nervous. Another one of those University types more at home in a library, or on a playing field, than in a city. He'd need watching out for.

"What happened?"

Ben listened as Arthur Bilks told him that a girl had been *"jumped by two hoodies"*. They'd knocked her to the ground, grabbed her bag, and then run off. A few moments ago Ben had been staring at Nelson, Big Ben and Her Majesty's Parliament. Now he was in the "Elephant & Castle" – an area with neither elephants nor castles – but seemingly rich in hooded thugs attacking poor girls. What sort of sick joke was SKB playing on him?

"Were they caught on CCTV?"

Ben had read that the British were the most observed people on the planet. What were the numbers, again – still resisting the continentals' beastly ID cards, but happy to be filmed on average six hundred and thirty-seven times a day, all in the name of good old security? The clever ones found a way around it. Like wearing hoods. Super clever, that. Well, effective, at least.

Arthur eyed up the new tenant.

"Your workmates are in Flat 412. It's on the seventh floor. Here: I'll grab your luggage. I have a pass key – I'll stick your bags in the entrance of your flat."

The small party to welcome Ben to London was probably another victim of the hoodies. Although tall and broad, Ben lacked self-confidence sometimes. He was starting to feel depressed at being outshone by a mugging. A little unfair and completely irrational, but perhaps understandably, in the circumstances, he felt that his arrival had been hijacked. *"Just get in the elevator,"* he told himself.

With his spirits dashed like the pebbles on the walls outside, he turned left out of the lift as Arthur had told him to, and stopped dead.

Well.

This was worth a look. This was a concrete box with a

view. He could see Parliament, the London Eye, St Paul's and in the distance Canary Wharf twinkled at him, like a mini Houston. He suddenly remembered why he had come to England. For adventure, as much as for a career move.

He found Flat 412 down a clinically white corridor, with a drab carpet. Squaring his shoulders, he knocked on the door. The door swung open to reveal a gabbling excited group, enjoying the drama in a brightly lit room.

"Oh my gosh, you must be Ben. I'm Kelly. Kelly Danvers."

There she was. The girl. There was always going to be a girl. You can't go anywhere, really, without meeting someone who grabs your attention, especially when you're twenty-six. What a girl. Ben's eyes widened as he took her in. Bright. Light. Tight. Brunette. In turn, her gaze arrested him and took down his particulars, in a curious but seemingly interested way. Her eyes were alive and dancing. He suddenly felt wide awake.

Chemistry was a beautiful thing.

Kelly explained that she had been supposed to meet Ben in reception, but when poor Crystal (*"She's been mugged!"*) tottered in, she (Kelly) had completely forgotten and brought her upstairs to look after her. Ben found her torrent of words entertaining: she talked so fast, and with a marked Southern accent. He grinned and nodded as she speed-talked him through recent events. He got the gist of it, but Ben was noticing Kelly Danvers' smile. It was perfect. It warmed the room. There was always something about a truly genuine smile. She wore the most stunning, daring red lipstick. Part naughty schoolmistress, part

French maid, and although he didn't know it at the time, a distant relation of Carol Vorderman.

She turned away, and he checked out her body. As any guy would. It was nice. Everything about it appealed. It seemed taut and coiled, as if she could sprint very fast or dance all night, at the drop of a pin. She had energy. She was going somewhere, or was, at least, about to introduce him to the others.

"Guys. Guys, this is Ben."

There were a dozen people in the room. The girl Ben supposed was Crystal sat in the middle, like the rhinestone in an oversized ring. The bandage round her calf kind of gave it away. Her sequinned miniskirt and low-cut top reminded Ben that he wasn't in SW1.

Ben went over and said hello, in the deeply concerned voice that he produced when faced with the unexpected and unfortunate. Eyes widening at his wholly acceptable looks and apparent sympathy, Crystal immediately asked him to sit with her. Amber, her kindly looking larger friend, gave him her seat. Crystal started to sob again; she couldn't understand why anybody could do something like that, just for a Fendi bag. Ben agreed, thinking that if the bag was anything like the rest of the outfit it was indeed a quite inexplicable crime. He could feel himself glazing over, as he nodded earnestly, desperately trying to convey sympathy as Crystal bleated on. For all his lack of confidence, Ben abhorred girls who threw themselves at him, especially when tears were part of the act. He started to feel empathy for the muggers.

Amber needed refuelling:

"Can I get you two a drink?"

Crystal's friend with the kind smile meant well, but Ben was not going to have one of the few safety lines ripped away from him like that. He needed a drink big time, but he also needed to go and get it himself. He told the girls he had to pick up his key from Kelly and go and check his bags in his flat, but that he would be right back.

He wandered over to Kelly, who was chattering away like a Gatling gun.

"Kelly, sorry – but do you have my key?"

He was relieved to hear that she did, and that he really did have his own flat in the Castle Lofts. Having escaped the immediate clutches of rampant sympathy-craving womanhood, he decided he could safely have a drink before retreating. Amber, who had appeared in the kitchen, thankfully *sans* Crystal, gave him a big smile. She passed him a large glass of what looked like orange-coloured beer with ice.

Ben held the glass up to the light:

"What is it?"

He'd never had a Vodka Red Bull. Amber told him it was the best drink ever. You didn't get too drunk, you didn't get tired, and it was legal. She called it "Ecstasy Light". Ben drank thankfully. It was a bit sweet and he couldn't really taste any alcohol.

Thirty minutes later, already onto his third, the conversation was flowing as fast as the liquor. Ben was now thoroughly enjoying his "*welcome to London*" party. He wasn't to know that Vodka Red Bull would prove to be a lifelong passion. He hadn't yet had it with a slice of lime, never mind mixed with half a flute of Veuve Clicquot. He had no idea that a whole wealth of otherwise mediocre conversations would become fascinating with the aid of this magical potion.

Amber was short and a little large, but she was such a sweet girl. She didn't work at SKB, mind you – but she was looking after him so well. He'd forgotten about the victim-girl with no bag, until Amber excused herself to go and check on poor Crystal.

Ben felt strong, happy and at ease. He talked to the other trainees, and time flew.

Kelly materialised by his side.

"So – do you want to see your flat then?"

He would like to see the guy who could say no to Kelly's smile. The party was winding down. He drained his glass, and followed her out the door, into the beige carpeted corridor. There were many of these corridors in the block, twisting and turning geometrically. The Lofts were enormous, like a wannabe spaceship.

Kelly explained that there were four residential blocks. A central building in the gardens housed a gym, swimming pool, saunas, steam rooms and café. Kelly recommended the café. She said the food was interesting, but good. She added that it was a great spot to meet up – it encouraged you to use the gym, too.

Despite its cosmetic challenges, this concrete box was getting better and better. Kelly told Ben that she had been at SKB in London for a little over a year. She shared her flat with a Fashion PR called Monique who was over in Paris seeing her family for the weekend.

"Here you are. Flat 80, The Castle Lofts. Your home, sir."

Ben could not imagine ever getting bored of the thrill of entering a new home for the first time. This was his first time in his own flat abroad. He felt a shiver of pure glee run down his spine as he turned the key. Or maybe it was the alcohol and the fact that he was taking Kelly Danvers into it. No, he would not let himself be taken captive by base instincts.

The flat was painted a deep terracotta colour, and had wooden floors throughout, with some large brightly coloured ethnic rugs – red and orange patterns. It had two bedrooms and nice big windows, as well as an enormous mirror in the main room. It seemed very clean and well kept – every cupboard opened silently offering something useful and functional. It seemed quite big, empty as it was, with nothing personal breaking up the space, or cluttering the surfaces.

"Well? Do you like your bachelor pad, then?"

He couldn't tell if Kelly was flirting with him or not. Ben wanted her to be. He wanted to throw his arms round her, drag her to the bed and let his alcohol-fuelled libido take over. He wondered what she looked like, naked. Instead of stripping her, Ben replied that he loved the minimalist lines, and, although he was only on the third floor, he liked the view of the Elephant & Castle shopping centre. Judging by the look of bemusement on her face, he probably should have gone with the libido option.

They stood around a little awkwardly as they finished the reconnaissance of the premises.

"How do you think Crystal will be?" Ben asked.

Privately Ben wondered if Crystal had been mugged at all and wasn't just milking the attention for all it was worth. He decided to share some of these thoughts. "The crying didn't seem that genuine to me", he said, just managing to stop himself from adding that the tears were as fake as Crystal's tan and tits.

Kelly was more sympathetic and made more civilised noises about the situation, which made Ben feel guilty.

"Apparently the poor girl had just been out for a quiet drink with friends, and out of nowhere she was jumped and thrown to the ground. It's rather alarming, to say the least" mused Kelly. Hence the blood on the door, thought Ben. He wanted to say that it was a shame they hadn't stolen her hideous clothes as well, but maybe Kelly would get the wrong idea. He cast around for a safer topic:

"Amber seems a really sweet girl."

Not trusting himself on the subject of Crystal, Ben focused his thoughts on her friend. He asked Kelly what Amber did and found out she was a nurse. She had come into her own tonight, neatly bandaging the scratches and scrapes on the afflicted leg. Ben smiled. He'd liked that girl from the start; he felt that he had an instinct for genuine people. The contrast between Amber and Crystal had hit him like a London bus. Even though she didn't excite the libido like Kelly did with her smile, he wanted to see more of big Amber. He told Kelly that he thought Crystal was fortunate to have a friend like Amber.

"Aha. You're into voluptuous blonde women, then, are you, Ben?"

He wasn't expecting that. He mumbled something idiotic about Amber just being a caring girl with a good sense of humour. Kelly laughed and told him she was only kidding and that she should get back to her flat.

"We know a nice place for brunch on the South Bank. Let's catch up tomorrow. My cell phone number's on my card – here you go. Sorry you've had a rougher landing than expected. But this is not the norm. Most Saturdays pass without blood-letting. Sleep tight."

She seemed to be gone very quickly. That was the drink speeding things up.

After walking round his piece of the castle a few times, Ben thought he would indulge a guilty pleasure – the occasional cigarette.

It was bad. It was very bad. He disapproved of himself. He took a packet of Marlboro Lights out of his case, found a lighter, his keys, and headed downstairs to the garden.

Now that he was inside the box, he rather liked it. He wanted to see what it had to offer. The discovery of its manifold secrets beckoned. The gym complex sounded great – as an originally skinny kid, working out had been an important part of his life for some time.

It was quiet now.

Ben felt peaceful and content as he stepped into the cool night air.

He saw someone walking in front of him. The shape looked familiar. A bit on the spherical side. It was Amber. One of the few people he was ready to see, he thought, with a smile. She hadn't seen him, and he was about to go up to her, when he realised that she was on the phone.

Her tone was somewhat different now.

"I deserve an Oscar for my sympathy, babe! You should've seen that cow tonight. Telling everyone that piece of shit bag was a real Fendi. I should leave it in a bin outside the Lofts. Not even a mugger wants that shit. At least the bitch cut her leg when you pushed her over. Next time she opens that big mouth of hers, she'll lose more than a bag. We'll make sure of that. Thanks, bro. No one – no one – disses Amber Bluett and gets away with it."

2

A brazillion reasons to keep fit

Rubens Ribeiro never felt more alive than when he was under the spotlights, with two thousand people watching him do what only a Carioca can do to music.

A good dancer never wants for an audience. The attention always made Rubens' skin tingle. Inhibitions dissolved like soluble vitamin pills. He forgot all his problems and lived in the moment. Intensely. Energetically. He danced for an audience that feasted on him with darkly glittering eyes. Dancing. Twisting and gyrating on the podium – a pedestal for his ego, show time for his statuesque body. He wondered. Was it the glare, was it the music or was it the ecstasy making him feel he loved and was loved by everyone in the world?

He knew there was no chance he'd be going home alone that night. Gabriela, his erstwhile girlfriend had got him started and wangled the job for him. It was what he loved best in life. Well, second best.

Estrella, the latest super club import from Spain, took over the old Landmark Cinema in Elephant & Castle every Saturday night. Rubens was one of the night's stars. He liked to think they loved his natural Brazilian rhythm, but he knew he wouldn't be there without his beautifully sculpted body, olive skin and smouldering good looks. He kind of liked that. He never understood why Gabriela always got offended when men saw her as a sex object. Rubens thought the problem was when people didn't see you as a sex object.

Tonight, Gabriela was wearing a painted on bikini top and one of those micro-thongs which led Brazilians to start needing a Brazilian. They'd met in Rio and it had been love at first sight. His mother immediately planned the wedding and gave thorough consideration to her favourite baby names. But Gabriela's modelling contract had brought her to London, and Rubens couldn't be without her.

He packed up and came over to Europe within two weeks of her departure. He had never been more grateful for his Portuguese grandparents. An EU passport made it all possible. Granted, it had been difficult. It remained difficult. Just because two people are beautiful doesn't mean they don't have their problems. She was always working or at model parties. Rubens felt like a lost boy in a strange big city. He was just Gabriela's boyfriend. Nobody was interested in him. He could feel her slipping away.

Things have a way of turning up, though. In time, Gabriela's agency did a show in Heaven for Gay Pride. Unwillingly, insecurely, a slightly sulky Rubens went along, trailing in her glamourous wake.

It was a new experience all round. Gabriela did not turn too many heads in Heaven. Rubens found that most of the club seemed rather interested in him instead.

Especially after he took his shirt off.

He needed this approval – oh, how he needed it. He felt good, properly good, for the first time since he had arrived in London. He liked all the attention he was getting from the men, particularly from a blue-eyed go-go boy named Karl. Karl had a lot of conviction for a young man. In fact, he had confidence that a con man would envy. There was no small talk or formal introduction. Karl had simply looked over, catching Rubens' gaze. Karl looked Rubens over deliberately, carefully and obviously assessing what he saw in a way that caught at Rubens' lower stomach muscles. Karl looked at Rubens' chest and at his arms, before allowing his gaze to fall squarely and heavily on Rubens' face. Karl's gaze felt like a touch, and his touch, when it came, was electric. When Gabriela had caught them kissing, Rubens knew his life would never be the same again. At that point, he did not know Karl's name, and also did not know that after that one first and only glorious night, after Karl had got what he wanted, he would never bother speaking to Rubens again.

"Hello? Hello! Mr Ben Barlettano? Open the door please!"

Ben came to, groggily. He thought the words "shrill" and "morning" were unhappy bedfellows, especially when combined with "Sunday". Was it normal in London to be punished after a lively Saturday night by the visitation of an evil banshee? He fell out of bed, fumbled his way to the hall, and opened the front door to a diminutive young woman clutching a clipboard.

"I knew you were home, Mr Ben Barlettano. I'm Miss

Pansy Ho, I'm the inventory clerk. Inventory today. Quick, quick, I have other appointment in 20 minutes."

Ho? You could not make it up. It was almost worth getting out of bed for a name like that. Mind you, Pansy looked anything but. She seemed viciously efficient, and there were no smouldering looks around. In his one minute's experience of her, Ben had been wakened by her shrieking, almost had his door broken down, and now was having orders barked at him. She was actually cute and sexy, albeit in a rather intimidating way – the way that women in control are. But Ben was never one to miss a good cliché, or even a potentially useful fantasy image. He took leave of any vestige of political correctness, and visualised Pansy as a stripper in Bangkok. Instead of launching ping pong balls, she would be launching hand grenades, dexterously pulling out the pin at the moment of ignition. And then shrieking with laughter as the grenades blew up those creepy, unpleasant ogling men who had dared to underestimate her. She definitely looked properly in control. He should keep on the right side of her. He didn't want to be on the receiving end of any grenades.

"Mr Ben Barlettano! What a big man you are! I see you are pleased to see me. I will call you Big Ben. But please put on clothes now."

Ben blushed bright red. Still half asleep he'd opened the door in his Calvins. With a semi. He prayed she hadn't noticed and was just referring to the fact he was six foot four and broad.

No such luck.

"Morning Glory, I think it is called, no?"

Another hope scuppered. Beyond embarrassed, Ben wrapped himself in his bathrobe. Businesslike, Pansy thrust a list into his hand and told him to start checking. He hadn't noticed all the marks on the walls and the floor until she pointed them out and carefully noted them on her clipboard.

"Be careful with this flat. You break anything you pay. You leave dirty you pay. Any more marks on floor or wall you pay. I hope you are very happy here. See you when you leave, Mr Ben Barlettano."

And then the noisy awakening disappeared. All that remained was Ben's copy of the inventory and peals of shrill laughter still reverberating around his throbbing head. And a vague thought that he should plan a vacation to Thailand at some point.

Slowly he remembered the night before. Ben still couldn't believe the conversation that he'd overheard. Amber... had organised the mugging? How could he have been so wrong about Amber? Should he tell Kelly? Maybe Crystal deserved a shaking up... No! That would be almost as bad as saying women who look too sexy are inviting rapists. He felt guilty for even having thought it.

He padded to the kitchen and opened cupboards aimlessly, locating in the process a packet of cereal with a post-it affixed to it. "You'll need this. Milk's in the fridge. Kelly." read the yellow tag. He smiled gingerly. That was thoughtful. It could only have predated the spark he hoped she had felt too. She was nice. He grabbed a bowl and the corresponding carton of milk and ate a modern English breakfast – complete with sugar rush.

It helped to achieve a degree of recovery. He still needed some fresh air. He thought about going down for a swim and then sitting in the steam room for a while. He didn't feel able to face lunch and conversation in this state. Yes, he would do it. After draining a pint of water, he went to the bedroom and unpacked his bag.

It was strange seeing his familiar belongings tumbling out into this new, still alien environment. In amongst the shoes and books and sealing wax he found his gym clothes. He threw them on, slightly creased as they were, grabbed his keys and a clean T-shirt and went downstairs.

The corridors were bright. The rumours about English weather seemed unfounded. Sunlight streamed through the occasional window, and Ben called the lift feeling unaccountably cheerful.

The gym was impressive for an English high-rise. Ben merely thought it was a little small, but would do. It was bright and well-lit, with new equipment, large mirrors, good air circulation and a good-looking man standing near the weights. Of course, Ben reminded himself, he could not tell that the man was good-looking. Ben was far too straight for that. But the gym instructor was a remarkable looking man.

Rubens strolled over, with feline grace.

"Hello, stranger. Are you new to The Lofts? I haven't seen you here before."

Ben was impressed that the gym had an instructor on duty on a Sunday morning.

On second thoughts, perhaps the instructor had been on duty on Saturday night, too. He looked overly wide awake and bouncy. This was generally true of gym instructors – but this one had something about his pupils. Ben picked up a restlessness about the man, a possible excess of energy. Ben never really liked gym instructors, especially the Men's Health cover guy ones like Rubens Ribeiro. Ben thought they all so obviously loved themselves. You *had* to love yourself, to get that buff, to care that much.

Such people made Ben feel inadequate. It would be so much easier – or at least possible, within the boundaries of his wildest dreams – to get that shape if he, Ben, were only five foot eight, instead of having his muscle cover over that extra eight inches. Ben consoled himself by thinking that the instructor was probably about as bright as a backward pigeon whose parents had moved about a lot when it was a chick. The man was looking steadily at him. Ben mumbled that he had just moved in the night before.

"Well, you look like you have spent many years in the gym. I'm sure you know exactly what you are doing. But if you want any help – I'll be here."

Had the self-obsessed pigeon brain just paid him a compliment on his physique? Ben smiled meekly and went off to work on his abs.

"So," he thought to himself, glancing at the walled mirrors, "I look like I have spent many years in the gym, do I?"

He felt good about the remark. It didn't really add up – but then again Ben had grown over the last few months into something nearer what he had hoped for all his adolescence. Growing up, Ben had been painfully skinny – dishearteningly so, at times. He always felt as if he was the last to be picked for any team. There had been skirmishes with bullying and being bullied. Acne and the inability to hold any amount of alcohol meant that his had been difficult teenage years. A slight nervous stutter hadn't helped, either.

Although by all accounts Ben was now a fine figure of a man, he still felt like that spotty teenager who was average at sports. He got more attention from women these days, and that was nice, but he still craved the acceptance from the jocks whose approval would have warmed his adolescence. Maybe he should take Pansy Ho's cue. From now on he would think of himself as Big Ben. An unlikely tag, but a hook to lift oneself with – anyway, what was there to lose? He would try.

More pressingly though, how was he going to deal with his dilemma about Amber Bluett and her attack on supposedly close friend Crystal Smith? Pumping iron usually helped him clear his thoughts, but not even the pec deck was helping him today. Was it even Ben's business to get involved? Did he care, one way or the other?

Should he ask Kelly?

He felt a stab of interest at the obvious opening. It was better than saying thank you for the Coco Pops. If nothing else, raising the question of what to do would be a good way of spending time talking to her. He immediately felt the thrill of the ulterior motive. She was hot. Manoeuvering comes easily when lust joins the party. It was not hard to believe that Kelly was probably worth it.

While he was sitting in the steam room forty-five minutes later, his thoughts turned again to Kelly. Pity that this is just for men he thought. Still, the Jacuzzi was unisex. And there was no one around on a Sunday mid morning. He smiled to himself imagining the scene. Time for a shower, he thought. A cold one.

"Excuse me, my friend. Your colleague is in the café waiting for you."

Ben turned round to see Rubens Ribeiro flashing pearly whites at him. The showers were open plan, and the Brazilian seemed quite amused by the Kelly effect. Ben grabbed his towel, covered a lingering tumescence for the second time that day, forced out a smile and a thanks, hoping that the heat of the steam room might provide a cover for his flushed face.

When he came out of the changing room, he saw Kelly and Rubens deep in conversation at the café counter. Rubens had his arm around her. As Ben approached, they started laughing. Rubens hugged her and kissed her on the lips, before walking over to a rather rotund man with rosy cheeks who looked like he needed guidance on how to use the "Super Abdo-flex".

"Ben. Whey-hey. Don't you look the all-American jock today."

Who was paying these people? First a fit Brazilian gym instructor, and now the girl of his fantasies, both massaging his ego in the space of one morning. He gave her a kiss – on the cheek, not being Brazilian – and asked her where they were going for lunch.

"I'm afraid the other two have let us down, so it'll just be you and me. Is that OK?"

That was fine. That was absolutely fine. Ben felt his spirits lift.

It was not long before Kelly and Ben were sitting outside in a tapas restaurant on the South Bank. It had remained a blissful day. There were no clouds, and the city was basking under a wide blue sky. Ben had never been to London in summer before, and was expecting day after day of grey skies with the occasional interlude for drizzle. That wonderful word. The rest of the world used it for a light application of olive oil onto rocket salad. In Britain, apparently, it was the prevailing weather.

Kelly was talking, occasionally glancing over at him to see if she was capturing and keeping his attention.

"I love London in summer," she said. "The city relaxes. It's no longer buttoned up and scowling... desperately trying to keep out the winter wind and rain, and the endless disappointment of the British spring. I always see it as a release for everyone. Finally, uptight Londoners let themselves go, and exhale."

She paused to stare with interest at a couple with alarming piercings and kind faces.

"Normally," she carried on, "it takes these people three pints of lager, or a bottle of Chenin Blanc, to chill. The English are a couple of drinks behind the rest of Europe. By Europe, mind you, they generally mean some hole on the Mediterranean. Most Brits' knowledge of Europe is defined by where My Travel will take them on a frightful package holiday. But when they do let themselves go, it can be fun. They teach the world to party. And there we have it. Contradictory little islanders."

Ben was amused. The word "frightful" was most entertaining in her Southern belle drawl. Ben wasn't used to hearing the word "frightful" very much back in New York. He wondered what other twists of phrase Kelly had picked up in her time in London. Would she use that omnipresent "cheers mate" with which Londoners littered their conversations? Maybe it was more of a man thing. He couldn't imagine using it himself. At least – not yet.

"You're not so keen on the natives then, are you, Kelly?"

"What do you mean? I *love* the British. This is my favourite city in the world. Of course it is full of tossers, but British tossers at least have a sense of humour and don't shoot you before trying to save your soul. You just get a mouthful of rather atrocious grammar, framed by some rather atrocious teeth. You'd have to be fairly unlucky to be on the receiving end of threatening behaviour."

It was always hard to find common ground – and yet so important to find it. You can't shag a discussion, even if a decent argument can fuel passion in unexpected ways. Ben steered the conversation onto smoother ground. In time he would get to know the Council House Armani Versace (CHAV) types Kelly was obliquely referring to, so named because they lived in what Ben knew Americans would call the Projects. Chavs seemed to distinguish themselves by spending their social security on designer clothes, never understated, steering well clear of the risk of being accused of possessing good taste. Thankfully, Ben would also get to know other British tribes.

Ten plates of tapas and four beers later, they were strolling slowly back to the Lofts.

"So do you use the gym often, Kelly?"

"Yes, as much as I can. I've never been that much into fitness, but it's so convenient. It's enormously convenient. And I guess you've met my gorgeous Rubens?"

This was less than satisfactory. So there was something between them. Ben had suspected it from the way they kissed. Damn that perfect Brazilian, with his smooth words and for sure even smoother skin. How could Kelly go for someone who was so obviously superficial? A mono-thought meathead? Ben didn't know Rubens but it was obvious behind the smiling façade, there was one large ego that loved Rubens Ribeiro even more than all the girls in the place. A gym instructor, for crying out loud. Rubens looked more like a male stripper than anything else. Should Ben even be thinking this? He felt jealous.

He wouldn't let on he was jealous. He could – and would – play the game. Ben would be relaxed. He must not show any sign of feeling threatened. It would boil down to perfect self-confidence.

"You couldn't really not notice a guy like that. He kind of makes Brad Pitt look like Colonel Ghaddafi."

"Don't knock the Colonel. Of all the leaders in the world he may yet prove to be one of the ones who were cute when they were younger. But Rubens… "

Kelly was about to say that of course Rubens was gay and that "my Rubens" was just a great girlfriend. But a strange look had passed over Ben's face when she had brought him up. She couldn't quite work out what it was, but it had definitely been there. In passing, like a shadow over the sun.

"So true." she declared instead, "Everyone loves Rubens.

But then, do I blame them?"

Ben was confused. Kelly didn't sound jealous. He guessed she was just that confident herself. Maybe that confidence would help him out with his Amber Bluett dilemma. He decided to leave the annoying Rubens for now and move to the disappointing Amber.

"Kelly, can I tell you something in confidence?"

Kelly wondered what dark secret she was going to find out. She told him that she was very discreet. It wasn't quite true, but she intended to give it a try. She was a little disappointed when Ben started talking about Crystal and her mugging. When it got on to Amber Kelly sparked up again, hoping to get a confession that he liked the larger lady. Perhaps gorgeous Ben was what Rubens would call a chubby chaser? That would be funny.

"Tell me," asked Ben, "how close are Crystal and Amber?"

Kelly really could not see where this was going.

"To be honest, Ben, I don't know them that well – or indeed at all. I have seen Crystal around. I felt sorry for her last night, and Amber is sweet enough, but they are... well, we don't have that much in common. If I am really blunt, I wouldn't really know what to say to them for more than two minutes. I mean, now that the incident is over, it is pretty unlikely that we will be speaking much again."

"OK. Well. That's as much as I might have expected. The thing is, though, after you left me last night, I went down to the courtyard to have a sneaky cigarette."

"A cigarette?" exclaimed Kelly, "All hail the last remaining idiot who wants to die of cancer!"

"Not the last just yet. Yes, I know I am stupid to smoke and should be treated like a leper henceforth – but that's a different point. Listen. Yesterday, I overheard a conversation. Specifically, Amber on the phone telling somone how she had set up the mugging. Oh – and she actually added something along the lines that if Crystal crossed her again, she would lose more than her bag next time."

Kelly couldn't believe her ears.

"What? That sweet Amber? Are you sure?"

Ben assured Kelly he was, as he had been right there when Amber was proudly telling the story.

"So," he asked, "what should I do?"

Kelly stared at him hard. This was not the dilemma she was expecting. She frowned.

"This is serious. You can't ignore this. We go and confront that evil little bitch masquerading as a caring friend. I don't really particularly like Crystal, but Amber is playing us all for fools and if someone doesn't stop her she'll probably do it again. Somebody could get badly hurt next time."

If Ben had known Kelly for more than a day, he would have known what her response would be. He displayed a lawyer's caution:

"But what if there is more to this story? Maybe there is a whole other side of things that we have no idea about."

"Ben, are you suggesting that getting someone to beat up a girl alone at night is alright?"

Ben realised that he had no way out of this argument. Luckily they had just got back to the Lofts and he had the excuse that he still needed to unpack.

"Of course not, Kelly. I just think we should think about this a bit more before taking any action. Are you free for a quick drink later?"

"Not tonight. I'm busy, I'm afraid Ben. But – let's catch up after work tomorrow. Maybe by then you will have thought it through and realised that we can't just stand by and keep quiet about crimes."

Kelly wanted to add that by then maybe he might have grown some balls, but it was the first day and she thought she would cut him some slack. This once. She flashed him that smile, kissed him on the cheek and strode off.

Ben's revelations troubled her, though. She needed to bounce her views off someone. She needed to talk to someone and she knew Rubens would still be in the gym. She decided impetuously to head down to see him – there would be few people working out Sunday afternoon and he was due off his shift soon.

She timed it right. There he was. As she walked into the gym café, she saw him sitting alone with a drink and his mobile on the table.

"Rubens, you'll never guess what I just heard… "

Kelly stopped dead as she saw Rubens' face. It looked as if he'd been crying. She'd never seen Rubens with anything other than a smile on that beautiful, carefree face of his.

"Rubens, darling, what's the matter?"

"Kelly, it's my mother. She has been sick for two years now and she needs all this expensive medicine and my family in Rio is poor. Meu Deus. Why do you think I work three jobs and all the extras? I've been sending money home so my father can look after her. But now the doctor says the medicine is not working any more and she needs an operation or she will die. I don't know what I can do; we need ten thousand dollars by next month. I really, really don't know what to do."

Kelly felt the full weight of Rubens' helplessness. For once, she did not know what to say. She gave him a hug and a kiss on the cheek as Rubens started to cry again. It was always a shock to see a grown man cry.

"My parents still think I am with Gabriela and that I am working with her as a model to get the money and that we will be going back to Brazil to get married. My mother has her dress already and she tells me that looking forward to my wedding is what keeps her going. Now there is no wedding and if she finds out what I do to get that money for her medicine it will kill her. Kelly, I'm sorry but what can I do? What can I do?"

3

All work and no PPLAY

Hartmut Glick always dusted his collection of Franklin Mint Fabergé Eggs on a Sunday evening. Dust – flakes of skin, and flint – got everywhere. It was better to keep dust in its place.

Dusting appealed to Hartmut's natural sense of order. He prepared himself for the challenges of the week ahead by lovingly caring for delicate and precious objects. Once the display sparkled and shone again, he would go to bed early. He made sure he got his eight hours before a six am alarm call. He needed the early Sunday night most weeks: PPLAY (Pleasure, Pain, Lust And Yearning) went on to the small hours on a Saturday night.

When he'd moved to London nearly twenty years earlier the bondage scene had been a pale shadow of his native Berlin's. He'd even had to go to gay S&M parties to get his fix. Hartmut only had sex with women, but he thoroughly enjoyed spanking a disobedient slave's bottom no matter what appendages they possessed. And in any case, the lines were always blurred at such parties, and so he could usually find some woman willing to tickle and torture his fancy.

Just then he noticed a card strangely out of place on his display cabinet. Instantly pained at the intrusion, he removed it. As he was about to throw it into the recycling bin he noticed a name and number on it.

Hartmut was a committed bachelor, married to his legal career and the care of his Fabergé eggs. How had he allowed himself to get a woman's number?

Caroline Napier Jones.

Yes. She was the tall, slim, brunette with the posh accent and the wonderful technique. They had met the night before and had immediately almost got into an argument, as they both wanted to spank the same cheeky scamp who had dared to take a drink from the masters' table. Luckily, Hartmut had managed to control his desire, subjugate it to his otherwise chivalrous nature, and offered up the peachy buttocks to the lady. She spanked with the strokes of a master, and Hartmut was filled with admiration and more. He had to get to know this woman. Dragging the slave along by its collar, he and Caroline sought out a private room in order to indulge their fantasies. The slave, whose name they obviously did not bother to ask, was superfluous and ignored; thankfully such rejection was just what it liked. The slave enjoyed the experience every bit as much as the protagonists did.

A shiver ran down Hartmut's spine as he remembered it. One of the most amazing nights in a lifetime of stimulation. Then he threw the card in the bin.

"You'll get to love the Tube in summer. It can get so hot that if you were to put cattle on the Tube you would be prosecuted by the animal welfare brigade. Apparently it is impossible to fit the London Underground with an air-conditioning system because of lack of space on the trains. That's one of those pieces of poor excuses that only the British would stoically swallow. We all know it's about cost. Londoners shrug when they hear that Transport for London has pretty much given up now, and advises people to travel with a bottle of water. Same thing when they accept delays on their overground railways because of "leaves on the line". It's like Fall surprises the British every year. Hilarious, if it weren't pretty tragic. You've got to ask yourself. How on earth did these people ever control one quarter of the planet?"

Monday morning, and Kelly was warming up. Ben loved the fact that he never knew what innocent observation would spark a tirade against a large portion of humanity, often the British. She had a point, though. They had travelled one stop on the Northern Line up to Borough and he was sweltering already. The suit didn't help. It looked good on a frame like Ben's, but it was not exactly comfortable, or practical on a train that reminded him of being in the sauna at the Lofts.

Still, he was looking forward to his first day in the new job. Something to take his mind off his twin dilemmas of the beautiful Kelly and the Fendi Affair. What to do in each case? He had no idea but felt he had to do something. After all this is why he had come to London – to get involved, to live life.

The office building was like a huge steel and glass coffin for an oversized and formally dressed giant. The building perched on its end like a begging dog. Begging for hours and hours of one's life. Devouring time like a black hole. Ben stared up at the glinting building and felt a little shiver. People looking like ants was no longer just a question of size. They actually looked insect-like. But Ben also felt excitement. This was new, and therefore could and should be enjoyed to the full. There was something sexy about it all too – the robot in Fritz Lang's Metropolis popped into his mind. He decided that it would look great with Kelly's head. Never mind her head. His eyes drifted to Kelly's body as she pressed through the doors ahead of him. He rather liked the way the skirt moulded her rather perfect derrière. The warmth of that image, as against the steel efficiency of the marble and stone entrance. This was not the most tedious journey to work that he had known. It had been hot in more ways than one.

He noticed that she had rather perfect breasts, filling out her shirt like two over sized stress balls.

The lifts were new and smooth, with big mirrors showing people what the gusty winds of London could do to their hair, and exactly how many years were etched onto their faces by the daily grind. No one spoke.

Ben and Kelly departed the ride at the eleventh floor. The reception desk gleamed into view. It was very large and very imposing. Ben noticed the thick carpet underfoot which muffled any sound. You moved from clattering crowds to lush, plush, cushioned quiet. A soothing ambience for a problem to come to.

After giving his name, Ben only had to wait for a few moments before an elegant woman materialised.

"Good Morning. You must be Ben Barlettano. Welcome to Stiller, Boils & Kumpelhauk."

Cornisha Burrows was a model office manager. Ultra-efficient and professional, she had an uncanny instinct for sizing people up. She was rarely caught out. Cornisha guessed immediately that there was something brewing lightly between Ben and Kelly. She decided she would need to look after that boy.

"Ben, let me show you to your desk. Mr Glick has booked a meeting with you at two o'clock. This morning, however, we'll be carrying out the first part of your induction. That'll give us some time to go through some housekeeping and the rules of the office."

Ben liked Cornisha's smile. Being a good Italian-American boy he always responded well to the mother figure, and she made him feel calm and secure. Kelly waved airily and disappeared through some large double doors.

The morning fled in a blur of computer systems, office machines, support staff introductions and a good gawp at the cavernous stationery cupboard – more of a vast walk-in closet, where anything from sticky white circles to firm-branded notebooks could be found, organised within an inch of their existence on cold white laminate shelves.

Lunch time seemed to come around quickly. The first sandwich lunch is generally quite tasty. There does come a time when they taste like misery on a bread base, as you cram another identical sample of slightly tired carbohydrates into your sad, pale, hungry mouth, knowing that every bite is probably thickening your middle like a blow up lifejacket, but no longer able to really care as you eat in order to stay awake – or simply because it is there. But Ben was some time off experiencing that yet.

The time for his first London meeting had come. Ben squared his shoulders and flicked crumbs from his jacket. He padded off to a conference room, which had been reserved for his first meeting with his new boss.

He knocked lightly and entered the room confidently. He saw a straight-backed man with immaculate silver hair and light piercing eyes. He was wearing a perfectly cut suit, and every detail looked correct – from the noticeably chunky but balanced silver cufflinks to a silk handkerchief in his top left hand pocket. He looked neither old nor young, but exuded authority with a slender hint of menace.

"So, you are the young man I must whip into shape. You may pick up some bruises on the way, but with industry and dedication you will enjoy your time here. Welcome to my team, Ben."

Ben had heard that Hartmut Glick, one of the more senior partners at SBK, was also one of the finest minds in law – a pleasing and oddly rare coincidence. Kelly had also told Ben that Hartmut could be a complete mindfuck if you got on the wrong side of him. Ben smiled nervously.

"I'm looking forward to learning a lot and contributing to the success of the firm in any way I can."

"Did I really just say that?" wondered Ben. He was aware that he had expressed the sentiment with great sincerity. Privately, he half meant it – but given that he had no idea what he would be doing or how, it seemed a lot of wishful thinking and a wild stab at the right thing to say to this elegant, po-faced man. The meeting went well and finished

exactly on the allotted thirty-minute mark.

All in all, Ben's first day was fairly easy. By six o'clock he had met several other trainees, and another Castle Lofts neighbour, one Harry Gumpert, another partner at SBK.

As it turned out, Harry Gumpert was the reason the trainees were mostly housed in the Lofts. One of Ben's new colleagues filled him in over a drink after work. Harry's wife wanted to live in Chiswick. All her friends and the cupcake shop were there, and it was perfect for starting a family. But Harry had stalled. He felt that he needed the buzz of Zone 1 to keep him fresh. Not for him, the safety and predictability of suburbia.

This had been a sore point, but the proximity to the West End and a few crafty moves on Harry's part had won the day. The Gumperts had bought a penthouse in the Lofts and decided to raise their young daughters in "up-and-coming" Elephant & Castle.

As Kelly pointed out, "up-and-coming" is really just a great English euphemism for "it's still hopeless but we're hoping". Harry was such a fan of the development that he had persuaded other partners to acquire flats there to house new trainees and young lawyers. Harry's little empire. His little buy-to-let dream. You pay the trainees with one hand and suck up their rent with the other, as if your other hand had its own currency vacuum hose. The very gentlest of pressure ensured that they realised that it was wise to rent from you, if they knew what was good for their advancement at the firm.

The return home on the Tube was even sweatier.

Kelly sighed as she hung onto a strap for dear life:

"You should get a bike, Ben. There is a shower at work, you know. I hear it is great fun playing tag with the lovely bendy buses. Which buttmunch had the idea to put eighteen-metre long vehicles in a city with a medieval street layout? Have you ever seen one crash? It's funny."

She looked so pretty when she said "buttmunch". Ben was getting used to Kelly by now. It was actually a pretty good crash course in learning about his new home. Her passion about everything was invigorating. She said these things in such a reasonable voice. There was nothing tame or fearful about her.

"Shall we meet in the café at nine? There's a pub round the corner from here. It's a bit faded but the beer is cheap – pretty appropriate for talking about Crystal and Amber. Oh, and Rubens will be joining us later. I need your help on something."

The Brazilian again. Ben felt an odd stab of despair. He decided abruptly that it was pointless to harbour desires for Kelly as she clearly either wasn't available, or just enjoyed playing games a bit too much.

It was good to get back into the flat. Ben realised that it looked like home, even if it did not quite feel like it yet. He swung the fridge door open. The shelves lit up empty, save for the duty free vodka and Kelly's carton of milk. Food shopping. The bane of the working professional. Refrigerators that reprimanded you for their barren spaces, bare save for half-used bottles of sauces and perhaps a rather elderly onion. He resolved to go to his local Tesco the following day but he was hungry now. Time to try out the café.

There were a few souls who appeared to have had the same thought, hungrily devouring a selection of rather nice-looking food. It was good to have a few people around.

Ben sat down at the counter and smiled at the woman serving food. She was white but wearing a turban. How utterly bizarre. This was Ben's first encounter with Millie Myers, militant vegetarian health café owner.

"Hi there, could I have a plate of that lasagna – with salad, please?"

Ben was about to find out that Millie mixed her metaphors like she mixed her ingredients – thoroughly. Occasionally one could not even find a trace of the original thought.

"It's vegetable lasagna. We do not serve meat in this café. We are ethical and do not believe in murdering poor defenceless animals just so that selfish human beings can indulge their carnal instincts. Did you know that apart from the inherent wrongness of eating living creatures, it takes ten times more land to produce a kilo of beef than it does a kilo of wheat? So it's bad economics as well as nasty. You see a bird in the hand really does cost six in the bush. Or actually ten. Will vegetable lasagna be OK for you? It's organic."

Being used to American customer service, Ben wasn't really expecting to be castigated for requesting a plate of lasagna, and certainly wasn't expecting the lesson on the economics of meat versus cereal production. But he hadn't quite got the measure of Millie yet.

"Well now. That sounds lovely."

45

Millie gave him a slightly haughty, superior smile.

"I'm glad you agree. Not everyone can appreciate the delight of the vegetarian lifestyle. After all, you can lead a horse to water, but a dog must be led. However, let me tell you this: when you train your first vegetarian dog – well, I can tell you – it is quite a source of satisfaction."

Rather mystified by Millie's philosophical cul-de-sacs, Ben smiled back and asked if he could get a Coke to go with his meal.

"I'm afraid Coca Cola does not fit in with the policy of this establishment. Why don't you try some organic dandelion and burdock? It is a traditional British soft drink, made by local producers. Alternatively, we have a range of ethically sourced soft drinks in the refrigerated cabinet. Of course, we also recycle the glass bottles here."

Ben replied that he would love to try dandelion and burdock, and asked to pay. Paying early meant getting away quicker.

Millie looked him over reflectively:

"Are you resident in the Lofts?"

Ben paused with his fork mid way to his mouth. The lasagna was very tasty.

"I am indeed. I just moved here from the US on Saturday. My name is Ben."

"Well, welcome to our community. I'm Millie. I guess I'll be seeing quite a lot of you then. You'll be amazed at what I can do with vegetables. Courgettes are my favourite. You don't have to have the sharpest tool in the village to kill two birds with one stone. Not of course that I would ever kill but one bird."

Ben had no idea what the hell Millie was going on about, but in fairness to her the lasagna was superb, even though he had to file the dandelion and burdock in the "acquired taste" category – rather as he did when his grandmother, Isabella Balocchi, tried to convince him of the delights of Chinotto when they'd visited her in Italy when he was ten.

He wondered what Millie's courgette surprise might be, and whether he had the nerve to ask her with a cheeky grin on his face. He thought better of it. Then, as he shovelled the last delicious mouthfuls in, he saw Kelly.

She came bouncing into the café, and the world lit up a little.

"Hi Ben, it's good grub here. I should have joined you – Millie's baked goods work for me. But there we have it. You can't eat all evening. Come on – let's go, then."

The Elephant pub was a local landmark. It had been there for ever and looked like it was still hanging back in the 1950s. Ben heard an old man order a pint of pale ale and a packet of pork scratchings, whatever they were. He and Kelly were apparently the only people in there under the age of sixty. He suspected they were also the only foreigners. At last he had found a spot in this city that actually seemed English. Charming, too, in its rather down-at-heel way. And they got a quiet table and were sure not to be disturbed.

The pale ale was a revelation. Why wasn't the place packed?

Kelly was focused on her subject:

"So. I have slept on it and I still think we should confront that lardy little liar. Alternatively, we could go to

Crystal and tell her. As long as we make her promise to go to Amber when we are present – I wouldn't miss that bitch fight for the world."

"Kelly, I agree with you that we can't just pretend I never heard the conversation. But I think we should be sensitive about how we approach the matter. After all we don't know the whole picture here."

"Ben, absolutely! After all I'm sure there's a perfectly good reason Amber got her brother to attack that girl in the street and steal her bag."

Kelly couldn't understand how Ben could be such a wimp about this. Wrong had been committed; the perpetrator had to answer. Period.

He held up his hands in a placatory way:

"OK, hold the sarcasm. I just mean that we should at least give the girl a chance to try to explain herself. In any case, I think we make *her* promise to own up to Crystal. Then it's up to them to sort it out."

"Alright then, Ben. Let's play it your way. I think we should go to her flat tonight. I'll ask Arthur on reception which flat she is in."

Although he wasn't looking forward to the conversation, Ben was relieved that Kelly was being reasonable about this. Then his thoughts turned to Rubens. His favourite Brazilian.

"So, what is the help you need from me? Do you need advice on how to deal with a man? Before your boyfriend joins us, I guess?"

Kelly nearly choked on her pint. Ben couldn't possibly believe she was going out with Rubens. Was he totally blind? God, her mother had realised Rubens batted for the other team within a minute of meeting him. It was kind of funny, though. She'd wanted to ask Ben how they could help Rubens with ideas on how, legally, to get his hands on the money he needed for his mother's operation. But maybe Ben wasn't the right person to ask about this. In any case Rubens had texted her earlier to say he couldn't make it.

"Rubens can't make it tonight. And I've solved the issue I had. I think we should just deal with our fake Fendi drama tonight. But nice to know that you can give me that kind of advice. Not many men can, you know. You're obviously in touch with your feminine side."

Ben wasn't sure how to take that last comment. There was something Kelly was hiding from him. But then they had only just met. He knew little about her.

"Fair enough. Should we be getting back to the Lofts? We don't want to leave it too late to pay our visit."

It did not take Kelly long to wrap Arthur Bilks around her little finger.

"Thank you so much, Arthur. I knew you would know. You are the best thing about this place, you know. You, and the view from the top floor."

How did women do it? Ben hadn't seen the full Kelly treatment before. He realised he didn't stand a chance. Maybe he should just wish Rubens good luck.

"Hold the lift please!"

Ben almost fell over as Amber Bluett jumped into the lift with Kelly and him.

"Oh, you're going to my floor already."

Kelly's eyes blazed. And she was off.

"We know the story. We know about you. We know about you getting your brother to beat up your supposed friend and steal her bag. You're going to go and tell her or we're going to the police. And remember we're lawyers. And we will do it."

Amber went pale.

"Kelly, I have no idea what you are talking about. How could you think such a thing of me of all people?"

Amber started to snivel. She looked over at Ben like a frightened puppy who'd just been smacked for no reason.

Kelly was unimpressed.

"Listen, you little actress. You were overheard. And you sure do deserve an Oscar for your sympathy on Saturday night. Do you seriously think we are going to let you get away with this?"

Amber's tears suddenly dried up, and her eyes flashed with venom.

"I guess that depends on whether you want to be looking behind you when you're walking home at night, honey. Remember this, you Yankee ho, this is my city. And I have a lot of friends here, many of them probably not the kind that your dear Mommy would like you hanging round with. They'd have a lot more fun with your pretty little ass than they did with that other piece of trash. If you're wise, you'll just shut the fuck up and start looking behind you at night. And Prince Charming, I'm sorry, I really like you, but you get mixed up in this and you are going down with her. Oh, I do believe it's my floor. Don't get out. In fact, stay away from me if you like your bodies the way they are."

She left the lift.

Kelly looked cross.

"I'm not a Yankee ho. I'm a Confederate ho."

Ben frowned:

"Frankly, my dear, that is the least of our worries now."

Back in the City, Hartmut Glick was leaving the office. He slipped into his navy blue cashmere great coat, and thoughtfully drew on his leather gloves. As he walked into the street, he almost collided with Harry Gumpert, who, with a blissful lack of self awareness of his own body space, was standing in the most inconvenient place possible outside the lobby, blocking the way, talking to a strangely familiar looking young woman. Attractive, conservatively dressed, yet now looking at Hartmut slightly oddly.

Harry smiled expansively:

"Hartmut, Hartmut, in a rush, as always? You should be careful, you could do someone an injury with that reinforced briefcase of yours. By the way, this is Caroline Napier Jones from Napier Jones, the PR agency three floors above us. She is also the daughter of an old friend of mine, and my next door neighbour at the Castle Lofts."

In a flash Hartmut recognised her. From killer heels to kitten heels, from a black rubber catsuit to a flowing Donna Karan dress, from a Bondara Deluxe black suede flogger whip to a brown leather Bottega Veneta handbag. It was certainly her, although this costume seemed a lot less convincing than Saturday's. He smiled weakly and gave her his hand. He didn't like surprises, especially not this type.

"So you are the famous Hartmut Glick. Harry has told me about you. One of the finest legal minds in the firm, I hear."

Caroline gave him a daring smile. So she knew me already, thought Hartmut. Did she know who I was on Saturday?

"It's an honour, Ms Napier Jones. My condolences, however, on your bad luck in neighbours. I have always said that Elephant & Castle may be very convenient, but you really never know who you might end up living next to. Forgive me, however, I must get home as I have an urgent case I need to do more work on."

"Oh, the pleasure is mine, Mr Glick. And don't work too hard. Remember: all work and no PPLAY makes Jack a dull boy."

For a second time, Hartmut smiled weakly as he heard her softly emphasise the double "p" of PPLAY. He had protected his secret double life to perfection for years and now this woman was toying with him. The worst part was that she was a neighbour of Gumpert's. He hoped she had as much to hide as he did. There was nothing else for it. He prepared himself for the distasteful experience of rooting for her card in the bin. Where was that slave, when you needed one?

4

Harry Plotter

Harry Gumpert remembered his Cambridge days fondly. A first in law, a boxing blue, and fiddling the election to become President of Magdalene JCR had made him popular, confident and happy. He could never settle on one woman, but then with so many available to such a self-styled intellectual stud as he was, he never saw why he should limit himself.

He met Sarah in his late twenties. By then he thought it was time to start a family. Many of his friends were tying the knot. The constant stream of traditional weddings caught at him like thorns, entangling him in the briars of responsibility and inhibiting his pursuit of the fun side of life. Yet marriage and a family offered a sentimental vision of the world that contrasted interestingly with his very English debauchery – very English in that it was something you never really talked about, especially not to those you play with.

Sarah was one of the few beautiful women he had met that he could bring himself to introduce to his friends. She was acceptability incarnate. In turn, she persuaded herself that he was a dreamy boyfriend and he was good in bed. On that solid foundation they took the plunge.

Sarah had always been devoted to Harry, in a slightly dull way at times, he thought. He rather liked it that way. After they discovered she was pregnant, and buggies, nurseries and other things foreign to him took on a strange and unwelcome presence in his life, Sarah started to try to assert herself, in the name of the family.

Harry wasn't impressed.

He was even less impressed when she started talking repeatedly of her friends' lovely houses in Chiswick, Barnes and Richmond. He could feel middle-aged respectability clawing at him with its myriad hooks – labrador puppies, sensible shoes, Audi estate cars and the obsession with getting into the right catchment area for Imogen and Annabel's education. The children became weapons of mass consumption. They guided expenditure like missiles. Sarah had a whole new set of targets, centred around them. Her strategy never varied. It was scorched earth. She grimly assaulted the plains of their future lives. They must get the best start in life. Parents must make any sacrifices needed, or else face the criticism of the most fearsome group of people ever to walk the earth. Other parents.

Faced with this threat to his lebensraum, Harry took charge. He made an about turn and sped off in the opposite direction, buying the largest penthouse in the Castle Lofts, a block full of single twenty and thirty-somethings. Lack of sleep there was more likely to be due to excessive illicit substance consumption than to a teething baby. Harry had consented to being tied down by

Sarah, but there were limits. And his limit would remain the edge of Zone 1.

From the first subtle frottage in the unisex Jacuzzi, Monique Mottin became one of Harry's favourite things in the Lofts. Kelly Danvers had brought her flatmate along to an SBK party. Luckily, Sarah had been at home with their twin daughters. The affair should never have got off the ground, but reliable baby-sitters were so hard to come by in SE1, and Harry and Sarah were usually out separately these days – especially at office events. With Sarah consistently not there when Harry was drinking, and Monique looking like a gloriously fresh version of Louise Brooks, Harry fell for the sensual young woman with the charming accent. More champagne and the thrill of the forbidden had egged him on.

Harry was an attractive man, with the experience, wealth and quiet confidence that forty years of success on planet earth had brought him. Monique was smitten by him in turn. She was devastated when Kelly had told her that Harry was married. She had felt so guilty the first time they had sex. But it had got easier. Especially when he had asked her to baby-sit.

As Amber stormed out of the lift Ben's frown deepened. This was giving him an uneasy feeling.

"We need to talk about this, Kelly. Your flat, or mine?"

"Mine. I think I'm better equipped. I may have more than cereal around. I think I need a drink."

He had to hand it to Kelly. She'd been threatened with the loss of body parts, and yet she was thinking hard, her eyes darting around as she weighed up the options. Ben pressed the button for her floor and they went up in silence. As they walked round to Flat 412, he thought of Amber's menacing stare.

"I hoped London would be exciting," Ben said, ruefully, "but I wasn't exactly expecting to be threatened unless I kept silent about a crime I had discovered. Do you think Amber is serious? You've known her longer than I have, Kelly."

"Well, she got her supposed close friend beaten up and robbed by her brother."

"Kelly, we're both supposed to be intelligent strong lawyers. A person like that can't tell us what to do."

Kelly nodded thoughtfully:

"We are right. Amber has broken the law. We cannot let her get away with this."

She grimaced:

"I'm not supposed to be intelligent and strong, though. I'm just supposed to look good and do the work adequately. It is a different measure altogether... but never mind that for the time being... "

Kelly normally knew what to do in most situations, even when she didn't really understand what was going on. But this time, she felt unsure how to react. She had never been spoken to like that before, and had never expected it to happen in the safety of her home. Her hand shook slightly as she put the key in the lock.

Her flat was warm and comforting. It was a classic girl's pad, neat and tidy, with plenty of elegant and interesting details – a painting here, some pretty lights there, and even week-old flowers hanging their heads like gorgeous forty-somethings after a night out.

"Hi Kelly, darling. Oh… who's your friend?"

Monique Mottin gave Ben a mesmerising smile. Ben couldn't immediately reply, but Kelly sparked into life.

"Monique, this is Ben Barlettano. Ben's just moved over from the US to work at the firm. He arrived the night Crystal got beaten up and then he overheard that bitch Amber Bluett on the phone telling her friend about how she had set it all up. We've just confronted her and she has told us that if we don't keep quiet something very bad will happen to us. Possibly involving loss of body parts. Or dignity. You'd probably lose some dignity with a body part."

So they weren't going to keep it a secret. Ben thought that it probably wasn't a good idea to object. Monique's eyes stretched wider and wider as Kelly filled her in with all the details. She shook her head in disbelief:

"I have never liked those girls. I think they are as bad as each other. I don't know how they even managed to get into this block."

Kelly shrugged:

"I think they just answered an ad. You know I love you, Monique, but we can't banish everyone to the banlieux just because they can't afford a real Fendi bag."

Monique gesticulated at Ben, pointing affectionately at Kelly with her chin.

"She always tries to make out I am a French snob. I am not at all. I just think people who so obviously are lacking grace and class should not poison my life. They force me

57

to have to look at their 'orrible clothes, their 'orrible hair and to hear their screeching voices. I mean, why live here, when they would be so much more comfortable in Zone 6? A nice little semi-detached house with a driveway for their Ford Focus, no congestion charge to complain about, and only a short drive to Lidl to fill the boot with family-sized packs of Walkers crisps and Sunny Delight. And don't get me started on the unemployed people who pay nothing to live in Zone 1, when a hard worker like me is struggling to pay the bills to live in Elephant & Castle and has to share with a girl from Louisiana."

Monique and Kelly both laughed. Ben couldn't tell if Monique was serious or just kidding him. She made sense and yet offended him at the same time. Or did she? It had a grain of truth in it – but she made an unlikely upper class warrior, with her bobbed hair, the string of pearls round an elegant neck and her slim five foot ten frame hugged by the essential little black dress. She was every inch the Parisienne, keeping Coco Chanel's torch burning bright, illuminating the darkness she found outre Manche. Ben could imagine Monique looking down on most of humanity, so she probably was being serious about the sartorially challenged specimens she found in London.

Monique got up to mix martinis. She knew what was needed.

"You obviously cannot let that girl get away with something like this," she continued, over her shoulder, "especially with you two being lawyers. American ones at that. I think we should actually tell that Crystal tart and then we stand back and wait for the fireworks. If we are lucky, they will fight and then get thrown out of the block. It could be our best chance to get them out."

Monique's confident smile convinced Ben that she was alright. This girl was gorgeous, and a real piece of work. He wondered if Monique ever fought with Kelly. He conjured up a picture of Celebrity Deathmatch. Kelly and Monique versus Crystal and Amber. That would be one dirty fight. He wasn't surprised that he couldn't concentrate on the problem at hand; he kept getting distracted by the women, the city, the situations around him. It was only day three in London. It seemed like half a lifetime already.

"What about if we let Crystal know anonymously?" suggested Kelly.

"Kelly, Amber would know it was us." said Ben.

Monique pouted:

"You Americans are so slow at times. Lawyers are supposed to be devious. It seems to me that you can learn something from a fashion PR. One of you needs to be having a further discussion with that Amber girl in a public place, whilst the other accidentally arrives with Crystal who happens to overhear everything. Oups. I had no idea!"

Kelly and Ben looked at each other. Maybe Monique was right. It could work.

"Monique, are you related to Hercule Poirot by any chance?"

"Oh, you minx. As you well know, he was Belgian, not French. Like fries. You may remember – in the Great War of 1914, the Americans came over, saw fries being cooked by French-speaking troops et voilà, one of the only things Belgium has ever given the world suddenly became French. You see, your country had no more idea of Europe one hundred years ago than that simple cowboy you didn't elect in 2000."

Monique was nothing if not forthright. How on earth, wondered Ben, did these two girls not kill each other? They must surely disagree a lot. Ben mused that London seemed full of foreigners who rubbed along pretty well together, even while possibly hiding vast wells of prejudices under the surface. Was this any different to home? Maybe it was just human nature to suspect and criticise things that were different. Either that or fall madly in love with it and want to distance yourself from the vagaries of your own culture.

What was really needed here was a decision about how to tackle the situation. Should he just let these two women decide?

Was he a feminist?

Kelly was already planning how to confront Amber again. She was used to Monique's little jokes. Ben didn't know that, behind the cool, slightly condescending façade, Monique Mottin adored the USA. In fact she wanted to move to New York as soon as she could persuade her boss to transfer her there.

A sudden, almost theatrical knock at the door made them jump out of their skins. Monique looked at Kelly and then went to answer it.

It was Harry Gumpert, coolly surveying the protagonist in his latest passion play:

"Monique. I say. Don't you just look perfect? Kelly. Ben. Quite the little gathering, I see."

"Hi Harry. We're having a council of war. Do please come in. We should probably ask for your professional opinion."

In the space of a few minutes Kelly had apprised Harry of the situation, including asking his view on Monique's plan. Ben wondered whether he would ever be able to keep up with Kelly. Maybe that was the basis of the attraction. Apart from her face, body and smile of course.

Harry looked at Ben. He looked a little too comfortable in the girls' flat.

"So, Ben. The very day of your arrival you manage to stir up a veritable hornet's nest here in our tranquil Lofts. I hope you won't get the same idea in the office."

Ben looked so worried that Harry thought he had better let him know he was only being sarcastic. He threw him a grin:

"I would agree with my honourable young friends here that something has to be done. I would also applaud the cunning method of leading the victim to make her own discovery, therefore clearing yourselves of blame and hence the tormentor's ire. But I do wonder whether you have the tools to achieve this. Do any of you know either Amber or Crystal sufficiently well to plausibly invite them anywhere?"

Ben, Kelly and Monique had to admit they were not lucky enough to have such enriching relationships.

"Sometimes I do fear for the future of our partnership. Have none of you ever noticed that Amber Bluett is a vegetarian, and surprisingly close to shy and retiring Millie Myers, our crazy basement lady? Crystal Smith, by contrast is a regular gym-goer. From what I have observed, she likes nothing more than instruction from the obliging Rubens Ribeiro."

Kelly looked delighted:

"Harry, that's why I love working for you. You're right. We just need to be organised. I'll get Rubens to do a special offer. He can arrange a free personal training session with Crystal. Ben, I guess you'll have to tackle Millie. Maybe we can lure Amber down with a new vegetarian recipe. That could work. That could work very well."

Rubens. So Kelly would get her boyfriend to help whilst Ben would have to tackle a militant vegetarian who he had only met that evening and had not been especially taken with. Ben must have looked a little sour, because Monique smiled over at him:

"Don't worry Ben, I will help you with Millie. Last week I bumped into her in a little café in Islington some way from here where she thought no one would know her. Anyway, the woman was only eating bacon, egg and a pork sausage! With that disgusting brown sauce they make here. I smiled so sweetly at her and told her that her secret would never pass my lips. Now, for some strange reason she has a thing for anything French. I think I can get her to agree, even though Amber is a friend of hers. Voilà. We have a plan. I feel extremely cunning. Anyhow, speaking of things French, Harry, can I come up and get that DVD you said you would lend me?"

Kelly smiled to herself as Monique and Harry left. She

may not have thought of involving Millie and Rubens, but she understood all there was to understand about the jousting between Monique and Kelly's boss. It worried Kelly to think that Harry might consider her stupid enough not to have noticed. Maybe she should confront him, not in the interest of honesty, but just for the sake of her career prospects.

Ben got up, slightly regretfully, still thinking about the Rubens question.

"I'm going to head off too, Kelly. It's been an interesting day. Let's talk tomorrow about our tactics for persuading Rubens and Millie to help."

"Ok. See you tomorrow Ben. And don't worry about them. Rubens can never say no to me, and Monique is extremely persuasive when she wants to be."

If he left the curtains open, Ben could see the main entrance to the shopping centre as he sat up in bed. On nights like this – alone, ruminating over recent events of note – he preferred to watch and think, rather than improve his mind with challenging reading, like the morning copy of Metro. Kelly seemed to enjoy talking about Rubens in front of him. Did she really have no idea that he, Ben, liked her? Ben wondered if he was obsessing. He should be careful not to stand too close a comparison with, say, one of those women from Sex and the City who analysed everything when they should just let things go and get on with life. Sex and the City, eh. Chance would be a fine thing. Gina, Ben's ex-girlfriend, had insisted he watch that show throughout all six series. He had only just escaped that sad fate of being the only hen-pecked straight man in the cinema when the films had come out. Even he had his limits. Why was he always attracted to strong, borderline bossy, women?

He moved away from Kelly. What was it about Monique Mottin? If she was typical, then he could understand why Paris had achieved such a legendary status in the realm of amour, glamour and sheer sex appeal. He wondered how many men before him had fantasised about staying the night in Flat 412, between the sheets with those two.

Sarah Gumpert had not been expecting to see "From Ladette to Lady" that night. Although she was completely hooked on the reality show that turned feral party girls into respectable scions of polite society by way of discipline, flower arranging and the ferociously disapproving looks of the teachers of Egglestone Hall, she was supposed to be out with the girls that night. But as soon as she had met Annabelle and Georgie she knew something was up by their flushed faces, happy smiles and what looked suspiciously like two orange juices and lemonade sitting on the table in front of them.

One pregnant friend would have been a celebration; two meant going home early.

Although it is possible to drink pints and pints of beer or wine in an evening, even the most experienced drinker quails at the third orange juice. So there she was, at home again, with only her trusty Bombay Sapphire and tonic for company, watching the matronly Rosemary Shrager scold her way through a cookery class with a group of ladettes trying their hand at pheasant plucking.

The key turned in the lock. Harry walked in with Monique Mottin.

"Hello darling, aren't you supposed to be with your Chiswick set?"

Harry looked surprised, but not yet uncomfortable. But he should be. What the hell was going on? Surely she couldn't have fallen for the oldest one in the book. Wife out with friends, husband bangs sexy French babysitter in conjugal bed. No. No. No!

"Hello Sarah, so nice to see you – oh, I love this programme too. I would love to be one of those teachers. I think most of London needs to go to that finishing school to learn some manners."

Monique didn't have the faintest whiff of guilt or embarrassment about her. Just that effortless superiority that comes with the unshakeable knowledge that you are actually better than most people around you, and that they probably know it too.

"I think I might have dropped my silver bangle here when I was baby-sitting last time. I let Chloe play with it on the floor. Maybe it is under your sofa."

Now Sarah felt insulted. Did they really think she was that stupid that she would fall for the "*I only came up to look for a missing bracelet*" tactic? She forced out a false smile and knelt politely to look under the black leather sofa she was sitting on. She had to pretend to buy it even though she was half ready to scream and half ready to burst into tears. She would wait for that French strumpet to leave and then Harry would get it. She should never have trusted him. Her mother had warned her against him. At that moment she glimpsed something. She reached for it. It was cold and hard and smooth. She pulled it out. A silver bangle, and not her own.

"Ah, mon Dieu. I am so relieved about that! It was a present. I was going mad trying to remember where I left it and then tonight I remembered when I saw Harry in reception. Thank you, Sarah. Well, I will leave you in private. Good night."

Sarah Gumpert felt the relief and guilt that was natural when one had wrongly suspected one's paragon of a partner. With the twins at her parents' tonight, Sarah might even be moved to show that there was some loving still left in her. Who knows, maybe she would be on orange juice and lemonade next time the girls met up. Surely with three children they might even get that cottage in Barnes.

Monique Mottin laughed to herself as she went back to Flat 412. She had planted the bangle there the last time she had been baby-sitting. She knew that evidence was always important in a case, and it had certainly fooled the jury that night. Poor Sarah was no match for her. Even if poor Sarah was going to be sleeping with the man Monique was in love with.

Harry Gumpert was feeling sexually frustrated. Sarah was nice. Monique was heaven. God, that French girl was good. How the hell had she done that? She was so smart, poor Sarah had no idea. He poured himself a stiff Bombay and cursed his luck at exchanging an hour of passion with

Monique for tales of the suburbs with his wife. But at least he still had a chance for some sex tonight. Something was as good as it got, at times like these.

5

Chic and chicanery

Nests needed to be feathered if the occupants were not to fly away. London flats needed a lot of feathers. Fortunately the city catered for everyone who flocked to it. From the out of town Ikeas to boutiques on the King's Road, from Harrods to Argos, each tribe could choose their own particular plumage. Plumage which would send important messages to friends, family and, of course, competitors.

It happened to be the seven year anniversary of Jamal Qureshi and Alex O'Connell's relationship. They were on Tottenham Court Road, where they seemed to spend ever more Saturday afternoons in the higher end furniture shops. There was just so much to finger and buy.

London had a designer version of every single item in the house and Jamal just loved it all. From the Missoni sheets in their bedroom to the Alessi mirrored fruit bowl in the lounge, from the Design Museum salt and pepper pots in the kitchen to the Valentino Egyptian cotton spa towels in the bathroom, Jamal insisted on quality – and quality invariably had a name.

It hadn't always been this way. Alex and Jamal met in an after hours party and it had been lust at first sight. The early years were a whirl of parties, clubs, vodka, sex and drugs. Designer-ware was strictly limited to Diesel clothes, Oakley glasses, Dolce & Gabbana anything. But with the growing relationship, and particularly buying their first home in the Castle Lofts they had done what Harry Gumpert had a visceral fear of. They'd settled down.

Not that they were alone. Apart from some of the old Trade regulars who actually worked in Habitat, Saturday afternoon saw a throng of respectable gay couples touring Tottenham Court Road, with just the occasional sneaky, cruisy look at someone else's Latin boyfriend who was still wearing well, before getting back to the more serious business of that new bathroom cabinet.

Although he was as house proud as the next middle-class gay man in a relationship, Alex occasionally felt it was all a bit too grown up. He would rebel by going out and getting far too drunk, and staying out all night in whichever den of iniquity happened to appeal to him. He would make a point of sometimes going out alone, just to prove that he still had it, and wasn't just an attachment to that lovely piece of exotica he happily chose to spend his free time with.

Although Jamal never consciously felt like he needed to rebel against the life and man that he loved so deeply, he was an instinctive creature. Sometimes those instincts drove him to take a short break from domestic bliss and wander back down the wilder side of life that he had gradually abandoned after meeting Alex. He fell into his old habits so easily; especially when he was out with his best friend, Rubens Ribeiro. Then again he would slip just as effortlessly back under the designer covers to the warmth of his man and their respectable, Home and Gardens-like existence.

Of course they still had the odd argument. Occasionally heated. Alex thought that it was normal. He was of the view that when you stopped arguing, you should start worrying. It was natural that caring so much, there could sometimes be a blow-up. Like a summer squall. Definitely preferable to watching passion die a lingering death when lovers slip into just being friends – and sadly sometimes not even that. Besides, when you stop arguing, you bid farewell to make up sex, and that was the sweetest thing of all. Even better if topped off by brunch in Covent Garden and the purchase of a chic, bijou item from one of their favourite shops in the West End.

"Rubens, my darling, I'm sorry I wasn't here yesterday but you have no idea what's been going on the last few days. Do you remember what happened to Crystal Smith last Saturday?"

"That poor girl! She is always nice to me. I love the way she dresses with so many bright colours, showing so much skin. With her, every day is like carnival, but in a very small town."

"Rubens, you're finally learning to be bitchy. Have you been spending even more time on the gay scene, or is it my influence?"

Rubens laughed. Kelly hugged him. From the outset,

Kelly had felt like the Brazilian's sister. It was surprisingly good to hang out with a man with no possibility of sex. Indeed, Kelly mused, apart from the lack of hang-ups and absence of sexual undertones that were natural in any woman's relationship with a gay man, Rubens was also straightforward and affectionate, to say nothing of being gorgeous to look at and hold. He had a naughty twinkle in his eye, but for her was as pure as driven snow. Kelly loved her blossoming relationship with her Latin brother.

The common bond of both being foreigners in a big city played its part, of course, but there was more to it than that. Understanding each other's emotional jigsaw puzzle featured large on the landscape. Although Kelly believed London to be one of the most open-minded places on the planet – where, generally, people didn't seem to give a damn about your nationality, religion or the colour of your skin so long as you paid your taxes, worked hard and obeyed the law – it was hard to get to know the British. They were like shellfish, keeping themselves to themselves, shutting down at the first sign of a risk of having to be sociable with strangers.

Most of the foreigners she knew hung out with other foreigners. Often, the British people they did know had in fact lived abroad themselves. Kelly felt comfortable with Rubens, in a way that she simply did not with many other friends.

Rubens sighed as reality bit. His mind was on his money problem:

"Kelly, have you come up with a clever plan for me to make some money? Fast?"

"Rubens, darling, I haven't forgotten that we need to have a long conversation about what you are, and also what you are not, going to do for money. But there is something else too. I need to talk to you about how you can help me."

"Sure Kelly, anything for you. Well, almost anything. Since I discovered the dark side you know I don't go certain places no more."

Rubens had the best collection of surprised noises of anyone Kelly knew. It was so satisfying telling him a good story. As she knew he would, he immediately agreed to the free gym session for Crystal.

"I will make a competition and her flat number will win."

"Perfect. Nothing like bribery and corruption to start off the day. Well, we have to wait to coordinate with Millie. Speaking of which, I do believe our secret weapon and her sidekick have just walked in."

Monique Mottin glided over to the café bar with Ben trailing in her wake.

"Millie – how are you, chérie?"

"All the better for seeing you Monique. I think you are one of the few people here who actually appreciate what I am trying to achieve. Still I owe it to the world to fight the good fight, even though it is hard to get through at times."

Millie directed a pointed grimace at Ben. Then she turned back to Monique with a smile.

"Where did you get that dress? It's from Paris, isn't it? I knew it. It's just stunning, Monique. But then, you need to have a figure like yours to carry it off. More than that still, you need to know how to walk. I watch so many of the women who come in here. They're slaves to their "Body Pump" classes and their low-fat meals, then they squeeze into their little size tens and their four-inch heels – and then what? They look like those awkward female sports stars when they are all glammed up for the awards ceremony. You just feel pinched all over for them. I can't help wanting to see them back in lycra and running shoes so everyone can breathe easy again, and stop feeling slightly uncomfortable. It's so sad, but then I suppose we mere mortals will never understand that *je ne sais pas pourquoi* that makes you French women so special."

Ben actually understood most of what Millie had said. Was he making progress? He certainly didn't agree with it all. In America the sportswomen were often hotter than chillis on a beach.

"Of course, you would be even better if you discovered the virtues of vegetarianism. When I went to Paris it was meat everywhere…"

"Millie," interrupted Monique, "I need to ask you a favour. An important one. And it is a very sensitive subject."

"Oh, Monique, of course. You know I am the soul of discretion."

Millie was one of the biggest gossips in The Lofts. She was like an extreme broadcaster, an ultra-specialised local news station, the ever-present reporter who not only knew her neighbourhood intimately, but knew who would be interested to know it too. However, as Monique told her the story, Millie's jaw dropped lower and lower. Ben wondered if it would actually land in the organic hummus.

"So you see Millie, we are in a very difficult situation, particularly my dear friend Kelly whom I am very scared for. Please do this for us. You only need to invite Amber down here at a particular moment. It would really save our... bacon."

As she said the word "bacon", a look of mischief crossed Monique's face. Even her threats were understated, elegant but so effective. She was a beautiful lily of the valley, radiating gorgeousness to all who saw her, but still poisonous if consumed. Subtly reminded of how she, a rather vocal vegetarian, had been caught secretly stuffing her face with sausage and bacon, Millie blushed and immediately agreed to do as Monique asked.

"Well, I think it is time to coordinate. Meanwhile, Kelly, Rubens, can I get your opinion on this organic lemonade please?"

They planned the set up for early Friday evening. Rubens said Crystal was pretty much always in the gym at that time as she wanted to look her slimmest for Friday night clubbing, and Millie would lure Amber down with a new vegetarian dish.

"In honour of my co-conspirator, maybe I could make vegetarian feijoada, Rubens."

"Are you seriously suggesting taking my country's national dish, and substituting pork, beef and sausage with your dreadful Quorn and tofu? What do you suggest next? Making a carnival in Blackpool with the dance troupes doing the conga in Kappa tracksuits and cagoules?"

Kelly wondered who Rubens was shagging for him to

have gained such a deep knowledge of British local colour. Ben just wondered what a cagoule was.

Millie shrugged – it took more than a nationalistic put-down to get her heated up. Rubens shook his head at her, but not unkindly:

"So, we make it Friday at 6.30pm. I am looking forward to it already. And now I must go and check that all your neighbours are exercising correctly. Ciao!"

As Rubens wandered over to the main part of the gym, Ben heard an all too familiar squeal fast approaching. He turned round and almost stumbled as Pansy Ho walked up to him boldly, with a second Pansy by her side.

"Mr Ben Barlettano. So nice to see you again! And with clothes on this time. I see you learn how to live here quickly. This is my twin sister, Ms Mildred Ho."

"Hello Mr Ben Barlettano. It is so nice to meet Big Ben."

And with that Pansy and Mildred erupted into shrieks of laughter. Monique looked irritated, Kelly amused, Millie concerned for her glassware.

Pansy was wearing tight pink towelling shorts and a red sports vest top; Mildred an identical outfit in yellow and pale blue. Their outfits were finished off with sparkly Tokyo Girls Collection pumps in matching colours. They looked interesting: a strange cross between the wide-eyed camera toting tourists in London laden with designer bags, and some middle-aged businessman's fantasy from "Asian Babes". Ben couldn't help but wonder whether that girly exterior was all for show. With the exception of the occasional decibel, Pansy Ho seemed to be in full control of all around her. That control thing again. There was more to that woman than met the eye. Although Ben knew deep down that it couldn't really be true, the overgrown teenager inside him wondered and hoped that maybe Pansy and Mildred did moonlight from inventory taking. Maybe he could get Kelly to ask.

Monique looked around the room and allowed herself a half smile:

"Oh, that is such a waste!"

Ben followed Monique's eyes to the new arrivals. One was a young dark-skinned guy. He walked into the gym with easy familiarity. He was followed by a blond man with piercing blue eyes, probably in his mid-thirties.

"Actually," Monique corrected herself, "I don't think they are wasted at all. From what I hear they are very popular and rather open-minded. I guess that is a polite way of saying they are a pair of tarts. Behold, Ben – yonder walk Jamal Qureshi and Alex O'Connell, our A-list gay couple in flat 432. They put us singletons to shame. They have been together for seven years, although in an open relationship. But then, look at them. They are easy on the eye, non? Apparently, they both pack a very mean punch to boot in the trouser department. I wish I could be a gay man for a night."

Kelly waved at them enthusiastically:

"Jamal, Alex, you gorgeous things, you just look good enough to eat. If you weren't so full of meat I'm sure Millie would have you on her menu."

As the men walked up, an orgy of air kissing, "darling, this" and "sweetie, that"" ensued. A friendly hubbub of touchy feeliness that the girls loved and Ben found a little distracting.

Finally, he got introduced.

Jamal seemed slightly distant, nodding at him with narrowed eyes. Alex on the other hand gave him a broad grin and a firm handshake which lasted just a bit longer than Ben was expecting, accompanied by a look deep into Ben's eyes, as if Alex were trying to get into Ben's head and stay there.

Ben felt hesitant. Surely Alex wasn't trying to flirt with him. Ben didn't like it. Being looked at as a sex object by an older man, pace an attractive one, was creepy and unsettling. Yet somehow it was also flattering, in its own way. Flattering, and yet uncomfortable.

No one else picked up on Ben's momentary discomfort, especially not the girls. They were used to dealing with such conflicting situations on a daily basis. Alex obviously was a player. Ben decided he wasn't going to like Alex O'Connell. Jamal also seemed a bit too aware of how beautiful he was. He must obviously be with Alex for the money. Ben bet Alex was a banker. He had that arrogant air about him. Why did Kelly like them so much?

"Well, I guess we had better get on with the workout. It's so much harder these days to keep this old carcass looking half decent, especially when I am out clubbing with guys who were born when I was already drawing the pension. Nice to have met you, Ben – I hope you enjoy your time here."

Alex's grin was sexy. He walked off with Jamal.

"He makes me laugh, that man." said Monique,

thoughtfully, "He does look amazing for forty, doesn't he?"

Kelly sighed and nodded:

"It rather sets the standard for us, doesn't it? But it must be a good thing. Why give up on looking as good as you can manage, for as long as you can? It surely enhances life."

"Where are they from?" asked Ben

"We're still prying. We're getting there. As far as I know, Jamal lost his father and two brothers in the Algerian civil war. He was the baby of the family. It's a bit of history we don't focus on, but over one hundred thousand people died in the nineties when the democratically elected Islamist party rebelled after being denied power by the Algerian army, probably backed by the French and the US. Anyway, Jamal somehow managed to finish his engineering degree in Algiers. After that, his mother saved up enough money to send him to Paris because she was so scared he would be next. He then came to London where he had to start working washing dishes in a bar because his English wasn't good enough for him to find a job as an engineer."

"Geez," said Ben, "it's Dickensian."

"Or Victor Hugo-esque. Certainly puts a student loan in context, hardship-wise," agreed Kelly, "Anyway, after a year of that and studying English he finally got a break into civil engineering, and now he has a team working for him. That guy has had it pretty hard, but he's a real fighter. I admire him. He has seen things that I hope never to see, like people being beaten in the street for not wearing the right clothes. And how angry must persecution make you?"

"Very angry indeed," said Ben reflectively, "What about Alex?"

"Alex is a bit of a surprise too. As far as I have worked out, he comes from a family of builders in Liverpool. He turned his back on the obvious option of taking over from his father as head of the firm and instead has worked for not-for-profit organisations since he left college. He's got pots of money, mind you – but he hasn't taken the easy way forward. He's got some extraordinary stories, most of which involve some escapade with the only gay in the village where Alex was digging a well. He was kidnapped in the Congo a few years ago and was given up for dead. Then, after six months in captivity, somehow he escaped. I saw a picture of him when he got back here. A fairly scary sight – skin and bones. And then, despite that, he went back two years ago. He's also been to Somalia, Darfur, you name it. Such impressive guys. They're more than the obsessively houseproud pair of walking libidos I used to have them down as. Then again, they haven't forgotten how to have fun."

Ben was not convinced yet. Jamal could yet prove to be a gold digger. As for Alex – yes, all very worthy – but sometimes women impress easily. There was more to this than met the eye. Ben thought he had better take his turn at pumping iron, to try to promote some heterosexuality around here.

It was time to warm up. The running machines gave a great view of the whole place. He could see Kelly and Monique still talking to Millie Myers, Rubens encouraging a rather portly middle-aged man to go for his fourth sit-up, Pansy and Mildred still squealing with laughter over something, and Jamal and Alex working out like machines.

What an odd community existed here in the Lofts. It seemed quirky to use the word in the context of a large concrete block of flats but Ben could see some sense in it. There was a distinct community in The Lofts. Ben had expected the anonymity of New York and couldn't get over how all these neighbours knew each other and actually socialised. Maybe they put a drug in the water. Or more likely it was that freaky Ms Myers and her "vegetarian treats" that turned everyone slightly strange. In any case, Ben felt protected and involved. Then he remembered the plan for Friday and felt a bit too involved. Maybe he should call his mother.

Gay dating sites seemed so last decade. Just hearing the expressions "Any face pics", "leave tracks" and "Gaydar years" took Alex back to his single days. A rough rule of thumb was that a 36 year-old on Gaydar would in fact be about 43. There was also the trick of putting photos on the site that were taken circa 1958. Alex often wondered why people did it. Did they really think that when the "date" turned up at the doorstep, expecting to find some muscular, youthful guy in his early thirties, and found himself facing instead some slightly lardy, lined man in his mid-forties, he wouldn't just turn on his heel and walk out, debating whether to go to advertising standards? Or maybe to just spread malicious truths about that abusive user?

But, thought Alex, from the optimistic user's perspective,

how would you even swing a date if you were not economical with the truth?

He shrugged, and leafed through QX Magazine. Not something he usually did midweek, as the gay clubbers' bible was usually only opened when the debauchery of the weekend needed planning. But oddly Alex was feeling up for fun that night. It was the periodic rebellion, raising its head again. He knew that he would have no problem persuading Jamal to either join him or good-naturedly to allow him to run off somewhere on his own.

The problem was that Alex had now leafed through almost all the magazine and there was nothing on that night that appealed. As he flicked through the last few pages where the male escorts stared out with telephone numbers and key dimensions, his eye was caught by a new guy in town. Kiwi. 23 years old. Model.

"I haven't seen that one before. Nice. Very nice!"

Alex hadn't realised Jamal was looking over his shoulder.

"There's nothing on tonight I fancy." Alex sighed. "Maybe we should do that thing we always talked about. You know. Phone an escort, to see what it's like."

"That guy is kind of tempting." admitted Jamal, "But it would be embarrassing when we inevitably meet him later at Afterlife."

Alex couldn't help but agree with Jamal. And yet there remained the issue of his desire that evening.

It was thus that Alex had gone online that Wednesday evening and had somehow transported back in time, back to the days of singledom. It was hard to believe how easy it was to dip beneath the vanilla surface of London life. After half an hour of fruitless searching through unattractive photos and unbelievable messages, he called Jamal over and they agreed to hook up with a couple of guys who were throwing an A-list only sex party in a penthouse in Clerkenwell. Very avant garde for a Wednesday night. Alex didn't think there was an underground scene he and Jamal hadn't yet discovered.

Boredom had overcome scepticism. They decided to risk the taxi fare. For once the bet paid off, as when they arrived, much to their surprise, the guys in the photos actually looked like their pictures. And they had invited a set of equally hot men to join them.

Alex had wandered in, enjoying the interest that he was generating. There is nothing like the feeling of being wanted – hungrily, immediately, mutually. This was a fierce and persuasive advantage of the gay scene. Frankly, you either understand it, or you don't. Some people don't need the reassurance of courtship. Sex does not have to be a negotiation if people are on genuinely equal terms.

Although Alex and Jamal had largely consigned the careless drug taking habit of their youth to the wastebin of the early noughties, tonight was about dipping back into the wilder side of their lost years – from which they had emerged largely unscathed. It was something to do with control of one's appetites and being fortunate possessors of non-addictive personalities. People who can have a cookie and not the whole jar. Alex and Jamal were indeed two of the lucky few. Plenty of others had not been so fortunate. They didn't see them around much any more.

Drugs tonight would be indulged in. A little GHB went a long way. Alex remembered discovering, years earlier, what the press now called "the date rape drug". He never quite managed to gain such moral high ground himself as G had helped Alex have some of the best consensual sex in his life, when, that is, he had got the dose right and not mixed it. He had also passed out, vomited all over himself and been rushed from a club, to which he could obviously never return, straight to hospital in the back of an ambulance. He would never mix G and alcohol again.

But that night everything had been perfect. After a more than satisfactory hors d'oeuvre with the hosts, they were just thinking about whether to go for a second round when a couple of new guests walked into the room.

"Thank God you listened to me, Alex." muttered Jamal, "I told you it would happen."

The man who walked into the room was the twenty-three year-old Kiwi model recently espied in QX. Alex was now definitely ready for the main course. And when he was hungry he rarely let the meal escape.

George was from Christchurch and had only been in London for a few months. He was straightforward. He had found that although he loved the glamour of being a male model he could make far more money if he let the clients touch him. They liked to use him, rather than just his image.

He was accompanied. His well-built friend had decent looks albeit in a rather conventional way. He was called Colin. He was a dentist from Doncaster. Whilst George oozed cool sex appeal from ten paces, Alex didn't really get Colin until things started. He'd always got bored when straight men talked about the things that certain women could do because they were so flexible. Now he understood. He would nickname Colin "Mr. Fantastic". The man could bend into incredibly convenient positions.

Jamal stretched out and ran a hand down George's thigh:

"You two make such an amazing couple. How long have you been together?"

Jamal was confused as George and Colin chuckled at his question.

"Mate," said George, looking at Jamal, amused, "you think we are together. Isn't it amazing what five hundred pounds and a good dose of G can do for you?"

"Sorry to ruin the illusion, Jamal," said Colin apologetically, "but I just got George's number from QX this afternoon. I asked him to organise something different for the next 24 hours."

Colin looked faintly sheepish as he straightened up.

"I'm only down from Doncaster for a conference".

Jamal and Alex just stared at them, wondering whether they should confess that they had had a similar idea. Probably not. If they did, Colin might ask for a contribution.

"Well I guess I must be pretty good at this then." said George, examining his nails. "Maybe I should think about moving from modelling to acting. It would be nice to be able to be honest with the folks back home."

"George," said Colin fondly, ruffling his curls, "whilst

I would love to see you headlining opposite Brad Pitt, it would be a terrible loss to the London gay scene. Think of your distraught clients. I for one would be devastated. You're an excellent escort – easily among the best in town. You get things done. Aside from being drop dead gorgeous, you bring me to this amazing penthouse and hook me up with these Donkey Kong studs. It's result upon result with you. It's not going to be the last time we see each other. Anyway, boys – are you going to join us at Mash later?"

"Nice to be asked." said Alex, "What is it, or should I know?"

"It's a new night down in Vauxhall." replied Colin. "The opening night was supposedly pretty good. We can then go for round two in Spartacus sauna before we head back off to my hotel for breakfast. Come on. We'll have fun."

It was tempting. But Jamal and Alex knew that on a week night they just – couldn't. It would knock them out. They were no longer students. Instead they exchanged numbers, with George promising to invite them round for dinner the next time Colin was in town. After thanking their hosts, they told their new friends to enjoy Vauxhall.

Alex and Jamal headed out to grab a cab home.

"Jamal. You know I'm always banging on about not being frivolous with money? We've done well tonight. We've saved the cost of hiring an escort, and met a few friends and the offer of dinner thrown in for free."

Jamal smiled at the partner who after seven years still knew how to keep him interested. His mind turned to another of the great pleasures in his life:

"Do you think George will make mutton stew?"

"Jamal!"

"I like mutton stew. And," persisted Jamal, "does this mean we can buy ourselves a proper anniversary present this weekend?"

6

Gorillas in the mist

"Oh goodness, this room odouriser has made me come over all woozy. Darling, please can you get Mummy a glass of water. I feel all light-headed. Liquid Gold. I've never even heard of it. And such a strange little bottle."

As Caroline Napier Jones rushed over to her mother with the glass of water, she wondered how she had been careless enough to leave a bottle of poppers out. It must have been from the escapades of Saturday night. She rarely took amyl nitrate, but the slaves seemed to like it. They became even more pliable in her firm, demanding hands. She would make sure the next slave was punished for this carelessness. And then she remembered. The poppers had belonged to Hartmut Glick. That inscrutable German lawyer who for some reason she found fascinating. And attractive. And who still hadn't rung her.

"Oh, that's better."

Eleanor Napier Jones waved a handkerchief at her errant daughter:

"Darling, I really must insist you stick to fresh flowers and lavender water, or even one of those ghastly scented candles I found here when you were at university. I knew we should have insisted upon Durham or Exeter and not let you come down here to London. But "Liquid Gold"? Whatever next? Will I be discovering a Tesco Nectar card in your purse, or fish fingers in your freezer compartment?"

Caroline often wondered how her mother would survive if ever she had to leave her rarified bubble of an existence and move into the real world.

Caroline had led a very sheltered existence until she was abruptly sent away to school at the age of eleven. The eighteen year-old who emerged was unrecognisable in every way, except in her mother's eyes, who still saw the innocent child. When Caroline arrived in London to read marketing and PR at University College London, Daddy had insisted upon finding her a nice flat where her mother could come and stay with her. Daddy's friend, Harry Gumpert, had found the place in the Castle Lofts. Harry had told Daddy what a great up-and-coming location it was. Harry, thought Caroline, was not a property guru. Eleanor Napier Jones had never forgiven him for bringing Elephant & Castle into her darling daughter's life.

As Ben stripped off his suit after another day at work, he surveyed his body in the bathroom mirror. Trying to look at his whole torso in what was effectively an oversized shaving mirror meant that he had to stretch on tiptoes. Even so, he was sure that he had lost a little off his pecs and his eight pack looked a little less sharp than just the week before in New York.

Damnation.

He resolved to throw himself into the gym and stay there. There was no time like the present to start, either. After all, if he was to lure Kelly Danvers away from that muscle-bound Brazilian he would need to be at the top of his game.

Ben flexed his right bicep and winced. No doubt about it. Rubens' arms were better than his. The son of a bitch was practically perfect. He still disliked him. It was doubtlessly unjust as Rubens had been really nice to him so far, but what the heck. All is fair in love and war, Ben told himself.

None of his new friends were in the gym when he went down, apart from the omnipresent Rubens who was actually working out himself that evening. He smiled at Ben and then got back into it. So serious. So focused. So it would be a challenge. Ben blocked everything out and went to work.

Working out intently was one of those strange things that felt so much better than one would expect it to. It was rather like revving an engine, and then feeling it roar into life. Once up and running the body took on a life of its own. Ben could feel each muscle strain and he tried to visualise the process of the smaller muscle fibres tearing so that they would grow back bigger, once he had finished and was downing his whey protein drink. Having been so self-conscious about his skinny frame for so long, Ben almost took a sexual pleasure from his body when he got a good angle in the mirror or was particularly pumped. This contrasted with the empty low on the bad days, when he could still see the skinny kid staring back at him. It was a very fine line to tread between insecurity and narcissism. Ben found the line hard to tread.

He deliberately avoided even looking at the Brazilian. The last thing he needed was to be put down by his rival. The effect of working out was undeniable. It really lifted his mood. An hour and a half of heavy exertion later, and Ben was feeling good. Damn sexy, even.

"A chocolate protein shake, skimmed milk, with a banana, hold the side of bacon, please Millie."

"Very funny, Ben. You sweaty Yankee doodle dandy. And we Brits didn't think that you Americans got irony. You can pull my leg now, but the boot would be on the other hand if you were that poor little veal kept in a dark shed all your life, or that goose that was force fed with paté so that its liver swelled out of all proportion. And then you don't even need it. I mean, no one asks for a protein steak after their workout, do they?"

Ben had immediately repented of trying to best mad Millie, and so sheepishly backed down. He downed his rather excellent shake in the face of the lecture, and went to get changed.

With aching muscles clamouring for attention like toddlers, Ben was looking forward to a good session in the sauna and steam room. Two very large middle-aged men were just leaving the communal showers as Ben walked in. He barely avoided brushing against their dripping fur. *Werewolves*. He thought it was so unfair that as men got older, hair seemed to desert the places where it was desirable and congregate in all the places that made women make that "ugh" noise. He wondered if he, too, would go bald and have to start shaving his back and trimming his ears and nose. Women went for sexy "Brazilians"; men needed a "back, sack and crack".

As Rubens Ribeiro walked into the showers, Ben wondered if that perfect, smooth, hairless body was the result of an all-over wax. Considering Rubens, it may even have been natural, although the designer trim on his groin gave the game away. The groin. Ah. Ben realised where he was looking – and Rubens had noticed – and Rubens was giving him that smile again.

Damn and damnation. Blushing bright red, Ben hailed Rubens in the most jockish way he could manage and headed off for the safety of the steam room. "Oh God", he groaned with embarrassment, clutching his head in his hands, as he recalled the knowing look in the Brazilian's eyes.

As Ben sat down, he realised he was not alone. Through the mist he could make out two large lumps, that still looked very hairy in the half darkness, and they were making strange grunting noises as they paced the small room. Feeling rather like Dian Fossey, Ben half expected the creatures he was observing to start beating their chests, or make threatening noises to establish their supremacy. Then the door opened and a different animal walked in. Completely naked, with his towel in his hand, Rubens came and sat right next to Ben.

Fantastic. Ben had the pair of intimidating gorillas pacing up and down in front of him, and the guy whose banana he had just been caught staring at, and who was going out with the female he wanted, sitting next to him, stark bollock naked to boot. This took the biscuit and the bacon. It seemed all so purposeful – as if Rubens was in fact illustrating with the work of art that was his body just why he was the alpha male, and why Ben should just give up. Ben had come down to the gym so he could feel better about himself, not to have it underlined that he was just a rather low-ranked member of the troop.

Just then with an extra loud grunt the two large silverbacks left the steam room.

A short silence ensued. Rubens leaned back, every inch the perfect looking man.

"So how are you settling in here, Ben?"

Rubens was very confident, and completely at ease. Ben was sure Rubens smiled at everyone just to show off his perfect teeth, and to draw attention to those lips that even Ben couldn't help noticing. Despite himself, Ben wondered how they made a kiss feel. He was sure everything was calculated with that guy.

"Pretty well, thanks. Everyone seems very friendly, although some are a bit strange. Take just now. I was given another lecture by Millie on not eating meat – and that happened the other day too, when I bought some food. That doesn't really happen in America. I've also been woken up early on a Sunday morning by a woman who barked orders at me whilst doing my inventory, and commenting on – ah – my state of undress. That was pretty novel, too."

"That would be Pansy, I guess. You're right, people around here take a little getting used to. But hey, you know – everyone has their own story and until you become aware of it, you really don't know the person at all."

This was seriously disappointing stuff from a naked man that Ben wanted to hate. Maybe Rubens wasn't as completely superficial as Ben had imagined. No. He could not afford to like the guy or give him credit in any way. That would be the bitter end of it all.

"But what about Kelly, Ben? Kel-ly. I love that girl. She is so direct, so strong, apart from being one of the most beautiful women in London."

So he did love her. Ben wasn't about to start discussing the girl of his dreams with the man of hers. That was taking submissive just a bit too far. He thought he'd change the subject.

"Rubens, man – how did you get a body like that? Have you been in the gym since you were about four years old or are you just a genetic freak?"

"I was a gymnast in Brazil. But it is nature. I train hard. I think I am lucky, too though, because I don't really ever put on fat. At least not now. But then my parents are… "

Rubens trailed off as he thought of his mother, and how he still had no idea of what he was going to do. He briefly clenched his eyes. However, this wasn't the time or the place. Still. He tried to relax. He really must get Kelly to talk to him. He had to.

"And your parents?" probed Ben.

"Sorry. Yes. Yes, as I was saying, they are very slim even though not so young now. I guess I am lucky."

"Yes, you are. I wouldn't mind having what you have. It's perfect."

"But Ben! You have an amazing body." Rubens' eyes were suddenly sharp and bright, and very black. "Flex your biceps. That's good. Very good. And now your abs. That is a real eight pack. And it goes all the way down."

Rubens looked Ben in the eyes without taking his hands off his stomach. Then Ben noticed what was happening between Rubens' legs. Then he noticed something happening between his own. What the hell! Before he could react Rubens' hand was down his towel. And Ben couldn't stop him. Or rather didn't. He finally woke up from his trance when Rubens Ribeiro showed him just how a kiss felt with those lips of his.

"What the fuck!"

"Ben, what's the problem?" said Rubens soothingly, "Not many people come in here and they wouldn't say anything anyway… "

"I don't mean that, Rubens! I am not gay! And what about Kelly? Does she know you do this? How the fuck can you even look her in the eye? Or does she know and she gets off on it? This is too fucked up, man! And will you please take your hand off my dick!"

Rubens still seemed to be smiling as he reluctantly removed his hand.

"Ben, I'm sorry. Don't swear. I thought when I kept seeing you look at me, even at my dick in the showers, I thought you liked me but were just too shy to say it. And – er – what has Kelly got to do with this? She knows I am gay and what I do in my private life is my business. She doesn't judge me like she doesn't judge any of her friends. Well, she does judge, but that's just Kelly."

"But she's your girlfriend, Rubens!"

For the first time since Ben had met him, Rubens

94

Ribeiro wasn't smiling. He looked shocked and then he burst out laughing.

"Caralho! You thought I was going out with Kelly. You crazy American! No way. No way! I joined the other team a long time ago, and I will not be going back."

Rubens passed a hand over his shaven head, still grinning:

"Kelly is fabulous, but not in that way. Well, not for me. But now. Now I understand. So you are obsessed with Kelly, thought she was mine and so that is why you were always looking at me. It wasn't me you wanted at all. Meu Deus. But if so, what was happening just now? It certainly felt as though you were enjoying it."

It had felt good. In fact Ben was still hard. What indeed was happening to him? He had always been aware of other men's bodies, or at least the fit ones, but he thought it was just a sign of his inferiority complex and wanting to be like them, not wanting to be with them.

He had never had an encounter like this before.

But then he had never met anyone like Rubens before. He was perfectly tolerant of gay men, but being gay himself? No, that one was not good. And anyway he liked women. He knew he did. And then he thought of the "b" word. But bisexuals were just either confused or plain greedy. Not him at all. Oh fuck! Oh fuck!

At that moment the two large silverbacks came grunting back into the steam room.

"I think it is time for a shower, Ben. Of course if you are able to get up."

As Rubens walked off lightly, Ben sat in a daze, newly

oblivious to the gorillas in the mist. What... had just happened there? Ben was suddenly wondering whether his obsession with his body, his muscles, his abs and more importantly how he measured up to the other guys was more than just his competitive nature. The fact of the matter was that not only had he not stopped Rubens from kissing him, but he had enjoyed it. Had he secretly been lusting after the Brazilian all this time? In any case he needed to get out of the gym and back to his room and think this one through. He hoped Rubens had finished showering.

Feeling like a nervous kid does the first time he's naked with other boys in the school changing room, Ben peered into the shower area. To his immense relief, it was empty. He didn't think he could cope with any more unwanted erections. After a quick wash he went to get dressed.

Rubens was there by the lockers, as relaxed as if he had just had a cup of tea. He saw Ben's stricken face and looked faintly sorry.

"Listen Ben. Be cool about this – it may not be what you were expecting but what happened, happened. And, as Shakira might have said, "dicks don't lie". Your head may not know what you want, but your little brother, he liked that and you have to carry him round with you every day. I was going to get married a few years ago, and then one night in Heaven changed everything. It wasn't easy. But you learn to deal with it. And gostoso, I can tell you that looking like you do, there will be a queue going round the block. Let's hope Kelly is OK with that."

And with that Hollywood smile flashing, Rubens left Ben alone in the changing room.

It was strange. Although Ben was feeling deeply confused, he rather liked that *queue round the block* remark.

Would he really be that successful with men?

What did Rubens mean by that Kelly comment? Did Rubens think that he was seeing Kelly? Or that he might?

Ben sighed. He wondered if they were open-minded enough to try a ménage-à-trois. Maybe that would be the only way to decide. He had to agree with Rubens' "dicks don't lie" observation. That was clearly true. The penis could not pretend and it had sent him quite a message. Communicative little sod. A sort of PR for the senses. Frankly, pretty much a PR at the best of times.

Maybe he was just one of those greedy bisexuals. What would his mother say? For the first time that evening Ben started to smile, thinking of all her bourgeois hurt and lack of understanding. That would be an Italian scene worth seeing.

But this was a real mess. That bloody Brazilian. Damn his perfect body, and to hell with those lips. They were likely to be the graveyard of a lot of good intentions and the birthplace of much guilt and confusion. Maybe that was all it was about. Big lips.

Perfect. He had the solution. He would get Kelly to have collagen needled into hers.

As his thoughts got more and more stupid, and less and less helpful, he decided that the best solution was the tried and tested British one, that he'd learnt about that week. He would go upstairs, make himself a cup of tea and watch Eastenders. He'd already caught the soap twice that week and could see that watching such a lot of miserable, unattractive people with sad lives couldn't help but make you feel better about your own existence. Happiness was indeed relative.

Rubens walked back into the changing rooms, handsome and confident.

"Listen. Here's my number. I don't usually do this. But even if you don't want to have sex with me, then you probably need the counselling."

Before Ben could reply, Rubens had walked out again. Ben really needed Earl Grey and Albert Square now. Time to switch the brain off and enjoy a soothing dose of schadenfreude. The sun would come out tomorrow.

Eleanor Napier Jones was rather partial to a strong Darjeeling tea with lemon and a scone with Cornish clotted cream of an afternoon. Caroline was well aware of her mother's habits, and thought that she could make up for getting her mother high on poppers by taking her out for a special treat.

The poppers incident would really just be another in the long line of disappointments that Caroline had caused her. Disappointments like not living in Belgravia; not having a holiday home in St Tropez; not having a Mercedes with chauffeur; and of course not marrying an independently wealthy, preferably noble, young gentlemen called Tarquin or Barnaby, who would whisk her away from the grubby world of actually having to go out to work at all.

"Even though it's not far, I've called us a taxi, Mother. I know you're not a big fan of the Elephant & Castle underpass, with neither scented candles nor Liquid Gold room odourisers to freshen it up."

"Thank you darling. I just find it so hard to ignore another human being asking me for money, but one doesn't really wear gloves in the daytime any more and the thoughts of making actual contact with the great unwashed... well, let's be clear. It might very well put me off my tea."

As they walked out of the flat, Caroline wondered whether eloquence and elegance made snobbery slightly more or rather less forgiveable.

"Darling, does the driver know where he is going? We don't appear to be heading for a bridge."

"Well mother, that is because we are staying south of the river. Believe it or not, but tea and cakes are not just a preserve of SW1."

Caroline watched her mother get more alarmed as the cab sped along the New Kent Road. Then her mobile rang.

"Caroline Napier Jones."

"Ms Napier Jones. Hartmut Glick here. I was fortunate enough to make your acquaintance on Saturday night and then once more on Monday."

Caroline's heart leapt like a salmon.

"Oh. Mr Glick. What a pleasure to hear from you. And – please feel free to call me Caroline."

"Actually, I prefer Ms Napier Jones. And I would like you to call me Mr Glick. It was an error to use first names and I would like it corrected. Anyhow, I am calling because I said I would and now you also have my number."

"I see. So this is an exercise in salving your conscience, Mr Glick."

"I believe in order, Ms Napier Jones. I will be at the

next meeting of PPLAY and I think that another successful liaison should be organised by using the method that we know to work. Arranging a meeting in another location would leave too many variables, too many things to chance. It might be… uncomfortable."

"Well, Mr Glick, thank you for your call. Much as I would love to stay and chatter away with you, I'm afraid I have business to attend to. I shall however look forward to seeing you at the next meeting. Have a nice evening, Mr Glick."

So the old dog had finally been shamed into calling her. But that act that she had liked so much on Saturday night… God, the man really was like that. What a wonderful caricature. One that may have gone quite mad. Did she like it, or was she freaked? No. Things were fine. She was chilled. She was not her mother. Damn. She'd forgotten all about her mother.

"Here you go, ladies."

"Caroline, what the deuce is this? That sign appears to be welcoming us to Asda, Old Kent Road, part of the Walmart family. I thought we were going out for tea."

The driver nodded helpfully:

"They have a lovely little café just by the checkouts. Very good value it is too. Me and the missus often go there for a nice bacon butty after the weekly shop. Sort of reward, you know. Treat ourselves!"

"No I don't know, actually." said Eleanor Napier Jones stiffly, "Driver, do you know where the Wolseley is? It's on Piccadilly just in case you don't ever pop in there for bacon butties. Kindly drive us there immediately."

"But mother I've booked a table here. By the window. We can't leave now."

"Driver, please ignore my daughter. She appears to be somewhat delirious. I shall have Antoine at the Wolseley get out the smelling salts. I believe the old-fashioned remedies are just what she needs."

Caroline couldn't hold back her laughter any longer. She knew that she wouldn't get her mother to ever set foot in a supermarket on the Old Kent Road, but she couldn't resist trying. The driver's comments had just been a bonus. He'd actually got her mother to use the word "butty". Priceless.

As they sped off to the safety of SW1, Caroline's thoughts turned to Hartmut Glick. For a naughty moment she imagined him disciplining her mother. Then she decided that was a bit too weird, wonderful as the prospect seemed.

7

A horny dilemma

Her three Martha Stewart White Phalaenopsis added understated elegance to the sitting room. She'd bought them because the online brochure had said they were also known as "moth orchids". Their exotic blooms resembled the grace of moths in flight. This was a distinct and cherished improvement upon the ungainliness of moths standing still – or horror of horrors, the unmitigated catastrophe of moths in one's cashmere jumper drawer. The presentation of the orchids, in matte black Skylands Foo Dog Planters, inspired by one of Martha's own planters, naturally added to the charm and tasteful interior that was a hallmark of Cornisha Burrows' Greenwich home.

Cornisha adored orchids. Whilst she loved picking up a pretty £15 bargain from Marks & Spencer, she also experienced particular excitement over the dendrobiums and cattelyas that she needed to procure from specialist vendors, to say nothing of her pride and joy, the scented Epidendrum Nocturnum from Costa Rica.

Even her holidays were influenced by orchids. She remembered her first trip to Singapore. Not only was it a paradise for an orchid addict such as her, but she had also discovered the VIP Orchid Garden in the Singapore Botanic Gardens. Dendrobium Memoria Princess Diana was a pure white beauty, Vandaenopsis Nelson Mandela a vibrant red, whilst Dendrobium Margaret Thatcher was a rather too ornate bloom in foxglove pink. In truth it would have clashed with the Baroness's ever present regal blue suit. But then it could have been yellow with red spots like the Renaglottis Ricky Martin. Cornisha wondered what the Latin macho man had thought when, long before he had shocked the world by coming out, he had been given a flower which looked like it had been inspired by a Flamenco dress. Clearly the gossip from Miami had even reached as far as the botanists of Singapore.

Cornisha always gave her floral children a full inspection before going to bed. It relaxed her, preparing her for a healthy sleep and the impeccable performance she would then produce in SBK's offices in central London. As well as being in control of all that passed before her, with an effortless ability to charm and coax the seemingly inexhaustible legal egos she dealt with every day, Cornisha was also the soul of discretion, hearing everything yet disclosing nothing, a skill essential for the Pandora's Box of secrets she had learnt and kept locked away at SBK. She didn't yet know that the arrival of Ben Barlettano, the boy she instinctively wanted to mother, would coincide with some explosive developments that would test that discretion to the full.

"Fuck. Fuck. Fuck."

Ben hadn't stopped swearing to himself since the day before. As it was difficult – nigh impossible – to smoke at work (in any case, he reminded himself sternly, he would never normally have more than three or four even on a particularly heavy day), at least he had his profanities to share his burden with. He tried not to swear too much, so that when he needed swearwords they really counted. He saw it as similar to his attempt to keep his alcohol tolerance low. The benefits were clear – it was more effective when you really needed the kick.

Ben hadn't been able to look Kelly in the face all day long. He'd even gone in early to avoid travelling together. For once, he was grateful for Hartmut Glick's total lack of interest in anything not strictly related to work. It was a relief not to be asked how you were. Strangely, the only person he did feel comfortable around was Cornisha Burrows. Even on a day like this, she managed to have a calming effect on him. Considering her rather full figure, Cornisha seemed to glide silently around the office, appearing from nowhere, with her perfectly coiffed long dark hair and elegant dark green dress, with a ready smile and a helpful word.

After a day dodging Kelly in the office, Ben decided he'd take the bus home rather than risking a painful tube journey. After looking at what passed for a map at the stop outside the Castle Lofts, Ben had decided that buses clearly weren't intended for the amateur and had steered well clear. He wondered how Londoners ever managed to get anywhere on them. He felt confused as soon as he looked at the supposed "route guide". But today felt like an emergency.

He sneaked out of the office early, and, as soon as he was a safe distance away, he settled on a bus stop. Fate was cutting him a little slack that day. The first bus that came along had "Elephant & Castle" on the front. The 133 took him over London Bridge. Looking at HMS Belfast and Tower Bridge, Ben thought it could be worth his while trying to figure out those bus routes, and put up with the 11 miles per hour average speed of London traffic. London was chock full of monuments that he had seen in guide books or read about, and you didn't really get to see much of them by tube.

Strata, or the Electric Shaver as Kelly called it, announced his arrival in Elephant & Castle. This was the down payment which showed that the Elephant still aspired to being an up-and-coming area. A forty-three storey modern skyscraper with wind turbines built into its peak – hence the shaver nickname – which clashed beautifully with the 1960s concrete monstrosities that Southwark Council had announced would be soon demolished. Those monstrosities did not include the Castle Lofts as, for some mind-boggling reason, this was a listed building, considered a fine example of postwar architecture, worthy of preservation for future generations. Ben was sure they would be ever so grateful.

Back in his room, Ben grabbed his sports bag and headed off down to the gym. He had decided to be bold and not to change his routine in any way. He needed to talk to Rubens, but he didn't want to appear too obvious. No Rubens as he walked in, so Ben went straight to the changing rooms. On coming out he saw Rubens sitting at a table in the café messing with his mobile.

Ben breathed deeply and went up to him.

Rubens turned and smiled at him:

"Hi gostoso, I thought you might be a bit shy today. Glad to see you here. See you in the steam room in about an hour?"

Rubens grinned broadly at Ben's look. Ben wished he wouldn't flaunt those perfect teeth, and those lips, my God those lips, so shamelessly in front of him. Ben had always thought women had played with him. Well, variety was the spice of life. Now he had a man playing with him. Did he have "plaything" written on his forehead?

"Listen Rubens, I can't deny what happened yesterday and of course a part of me was quite happy to go along with it… "

"And I know which part, gostoso."

Rubens started laughing at him again.

"Rubens, I'm trying to be serious here. This is pretty heavy for me to deal with and at the moment my way is to think about it in private and pretend it didn't happen in public. Give me some time."

"Hey, I told you. You got one hour to work out and then, ding ding, round two."

Ben wondered if Rubens would ever stop laughing at him. He felt tired: the Brazilian never seemed to be able to take anything seriously.

"Listen, Rubens, can't you see this is serious shit here? All you can do is dick around with me. Not all of us just float through life without a care in the world, you know."

"Serious shit, you say, Ben."

Rubens got up and stared thoughtfully at Ben.

"Well, Ben," he finally ventured, "If this is the most serious shit you have had to deal with, then maybe it is you who has been just floating through life, my friend. You got a hard-on when you didn't expect it. Hey, you might actually like something you never thought you would. Big deal! I reckon you have no idea what serious shit is."

Ben didn't know what to say. Although he felt somewhat turned inside out, Rubens was right. No one had died, no one was even hurt. Ben hadn't lost any friends, a job, money or even a favourite possession. He was freaking out because his self-defined masculinity had been shaken.

Why should it be such a big deal? Maybe Rubens was right and he should just chill out and enjoy it.

... what was he saying? Ben had no problem with gays, but Barlettano was not a cocksucker! It *was* serious shit!

"OK, Rubens, maybe it is not worthy of the BBC News, but this is serious for me. I'm asking you as someone I hope can understand. Just give me some time. You said you had been through this. Then you must know what I'm going through."

"Man, I'm Brazilian, not some problematic American. When I discovered the other side to life, I just made love, had fantastic sex and I was happy. Why should I have been troubled when I discovered the best sex of my life?"

Once again Ben didn't know how to respond. Were Americans so full of problems? Was that a racist comment? Should he just stop thinking about this and take refuge in the gym?

"OK, that may make me a troubled American who

107

thinks that an erection is the end of his world. You may think it is nothing, but it is pretty difficult for me to adjust to the person I may be and where it might take me. Please respect my need to deal with this my way."

Ben turned away angrily, but Rubens reached out a steady hand.

"OK, Ben, I am a bit hard on you. I can understand that it is not easy. You got me at a bad time. Problems at home. Real problems. Ones that for once I cannot resolve on my own. Ones where someone may… not make it. I just compare the two things, and this does not seem in any way important. I guess human beings always have problems. If you don't have big problems you exaggerate the little ones until they seem like big ones. Human nature. I should understand that."

Rubens' face looked somehow different when he said things like that. Interesting, mature, yet with more than a hint of vulnerability, all at the same time. Ben wondered if he was starting to look at the Brazilian the way he usually only eyed up girls.

On the other hand, this was infinitely less awkward than it might have been and the Brazilian deserved full credit for that. Ben forced out a weak smile.

"I guess I am over-reacting too. I just need some time to work things out. Oh, and I'd appreciate it if this stayed our secret."

"Of course, Ben, I understand. In fact I made Kelly promise not to tell anyone about this."

"You told Kelly? For fuck's… "

Ben stopped as Rubens laughed again. It was infectious.

Even Ben could see the obviousness of the cue and response.

"You like playing with me, don't you?"

"Well, it's so easy, gostoso. I mean you even give me lines like this, I don't even have to try."

The two men looked at each other. Although Ben tried not to, he couldn't help thinking about Rubens' lips, and how a deeper kiss would have felt, and then about what else those lips could do. He self-consciously had to adjust himself as his libido started to run away with him. How would they feel around his dick? The guy was just beautiful. He didn't know that Rubens was thinking exactly the same thing.

"Have we interrupted something, boys?"

They hadn't noticed Kelly and Monique come into the café. From the look she gave them, Ben could feel that Kelly suspected something was up.

"Monique, Kelly, darlings! Ben and I are just getting to know each other. We're finding we have all sorts of things in common."

"Really? May I ask what?"

"Well Kelly, apart from being totally devoted to you, we are both addicted to the gym, and just love a good session in the steam room afterwards. It stimulates blood flow, you know."

Ben rolled his eyes and smiled awkwardly. He knew better than to rise – oh no, no pun intended – to this now. Rubens would always have said things like this. There was no need to be oversensitive. Perhaps more importantly, there was nothing he could do about it.

"Oh you boys, getting all pumped up, comparing your biceps, admiring your hard bodies. So homoerotic! You'd better watch out, Ben, or Rubens will be introducing you to the delights of Spartacus Spa on a Sunday morning."

Had Rubens perhaps already told Kelly? Ben felt like he was being cornered. He decided to change the subject.

"So, Monique, are we all set for tomorrow night?"

"The lovely Amber will be down here at 7 o'clock to try some appalling new tofu recipe that Millie is cooking up. I think if Amber actually eats it, it would be punishment enough for what she did."

"And that will be just halfway through Crystal's workout session with me." said Rubens confidently, "She was so pleased when I told her that she had won my special prize. I think she nearly fainted when I told her she should feel particularly privileged as very few people ever get the pleasure of experiencing the Rubens Ribeiro special stimulation session. I was trying to convince Ben to go for it yesterday, but I think I still have some work to convince you, don't I, gostoso?"

Rubens grinned gleefully as he looked at Ben. Kelly snickered. Rubens was a massive flirt when he found someone he liked, although Ben looked even more embarrassed than usual. Why? She was intrigued.

Monique waved a carefully manicured hand around expansively as she contemplated the set up:

"Rubens, you should be careful if you will be specially stimulating her for one hour. That girl is always so, so... shiny! I need to put on my dark glasses before I can look at her. And when she goes out at night it is just ridiculous.

She is singlehandedly supporting a whole industry of high visibility sequins and shiny things. You could certainly never miss the woman. Her lipstick would make a baboon's backside scream for subtlety. Her skirts are usually so short – I think they have an allergy to her knees. That at least is understandable. I myself come out in a rash if I even get close to the girl. And why can she never find a top that is as long as her body? I see that girl's belly more than I see my own. It's deeply off-putting, and dimpled to boot. And that piercing! Awful. I do not like that girl!"

"Well, we would never have guessed, Monique." said Kelly thoughtfully, "You must get off the fence and let us know what you really think, sometime. She probably only needs a friendly word of advice in the wardrobe department. Maybe after all this you two should become friends? You should take her shopping down Bond Street – or maybe lend her some of those little designer dresses in the wardrobe that you never wear?"

"Kelly, I will personally rip up every piece of your clothing if you even suggest such a thing again. Me, being seen outside with her? It is bad enough saying hello in the lobby here. People might think we are more than just very casual acquaintances. And lend her my clothes? For a start, it does not matter how many "special sessions" she has with Rubens, she would never fit into my clothes. You cannot slim down "big bones" especially when they are the ones that are made for bearing children. Have you ever seen a pear-shaped Prada dress?"

Monique probably had more views on the topic. Ben did have to admit that Crystal was pretty shiny. Some women were like magpies – show them a sequin and they bought the whole shopful. Was there anything wrong with wearing a lot of sparkly, colourful clothes? Crystal and Amber certainly did make full use of the rainbow. With huge fistfuls of glitter added.

Rubens glanced at his watch:

"Anyhow, my beautiful people, I must leave you now."

Rubens gave Kelly the usual kiss on the lips and Monique a more elegant two cheek variety. He then moved towards Ben with an impish grin.

"Gostoso, come here. No cold formal American boy any more, now you are part of our family. I kiss all my friends, especially the straight boys."

Ben passively proffered his cheeks as those lips came in. He tried to imagine it was Angelina Jolie, but not even the goddess herself could block out the feel of Rubens on his skin, again.

"Is there something I should know about, Ben?" teased Kelly, "Rubens was rather fresh with you today."

"I thought all Brazilians were like that, Kelly. I don't see you kissing many men on the lips like he does with you."

"Are you jealous? I'm sure he would to you to if you asked nicely. See you tomorrow, darling, we can do some last-minute plotting at work. I'm sure Harry will want an update."

As Kelly and Monique disappeared, Ben thought about his impending Friday night. The trap was set. Crystal would be working out with Rubens from 6.30 pm onwards. Monique would be sitting at a table in the café. She would text Kelly when Amber came down to sample Millie's new delight. Monique would then text Rubens who would bring Crystal to the bar for an essential energy drink, of course part of the special stimulation prize. Unfortunately, Crystal would overhear the conversation that Kelly and Ben would initiate, the two girls would get into a massive fight, they would both be thrown out of the Lofts and Monique could stop texting. It was a perfect plan.

Perhaps Ben could then get on with resolving his Rubens problem.

James Burrows met Ashia Daka in Dar es Salaam in 1961. It had been love at first sight. The illicit relationship between a poor servant girl and the assistant conservator of forests in the colonial service of pre-Independence Tanganyika had met with polite society's disapproval and the ostracism of James' father, Prescott Burrows, who could not bear the thought of his only son's betrayal of his race.

As a fervent eugenicist, Prescott reserved more than a little sympathy for the Nazi experiment, although he was wise enough never to own up to this sordid secret after 1939, and political enough to feign all the appropriate public moral outrage and disgust after 1945. But the fact of his son mixing the Burrows bloodline with a woman from the colonies – well, that was one bitter pill that Prescott Burrows refused to swallow. When James' letter refusing to comply with Prescott's order to abandon Ashia arrived at the family home in Hampshire, the matter was decided. Prescott instructed his secretary to officially inform James of his disinheritance. They would never meet or even speak again.

As a boy growing up in a modest terraced house in London's East End, Conrad Burrows was only hazily aware of the family feud poisoning the generation above him. His mother Ashia had lived with the guilt of splitting her darling James from his family and reducing him from wealth to something closely approaching poverty. She would just fall silent if her son asked her to talk about the family. As for James Burrows, he was a typical Englishman of his generation. He would think nothing of embarking upon a two thousand mile journey across uncharted jungle or savannah, and had unhesitatingly given up a life of luxury for his principles and the woman he utterly adored. He was however quite incapable of discussing such terrors as emotions, his feelings or, of course, anything to do with the physical aspect of the human body.

It was only upon Prescott Burrows' death that the breach was healed. James Burrows saw his own mother again for the first time in fifteen years. When Granny Nancy sat the teenage Conrad down and explained the whole history, he felt tears coming. His parents had gone through so much hurt because of their love and his father's principles. He vowed he would never do anything to upset his father and would try to make up for all their pain.

Cornisha Burrows smiled ruefully to herself. Maybe sons were destined to turn into their fathers and to re-tread their paths. But somehow there was always a twist. Conrad had been a perfect son, the apple of his mother's eye, and a source of pride for his father. But perfect sons often have a secret deep down. Conrad was no exception. His mother had laughed the first time Conrad asked to try on one of her dresses and then did a little dance around the room. His parents had become less happy, when he fully embraced the "gender bender" movement of the early eighties. He avoided telling them that he had progressed to being a full on transvestite. But he couldn't hide it forever. His mother started sobbing and his father just stared at him when Conrad told them the truth about his secret life.

Despite his stiff upper lip, James Burrows was a kind and decent man. He was cut from different cloth to his father, Prescott Burrows. James had no intention of imitating his father's narrow-minded vindictiveness. After a large glass of Scotch, he told his son that he loved him no matter what. He asked Conrad to explain everything to him. It was James Burrows who accompanied Conrad to the hospital in Sao Paulo. He was there when Conrad finally became Cornisha.

8

Tofu Surprise

The man of both Crystal and Amber's dreams, Kerwin James, knew what he wanted. Long before he'd turned his mind to women, he'd wanted an Aston Martin.

He could still remember seeing one for the first time. He was ten years old at the time. The car had swung into view, a smooth, sleek beauty, cruising down a slightly dirty, messy, wide London road. Like a beautiful alien. Entirely mismatched to the setting, and all the more remarkable for it. Even then he had felt pure lust for the car. Now, here he was, ready and able to buy his own. After closing the biggest deal of his life he felt he deserved a reward. A proper one.

He'd kept his head down, working steadily all these years. All around him friends had taken a different path. It was less of a stretch to just go with the flow, avoiding deadlines or any sign of initiative or challenge.

Kerwin's first job had been the cold-calling classic, the initiation rite of any salesman and the graveyard of many. He'd started low-key, dealt with the brush-offs, developed a style with immeasurable patience and conviction. He knuckled under, pulled in the sales, multiplied the sales, and got noticed. Kerwin was careful to credit his leaders. Promotions followed: seven years later his business card described him as a "Global Account Director" – known as a *GAD*. The telecoms world always had to reduce everything to a ridiculous *TLA*. That would be a Three Letter Acronym.

Kerwin's grandfather had been a trader, back in Ghana. He moved to London when Kerwin's mother was in her early twenties. Grandad had a natural ability to listen. He understood that people liked to talk, especially about themselves. That was the way that you found out about them and about what they might need. Kerwin's Grandad gave him many pieces of advice. One which struck a chord was that God had given him two ears and just one mouth for a reason.

Kerwin never worked out who he got his methodical mind from but it was probably from a woman. He was ruthlessly organised and never let anything slip. He had action lists, contact lists, contract lists and even lists of his customers' favourite drinks, and other foibles. These were all meticulously updated, backed up and stored on the appropriate database.

Kerwin was a pleasant man, and his manner did not betray his ambition. His customers loved him and could relax around him. It did mean that his mobile could demand him at any time, like a shrill and needy girlfriend, but that was a price he was happy to pay for success.

Out of work, Kerwin unleashed a cheeky grin and a love of cool threads. With his sharp suits, Armani ties and essential eyewear, his workmates often pigeonholed Kerwin as a smooth talker who would try to sell sand to the Arabs. But they didn't know about his almost psychotic obsession with schedules, nor his grandfather's advice. Kerwin liked to think of himself as a dark horse, shocking all those condescending second-raters when it came to the monthly numbers. The sales numbers. The ones he always excelled at. Because, in contrast to most of his colleagues, Kerwin had listened to what people wanted, obtained it for them and followed up to check that it had been delivered. Correctly.

His Grandad had taught him one other thing. The cornrow, the clothes, the watch were all cool, and Kerwin loved them, but you had to look deeper and ask yourself if there was a man underneath all that paraphernalia. Grandad was clear on this. Look into your own eyes in the mirror. Ask them what you had done that day. And what if someone had done that to you? Could you sleep with that? If you couldn't, change things the next morning.

Kerwin invariably slept very well. That was when he slept alone, which wasn't too often. He loved the ladies and with that grin, those two ears doing all that listening, and a mouth superbly skilled in things other than just talking, the ladies loved Kerwin James. He had from time to time been called a male slut. Maybe he was, at times.

The ladies should appreciate him even more with his DB9. He'd thought about buying an M5 but a BMW was hardly an original choice. As beautiful as it was, the Jaguar coupé had been discarded for the same reason. Kerwin could have stretched to a Bentley Continental or even an old Ferrari or Lamborghini, but they were just too flash. Like himself, the car needed to be understated, clearly cool, and not something you came across every day. It had to be the DB9.

It was being delivered Saturday morning. He couldn't wait. And neither could Crystal Smith who'd bought a replacement Fendi especially for the occasion.

"Yes, Rubens, yes. I can feel the burn!"

"My special stimulation is going to make you burning hot all night tonight, menina. You are going to see how those men will be all over you in that club."

"Oh this hurts more than waxing! What else – phew – should I expect from a Brazilian?"

Rubens was a master at laughing out loud to really poor jokes. It was a skill shared by good personal trainers, hairdressers, bartenders and salespeople everywhere. The goal was to make the client believe that your smile or laugh was totally genuine, and that you had priceless fun with them. It made business sense to convince them that you were just like them, and had so much in common. If they thought that, the rest of the selling came easy. More sessions. More money.

Rubens had taken a while to learn how to do it, and when he did get it, he was amazed at how simple the key rules were. Whenever you smile at someone, or laugh at their joke, hold that expression for a few seconds longer than you would normally. When you turn away, do not let that smile vanish, because somehow they'll notice. Keep it plastered on your face even when they are not looking because they will pick it up. Rubens now did this brilliantly. He was so much more than a pretty face.

He smiled encouragingly at Crystal:

"Darling, you are doing so well, and becoming more gorgeous by the minute. I think a little more, and then it will be time for the special stimulation reward."

Over in the café, Millie was playing her part.

"Is that a new dress, Amber? It's lovely! Where did you get it?"

Millie Myers had never mastered Rubens' smiling techniques, but when she wanted, she too could deliver an insincere compliment with heartfelt sincerity. Millie actually thought Amber looked rather like one of those 30kg sacks of organic potatoes she bought once a month for the café. That is, if potatoes came in nasty electric blue polyester sacks with sequins stuck randomly all over them.

Amber beamed with delight.

"Thank you Millie! It is new – and it is going to get me a fine fella tonight. I can feel it in my bones. I got it from my favourite shop down the Walworth Road. You know the one? Opposite McDonalds? It makes me feel proper fashion forward, even if I paid a bit too much for it."

"Well," said Millie confidently, "I always say that more is more and less is less and gild looks lovely on a lily, which is a rose by any other name. And you are certainly going to be a rose between thorns tonight, Amber. Mark my words."

"Oh Millie you are always so lovely! Speaking of lovely, what is this wonderful new delight that I just have to try?"

"It's spicy plantain, yam and tagliatelle tofu surprise. Do

you know, I think it has your name just written all over it."

Millie served Amber up a generous portion of the yellow and orange mush. Amber feigned enthusiasm – but, as with much Millie made, it tasted far better than it looked.

Seated elegantly at a café table, Monique Mottin watched proceedings stealthily. She took out her ice pink mobile phone and texted Rubens Ribeiro: "*Sack of potatoes at three o'clock*".

Rubens glanced at his phone and led Crystal over:

"Crystal, this is the one you should be drinking; the "Extra Slimulating NRG Plus Shake". Now would you prefer Ugandan Chocolate, Wild Forest Loganberry or Brazilian Beanfest flavour?"

"That's easy, Rubens. You know how fond I am of anything Brazilian…"

Rubens turned on the professional laughter. Crystal smiled back at him, and then she noticed the electric blue blob at the counter.

"Oh hello Amber! How strange seeing you down here in the gym. Have you come to work out? Oh, what am I thinking? The gym is incidental! It's hungry o'clock, isn't it?"

"Very funny, Crystal. Actually, Millie made this dish, thinking especially of me. It's good for you and real tasty. Oh, just like me. But enough about me, already. How *is* your poor leg? I'm so glad to see that you are able to walk on it again."

"Well, luckily it hasn't got so much weight to support, so it's fine."

"It must be a lot easier without that heavy bag of yours, Crystal. After all, the genuine article always does weigh more than cheap imitations."

The two girls faced off, each daring the other to up the stakes in the war of attrition that they had been conducting ever since they had met and clashed over Kerwin James, with just a brief ceasefire after Crystal had been wounded in the Battle of Fake Fendi. Of course, they were pro enough to play the game to perfection. Throughout, both maintained a broad smile plastered on their heavily lipstick laden lips. For that to vanish would be a sign that a shot had hit target.

At that moment, Kelly received Monique's next text: *"Fashion disasters in position"*. She and Ben were in the reception area, and they immediately headed off towards the gym. Never keen on confrontation, Ben was feeling nervous already. Then he heard an all too familiar screeching sound.

"Hello, Kelly. And say, hello Big Ben! You go for workout now? Before you go Mildred and I need to ask you something. We are going to New York for holidays and we want to know where are the best places to go shopping."

Pansy and Mildred Ho arrested his progress like two militant Barbie dolls. Ben took a step back.

"I'm afraid I am not very big on shopping, Pansy, especially not for girls' clothes. I wouldn't really know."

"But you must have girlfriends in New York. You from there no?"

"Yes I do, but maybe they don't have the same taste as you."

Ben was quite sure his friends did not have the same taste as Pansy and Mildred Ho. And in any case they did not have time for this nonsense. Kelly looked as if she were about to punch the Hos. They had to get to the café before Crystal left.

"But we want New York style. We know London style and we want something different. Your friends can help us to get New York look."

A cute smile framed Pansy's request. Kelly saw Ben wavering and motioned towards the door. Ben smiled uncomfortably.

"Listen, Pansy, I really don't think I can help you. But all the guide books have sections on shopping. I'd start there, if I were you."

Pansy and Mildred looked at him. Their faces registered surprise and enormous disappointment, before the Ho ebullience raced back.

"OK, we understand. You don't want to help us at all. Anyway, Mildred, he is type of man who comes to door in underpants and always wears boring suit or boring sports clothes. I am sure his girlfriends dress really boring too. We don't need help like that."

"Pansy, you're right, I'm really not very good with clothes. I would probably send you to the wrong places entirely."

"Don't worry Mr Ben Barlettano, we'll be fine. Just take good care of little flat, because I remember this when you looking for help because of marks you put on walls or plates you break. I always remember. Not good for you to be on wrong side of a Ho."

Ben couldn't believe he was being threatened by Pansy,

all for the sake of a shopping recommendation. What was she, a lawyer or something? For a moment Ben wondered whether he should give Pansy and Mildred his mother's number. Just for the sheer hell of it. Maybe not. Remember the inventory. Be diplomatic.

"Pansy, Mildred, OK, OK. I'll see what I can do. I'll call a couple of friends this weekend. I'm not promising anything – but I'll try."

"Oh, Big Ben, we knew you were friend really! See, Mildred, if people do not want to help you straight away, no use in going all girly and start crying. Much better to threaten them with an angry Ho's revenge, and they soon see right way. Thank you Big Ben!"

Ben gave Pansy and Mildred an awkward smile as Kelly practically dragged him down the corridor to the gym. However, like so many other unplanned shopping trips before then, Pansy and Mildred's New York jaunt had caused a fatal delay. By the time Ben and Kelly practically ran into the café, almost knocking over Amber and her tofu surprise, Crystal had already retreated back into the gym area and was working out hard, sounding like Venus Williams about to win Wimbledon. Ben turned and gave Kelly a helpless look. Ignoring him, Kelly stared balefully at Amber.

"You just tuck in there, Amber. Don't let us disturb you at the trough."

So this is how it would start. Amber almost choked on her surprise.

"I thought I told you to stay away from me. Maybe I should buy you a lead, Ben, so you can keep your little bitch out of trouble?"

Ben made a placatory gesture:

"Amber, we don't want to have any problems, but we did want to ask you if you had re-thought whether you would be talking to Crystal about... well, you know full well what it's about."

Amber's face almost turned purple. Her eyes flashed with fury as she just glowered at the Americans without saying a word. Then, with a visible effort, she decided to change tack.

"Listen, Yankees, this is not the place for this conversation. In fact I don't want to talk about this at all. But in any case keep your voices down as I do not want this broadcast to everyone in the Lofts."

"I'll bet you don't want to talk about it. If I'd done what you had, then I would want to keep it a dirty little secret too."

Amber looked as if she may smack Kelly in the mouth, or perhaps explode on the spot, showering everyone with garish red lipstick, blue sequinned polyester and tofu surprise. Again, though, she managed to bring her rage under control. She spoke in a low menacing tone:

"If you two do not shut up right now, you *will* pay the price. And that is a P-R-O-M-I-S-E."

Although Ben disliked arguments, he couldn't help but register just how tacky Amber's threat was. She sounded like a schoolyard bully, not a grown woman. And certainly not one who was supposed to be a nurse.

From the other side of the café Monique had been nervously watching the scene unfold. She couldn't believe that Kelly and Ben had managed to undo all the good work by arriving late. As she was debating what to do, Rubens Ribeiro was also keeping an eye on progress.

"Well done Crystal. Now take a one minute break. Oh, look. There's Kelly having fun with Amber. They do not look too happy. I wonder what's going on between them."

Crystal followed Rubens' gaze to where Amber was standing with Kelly and Ben. Now that her attention was drawn to it, Crystal did wonder what the hell was going on. The normally placid Amber Bluett looked furious. Her fists were clenched on the counter, almost as if she were going to attack the American girl. Crystal couldn't quite hear what they were saying but it certainly wasn't friendly.

Kelly was also fuming. Ben had really messed this up with that ridiculous conversation with those Hos. She wouldn't listen to him any further. She glanced over and noticed Crystal staring at them with a curious look on her face. Kelly realised that she was too far away to hear them talking and so decided that desperate measures were called for. She shouted out across the gym at the top of her voice.

"Crystal! Please could you come over here? We have some very important information for you. It's about your handbag and what happened last Friday."

Ben looked at her in disbelief. What had happened to the plan? Did she know what she was doing? It was difficult to see the join between shock and fury on Amber's face. Monique smiled to herself as she imagined what would come next.

Crystal walked quickly over to the group, wondering what Kelly had found out. Rubens decided he had better go along too. Monique maintained her dignified distance at her table.

"So, what's up then?" asked Crystal with interest.

"Crystal, I'm sorry you have to hear this way, but your lovely friend Amber set the whole thing up. The whole attack was a fake. Ben overheard her on the phone to a friend after leaving your party last Friday. It seems it was Amber's brother who attacked you."

Kelly did not get the immediate reaction she expected. Crystal stayed calm. She turned to her supposed friend and gazed at her in silence for a moment. Amber had a shocked and hurt expression ably pasted on her face.

"Amber? Tell me this isn't true."

"Crystal, we've known each other for years. How could you think I would ever do something like that? And you've met my brother! I don't know what is going on here. But as for this one – she has always been a troublemaker. Ben? Give me a break! He hasn't even been here long enough to understand English properly. I have no idea what this is about. He may have thought he heard one thing, but that was not what I said."

"So, you have nothing to do with it then?"

"Crystal, why would I do such a thing? You're my girl! We're always out together, with the gang."

"So, you're not upset about me and Kerwin then?" Crystal folded her arms. "You see, when it happened, when I was attacked, after I got over the shock and then the anger, I started to ask myself if it was because of something I'd done. Sure, there's, like, random violence, but most of the time when someone does something bad to you, it's payback for what you've done to them. So what did I feel bad about? What did I feel guilty about?" She shrugged and then zeroed in on Amber's face: "But then I had a thought. That's when he came into my mind. The man who chose me over you. Kerwin James. You used to really like him, didn't you?"

Although Amber was a true pro in the faking stakes, Crystal's final remark made her blood boil and for a split second a look of sheer hatred passed across her face. Unluckily for Amber, Crystal Smith was a lot more perceptive than people gave her credit for. She noticed it. So it was true. Amber did hate her. And that... *bitch* had got her attacked.

Now it was Crystal's turn to explode.

"You cow! It's true, isn't it! How could you do such a thing?"

"Crystal, this is crazy! I would never do something like that! I'm not that kind of girl. I don't even eat meat for heaven's sake!"

Remembering some of the stories Amber had told her and the girls about people who had got on the wrong side of the Bluetts, Crystal had no doubt about what Amber could or couldn't do.

"You must think I am a complete airhead, Amber. Do you think I don't remember the stories you've told us about the poor sods who crossed the Bluett posse? You're not that kind of girl? Bad enough you get your brother to attack me in the street, now you're even insulting my intelligence. But wait, I must be wrong. After all you don't even eat meat. Chow down on this, you vegetarian bitch!"

With that, Crystal snatched up Millie's tureen of tofu surprise from the counter and deftly tipped it over Amber's head.

It made a very satisfying slithering, sloppy noise, like a hot mud pool burping contentedly to itself. Overcooked tagliatelle cascaded down Amber's head, lumps catching in her extensions. Gobs of creamy sauce with squidgy tofu and chopped yam and plantain pieces dripped off her chin and nose, covering her beautiful new blue dress in a gooey orangey mess.

For a moment there was a stunned silence, until it was broken by an elegant giggle from the other side of the café. It was strangely, identifiably French even from a distance.

"Oh no, Millie, your fantastic new dish! Oh – and Amber, it looks like someone has vomited all over that... dress of yours. What a shame, it will be ruined!"

Ben was now desperate to burst out laughing. He avoided looking at Rubens and Kelly, who he couldn't believe was managing to keep a straight face, and just focused on Amber who was slowly turning purple with rage again.

No one had ever done this to Amber Bluett. Ever. Amber had half a mind to leather her foe into the ground. But there were too many witnesses, probably even bloody CCTV. She had to control herself. Should she start crying and continue to protest her innocence? Crystal wasn't that stupid. Stupid, yes, but not that stupid. Amber snapped through her mental Rolodex of fierce tricks – "*Quick girl! Do something*" she thought.

Indecision rarely dwelt long in Amber Bluett's mind. This time was no exception. The game was up. She had to go for damage limitation now, and pick off her enemies one by one later. She turned to Crystal and spoke to her in a low serious voice with an upset look on her face, annoying Monique in the process as she couldn't hear from her table.

"Crystal, you and I have been friends for a long time now. We've always been out together, had great times with the girls, even been on holiday. How could we ever forget Ayia Napa? But you were always the one with more success with the guys. I don't know what you do, but there's always a queue for you, but me… well, I have to take the leftovers."

"Looks like you've still got some of those stuck in your hair, Amber."

Amber glowered at Kelly, mentally noting she would pay for that comment (after she had paid for everything else), and tried to get a bit more tofu out of her hair. She ignored her for now, and continued:

"Then finally one sweet, cool guy who treats a woman right comes along and I feel happy. Sure it's just the start, but I can see it working out. But that wasn't counting on you, Crystal Smith, coming and turning his mind upside down and his head inside out. When you stole Kerwin away from me, it was just too much for me. I lost my mind. And I put on weight."

Amber started sobbing. With a piece of yam stuck in her left eye and her right eye full of that spicy sauce, the stinging was so bad that tears had naturally started flowing down her face.

Rubens, who had been silent all the time, suddenly felt a little sorry for Amber.

"Don't cry, Amber. Here – do you want a tissue?"

Kelly re-entered the fray.

"She'd probably prefer a paper napkin. That way she could take some of the tofu home to eat later."

Millie threw her hands up:

"I can always make some more!" she announced unnecessarily, "Although I must say that I must protest at such a waste of good food. Do you know how many people don't have the chance to eat a nutritious meal like… "

Millie fell suddenly silent as everyone turned and stared at her, silently informing her that it was time to zip it.

As Amber wiped some of the sauce out of her eyes with Rubens' tissue, she vowed again that the American woman was going down. But first she had to take care of Crystal.

"Oh, Crystal. I've been feeling so bad since Friday. I only wanted my brother to give you a bit of a shock and then when I saw your leg, I couldn't believe what had happened. I know you will probably never be able to forgive me, but you must believe me. I am so sorry about this stupid thing I did and I will do anything to make it up to you. Even though I know you will never be able to trust me again."

With that Amber started bawling into her creamy tissue. By now Millie's concoction had started to dissolve Amber's cheap mascara, and she was starting to look like an extra from the Thriller video. She was even starting to smell like one might.

Although Crystal was still furious and shocked at her friend's actions, the sight of Amber looking quite so pathetic did have its effect. She knew how she had suffered in the past when she had not got her man, and this was a way of life for Amber. Worse yet, Amber had to look straight at the success story that she imagined Crystal Smith was. And worst of all, Crystal had stolen her man. Amber had had a moment of madness, but it didn't mean that she, Crystal, could not forgive. And although being knocked to the ground was awful, Crystal had always wanted to pour a bucket of slop over someone's head. God, it had felt so good. Shame she didn't have a camera. But wait. Would it be insensitive to take a photo with her iPhone?

Before Crystal could decide whether to go for it, Amber decided enough was enough.

"Crystal, we need to spend some time alone, away from these people. Nobody else can understand what we have together. I'm sorry we had to do our dirty washing in such a place."

"And that's quite some dirty washing you have there, Amber. You'll need a pretty good stain remover to get all that nastiness out of such a delicate material. That goes with the territory, I suppose, for a wolf in cheap clothing."

Would that American never shut up? Amber gave Kelly a forced smile, and focused back on Crystal.

"I'll call you, girl. I am so sorry and I swear I will make it up to you. I don't know how, Crystal Smith, but as God is my witness, you will see that I am a true friend who just made one really bad mistake and will regret it for the rest of her life. Kelly, can I have a word in private?"

From the change in tone when Amber said the word Kelly, Ben sensed that, although Amber may be all contrition with Crystal, the real Amber was a millimetre under the surface, ready to burst through the skin like some vulgar alien. He stayed near to Kelly as they stepped aside.

"This ain't over, bitch." said Amber neutrally. "In fact it just got started. You have no idea what is going to come raining down on your pretty little head. I warned you not to get involved but you had to open your big mouth. But you will see. Me and Crystal, we go way back and I know that girl. She'll come round and we'll be best friends again before you know it. But you, Miss American Pie, you got yourself one enemy that never forgets and always gets her revenge. You're going down. Just keep looking round the corner, because you're not going to know where it's coming from. You're going to be Miss American Paella when I am through."

Somehow Amber managed to have attitude even with scraps of plantain in orange sludge caked on her skin, like some particularly ineffective mud pack. Kelly gulped a little. Dealing with sheer venom was not easy. With a last dark look, Amber stormed off towards the lifts.

Arthur Bilks barely raised an eyebrow as she trailed through reception. He hoped she wouldn't drip in the lift, but he knew far better than to say anything to that one.

Amber was raging. She knew she could bring Crystal round, because that girl was too dumb and too soft for her own good, however much of a slapper she was when it came to men. But Amber's anger was volcanic – the Eyjafjallajokull of the chav world – and it meant consequences would follow.

Crystal felt upset but knew what she had to do, which was to finish her workout so she would look her best for her date with Kerwin later that night. She asked Rubens

133

if they could carry on. She would have time to think about the whole Amber situation later.

Rubens had thought for a while that he was back in Brazil in one of Globo's telenovelas, albeit one of the really low budget ones. Maybe Millie should have tried her tofu feijoada after all.

Monique closed her mini video camera that had discreetly been recording the whole scene, hoping that the microphone had picked everything up. She would watch that again later, maybe with Harry.

Millie Myers got out her mop and sadly started cleaning away what had indeed been a surprise for Amber. Should she make it again or would that just be a reminder of an unpleasant evening? Damn that American girl, taking the whole night's focus off her vegetarian cooking. If it wasn't one thing, it was another, in the battle against meat.

Kelly, for all her bravado, was disconcerted and worried about what she had unleashed. She smiled nervously at Ben and gave him a big hug. He hadn't needed to follow her out with Amber but she was so glad he did. She'd been a bit hard on him. He may not be the action hero she had always dreamed of, but he seemed like a caring guy who would be there when you needed him. And maybe having someone who thought before he opened his mouth would not be such a bad thing.

It was the first time she had properly felt the body underneath Ben's clothes. There was a lot of it, in all the right places. It was as firm and tight as a twenty-something gym addict's body should be. It felt strong and she felt ready. The hug went on longer than she expected. For the first time she started to see what attracted Rubens Ribeiro to Big Ben.

Rather incongruously, Ben was thinking that he had had quite an exciting first week in London. It had actually only been six days. He was alternating between being shocked at what Kelly had done, and wanting to crease himself laughing at the state of Amber Bluett, who had played out the whole performance looking as though an entire football team had barfed all over her.

It was a strange state of affairs. He would have to watch out for Kelly now. He felt a difference in her in that moment, a sudden vulnerability that he hadn't noticed before. Maybe the girl from Louisiana was human after all, and she needed a big strong man like him to look after her. He could even turn the Amber Bluett fiasco to his advantage. This would be a superb way of getting closer to the girl of his dreams. After his customary moment of guilt at using misfortune for his own selfish ends his mind skipped busily to the boy in his life. Kelly's skin wasn't quite as smooth as Rubens' and although her arms were beautifully toned, they weren't Rubens' massive guns. But then Rubens didn't have a pair of tits like the ones that were now pressing into Ben's chest. Pecs were nice but nothing gave the feeling of a perfect rack in your hands, in your mouth, on your dick, oh God, what she probably could do with those tits of hers...

Ben forced himself to slow down, to control his accelerating thoughts. He felt, as he always imagined at this stage, that blood was starting to drain directly and rapidly from his brain to his dick. It was medically inaccurate, but it still seemed all too real to Ben. Any less circulation in his head must inevitably lead to the "I've got the blood flow so I rule the body!" phase of cock ruling head, and worse still, hard cock ruling willing head. Kelly was that bit too close. Some elegance was needed to stave off the prospect of a damn big bulge pressing into Kelly Danvers' groin and his brain going soft on him even as his cock did not.

Ben could never think straight when he had a hard-on. Considering that there was the best part of a pint of blood that was missing from the rest of his body because it had gone to power his erection, he always had imagined that therein may lie the reason for the loss of brain form. He wondered if well-hung men lost their reason more than those with a mini-me wiener when they got excited. But hang on. People gave blood all the time and a good idea that was too. They did not suffer impairment. You usually got a cookie. Maybe he needed a cookie? Still musing over the relativity of loss of brain capacity due to erectile function, Ben suddenly realised he had been hugging Kelly for quite some time and she hadn't pulled away from him.

He debated whether he should actually go for the inappropriate hard-on, before deciding against it, and then taking the lead and disengaging himself from her still hugging arms.

Kelly gave Ben a tender look, and then kissed him impulsively on the lips. It might have been the double shock of tenderness from Kelly and then the fact that she had initiated a kiss. Or maybe it was the effort of still weakly fighting that erection. Whatever it was, he just stood there motionless as Kelly tried to get some passion into the kiss.

Before he knew it she pulled away, as suddenly as she had started. Kelly was fazed at the mere fact of kissing Ben, embarrassed at doing it in public, and mortified at the fact that he hadn't kissed her back. Blushing bright red, she turned away. There were a couple of awkward seconds, before she gathered herself together. She patted him on the arm, then hurried back to grab Monique, telling Ben over her shoulder that she would see him in work the next morning.

Kerwin lay back contentedly, an arm around Crystal:

"See baby, I told you it was worth us coming home early just the two of us, instead of staying with all those drug-addled losers at that party. You and me have much more fun alone. Who needed a late night when tomorrow we'll be celebrating?"

Crystal hugged Kerwin tight. He was one of the good guys who actually checked to see if she wanted to talk after sex, rather than just rolling over and going to sleep, or taking another line, or worse, just leaving.

He was so excited about his new wheels. But then, so was she. Kerwin was getting this expensive new sports car. She couldn't remember what label it was, but it was pale blue and she had bought herself a new outfit especially to go with it.

Crystal hadn't told him about what had happened with Amber. She was trying to work it all out in her own head first, processing the facts, all those words, all those new thoughts she had had. She had been feeling guilty about what had happened, even though she had been the ultimate victim. She couldn't stop thinking that if she hadn't been such a competitive flirt, and rubbed Amber's face in it, to say nothing of making a raucously flagrant point at every opportunity about Amber's expanding waistline, then she wouldn't have provoked her into doing such an awful thing. Surely it would be weighing on Amber's conscience now.

Amber had become a bit of a bloater, though. But every girl likes a fat friend, to make her look good. A gay friend is useful too, for the truth about whether one's bottom really does look bonkable in that new outfit.

Crystal frowned. Maybe she should adopt Rubens. He was a bit too sexy, though. Having a friend that she fancied so much would almost feel as if she were cheating on Kerwin, even if Rubens were gay.

But she needed to get back to the point. Amber.

She propped herself up on her elbows, and looked at Kerwin searchingly:

"Why did you choose me over Amber, Kerwin?"

It just kind of came out like that. She hadn't intended to ask such a direct question, but in fact she did want to know. Kerwin was taken slightly aback. He wasn't sure where this was going. He kissed Crystal softly on the lips and looked at her for a few seconds before replying.

"Do you mean apart from the fact that you're so sexy it hurts?"

"Man, that's bad. You got that from a "Booty Luv" song!"

Kerwin laughed as she pretended to clip the back of his head. He was always so full of fun. Another thing she liked about this guy.

"But seriously, you seemed to be into her, and then I find, luckily for me, nothing's going on any more."

"Baby, it's true I always noticed you. I can't help it, I'm a man. A sexy woman like you? She would always catch my eye. You're right. There was something going on between me and Amber at first. But then problems started. It wasn't the weight. That came later. I'll admit that didn't help. True enough, I was getting worried that she just wouldn't stop growing… stop laughing now, Crystal. No, there was something else. I never felt that she was really interested in listening to me."

Kerwin stopped, almost in mid-thought, as if he had changed his mind over saying something.

Crystal was perplexed, but decided to play it with a light touch:

"So she didn't flatter your male ego enough? Maybe it's because she didn't like listening to all your bullshit about your new car?"

Now it was her turn to start laughing as Kerwin pretended to hit her with a pillow.

"Who told you about my new car? Do you want to hear all about it? Well, it's…"

They both laughed again. Crystal laughed a lot with Kerwin.

"For real though, Crystal. It was more than that. I felt that she would pretend to listen to what I said. But actually it was all about her. Once we got together, I was merely a pawn in her plan. I started to get a weird feeling being around her. And then, there was that family of hers."

Even though she had known Amber for a long time, Crystal had rarely met her family. Kerwin's words reminded her of her last contact with them, and suddenly she didn't feel like laughing. He was right. There was something wrong there. Maybe she didn't want to spoil a perfect night with Kerwin by talking about Amber and her family – especially not those Bluett brothers. They were not people you'd want to come across in a dark alley, damn their eyes.

As Crystal fell asleep in Kerwin's arms, loving and being loved, little did she know just how criminally minded the Bluett gang really was.

9

Guns for hire

"Paulo." Rubens whispered his brother's name.

Rubens Ribeiro rarely got his few family photos out, because it usually ended up the same way, with him feeling raw and in tears.

Paulo was three years his senior. Rubens had always looked up to his big brother. Their parents had showed them so much love, even though Rubens suspected that his father had secretly favoured the clever brother who studied medicine at the Universidade Federal, rather than the slower one who excelled at sports. Whilst his mother was planning Rubens' wedding to Gabriela, his father was planning Paulo's career.

The family lived in a tiny house in the Western suburbs of Rio de Janeiro. Money was tight, always, as his father's salary as a low level bureaucrat in the city administration was barely enough to support a wife, two boys, and Rubens' baby sister Anunciata. University fees made things tighter. But, as he knew his brother was sick of hearing, the father stuck with a well worn mantra. *Paulo would soon be a doctor, and then the family would be OK*.

Rubens remembered the day the new washing machine arrived: Paulo brought it in his friend Antonio's van. The family did not realise until that moment that Paulo had been working part time to earn some money to help out. Rubens remembered how his mother cried, and how his father embraced Paulo. He also remembered the almost imperceptible look of disappointment that was directed at him.

Rubens had tried to emulate his brother, but jobs were hard to come by. He asked Paulo off-handedly if he could get him a job working in the bar with him. Paulo couldn't help, and Rubens pretended that he did not care one way or the other. In fact, Paulo wouldn't even tell him where the bar was. He didn't even appear to want to talk about it, as though he felt that needing to have a job was embarrassing. Rubens guessed it couldn't be easy for his brother when most of his friends now were the rich kids of Rio. Some students arrived at University in BMWs and Mercedes. It wasn't easy for Paulo with his bus pass. You could try to pretend that it did not matter, but it did. It did. Brought about by wealth, imposed by inheritance, there was a world of distance between the life Paulo aspired to, and the one he was trying to leave behind; Paulo was careful to conceal from his devoted parents just how difficult it was to bridge that gap, and how much pressure it piled on his father's blue-eyed boy.

Feeling like a spare wheel himself, Rubens consoled himself with his football, his girls, his friends and of course the beach. Maybe he didn't have a Rolls Royce of a brain like his brother, but he had the Ferrari of bodies and everyone wanted to take it for a ride. Rubens had had a whole string of women drivers who, after enjoying the good times that marked a fling with Rubens Ribeiro, had tried to park him, and get him to settle down. Yet no matter what manoeuvres they tried, Rubens had always felt there was something missing. But life was good. He had fun. Then he met Gabriela. She took his world apart, and then put it together again, furnished with new horizons. Rubens had gladly let her take control. She was ready to drive him all the way to London.

It was Gabriela who first asked him if Paulo was on drugs. Rubens had laughed crossly at her, thinking how *stupid* she must be to think that the brother Rubens looked up to, the doctor-in-waiting, would take drugs. Just because Paulo was sometimes a bit absent-minded when he was spoken to. Just because he suffered mood swings. What did Gabriela know? Paulo was under pressure! That was because he was an intellectual, a thinker – not some average José.

Back then, Rubens didn't know much about Gabriela. She was far-thinking. She observed things and people. She wanted to know the background to the family she was mixing with. She was also genuinely worried about Paulo. She thought Rubens should know what was happening to his brother. So she made enquiries.

Rubens had wondered why Gabriela had chosen to take him to such an awful bar. When he saw Paulo, Rubens looked at Gabriela. She squeezed his arm, and told him quietly not to let Paulo see him. She knew how embarrassed Paulo would be if his little brother caught him at work.

Rubens could understand why Paulo didn't want him

to know he worked in such a terrible place. Rubens even smirked, thinking to himself that he would understand if his brother dabbled in drugs now and again, just to pass the time in this hellhole. Then he noticed that Paulo hadn't left the table he was sitting at. Different people were coming and going. Then Rubens saw the money go one way and the package the other, with but the barest attempt at concealment.

When Rubens confronted him, Paulo reacted by sneering:

"How in God's name did you think I paid my way and got the family all the stuff I do? You're so innocent, baby brother. I never asked you to interfere. But don't you worry! It's off your plate. Paulo's got it all under control. I deal, I don't do. The day I graduate, this stops."

Maybe Paulo really believed it. He probably felt wholly in control. But he wasn't in control of the gun that ended his life. The police didn't even bother investigating properly. It was another gangland killing in the favelas. One piece of dirt that they didn't really need to clean up.

Rubens never told his parents that he knew what his brother did. Could he have stopped it? He had worshipped clever Paulo, the future saviour of the family. Rubens wouldn't have been strong enough to stop him.

But now the burden of supporting the family fell on his shoulders.

The guilt and pain wasn't easily appeased. It seized Rubens daily like a stomach cramp. He wept for hours, till his eyes felt hot and dry, and his cheeks stung. But despite what felt like a yawning hole inside him, Rubens Ribeiro was tough. He knew things were not going to change unless he did. He embodied the *espiritu brasileiro*. The sadness he felt inside would not stop him from celebrating life and living for today, because who knew what tomorrow would bring? Seize the day, every day – Rubens embraced the attitude that made the Rio Carnival so inimitable, despite the world's best efforts to capture the celebratory feeling elsewhere. The visiting stranger would not easily guess at the hardship and sadness that hid behind the fantastic masks and costumes. Carnival remained a celebration of joy in its purest form. Tomorrow, alone in your home, you could worry, but today was time to party and show the world your happy face. And so it was with Rubens. His smiling face became more beautiful every day, even as his heart struggled to rebuild itself from the shock and pain of his brother's death.

London had been an instant band aid, and a vital part of the healing process. Until of course he had heard of his mother and the operation the family couldn't afford.

Kelly felt empty. It was the first time in her life she had not been kissed back. You always remember your first.

She shuddered as she remembered the moment again. Ben's reassuringly masculine arms had woken up the latent passion in her – and, just as suddenly, his apparently shocked, immobile lips had doused the flames with a lakeful of cold water. She could still feel his entire body stiffening when their lips had touched. Everything except the one desirable stiffening.

What had happened? She thought she had read the

signals. She normally knew when a guy was interested. Even though it had taken her some time to realise she was into Ben, she felt from the start that he was attracted to her. But maybe she was wrong. After all, there had been something going on between him and Rubens. There just had to be.

Had she really fallen for a gay guy? What sort of a mistake was that for a cosmopolitan girl about town? These days, hanging around with Rubens, she was practically turning into what he (and the rest of the world) termed a fag hag: a sometimes – though not always – charming female, who spends a suitably substantial proportion of her life with gays, and then usually complains about not being able to get a man. Occasionally – in the extreme cases – she might gently try to "convert" the splendid specimens of manhood gathered around her like cushions on a sofa, into less soft pieces of furnishing.

The thought was too uncomfortable to dwell on. Putting her lawyer's hat on, Kelly decided that there was insufficient evidence to make a decision, and such evidence as did exist was purely circumstantial. She would need to do more investigation and the best way to do this would be to study the subjects together. She had been feeling guilty for some days now that she had not yet had the conversation with Rubens about getting money for his mother. Now she could kill two birds with one stone by inviting Ben along too. She snapped open her mobile telephone like a 1950s compact.

Kelly was a woman of action. The next afternoon found her relaxed, as if nothing had happened, sunbathing in the sunshine in Victoria Park with Ben and Rubens. The park was almost beautiful, and certainly worth its weight in gold, a little lung on the northern bank of the Regent's Canal, just north east of the City. Hard by trendy Shoreditch, and artsy Hoxton, and with the new London overground line bringing trains to Hoxton, Haggerston and Dalston, the whole of inner Hackney was undergoing the kind of rebirth that Elephant was still dreaming of, overseen by a warming Olympic glow.

Being on the right side of trendy himself, Rubens lived in Shoreditch. He liked dragging the poor concrete jungle dwellers to the slightly more agreeable parts of his neighbourhood. It was certainly good to skip away from the Lofts for a while and show Ben a London the tourists never get to. This was London with a touch of mascara on, prettier than you might think.

Rubens stretched out on the grass:

"I love cycling into the West End from here, even though I have nearly ended up in the canal a few times."

He flashed his dazzling white teeth as he smiled widely. Ben felt momentarily distracted from his thoughts on the Regent's canal. Yet he was interested in these London waterways – he'd read about them in guidebooks: how the canals' short life as the arteries of England's Industrial Revolution had been followed by a long decline, before a new spring into life, now forming the backdrop to converted warehouse apartments with balconies, nice young middle-class families with three-wheeler buggies, the trendier-than-thou contingent hurrying to Hoxton, the latest uber-cool bar in Dalston, and, of course, the cyclists.

Cycling in London seemed to be a very serious business. If the classic image of Amsterdam, still ahead as the Cycle City par excellence in Europe, was one of a sedate, upright rider taking his or her time to manoeuvre round the canals, Londoners all seemed to be inspired by their Olympic medal winning team. The streets were mean and speedy. Far too much lycra dominated for Ben's taste – violent purple and yellow tight fitting suits that struggled aesthetically with the shapes crammed into them. Almost being hit on the canal and being told to "*get out of the fucking way*" by some sweaty oik on two wheels didn't impress Ben. It also jarred really badly with the relaxed Saturday lunchtime feel of Shoreditch.

Ben's reverie about wheels was suddenly interrupted by the appearance of a rather large man in a mini dress, huge blond wig and far too much make-up, accompanied by a couple of skinny boys in shiny tops. The apparition flounced over to them with what must have been intended to be a winning smile.

"Darlings. Darlings, my name's Miss Victoria Park and I do hope you are enjoying my eponymous garden. Now I'll only keep you a moment, but you do look like the type of people who know a good time when they see one. May I offer you special invites to the "Beauty and the Beast" party at the Dalston Superstore tonight? It is unmissable. Entertainment will be provided by the glamorous Farrah Faucet from Philadelphia – the Beauty – and her cousin the tawdry Tammie Tap from Tamworth – the Beast. I hope you mouth-watering treats will add to our beautiful contingent tonight. Do please do me the honour – I'd be pink with pleasure about it. Right, girls – let's go and find some beasts – shouldn't be too difficult, looking around us."

With a wave and a smile and a quick twist on her sparkling heels, Victoria Park strutted off across Victoria Park, with her equally be-sequinned organ grinders in tow. Kelly and Rubens smiled lazily after her. Ben looked at the invitation he had been given. A drag act and themed party night. So this was the East End scene he had heard about. He wondered what "mixed up filthy beats" meant. Maybe he should check it out. Not because he was gay, because he wasn't. He simply wanted to soak up the London scene.

Rubens rolled over onto his front.

"Funny, I've never seen drag queens doing promotions in Victoria Park before. Do you think there must be a little gay corner to this park? Like the muscle beach by the male bathing pond on Hampstead Heath?"

Ben couldn't tell if Rubens was making it up or not. That sounded a tad intriguing; a muscle beach, by a male bathing pond? Ben still didn't feel gay. This was nothing to do with being gay. It was just an appreciation of further facets of the city that he was making his home.

If nothing else, it might be good for a few admiring glances and maybe even an unsolicited compliment or two. Ben was certainly man enough not to feel threatened because a gay man found him attractive. He made a note to self that he would have to get Rubens to take him there, with Kelly too, of course.

Kelly was yawning:

"Amongst all these young families, we are the little gay corner, Rubens. You two are making me look like a fag hag

149

sitting with a pair of Muscle Marys, proudly displaying your bulging pecs and iron abs, all waxed to within an inch of their life."

Ben wondered what a fag hag was. And what a Muscle Mary was. Kelly saw his look of bemusement.

"Oh, of course Ben, you're a neophyte at all this, aren't you?"

Ben shrugged:

"I am, sweetheart. But you are dying to educate me."

Kelly frowned:

"Don't be like that. It takes away the fun of educating Rita. And you do need to know what's what. I got it all mixed up for a while – mainly because I did not want to ask. A Muscle Mary is one of those gay men who is all pumped up on the outside but still a bit of a Mary on the inside. You know, a bit sensitive and vulnerable – a sort of skittish Incredible Hulk. *You wouldn't like me when I'm angry, because I'll burst into tears.* Also known as "Walks like Tarzan, talks like Jane". A fag hag is a girl who spends all her time with Marys, muscled or not."

Ben couldn't decide whether he was more annoyed with the gay Mary connotation or gratified by being called muscular. It was cool that he stood the comparison with that Brazilian mega-body. On the downside, if Kelly thought he was gay, it would kill his chances of ever getting hold of her affections, to say nothing of those phenomenal tits of hers.

Ben decided he would play it dumb. So dumb that he couldn't even think that she was implying anything about him other than he was gorgeous.

"So I look that good? I knew those hours in the gym

would pay off for me. I never thought I'd be buff enough to look gay, Kelly."

Rubens tried to work out what was going on between Ben and Kelly. There was tingling tension that came and went, like a polyester sweater being rubbed on cheap carpet. The American was obviously still thinking he was in love with the girl. Rubens did not know what he felt about that either. He too would play it cool and get to the reason they were there in the first place.

"My friends. I thought today was supposed to be about you two great legal brains working out a way that I can get eight thousand pounds together quickly?"

Kelly turned her eyes to Rubens. He was struck by the intensity of her gaze. It was oddly comforting, the way it is always to be with somebody who actually gives a damn.

"Unfortunately we have not got very far. To state the obvious, the simplest solution is a bank loan. Ben has only just arrived but I have tried my bank and been given three thousand. It's a start."

Rubens stared at Kelly. He was dumbstruck.

"You have got a £3000 bank loan for me?"

Kelly smiled and blew Rubens a kiss.

"Rubens, I do have a heart you know. I know you would do the same for me if the roles were reversed."

Ben was equally surprised. As if it were nothing, Kelly had just announced she was lending Rubens £3000 she didn't have. Who even knew if Rubens would be able to pay it back? He hated himself for immediately thinking she was so much more than a brain on a rack. It was a breathtakingly generous offer. Should he offer his $2000 rainy day savings? He'd only known Rubens for a week. But it had been quite a week. And he had to come back with something to look good in front of Kelly.

"I've got a $2000 emergency fund that I won't need now I'm settled here and earning. I want your mother to have it."

Rubens was even more dumbstruck now. He didn't know if he could accept or not. Kelly decided to take control.

"So," said Kelly intently, "We need another £3500. Either we ask someone, or we do something illegal. Given that we are in London drug dealing could get us there." She smirked: "Or looking at you two boys, maybe prostitution."

Ben had no idea what to say. Was Kelly being serious? Would people pay money for him? Then he noticed Rubens' face.

The Brazilian didn't know if Kelly meant what she said, but just suggesting selling drugs was like a knife plunged into his chest. He had never told her how his brother had died; it was still too painful and sharing it with others made it more real. He usually dealt with it by pretending it had never happened and just suffered through the occasional reminder like this. Kelly saw the look on his face, and knowing him, realised it wasn't the prostitution that concerned him:

"Rubens, I wasn't seriously suggesting that you sell drugs. What I meant was that I think we need to ask someone. Between us we must know people who can lend us the money."

Espiritu brasileiro to the rescue. The private thoughts had been put back in their safe, and Rubens' dazzling smile made Kelly wonder if she had even really seen that fleeting look of pain.

"Kelly, borrowing money off you two is hard for me, but I will do it for my mother and I will thank you both for the rest of my life. But I will not go begging to other people. And I don't want you to either. I need to get the rest of the money myself. I have to look after my family no matter what. But, forgive me for reacting – not drug dealing. No way! No way! But using what God, my genes and the gym has given me, well that is something I have thought of. Well, actually more than thought of. But just a couple of times. When it happened. Not as a consistent... job."

"You're an escort, Rubens?"

Rubens looked back at Kelly. His big dark eyes looked like those of an Alsatian who knew it shouldn't have jumped on the table and eaten the sausages, but was still hoping – against hope – that his mistress would melt in front of its liquid gaze.

"Oh my God, Rubens! You are, aren't you!"

"Kelly, I've done it a few times, that's all. After the club where I gogo, sometimes I get guys coming up to me and offering me money. Good money. How much do you think I earn from dancing and personal training? I'm not a lawyer like you two."

"But Rubens, there are plenty of people who have normal jobs like working in Tesco, but they don't go and sell their ass to the first dirty old man they meet in a club, so that they can go and buy themselves the latest pair of D Squared jeans. There is a difference between shelf stacking and fudge packing, you know."

For a moment the Alsatian looked as if it was going to attack. Kelly retreated:

"Rubens, I didn't mean that quite the way it sounded... I am really sorry. Baby I love you and I hate to think of you doing something like that. I take it back. I am really, really sorry."

Slowly controlling a sense of outrage and hurt, Rubens started speaking in a very low, serious tone.

"Kelly, you know about my family problems now. But there is a lot that you don't know about. I am Rubens with the happy face and carefree smile and everyone has fun with me. And that's the way I want it. Most of the time. But behind the smile, especially when we are talking of my life in Brazil, even a friend like you has been hidden from this. You think I do this for a pair of jeans? Caralho, you have no fucking idea."

Rubens suddenly stopped himself. He had been about to tell Kelly to stick her money where the sun didn't shine, but then it occurred to him that it was he who had always hidden his life away. It was he who gave the impression that everything was fine, everything was fun, everything was beautiful and cool on Planet Rubens. He couldn't really blame Kelly for not suspecting that there was another side to his life. Just like he couldn't blame that innocent, but not so innocent, gostoso de Nova York sitting next to her. Americans! They thought the problems of the world were on their shoulders, but they really had it so easy.

Kelly couldn't speak. She felt guilty and was concerned about making it worse. Ben wondered what Rubens' real story was. The more he heard, the more he wanted to know. He noticed Kelly's uncertainty, and how upset Rubens still was and decided to take action. Big Ben coming out again. Not in that sense of course. Not in any gay sense.

Grabbing Kelly with one hand and Rubens with the other he pulled his two friends closer and gave them each a kiss on the cheek.

"Kelly, that was a completely stupid thing to say and you will be apologising for that for a long time. However, Rubens, we are not mind readers and you do look like you have a pretty fine life. Kelly cares so much for you, and if she says that, it's because you are like family. You remember that community we talked about? Well, I feel it here after just one week. If I found out one of my brothers was an escort I would have a strong reaction too. So you two, you hug, kiss, and make up – we need to decide what to do here, and we have all got to be on the same side."

Kelly and Rubens were taken slightly aback by Ben taking charge. He felt surprised too. Maybe London was helping him to find himself? He was questioning a lot of things he had taken for granted, conclusions he had easily and swiftly jumped to, comfortable "truths" that concealed a pack of lies. Nothing new there: black and white usually faded to grey if you looked hard at it. This city was glamour and grime, friendship and deceit, Beauty and the Beast... He felt himself drifting off as he mused on the oddity of it all. Rubens brought him back down to earth.

"Anyhow, so far I have only done it a few times when people come to me. But now I need more money. Quickly.

I think I should put an ad in one of the gay magazines here in London. £50 for the ad and I can get a couple of hundred pounds just from the first trick."

Rubens was one of the legion people who lived London's Janus face every day. That beautiful fitness trainer and dancer who was just so unattainable could be yours for an hour, for £200 plus taxi fare.

"Are you sure about this, Rubens? Isn't it dangerous?"

Kelly was nothing if not practical. The D Squared jeans comment was forgotten. Rubens wondered how he could have got so momentarily angry at her when he knew she was a sweetie inside really. And she cared for him in a way that mattered.

"It's not something I am happy to do, but I have friends who do it. Unless you are very strong I think it can change your attitude to sex, but in London for a man it doesn't seem so dangerous. I haven't heard too many bad stories about men. I guess at least with male escorts, they are usually stronger and more muscular than the clients. I can take care of myself."

The grin was back. But then Rubens had a point. Ben would like to see the man who could overpower the Brazilian. He'd like to watch. Purely from a sporting perspective.

He felt a summing up was in order:

"Well, I guess if you won't let us help you to get some more money then we don't have anything else on the table at the moment."

Kelly's phone rang. She walked off to take the call. She was back in two ticks.

"Boys, I forgot I was supposed to go to a dance thing on the South Bank with Monique this evening. I must dash. You finish your beers and we'll catch up tomorrow. I'll call you."

Rubens waved her off: "So boring when performers keep their clothes on," he called after her. "And they earn more than I do. *So* not fair!"

As Kelly hurried down the canal towards Hoxton station, she thought about the afternoon's conversation. She was still ashamed of herself for being so hard on Rubens. It must be harder than one thought, facing money worries, even without everyone else piling in with a view. She was also getting more and more impressed with Ben. He may look like a gay man, and be sensitive, but she felt that she was actually wrong when she had suspected him before. She could feel something between them. She'd never felt that with Rubens. Maybe she should drop in on him later after the show. To discuss the plan to help Rubens. Well, that would be the excuse. Maybe she would bring a bottle of wine?

Kerwin and Crystal drove round London for most of the day. It had been exceptional. The car was a dream, and they were getting on brilliantly.

They had dropped back in on Crystal's flat so she could gather belongings for the next day.

The DB9 had lived up to everything Kerwin had aspired to. His friends were impressed, his mother had cried, his father had beamed with pride, and Crystal, well, she was sure going to give him plenty of sugar for making her feel this way today, riding round like a princess. This was what Kerwin James worked hard for. Moments like this justified all the knocks.

Leaving the Castle Lofts, he waved at Arthur Bilks who opened the gate for him, and nearly knocked over a couple of men who drunkenly stumbled in front of him as they went into reception.

"Rubens! Sweetie! Do you like our new car?"

Rubens, who had almost ended up under the DB9, didn't hear Crystal calling to him. He was busy trying to keep Ben upright. They had been drinking all afternoon in the park and then gone for dinner with more alcohol, and then topped it off with a couple of vodkas in a bar in Shoreditch. Saturday night cab curse had struck with all its usual might; they hadn't been able to find a minicab for Ben, and so Rubens had offered to bring him back to Elephant on the bus. Maybe he would get a little reward? Rubens unaccountably felt as if he needed a hug. Ben had been chattering something about Kelly keeping a bit of distance from him today, and that he was a bit confused. Rubens reckoned that tonight would be a good night to clear Ben's mind.

Kelly didn't normally drink sparkling wine, but she liked the look of the Cava on special offer at Costcutter. A good cava went a long way. She was after all a debtor now. As she walked into the Lofts clutching her prize bubbles, she saw that Ben's light was on, high above her head. It lifted her heart, she felt that all was well, and that making her move again would be a natural progression. Things were all right. She was a confident, modern woman, with needs. The feeling lightened her spirits and directed her steps. She would just do it. Although she couldn't really believe that she was taking a bottle of wine to Ben's flat on a Saturday night, with intent, what was the worst that could happen?

Had the world turned upside down? She was terribly forward. Perhaps, but it seemed to be quite an ordinary thing to be.

As she knocked at Ben's door, Kelly rehearsed what she would say. *I needed to talk about Rubens' plan again, but I didn't want to say anything in front of him. I'm just so worried.* She smiled at the all too familiar mental rehearsal. People were so duplicitous at times, disguising true intention, even to themselves, even where it was blindingly obvious.

It was taking Ben a long time to answer the door.

A doubt washed over Kelly like a tsunami. Was this in any way all right? She hoped she hadn't caught him reading a magazine on the toilet, or, worse, masturbating. Men could be such passion killers at times. She knocked again and called through the door.

"Ben, I know you're in there. I saw the light on. It's me. Kelly."

After another minute the door opened. Christ, she had been right! Ben only had a towel on and she could see the bulge betraying the fact that he had indeed just been cracking one out. What to do with the wine? Then she smelt the alcohol coming off his breath. With the door half open, she could see part of the lounge; last time it had not had clothes thrown all over the floor. Men!

"Er... maybe this isn't such a good idea, Ben. I thought we could talk about the conversation this afternoon, but I can see this definitely isn't such a good idea. Here. Take the wine – we can drink it next time."

Ben tried to say something but words were not his friends that night and he just managed instead to stare at her in silence with a slightly bemused look on his face. Then the silence was broken by something being knocked over in the bedroom.

"Oh my God… you're not alone, are you?"

Looking past Ben at the mess in the lounge again, Kelly realised that she had seen that blue Dolce & Gabbana T shirt now on the floor a few hours earlier. But it wasn't Ben's. It belonged to a Brazilian.

Suddenly Kelly really needed to know, and, doing something else for the first time that she never thought she would ever do in her life, she pushed past an ever more bovine looking Ben and charged into the bedroom.

In different circumstances, Kelly might have found the sight of a man like Rubens Ribeiro totally naked and sporting what could only be described as a pretty generous erection, to be on the continuum between sexy and sexy. But not tonight. She threw the first thing to hand, which happened to be a sneaker, straight at Rubens' bobbing cock, and with a shriek worthy of Pansy Ho, spun back into the lounge, slamming the bedroom door behind her. Although not officially spurned, Kelly was furious as hell with herself for getting it so wrong about that weak-willed, confused, bisexual, wet, infuriating, gorgeous

160

New Yorker. As she again pushed her way past him, she snatched back the wine, and fired a parting salvo in his direction.

"I knew it. I knew I felt like a fag hag in that park. I should have known from that frozen kiss you didn't give me last night. And to think I was really starting to like you! I must be so goddamn stupid!"

10

Boyfriend Clinic

Sunlight streaming in onto a canary yellow wall didn't help Rubens' sore head at all. In a daze he wondered where he was. *Chitty on Contract*. A copy of *Time Out* magazine. A picture of a middle-aged woman wearing a mink coat and a bit too much make-up. Then he heard the breathing behind him. He frowned lightly. Who on earth had he gone home with last night? As he turned over and his eyes found Ben's naked body, it all rushed back to him.

Oh yes. That was it. He grimaced. After the initial thrill of getting the unattainable man into bed, it hadn't turned out to be one of the more spectacular shags of Rubens' life.

Some gay men really got off on chasing "straight" men around, but Rubens always preferred a guy who knew what to do, rather than feeling as if he were teaching an eighteen year-old to suck eggs.

Although the American had been very drunk, Rubens could tell that Ben wasn't exactly an accomplished Casanova. His kiss had been far more enthusiastic than sensual, and his fumbling hands seemed confused as to where they wanted to be. Rubens laughed to himself as he remembered how Ben had struggled to take off Rubens' belt and pull his jeans down. God only knows how he coped with a bra.

Underneath his clothes Ben certainly measured up, but after finally getting naked things took another turn for the worse when Ben decided to lunge in for a blow job. Rubens winced as he remembered. Ai ai ai. Ben seemed to have completely forgotten that he had thirty-two perfectly formed pearly white teeth in that mouth of his, and that they needed to be pulled well back. It seemed doubly ironic, given that Ben himself must have suffered from blow job enamel abrasion at some point, given how thick his nine-inch nail was. Unless of course he chose girls with particularly big mouths. Hmm. Maybe Kelly would be a good match for him?

Oh God, Kelly. She had walked in on him naked yesterday evening. Then she'd thrown a shoe at him and run off screaming. As you do.

After Kelly ran out, the men had felt concerned for a matter of seconds and then had been all over each other again. About five minutes after they restarted it was all over for Ben. Overexcited, and still ruinously drunk, he had shot his load and fallen asleep almost instantaneously.

All in all a pretty disappointing night for Rubens. Maybe he should give Ben another chance this morning. He gently shook his companion awake.

Ben came to, blearily.

If Rubens were hoping for an erotic grin, it was not forthcoming.

"Oh... my God," mumbled Ben, "What are you doing here? You're naked? So am I. Oh my sweet aunt. Oh no. I'm starting to remember."

Rubens rubbed his eyes. At least Ben was whispering. Rubens looked at him and neatly crossed his arms:

"Ah. Ben. Good morning. Can you remember how you tried to bite my cock off and then got so excited you prematurely ejaculated and fell asleep? You should be amazed that I stayed overnight. I'm only here because I thought it would be charitable to let you try again this morning, before I go and tell all my friends how rubbish you are in bed."

Ben's eyes looked like black holes that had forgotten how to suck in matter. He was dumbfounded by Rubens' salvo. He was starting to remember.

It was deeply troubling. From what he could recall he had been *masterful* the night before. Rubens' belt did have a pretty strange buckle but apart from that he had been fantastic, not even letting the interruption of Kelly divert him from his purpose.

Oh God. Kelly. She had walked in on Rubens naked yesterday evening. The game was up now. What should he do?

"Gostoso, I'm waiting? One of us didn't come last night. I love having sex in the morning. I simply love, love, love it."

Rubens had startlingly lovely eyelashes, skin like cocoa butter and the confidence of a con man. He'd learnt from the best. Being close to him felt very good – Ben could not deny it. It seemed to make sense. The emotional conflict faded as he felt Rubens expertly drawing him closer. God, that felt good. Certainty is nine-tenths of seduction. Like men the world over, Ben's mind was powerless to resist when his dick was on a mission, and he willingly gave in to his desire for straightforward unsophisticated sex.

"So how big was it, anyway?"

Monique had tried to show Kelly all the required sympathy, but she wanted some supporting evidence for one of her theories. She held a long unsubstantiated view that most bodybuilders were merely trying to compensate for a lack of muscle down below. The M4 syndrome, as she had once heard it described: *Maxi Muscles Mini Member*. Did the stupid men not realise that having thighs the size of a large Prosciutto di Parma only made their pathetic penises look even smaller?

"It wasn't bad actually, Monique. But please. That's not the point here. I finally decide to do something about that damn New Yorker, and I find he's been playing hide the Godforsaken sausage with one of my best friends!"

"Well at least we can enjoy that rather nice bottle of wine. Cava can be surprisingly delicate. It would have been wasted on your frat boy, who is clearly an ass half-full rather than an ass half-empty kind of guy."

It wasn't the first time the two girls had spent Sunday morning on the balcony of their flat overlooking the Castle Lofts gardens, discussing the romantic disasters of the night before. In fact, *Boyfriend Clinic* was a pretty regular fixture in their calendar. The agenda had some regular features. The first point of order usually came from Kelly, who was often found getting bored with the latest guy that was paying court to her. They then moved to discuss how to let him down gently. It was, however, the first time that Kelly herself had been left high and dry by her man choosing another man. Worse yet, her man had chosen Rubens Ribeiro, her best friend, whom she had now assaulted in the crotch region with a Nike trainer.

"Seriously though, Monique. How am I going to be able to look either of them in the eye again?"

Monique smiled lazily:

"You have the techniques for that. No self pity allowed in the Clinic. You've lived in England long enough. Pretend nothing has happened. Ben was so drunk that he will not remember, and Rubens I think is used to being naked in front of men, women, goldfish... whatever. He will not care at all. It will only be embarrassing if you make it so. Just think. If you had found out about Ben's leanings *after* you had had sex with him, that would have been far worse."

Kelly made as if to protest, but Monique was having none of it:

"Don't look like that, as if you are all innocent! I think you were horny, then frustrated – and that is why poor Rubens may be mincing around today."

Kelly started laughing in spite of herself. Monique knew her so well. She had of course felt horny the night before. She had been thinking about Ben ever since that embrace after the confrontation à la tofu.

Monique was right. Maybe she should just take it on the chin and be grateful she had found out before it was too late. She shouldn't blame either of them. In fact, Kelly reminded herself, she had been the instigator, leaving the men together, drinking together, knowing – or at very least suspecting – that there was a spark between them. Last night was just a logical consequence when you mixed any two young sluts with alcohol and opportunity. A lethal cock tale. They hadn't wasted any time. They were a pair of self-indulgent bastards and they probably deserved each other. But that didn't mean she couldn't still be friends with them.

Monique made it seem simple.

Kelly sighed:

"Yes, my frog princess. I guess I was up for it last night, and my ego has taken a knock. I've never been left for a man before, not even one as good-looking as Rubens."

"I'm not sure I can allow that. Kelly, you cannot be left by someone you are not even with. My God, just because in your mind you are thinking of the boy does not mean that he has understood, you know. They can be pretty simple, these men. You know, sometimes their ESP just does not work."

Kelly started laughing again. Monique was right again. She had a way of making fun of Kelly that always brought her back down to earth.

Monique held out a hand and looked at her perfect nails.

"I am the one with the problem, Kelly. I have fallen in love with a man who has a wife and children. He just

167

wants to keep me on the side, like a trophy to show that he is still young, sexy and successful. And I am so stupid that I cannot bring myself to leave him."

With an effort, Kelly focused on what was indeed a more challenging problem.

"I thought you liked it that way, Monique. Keeping your distance, your freedom?"

"Some days I do. It is fantastic. But then there are the other days. The ones when I start to think about my future beyond the next beautiful meal, amusing conversation, or of course wonderful shopping trip. That reminds me, by the way. We are long overdue for one of those. But let's face all facts, shall we? What will my future be? Can you imagine me at forty-five with a sixty year-old boyfriend who is still hiding from his wife, probably with children who know about me and stick pins in a Voodoo doll of me because I have ruined their mother's life?"

That joke fell flat. Kelly knew that this was the age-old conundrum about the workings of monogamy, and that it was a real question:

"The short answer to your question is no, I cannot imagine you with Harry at forty-five. But are you really that into Harry anyway? I mean, don't get me wrong. He is an attractive man. There's something about the power, and he is clever, but he's not that much of a looker. He's... well, old."

"The problem is that I am into him. We have a connection. I fell in love. It's all so dreadfully predictable. They all tell you you shouldn't, but you just do. Sure, your Ben – sorry Kelly, I mean that New Yorker friend of Dorothy's –

168

is a handsome, attractive, fit young man. Sure, Rubens is perfect, and there are plenty of other young single guys in London, but they do not offer that connection. Harry does. When he is there, he makes me feel very involved – very special. I feel properly alive with him. And, much, much more than that, I don't get bored. Maybe it is the mix of intelligence and unattainability – oh my, that is a word – that gets me."

Kelly patted Monique's hand. At that moment, slightly incongruously, faint peals of happy laughter floated up from the gardens seven floors below. Monique and Kelly looked down to see who was so inappropriately joyful, interrupting their pensive moment. Crystal Smith was walking hand in hand with Kerwin James towards their new DB9 in the underground car park. As they approached the car park entrance, Kerwin chivalrously held the door open for his adoring Crystal. Monique's face took on a strangely thoughtful look.

"I cannot believe this. I am now feeling envious of that girl. Last weekend you and I were pitying her with her bleeding leg, trashy clothes and vulgar ways. We felt so superior. And look. Who's laughing now? She is happy with her successful boyfriend. Unlike our messes, he stayed overnight with her, and appears to treat her like a lady. And of course she gets to drive around in that car. I have never spent a whole night with my man. He hides, and then runs off to his irritating wife. Still, in this sad self awareness, I am not alone. You have just discovered that your "boyfriend" actually prefers having sex with a muscle-bound male prostitute. *A chacun sa merde*. Is it too early to open a bottle of wine?"

The two girls weren't the only ones to see the happy couple drive out of the Lofts. Amber was walking out of the reception when she caught sight of the Aston Martin. She stopped dead, and after a look of rage mixed with venom that only Arthur Bilks noticed, she summoned up her best Oscar-winning skills and forced out a beaming smile. Her gleaming white teeth were framed by her generous lips plastered in Cherry Kiss Liplicious Ultra Shiny Gloss.

"Crystal, Kerwin, how lovely to see you. Oh my God, this car suits you so well. It is beautiful, stylish and fierce!"

"Amber, jump in, we'll give you a ride."

"Oh I couldn't. You two look so perfect in there together, and I don't want to try to come between you. I think I've messed up enough already. You go on and paint the town red! I'll be fine on the tube. Let's catch up in the week."

Amber was a master of the false gush, but she knew that with what was going on inside her head the mask may crack if she kept it on for too long. She had to manage her feelings and stay away for the time being. Behind her Liplicious smile was a longing to grab Crystal by her weave and throw her out of the car, before driving over her – and then reversing – in that bloody Aston Martin. But Amber would need to bide her time. For the moment, it was time for feigned contrition, fake guilt and an insincere desire to start afresh.

When the time was right, revenge would be sweet. The plan was all-encompassing. She'd also let the American girl think the storm had blown over. However, Amber

170

had already started talking to her brother about what was going to happen to pretty Kelly Danvers one night when she got just too drunk for her own good. And she'd make sure that Prince Charming wouldn't be there to save her this time.

That morning the Prince Charming in question had decided he really wasn't very interested in damsels in distress. He found that he had rather liked playing the role of Sleeping Beauty, and being woken up by his own handsome Prince. Although still not exactly an expert, Ben was at least sober this time and he was able to ensure that Rubens Ribeiro was finally satisfied. With a post-coital glow fresh upon his brow and a spring in his step, Ben did what all good New Yorkers would do. He invited Rubens to brunch.

Of course then there was the problem of where to go for brunch. Ben didn't really have any idea of where to go for brunch. Millie's Health Café did not seem quite the ticket, given developments. Ben did not think he was ready for such a public outing with Rubens. No, it would be better to sneak off into town, have a nice meal and discuss what happens next, like mature adults.

Rubens was pulling on his clothes:

"Listen gostoso, I know exactly where we can go where you will not run into your friends. Good food, good prices and fun. Do you trust me?"

Ben leant out of the bathroom:

"That sounds perfect. You could tell that I wasn't exactly overflowing with ideas then?"

They laughed. As Ben looked at Rubens he felt strangely light-headed with what felt like butterflies in his stomach. God, was he turning into some weirdo lovesick fag? Would he be starting to shave his legs and watch old musicals? No, the hills were not alive with the sound of music. He was probably just really hungry and needed to feed. He half winced and half smiled as he remembered what he had done that morning, what he had never thought he would end up doing, especially not with another man. But what a man. There went those damn butterflies again. *Ben, you are just hungry*.

They took a cab. It was good to be out and about. Heads had cleared.

It is a small world. The café in Old Compton Street chosen by Rubens was delightful – small and discreet yet buzzing with atmosphere. But the first thing Ben saw was a familiar face. Although he had not seen a smile soften the stern features of Hartmut Glick's face before, Ben could hardly fail to recognise his boss eating with a slim dark-haired woman, when he was only standing twenty feet away from him at the back of the café. He knew immediately that Hartmut had recognised him too.

Maybe it was the lawyers' instinctive sense of discretion or some automatic appreciation of confidentiality that caused both men to immediately avert their eyes. A tacit agreement to pretend the other one simply wasn't there had instantly been ghost signed, countersigned and copies circulated to concerned parties for their records, there and then. Ben muttered his embarrassment to

Rubens. Thankfully, Rubens knew the café manager so after a moment standing there exposed like a starlet in Cannes, Ben was dragged to one of the outside tables, just out of sight of Hartmut's table inside.

Although the café was a pillar of the Soho gay-stablishment, on a Sunday lunchtime it let it all hang out. Respectable middle-aged straight couples tucked into their full English breakfasts alongside trendily dressed gay boys. Some customers were theatrically debating the relative merits of Alexandra Burke and Leona Lewis over their skinny caffé lattes. Those were not the tourists. America's "Melting Pot" would find its ideals fairly well captured in this little street, where various tribes seemed to rub along really rather happily – so long, that is, as they got a decent table and quick service. Not that people weren't there for the show, of course. Ben noticed a demurely dressed woman in her sixties nudge her husband to make him look at the beefy Monster Mary (Rubens had told him that that was the terminology to use when a Muscle Mary had overdone the steroids) on the next table. But rather than being disturbed by the sheer quantity of metal the guy had in his face, it transpired that she was merely summoning up the courage to ask him to agree to a photo with her. It certainly would capture the spirit of London, to be shown off to the folks back home in South Dakota.

Old Compton Street somehow kept its allure for London tourists, like a fading actress with plenty of spirit in her yet. Apart from being a gay Mecca, and although Londoners often made fun of it as being only good for visitors, it was an essential visit for anyone who wanted to see the last remnants of London's Red Light district. These remnants now rubbed shoulders with trendy café bars, exotic restaurants and the couple of theatres which had been here even before the streetwalkers. Possibly the best time was when the show finished at the Prince Edward Theatre and crowds suddenly started streaming out of the auditorium, dressed for the evening, on the quest for one last martini before a taxi home. Next door to all that jazz was the G.A.Y. Bar, one of the busiest queer watering holes in the city. The two crowds would merge like the confluence of two mighty rivers, but like the Ohio and the Mississippi you could still see the different colours showing their origin for hundreds of yards downstream before they eventually blended and faded, each to their own, into the London night.

From Ben's vantage point, two doors up from the G.A.Y. Bar this lunchtime, the crowds were more sedate, but still sufficiently variegated to make it a compelling people watching experience. The overprepared elderly couple with cagoules on a sunny day; the lipstick lesbians hand in hand, making the builders drool; the gym addict with the compulsory lycra vest, showing every sculpted bulge; the group of girls looking for fun presents for the hen party next weekend; the drag queen in daywear; the tourists with cameras and maps at the ready; all wandered about. There was an occasional cruisy look at a sexy young man, but most were too busy going about their own business to care about what the others looked like. Then the sparkling touches of real fun – the small crowd of people dressed as angels, in pretty silver costumes and glitter, the happy groups catching up, in this half-way house between their respective London villages. Ben loved his home in SE1, but he was rather pleased that he too could now escape to the anonymity of the West End. It was, always and maybe forever, a concrete garden of theatres, bars and restaurants running from Covent Garden to Mayfair, steeped in character and perhaps even tinged with greatness.

Occasionally disappointing, too. Hartmut Glick was somewhat displeased at the failure to achieve anonymity that Soho had afforded him that morning. After his clearly expressed wish on the telephone to restrict meetings to defined night-time events, it had taken all Caroline's persuasive abilities to convince him to meet her before dark. Hartmut had never before met a creature from PPLAY in the daytime, but then Caroline Napier Jones was one of the finest creatures that he had clapped eyes on in many a year. The thought of her derrière weakened his Teutonic resolve. He had succumbed.

"So, Ms Napier Jones, I am very happy to see you. It is not in my usual habit to frequent cafés, but it is quite congenial in your company."

"Mr Glick, the pleasure is all mine. It is rare to meet true gentlemen like yourself."

"Of course, Ms Napier Jones. Nothing else would do. For you I would possibly even offer up my very last slave."

They both grinned at the simultaneous appropriateness and inappropriateness of Hartmut's comment.

"Mr Glick, with both our proclivities, maybe it would be easier if we had a few slaves on tap."

As both Caroline and Hartmut were clearly masters and

not slaves, if a relationship were to grow it would offer its challenges. Hartmut tackled this head on:

"Although this is most agreeable, Ms Napier Jones, I have not come here today merely to discuss pleasantries. At first glance it would seem that there is a fundamental problem with the idea of our frequenting each other on a regular basis. Indeed, we should be two repelling poles. However, there is something about you which intrigues me and even stimulates me. At the risk of sounding indecorous, I feel I would like to explore certain formerly forbidden paths with you, Ms Napier Jones."

Caroline wondered if Hartmut Glick could possibly be the human incarnation of some long-lost Dickens novel, masquerading in human form. Perhaps "The Mystery of Edwin Drood", Dicken's unfinished novel, alive and open to re-writing? Hartmut certainly wasn't an open book. Maybe she could use the name Edwin as code to describe her mystery lover. Did she just think the word "lover"?

Hartmut for his part was in reflective mood.

"This situation requires the modification of thoroughly ingrained behaviour. Habits framed over the course of quite some years will now be demolished and required to re-form in quite the opposite way. A successful conclusion to this matter will be no small undertaking, and is certainly no foregone conclusion, Ms Napier Jones, no matter how much mutual intrigue there may be. It will necessitate ruthless organisation, for otherwise we shall be lost."

Although she was quite the dominatrix when robed, Caroline was relaxed in conversation and was rather enjoying Hartmut's speech. He continued in a steady melodious voice.

"I wish to treat this endeavour as I would a particularly important case. I believe preparation to be the key, Ms Napier Jones. To that end I propose a series of events through which we may begin to deepen our mutual understanding and knowledge of each other. We should conduct daytime meetings such as this one and we should also continue our sorties after dark. After each event I believe we should each review how satisfactory the experience was and then we should compare notes. It will be essential for us to act with complete honesty, particularly when it comes to the matter of... let us say, leading. If at the end of a few weeks we find that our reviews have been satisfactory I propose that we go and stay with my sister, Ursula Himmelfarb, in Berlin. She has a very large house which is most conveniently located for the KitKat Club, should you be interested in attending."

Caroline couldn't quite believe Hartmut's approach to dating, but then she couldn't fault its logic – even if romance didn't seem to be overly high on his agenda. She wondered what she would need to do in order to achieve a satisfactory grade. She wanted to laugh out loud but she feared that that would meet with Hartmut's disapproval and immediately gain her a black mark. So she repressed her urge to giggle and instead focused on Ursula Himmelfarb, her hostess for the infamous KitKat Club. She had read about the biggest fetish party in Berlin but had never been there. Maybe there was some romance in what Hartmut was suggesting after all.

"Mr Glick, I should thoroughly endorse your plan. I hope that we shall have a series of satisfactory encounters, because it would indeed please me to visit Ms Himmelfarb in Berlin."

"Super. Ms Napier Jones, although I will score this encounter in greater detail when I reach my home, I feel confident in saying to you that this has been most tolerable from my point of view. I will nevertheless give greater feedback when we meet next, as I hope we shall. That will depend solely upon your verdict on our little luncheon. Now might I accompany you to your car, or hail you a taxicab?"

Hartmut smiled again. Caroline had really rather enjoyed the whole charade. The only thing was, Hartmut Glick wasn't acting. This was the real thing. And that was absolutely marvellous.

After his brunch in town, Ben said goodbye to Rubens. He spent some time in the National Gallery in Trafalgar Square. He thought that after a night of drunken debauchery, he should get some balance back in his life. Culture was a soothing reassurance. Cities really were fantastic – sex and brunch and food for the soul.

He looked around Trafalgar Square and recalled his excitement at seeing it again during his taxi ride in from the airport. On foot it seemed a more stately place. The sky was grey but streaked with hazy ribbons of pink as the sun started to set. It resembled a Turner painting. He sat on the museum steps and looked across the square. He felt at peace. Even urban landscapes offer the chance for reflection on the inconsequence of most things.

After watching the pigeons for a while, Ben headed back home.

There seemed little to be gained by staying in his rooms for any more time than strictly required. As a man living alone, Ben had always spent more time out than in. (Not in a gay sense, mind, until now). Ben headed down to the gym. If he planned on spending more time with Rubens then he would need to train his body pretty hard. Keeping up with Rubens was probably going to be good for him.

"Hello Ben, how are you settling in?"

Ben wasn't exactly pleased to see Alex O'Connell. He found him a bit too smooth. Alex made Ben uneasy. Wasn't Alex supposed to be playing with people of his own age? What did Alex *want?*

"Pretty good thanks, Alex. I'm settling in fine."

"Good. It's a surprisingly nice environment. We've got quite a community of sorts here. I think the Lofts are conducive to it. We're taken care of in unexpected ways. Without Arthur, of course, the place would be chaos. And there is the winning combination of Millie's cuisine and Rubens' smile. It must be said – they both get people talking."

Did Alex know about him and Rubens? How could he? Maybe Ben was just being paranoid. And anyway, did Ben care? Was he going to come out as gay or bisexual? As Kelly already knew there probably wasn't much chance of hiding. It hit Ben suddenly: what about work? He wondered how London was for working bisexuals.

It struck Ben that he had been presented with a golden opportunity to make some discreet enquiries.

"What's it like being openly gay in London, Alex? I mean, are people generally out at work?"

Alex shot Ben a keen look. Where had that question come from? Was there something he wasn't aware of? Ben looked more than just idly curious. Alex thought it might be interesting to find out.

"We have pretty strong anti-discrimination legislation in this country. If you are working in Central London, you really shouldn't have a problem. Of course, if you're a builder or a footballer you may not want to flaunt it so much. Why do you ask?"

Ben didn't know what to reply without giving the game away. Alex noticed his awkwardness.

"We're quite civilised here, Ben. Quite lucky for people like me, really."

Ben was thankful for Alex's smile and his politic assumption that the question was all about him. He suspected that Alex had picked up on some obscure embarrassment and had helped him out of a hole. That was nice of him. Maybe Alex wasn't so bad after all.

Ben changed the subject:

"So where's Jamal tonight?"

"Oh, he's moonlighting tonight."

"Moonlighting?"

Ben wondered what Jamal might do in his spare time. What strange gay things did gay men do at night? Alex noticed Ben's puzzlement, and smiled at him.

"You know Jamal is a serious engineer, right? Well,

tonight he's dancing with Rubens at the After Dark Club."

"Really? Is Jamal a go-go boy as well?"

Alex smiled again:

"Jamal wouldn't be happy to be described as a go-go boy, but, basically, yes. He used to dance all the time before he managed to get a proper job. Not that dancing isn't a proper job, but you know what I mean. It's not quite one that pays the bills and offers holidays. That's how we know Rubens. Jamal and Rubens worked together all the time, way back when. They are great friends and usually a pretty bad influence on each other. Who knows what those naughty boys will get up to tonight without me there to be all boring and sensible."

Alex raised a confident eyebrow. Ben looked disconcerted. Rubens had told him that he was working in a club that night and had even asked Ben if he wanted to come along. Ben had turned the opportunity down, thinking it might be uncool to be perceived to be a hanger-on. Besides, Ben was tired and he needed to catch up on some sleep. It struck him now, though, that the new object of his desires was going to be dancing almost naked with a very sexy friend – one in an open relationship, to boot – and that they would in all likelihood encourage each other to do things they shouldn't.

Ben had heard gay men paid less attention to restrictive societal customs such as monogamy. *OK. They were sluts.* But surely Rubens wouldn't go off with someone else on their first day together. Maybe he should call him?

Alex was picking up on something:

"Don't worry," he said airily, "they're not that bad. Do

you think I'd let Jamal go off and get into trouble? And Rubens is a smart guy behind his frivolous façade. They'll just end up taking a few too many drugs and staying up all night. Don't worry about your friend Rubens – he can handle himself. And the After Dark isn't such a full-on club."

It definitely felt as if Alex were trying to reassure him. Ben wondered if he should confide in Alex after all. It was an option. But – on reflection – not yet. Ben settled on doing nothing. He wouldn't call Rubens. Remember "Sex and the City". Do not turn into the needy one. Whatever else happened, needy was always "Unsexy and the City".

Rubens wore a pair of Calvin Kleins stretched to snapping point, showing everything Calvin had hoped they would ever show. Jamal was by his side wearing an equally stretched pair of AussieBums.

The After Dark was an intimate venue down in Vauxhall. It did not boast the glamour of the West End, but served the kind of guys who loved guys and wanted to get loving without wasting too much time discussing designer T-shirts and spinning around to Girls Aloud.

Rubens and Jamal were being eaten alive.

Not literally, of course. It helped that they had decided to take the extra money for dancing tied-off. They had each tied elastic, softened in baby oil, tightly around the base of their cocks so that their erections would stay for the duration. Go-gos who tied off and then showed it all would get twice the rate of the flaccid and merely muscular.

The crowd had been warmed up nicely with a pair of M4s (*Maxi Muscle Mini Members*) on basic pay. Now the club produced its heavy artillery. The crowd knew what to expect. They had been watching the warm-ups and were now starting to want blood. Of course, there was no baying – no screaming or any overt show of eagerness. That would have been deeply uncool. Indeed, it would be desperate to show oneself too keen to see the go-gos' cocks. What would that hint at vis-à-vis one's own? It was all done in silence. Jamal and Rubens could feel the unmistakable tension, however, and were feeding off it.

They had done innumerable mock sex shows before with each other. It was all theatre. Although they appreciated the beauty of each other's bodies, and neither was averse to a large erect penis, it would have taken an unusually strong dose of GHB for them to seriously start getting into each other on stage. Tonight they were fully under control.

The show was all the better for it. As they rubbed up and down against each other, catching the gleaming eyes of various hungry men in the crowd, Rubens had been telling Jamal about his night with Ben.

"You're saying he needs a bit of breaking in then, Rubens? A bit of civilising?"

"Precisely. I've got used to pretty good sex. It's tough to step back to being a teenager again."

"But this could be the man of your dreams, babes."

"Maybe. Maybe. But I have a lot of dreams. There is just so much choice on the stalls here in London."

"Tell me about it," mused Jamal, "I'm not sure I would

know what to do if Alex wasn't as keen on an open relationship as I am. How could *anyone* think of having sex with just the one person for the rest of their lives? Why *on earth* would you do such a thing?"

Rubens nodded thoughtfully as he spun around:

"Yes, well, that's a whole other question, my friend. I think it's time by the way. They're going to start booing soon if we don't get them out. Either that, or they'll get up here and rip our clothes off. Hmm, could be fun. Do you think Mark would pay us more if we got them to do that?"

"No, he'd probably want money back to replace these bloody underpants, he's so mean."

Trying not to laugh, as that didn't fit with the image of the moody, super horny sex toy, the boys parted and faced the crowd. Mirroring each other to the inch, they put their fingers inside the waistbands of their designer briefs and started playing with the elastic.

After all this time, the act was as accurately synchronised as the mechanism of a Swiss watch. Rubens turned to Jamal, raised an eyebrow and looked down intently at Jamal's bulge. Jamal responded by lowering the waistband slowly so that his helmet appeared. He then turned and stared at Rubens who followed suit. Moments later, the underpants were in their hands. Jamal had learnt from Rubens how to move his hips so that their cocks seemed to be gyrating in perfect harmony. It was their thing. Playing on the fascination with twins, brothers, anything, Rubens and Jamal created the illusion that they were two halves of the same sex toy, availability incarnate, the object that would make your fantasies all come true. The truth remained that they were too alike to be anything other than partners in crime, uninhibited boys who egged each other on, but who had never gone so far as most of the men on the dance floor were silently begging them to in their minds. A few minutes of dick Olympics later, they were safely backstage with towels round their waists, and a Red Bull to wash down the second E of the night.

"So," breathed Rubens, "are we going to Scream after this, Jamal?"

Scream was one of gay London's better known after-hours clubs, and it took punters through to Monday morning. The true clubbers preferred to start at 4am, leaving the regular clubs for the amateurs who didn't know how to sort out either their sleeping patterns or their drug intake.

"I'm raring to go. What are you thinking? Do you think I've just taken an E so that I can go home, wake up Alex and debate the finer points of government policy in Darfur?"

"Excellent. I think I need you tonight. I want to try to be a good boy, at least as far as sex goes. I did only get with the American last night. I think he deserves a few days of my full attention."

"But Scream is such a treasure trove of men, Rubens. Ha. You must really like him."

"I might liké him. I might. Who knows, though? I like a lot of guys, and now the chase is over. We'll see. Tonight I will be a good boy, maybe help you meet anyone who catches your filthy eye. I'll tell you, though, if Big Ben doesn't learn how to use that Magnum of his pretty soon, then I think I will just have to go searching for satisfaction elsewhere. Anyway, get your jeans on, bija, and let's take a tour round this place before we head off to Scream. The boys are calling."

11

A Helping Hand Job

It might be stretching matters somewhat to say that Millie Myers' tofu surprise had changed Crystal Smith's outlook on life, but it was certainly true that the day of the confrontation had marked a watershed for her. Crystal had never wasted too much time thinking about irrelevancies like the consequences of her actions, not while there were so many beautiful things to acquire, experiences to be had and men to attract. But Amber's reaction to her one-upmanship over Kerwin had made Crystal realise that what she did had an effect on others – and that it could even backfire on her.

She had thought about it. She made a promise to herself. From now on she would be more aware of what she did. She would endeavour to treat others better, and she would also try to be grateful for what she had, rather than constantly pursuing the next bag, pair of shoes or compliment. She was already so lucky having friends, a decent job in a department store, and an amazing man like Kerwin who seemed to like her for more than just her breast implants. Yes, perhaps the time had come to see if, somewhere in her large handbag, there was a new leaf that could be turned over.

Crystal had spoken to Arthur Bilks a couple of times, but only ever to ask if a parcel had arrived for her. It was very useful having a concierge to sign for things. Fortified by resolutions, however, that morning Crystal decided to say hello to him and ask him how he was. He had been kind to her on that dreadful night. It was the least she might do.

"Good morning Arthur. How are you?"

A man with less experience would have been taken aback by the unexpected smile and concern for his wellbeing, but Arthur Bilks had seen it all before. He had observed the outward signs of a happy relationship – cemented by that handsome car – develop over the past few weeks. The glow lit Crystal up like a bedside lamp. In that state of sexual bliss Arthur could imagine Crystal even smiling at the bus driver, usually a being invisible to Londoners armed with Oyster cards. So he wasn't particularly surprised to see her hold the door open for an elegant lady. The visiting woman was around fifty, thought Arthur. Crystal smiled sweetly as the lady thanked her.

Arthur looked up to find the visitor before him.

"Good morning. I have a delivery for Harry Gumpert. Flat 500?" She looked around, intrigued, "I trust I am in the right place. Is this the Castle Lofts?"

Although not in the first flush of youth, the woman was impeccable in every sense. Arthur felt himself stir. Things have a wonderful way of perking up when what appears to be a kindred spirit waltzes into view. Why this happens is a delightful mystery – but chemistry had always been a mystery for Arthur. He admired the visitor's fuller figure, the way the fitted green dress shaped her ample bosom and generally made her curve in all the right places. Her hair was perfect. She was wearing tasteful, expertly applied makeup, and she had a pretty face. Although her skin tone hinted at dual heritage – Arthur did try to keep up with the latest politically-correct lingo – the lady reminded him of a swarthy Meryl Streep. The way she spoke also clearly marked her out as a lady. Arthur was momentarily distracted, but soon regained his professionalism.

"Absolutely, Madam, this is the Castle Lofts. Mr Gumpert indeed resides in Flat 500. Allow me to ring up for you. Who may I say is calling?"

"Oh, that's very kind, thank you. My name is Cornisha Burrows. I'm a colleague of his."

Cornisha's smile distracted Arthur again and for a moment he just stared at her. Suddenly conscious that he had not rung the number yet, he repeated her name back to her and rang up.

"Oh hello, Mr Gumpert. I have a very lovely lady called Miss Cornisha Burrows to see you. Would you like me to send her up?"

Cornisha registered the "very lovely lady". She blushed slightly. It confirmed the suspicion that Arthur's staring had awoken moments earlier. She'd been here before. Men were often taken by her looks only to be rather less than enamoured when they discovered that she had once been one of them. She sighed as she weighed Arthur up. At first sight, he seemed like a typically salt of the earth Eastender. Just don't attempt to persuade such types to overcome their built-in prejudices, and you'll be fine. She would spare the poor man the heart attack and not take the bait. Even though there was something about him.

Cornisha thanked Arthur and directed a warm, but not too friendly, smile at him as she walked to the lifts. *Men!*

It was with men that Arthur spent most of his time since his wife had passed away eight years earlier. Apart from John and Bert, his two childhood friends who he met down the pub, and of course his brother Charlie, Arthur didn't see many people outside of work. In work, whilst he saw everyone, there were very few people he thought saw him. Rare indeed were the ones like the lovely Kelly Danvers around whose little finger he rather enjoyed being twisted. In fact, Arthur had settled for being another one of the invisible people that some Londoners treated as an extension of the building. He had had his time in the sun, and he had also enjoyed a good life with Phyllis until breast cancer had carried her off. He still considered himself the luckiest man on earth to have had thirty happy years with a woman like that.

Every so often, though, close contact with a lady like Cornisha Burrows reawakened the man inside Arthur Bilks. He lived half-asleep most of the time, deep frozen in the happiness of the past. He wasn't miserable, but felt like a bystander, always on the sidelines, watching others play. This morning, Arthur felt something he hadn't felt in a while. A spark of life.

"Bija, we are dangerous when we get together! I'm surprised Alex lets you out with me any more!"

Jamal laughed and steadied himself:

"I was wondering last night whether I'd be putting you into a taxi with that sexy rugby player from South Africa, or into an ambulance with that miserable paramedic from South London. And as it happened you drew a blank. The devils are in despair. Somehow Rubens Ribeiro, London's number one slut, left both the players and the doctors in peace. Your American has turned you into a good little boy!"

"Jamal, I love you to death, but sometimes you can be so shallow for such an intelligent guy. Are you deaf? I actually like him. Sure, I still look, but for the moment – that's it."

"Speak of the devil and up pop his horns. Look – see the cute couple in the café? Seems as if Ben is making amends with Miss Kelly. What do you think they were talking about?"

Although Kelly had not followed Monique's advice to the letter, she agreed that she had been lucky to escape before getting anything more than her ego hurt, and that it wasn't worth throwing away two friendships for. So she had visited Ben that day in the office and invited him for coffee that evening in the Health Café. He had accepted gladly.

Kelly wanted things to be normal, no subterfuge, no embarrassment and certainly no hiding. She would acknowledge what she had seen, tell him all was fine, and then they could pick up from where they had left off.

It was more straightforward than she had thought it would be. Nothing seemed to have changed, and in fact she felt quite at ease with him. She looked up at him with questioning eyes, and Ben felt a strange pang as he took in her calm beauty.

"Kelly, I really don't know what to say."

Unexpectedly, Kelly laughed.

"Reverting to type, Ben? Lost for words, again? Don't let me down with a show of awkward silence. You seemed to be making so much progress. Damn you, I have vowed to myself that I would not have a go at you for deciding you preferred a Brazilian muscle boy to me. But I guess you are going to have to suffer a few barbs for having wounded my pride like that."

Kelly's warm smile confused Ben. So Kelly was just suffering from a bruised ego because he hadn't fallen at her feet? Or was it something more?

"Kelly, you must know that I felt something for you from the start, but I never seemed to get back what I was looking for. You just didn't… "

"… have a cock? Sorry, Ben, but given what I saw on Saturday night, it didn't look like Rubens was there trying to help you with a chat up line to approach me with."

"Kelly, you're right. I was completely drunk and obviously I'm not completely straight."

"You don't say. You should be a detective. Lordy Lord, Ben, is that the best you can come up with?" She crossed her arms, and then uncrossed them, leaning forward.

"Look, it's not as bad as it felt at first. Just admit that

you are gay and you needed to escape from your mother to be able to explore your sexuality. We've all heard about this Italian guilt thing, you know."

Was it true? Did his mother have anything to do with it? She was coming over to visit soon as well. Would that unleash more unexpected reactions?

"OK, Kelly. I guess I am at least gay in part. But believe it or not, I do like girls as well. And you should know that you are one of them."

Kelly smiled woodenly:

"Gee, Ben. Thanks. I love being *"one of them"*.

"There are not thousands like you – or hundreds, or tens. I liked you the first time I saw you, so much so that when you kissed me I froze because what I really wanted to do was to rip every piece of your clothing off and make mad passionate love to you there and then in front of everyone."

What? Had he really said that? Ben had never been so upfront with a girl before. Especially not to one he liked.

What? Had he really said that? No one had ever told Kelly Danvers so unceremoniously that they wanted to rip her clothes off and make mad passionate love to her.

They stared at each other in silence for a moment.

Kelly laid a hand carefully on the table.

"So – let me work this out. I guess I am just unlucky. You decide you want to rip my clothes off and when you finally summon up the courage to do it, *oops* you accidentally rip the clothes off the gym instructor instead and make love to him."

Ben wondered whether it would be inappropriate to say

that they both had the most marvellous chests and butts. He erred on the side of caution.

"Ben," continued Kelly patiently, "in any case, even if you are bisexual, or maybe a rather rubbish heterosexual, I'm not sure I want to compete with every attractive person on the planet. It's bad enough worrying about the threat posed by other women, but in a city with as many buff gay men as London, I don't think I can face worrying about them too. Tell you what: I'll savour the compliment that a good-looking, sexually confused young man finds me worthy of shredding my Prada tops for and go for the friendship option. I'm cool with this. Me, my libido and my ego will all survive in our village. What do you say? Does that make sense to you, too?"

Before Ben could say anything, he had to digest the fact that Kelly had referenced her libido. Did that mean that she wanted him too? This was exciting. Blood started to flow down to his groin again. *See, it's true, I do fancy women!* Ben wondered whether he should tell Kelly that she was giving him an erection. Maybe that wouldn't actually be the most romantic thing to say, even if he was trying to prove his heterosexuality. Perhaps he should just wait. Of course – what about Rubens? He had felt in love with him yesterday and had been thinking about him at work all day. He should definitely wait.

"Kelly, you're right. If nothing else, I need time to decide what I am. And what we want. All of us. I guess I have to think of Rubens who I don't want to play along either. Oh, and there he is with Jamal."

As Monique had correctly predicted, Rubens Ribeiro

showed no more embarrassment seeing Kelly in the café than he had in Ben's flat a few nights earlier.

"Kelly, darling, how are you?"

"Just fine, thanks Rubens. I'm finding out all sorts of interesting things about your new man here."

There, it was officially out in the open. Ben had just been described as someone's "man" in a public place. Even with those broad angular shoulders of his, there would be no scuttling back into the closet and pretending to be a coat hanger any more.

Kelly sighed and turned to the one person in the group who had no idea what Ben looked like naked:

"So how was After Dark the other night, Jamal? I hope you two didn't do anything the rest of us wouldn't."

Jamal considered asking Kelly if she and Ben would contemplate simulating sex on stage in front of five hundred people, but thought better of it.

"Oh, you know, it's the usual parade. We shake our booties in some tight little shorts and get men to throw their underwear at us. Sometimes we get some nice stuff on stage. AussieBum, Calvins, D Squared – you know. Brands from the branded."

"I hope you wash it before wearing it, Jamal."

"Come on Kelly, he's not being serious!" scoffed Rubens. "Gay men may ocasionally be desperate, but trust me, they would never waste a pair of designer briefs like that. Anyhow, as I have three of my most important people here, maybe I could get your help with my issue. Jamal knows everything by the way, guys. I've asked him not to mention things to Alex – I think I ought to pull together the rest of the money myself, or I'll never be able to pay you back."

"So," asked Kelly, "have you done anything about what we talked about at the weekend?"

"Sure thing, Kelly. The magazines may be weekly, but the wonders of the internet mean you can choose a new career Monday morning, have four adverts online Monday afternoon, and go to bed Monday night with four hundred pounds in your back pocket."

Jamal raised an interested eyebrow:

"So how many blow jobs exactly does that equate to?"

"Jamal! You are getting so crude. It was three, actually. But I only had to give one of them."

Kelly grimaced:

"Boys, I think this is a little too much information for me. I am very happy for you that you are men who like men – and even men who get paid for liking men in your case, Rubens – but I'd rather not have too many details. Bit gag-worthy. I might be a bit jealous, too."

"Sorry, Kelly. You're right. I blame Jamal for dragging the conversation into the gutter. He used to be such a respectable boy before he found out just how much he liked fellatio."

"Well," retorted Jamal, "at least I'm not Mr Rentboy.com selling my ass, and everything else, habibie, or should I say *Paulo Pauzao*?"

Jamal and Rubens glared at each other, daring the other one to continue, before chuckling and giving each other an exaggerated double air kiss.

"If I didn't know your boyfriend, Jamal, and I hadn't

seen you in a certain person's flat the other night, Rubens, I'd swear you two were working up to being more than just friends."

"Kelly, darling, I love Jamal immeasurably, but in all seriousness – what would we get up to in bed? Knitting? We are too, too similar, baby. He's my sister!"

"Good. I think I'm on camp overload now, boys. Did you actually want to discuss something serious, Rubens, or are you just trying to initiate Ben into how to be a card-carrying London queen?"

"Kelly, you can be so brutal at times. What an *animal*. Jamal and I are just joking." Rubens sat down, and looked at his friends in turn: "People, I do have something serious. I am making money, but I have the chance to make more."

He paused. How would the group take this?

"Don't take this the wrong way, now. It's just a thought. I had this client a couple of days ago. Unfortunate guy with a lazy eye, a really tiny penis and one of those man pregnant bellies, but at least a healthy wallet. Anyway, Squinty Smallcock knows some City big shot. By all accounts someone who finds it hard to get his kicks. A cold, tedious creature, Squinty said. But apparently City Man knows what he wants. His fantasy is discovering two guys making out and then watching them whilst he enjoys himself. Squinty said City Man just loves Brazilians and then actually asked me if I knew another person to have sex with while City Man would watch. This City Man has so much money that he never even calls the boys himself; he gets Squinty Smallcock to organise everything, paying him to do the research, which Squinty enjoys. A lot. It all sounded a bit twisted to me and I said I did not do that, but he insisted that I should think about it. Squinty offered me a *huge* amount of money. I don't think he has a *clue* about the going rate. But now I need to find someone… "

"Don't even think of looking at me habibie!" scoffed Jamal in disbelief, "Unless of course he wants to watch us knit."

Kelly was also incredulous:

"This is one time when I am really glad to say that I'm missing the right equipment, here."

Ben suddenly realised the other three had turned and were looking at him. Surely not.

"Well, Ben, as you are the only one here who seems more than happy to make out with Paulo Pauzao for free, why not do it and get paid for it?"

Jamal must be joking. For God's sake he had only had sex with a man for the first time a few days ago and now it was being suggested that he become a gay prostitute. There was tolerance, and there was the intolerable.

Rubens caught his arm. His eyes were dancing.

"Ben, Ben, think about it at least. You would be helping me here and this guy would not touch you. *All he would do is look*. You could pretend he wasn't even there. I know it's not what you're used to, but it would be really, really easy. Oh, and apparently City Man likes the generously proportioned members, so you should even help me get a big tip, gostoso."

Ben's face was a picture.

"You guys are crazy. Crazy. I came to London to broaden my horizons, have fun and get on with my career, not

198

to perform a sex act for money in front of some skanky pervert, who's too damn lazy to organise his own... perversions!"

"Don't be so judgemental, Ben," coaxed Rubens, "We wouldn't even know he was there. We start making love, a door is left open and you won't even notice when he comes in and watches us. It would be so, so easy... "

"Easy? Easy? Let's do it right now then, Rubens! I'm up for a practice run right here, right now! Man, what are you talking about? Is this the only reason you decided to get off with me in the first place? So I could become your... your... I don't even know the fucking word for what you want me to become!"

Kelly could understand Ben's anger, but she was also stifling a laugh. This was *priceless*. Rubens' request was *totally* outrageous. But then, had Ben thought about how *outrageous* it had been of him to lead Kelly on like that and then drop her for the Brazilian? That is very much how things had stacked up for Kelly. Maybe this was sweet payback. If Ben really was that into men, then this shouldn't be such a big deal. However, thought Kelly, if he was just dabbling, or *confused*, then it might just put him off this whole ridiculous sortie into the homo-sphere.

Maybe Ben wasn't gay after all. Maybe there was some room for manoeuvre here? She leant forward, sweetly reasonable, like any negotiator about to make a preposterous point:

"Listen Ben, this does sound pretty unusual at first blush. But I think there is quite an interesting point to be drawn out here. Think, for example, about how we prostitute our brains, our ability, our very beings – *every day at work*. We think about other people's problems – I should say other *imbeciles'* problems, given some of the self-inflicted situations that we face – for eight to ten hours daily. *For money*. I look at that situation, and I look at this situation."

"They are not the same at all!" cried Ben, outraged. Kelly ignored the interruption:

"With the promise of cash we switch off all interesting and truly useful thought. Then, when our dreary day is done, we immediately attempt to think about something else – mainly how we are wasting the best years of our lives for cash. We don't do it because we really want to. We'd all rather be elsewhere, or being creative, or useful to the world. We are prostitutes of the realm of thought. Is this *really* that much worse, once you've got over the vapid morality arguments? In fact, maybe this proposition is more honest. After all, you're doing genuine good by it. It's... *utilitarian*. The end does justify the means. You *do* kill one child to save a whole village."

Ben cocked an eyebrow at Kelly. What absolute tosh. But she looked good saying it. It made him think for a moment. Before he could regain his sense of outrage, Jamal came in with the killer blow.

"It's more like being a porn star really, Ben. With an audience of one. It's quite a compliment. Think of it in those terms. A guy is willing to pay *all that money* just to see you make love. Doesn't it make you feel kind of good?"

Jamal's point was crammed full of logical errors, thought

Ben. The person in question just had to be some sad, lonely pervert. But... a porn star?

Ben was not wholly displeased with the concept of having the potential – accepted unquestionably by all these attractive people – of being a star of the realm of pleasures of the flesh. After all, he *was worth it*.

Could he pass off as one?

From time to time, men he had known boasted – with a fair degree of regularity – about how great they would be if called upon to perform on camera. Ben's fragile ego attached itself limpet-like to the implied compliment. Well, now, here was a turn up for the books. He was beautiful and sexy enough for someone to pay just to watch him make out.

Nice.

Ben's rational side tried to counter, but his ego had just downed an upper and it would brook no argument. The other three could see Ben wavering.

Jamal found this all hilarious:

"It's actually kind of cool in a way, Ben. I mean, releasing a porn video on the internet was so last decade. You get the chance to be paid for a sex performance with a guy you like anyway, and then even better the money is going to charity. I mean, if it were starving children or the rainforest instead of Rubens' poor Mum then we'd probably have Bono and Sting lining up to do it."

"Would we? I hadn't thought of that. Hey, we could call it *Sex Aid*. A whole new meaning to Feed the World."

"Let them know it's Kiss-mas time," said Kelly.

Kelly and Jamal kept a straight face. However, despite the

apparently ludicrous nature of it all, Ben was thinking about it. Rubens' indecent proposal was now an opportunity for the American to validate his masculinity and – somehow – be a better person at the same time.

"If I agreed to do this, Rubens, the guy wouldn't come too close to me, would he? Where would it happen? Would we use your flat? And... what exactly would I have to do?"

"Baby, we would do just what you wanted, where you wanted. This guy gets off on watching us enjoy ourselves so that means we choose what happens. And, gostoso, I think I already have a pretty good idea how to make you happy. Once I get that shirt off, those pants of yours slip down and I start playing with your... "

Kelly held up her hands:

"OK, OK, Rubens, stop right there. I think I preferred the camp overload. I'm a girl, not used to all this detail. I thought being a fag hag would be trips to Habitat, watching Glee together and getting advice on which shoes went best with my outfit. Not ready for what you two do in bed. Really not ready for that."

"Glee! My God, what time is it? I need to go. "America's Next Top Model" is about to start. Alex and I are addicted to Tyra. See you tomorrow, guys."

Ben couldn't quite figure out Jamal Qureshi. This guy had supposedly been through a civil war and was now some important engineer with a large staff. He was responsible by all accounts for major building projects. When they had first met, his expression was almost forbidding, it was so serious. Yet mix him up with Rubens and he turned into a turbo charged go-go boy, camping it up like a Glastonbury field before rushing off to watch Tyra Banks present a show about hair and make-up. Maybe all serious, intelligent people had wild alter egos. He suddenly got a disturbing picture of Angela Merkel on E dancing madly to German techno king Scooter. Or Barack Obama prancing round in Michelle's frocks whilst RuPaul taught him how to walk in high heels.

Nice.

Rubens moved closer to Ben.

"So, baby, am I going to get an invite to stay over tonight so we can practise some moves?"

Kelly sighed:

"I think that's my cue to leave. Ben, I think you should do it. Rubens, just remember that I am Kelly, not Jamal, and need treating a little more gently please. Have fun."

When the lift arrived for Ben and Rubens, a familiar green dress swept out majestically.

Ben did a double-take.

"Hello, Cornisha. What are you doing down here at The Lofts?"

"Hello, Ben. Just dropping something off for the Lord and Master of us all."

Ben looked nonplussed.

"Mr Gumpert," explained Cornisha patiently.

She looked over at Rubens expectantly, with a serene smile on her face.

"Oh, Cornisha, sorry. This is Rubens Ribeiro. Rubens, this is Cornisha Burrows, a colleague. Rubens is the gym instructor here. He's a key member – key *part* – of the building facilities. Rubens, Cornisha has the wonderful job of trying to keep the SBK office on the road, and seems to manage it effortlessly."

As Rubens shook hands with the elegant lady in front of him, he thought her face looked familiar. Had they met before? Or was it just the work he recognised?

Cornisha wondered why that nice young New York trainee should be taking a strapping great gym instructor upstairs. What had happened to Miss Danvers? Cornisha hadn't seen that one coming.

Unfortunately, musing on the unexpected brings more of the same. Cornisha hadn't seen the slight step between the lifts and the reception desk. Her toe just caught the lip of the step and she toppled over, banging her knee painfully on the marble floor, her handbag skidding off into Arthur Bilks' desk as she in vain tried to save herself with her hands. Moving fast for a man of his age, Arthur was at her side in a trice.

"Madam, are you alright? Are you hurt?"

"It's just my knee," said Cornisha, shakily.

"Can you get up if I help you?"

Cornisha was surprised at how easily yet gently Arthur helped her to her feet. He was a rather strong man. Arthur couldn't help but feel that under that matronly exterior, Cornisha seemed to have the body of a younger woman. He didn't know at the time that bits of it were actually quite a lot younger. He was also entranced by her wonderful fragrance.

"Come and sit down, Madam. Do you think you can walk a few steps? Can you put any weight on that knee?"

Leaning heavily on Arthur Bilks, Cornisha made it to a soft seat by the reception desk.

"Now may I ring through to the café and get Millie to bring you in a nice cup of tea? I might even be able to locate a little flask of Teacher's if you fancy something a bit stronger."

"That is so kind of you! A cup of tea would be lovely. And a little medicinal nip of whisky might also help my knee. That is very gracious of you."

"I'll call right away, Madam."

"Oh, please call me Cornisha."

"Delighted, I'm sure. I'm Arthur. I am delighted to meet you, Cornisha."

Arthur was indeed delighted to meet Cornisha Burrows. As he rang through to the café, he discreetly admired Cornisha from the safety of his reception desk. For her part, Cornisha was charmed by the attention that Arthur had lavished upon her. He was so kind and chivalrous, as well as being a rather attractive man, who had obviously taken good care of himself. She scolded herself, feeling she was reacting like a silly schoolgirl. What was she doing, imagining getting to know Arthur Bilks better? But she couldn't help it. She liked him. She just did. He was strong and caring and he had been there for her in a flash at a vulnerable moment. Liking people was not a hard decision. It did not have to be complicated.

Yet Cornisha knew full well that a man like Arthur would be shocked when he found out. She should gather herself up, compose herself and stop dreaming. There was no room for her to behave like a ninny.

As Cornisha sipped the tea that Millie had brought, she started to feel better. Maybe it was the good stuff that Arthur had added, giving her a big wink as he did so.

"I always used to add a dash of Scotch to the tea when I went to the seaside. Frinton-on-Sea wouldn't be the same without it."

"Oh Arthur, Frinton! I love Frinton. It just captures something about the quaint old charms of the English seaside. Do you go there often?"

Arthur hadn't been there for eight years. It had been Phyllis Bilks' childhood home and Arthur cherished the happy memories of the days out there.

"I haven't been for a while. It was my wife Phyllis' favourite place. It isn't the same on your own. And it would be a bit odd taking anyone else for a day out at the seaside."

Arthur's expression had been so sad when he mentioned Phyllis, but he had recovered his smile.

"Oh, Arthur, I'm so sorry. I've just completely put my foot in it."

"Cornisha, don't be. Phyllis passed away eight years ago. There isn't a day goes by that I don't miss her, but we had a wonderful life together. My memories are happy ones. I guess I want Frinton to stay special. Maybe I just need a good reason to go back there."

The unexpected twinkle in Arthur's eye made Cornisha come over all giddy again. Why shouldn't she behave like a schoolgirl if she felt like it? After all, she had never had the good fortune to be one, despite all Conrad's secret dressing up.

"Arthur, please will you let me take you for a cup of tea one day? After I have finished thanking you properly for saving a clumsy old woman from feeling too stupid, we can think up some particularly good reason why Frinton needs a visit. And make sure you have the hipflask handy."

12

Eminence Grise

Nicholas Casterway was thoroughly enjoying being in Egypt.

The country had seven thousand years of recorded history. It had produced such marvels of human achievement as the Pyramids of Giza, the Valley of the Kings at Luxor, St Catherine's Monastery, the irrigation of the Nile Valley, the Aswan Dam, and "The Mummy Returns". Then there were the natural wonders of the Red Sea. Above ground all was harsh and arid. Although the five star hotels of Sharm el Sheikh and Taba Heights had allowed a thin veneer of luxury to blossom in a narrow strip along the coast, there was still much desert to contend with. Once under the water, though, the magic of the coral sea came to life, and the true beauty of the place was revealed. The five star natural wonder beneath the sea was a marine Garden of Eden where thousands of brightly coloured fish enticed thousands of fading humans to shed their workaday personalities and let their better nature blossom.

Nicholas Casterway, however, had not come to Egypt for any of these reasons, although he could appreciate an attractively carved tomb or a playful blue tang as much as any person on a package holiday. No, what made his sojourn in Egypt particularly enjoyable was the wonderful servility of the staff in all the hotels. No one could do enough for you. They called you *sir* and meant it. They knew their place. Nicholas felt he could probably buy most of them if he wanted to – if his wife weren't there to cramp his style, that is.

Britta Casterway tried to keep him from lording it over the natives too obviously, but Nicholas couldn't help but revel in his own private post-colonial experience. He was in truth somewhat peeved that he had been born too late to enjoy a posting in the greatest empire on Earth. It would have been a natural fit. He imagined himself with a retinue of servants at his beck and call, and a host of further underlings, all there purely to carry out his orders. He would have had a direct line to Cabinet back in Blighty. He could see Britta as the foreign wife of the Viceroy – with the libido of a stone statue, mind you, not one of these women that actually enjoyed herself. Heaven forbid that she should try. Blondes may have more fun but not with their husbands, thought Nicholas bitterly. He dismissèd thoughts of his wretched matrimonial sex life, and focused instead on his imaginary colonial alter ego. There he was again: a clever and linen-suited benevolent dictator, dispensing justice and good governance, but also making sure he took full advantage of what the land had to offer. What goes on in the colony, stays in the colony – other than dysentery and a few other pesky disorders.

Holidays in the Arab Republic of Egypt were a small consolation for having missed out on the life that Nicholas should have had. When he watched the Egyptians scurrying around to make sure everything was just right, he was transported to the place inside his mind where he exercised real power and men would kneel before him.

Yes, indeed, Nicholas Casterway was thoroughly enjoying his time in Egypt. What a pity that it was the last stop in his round the world tour. Soon his four-month long sabbatical would be over, and he would need to return to his life as a senior partner at SBK in London, England.

"You must try this, babe. It is amazing!"

Crystal pouted her crimson lips before seductively eating the oyster from Kerwin's outstretched fork. To be fair, she had a moment of doubt. Removed from the pearly shell that nestled on a bed of ice, it did not look that great. It hung on the end of the fork like a grey flabby... thing. But when in Rome, have the orgy. She closed her eyes and opened wide.

Kerwin had managed to get a table on a Friday night at La Grande Bouffe. Neither he nor Crystal had ever been and, sprinkled with the stardust of more-than-just-good-friends, it was turning into one of those special evenings. Evenings where he thought she might just be the one, and she thought she could start dreaming of that honeymoon in the Caribbean, and even a house with a proper dining room. She thought she should take special care eating the dessert, just in case there was something hard in there. Like gold. Like a ring. Why shouldn't she have those dreams? She was here, looking over the River Thames. London was at its most magical, and she was close to a man who had swept her off her feet, and was still there to hold her up.

Kerwin had stayed over a couple of nights in the Lofts

that week. Wednesday night they had actually cooked dinner together. She hadn't really progressed far beyond late night kebabs on the Walworth Road with a man before.

Kerwin was a dab hand in the kitchen. He showed off to Crystal and enjoyed it. He told her he had always listened to what his mother and grandmother had told him about cooking. He talked about listening a lot. Crystal didn't know if it was a hint, as she was rather partial to talking, herself, but in any case it had plainly worked for Kerwin. So it was worth paying attention to. She was trying to pick up some tips from him. The new recipes were a bonus. She would surprise Amber when she came back from her week with the family in Basildon.

But back to the sad oyster.

"Kerwin, that is almost as good as you are, honey! Salty, mind. And slippery too. Am I going to be able to thank you for all this by making you one of my extra special breakfasts tomorrow morning?"

Crystal gave Kerwin her most winning smile, with just the sweetest hint of insecurity as to whether he would spend the night with her. Being a bit of a romantic at heart, to say nothing of having a weakness for any attractive woman, there was no doubt in Kerwin's mind.

Kerwin smiled right back:

"You can count on it, baby. Hell, I wish Amber spent more time with her family!"

The week in Basildon was a double celebration for the Bluett family. Sally Bluett, Amber's cousin on her father's side, had married a certain Barry Silverton on the Saturday, and Darren Bluett, Amber's older brother had been released from jail on the Thursday.

Amber had decided to stay at home for another week. The act with Crystal was getting harder and harder to pull off. It was bad enough seeing her so soppy and in love, but the fact that it was with Kerwin, Amber's targeted man, just made it unbearable.

Amber knew Kerwin had a bit of a wandering eye and she was just waiting and hoping for it to engage so that she could be there for poor dear Crystal.

More pragmatically, she needed time to speak to her two brothers about how she was going to get even with Kelly Danvers.

Darren Bluett was a well-built man with whom you would not want to pick a fight. His cropped hair was typical of many British guys of his age. His clothes drew heavily from the gangster style, except for one thing. Unlike his younger brother, Darren did not get why any man would want to walk down the road with the back of his jeans down round the top of his thighs, and his arse hanging out, advertised for all to see. He had tried convincing Nathan to invest in a belt, but the younger Bluett brother thought that his perfectly-formed butt made him even more attractive to the ladies, and deserved to be shown off. Just like his arms in the cut-off tops he wore. Darren despaired at times.

After Amber had finished telling Darren the whole story, including the part where younger brother Nathan had mugged Crystal, Amber waited expectantly for Darren to respond. He just sat there for a minute, dragging hard on his Benson &

Hedges, looking alternatively at her and at Nathan.

"So, what you got planned next then, sis?"

"I want to hurt the bitch so badly that she's afraid to go out at night," said Amber shortly.

Darren took the last drag of his cigarette and stubbed it out in the un recuerdo de Gran Canaria plastic ashtray. There was a small round brown burn mark where the camel's head used to be. It accurately reflected how the Bluett's felt about anything that wasn't family.

"Sis. Do you fancy ending up where I have been the last six months?"

Amber stared at Darren and looked over at her brother Nathan, who was slouching in her father's favourite armchair.

She'd always hated that armchair. In fact she hated the whole room. Only her parents could live in a sitting room with a pink chintz three-piece suite, red patterned shag pile carpet, flock wallpaper with multicoloured tropical birds on it and lime green curtains that had belonged to Amber's granny. The rest of the house wasn't any better. The worst was probably the bedroom suite in black and gold with elephants' heads in relief framing the mirrored headboard. Thank God she had escaped to London, even if she was sharing with Crystal.

"Sis, are you listening to me, or just staring at me like a retard?"

Amber was back in the room. What did Darren mean?

"Listen, Amber, you want to hurt someone that has crossed you. I get that. What you need now is a plan. It's not smart making it obvious you want revenge, because then when you do the deed, the pigs know exactly which door to come knocking at. Be smart, sis. Make peace with the woman. For now. She'll be thinking it's all water under the bridge, but meantimes you keep your eyes peeled for an opportunity. Then we catch her off guard. Nail her good and proper. No evidence, no trail, no trouble."

Nathan nodded earnestly:

"Darren's right, Amber. We were lucky to get away with jumping Crystal. I don't want to risk that again. I'm too young and pretty to go to jail, if you get my drift."

Nathan was indeed far too pretty to risk prison, especially with his penchant for displaying his pertly-bulging underwear.

But Amber's younger brother had a point. They had been lucky. Amber was letting her fury with that American girl blind her to the chances of actually getting away with something like that. But if she followed Darren's plan then she would have to be nice, maybe even apologise, to Kelly. It was almost unthinkable.

Darren smirked at the expression on Amber's face:

"Sis, relax. You don't have to be too nice to her. That's, like, too suspicious. You just want to let her know that what's done is done. You don't want to have anything to do with her. Just stay out of each other's way. The war is over. Finished. Until you find that opportunity to get her alone, no witnesses, no suspicions and then pow! Nathan and me. We'll be there for you, girl."

Blissfully unaware of the plotting taking place on the floral velour, Kelly was at lunch with Ben. They didn't normally have time to leave the office, but it was Friday, and it was also the penultimate Friday before the return of one of the most senior of SBK's partners, the infamous Nicholas Casterway.

"Kelly, why is everyone talking about the return of this Casterway guy?"

Kelly paused:

"He's an important partner, obviously. But he's also, by reputation, the most devious. He's stupidly well-connected, too. He seems to have quite a network and finds out about everything that goes on. As far as I've gathered, he can be completely ruthless when it suits him. I think there is more blood on the carpet thanks to him than to any of the other bullies that stalk this place."

"So kind of Machiavelli's Prince crossed with Orwell's Big Brother?" ventured Ben.

"Rumour has it that he doesn't see eye to eye with some of the other partners. Like Hartmut. You've seen Hartmut Glick. You could get more warmth from a frozen pizza, but I think Harmut is brilliant. He's straight down the line, and plays everything by the book. The total opposite of Nicholas Casterway, who seems to be scheming his way to what he fondly imagines is greatness."

Kelly sighed. It was depressing to think of such insignificant human beings wielding such disproportionate power – and wielding it so so badly. It wasn't much consolation to think that, in reality, they had the judgment of lemmings at jump-the-cliff time. The very fact that such people had any say in anything at all is enough to make one turn to crime. But law is practised privately.

Private practices get away with murder.

Kelly chewed absent-mindedly on a fingernail:

"Casterway has no way of controlling Hartmut Glick, and he doesn't like independence around him."

"So, we're saying that Hartmut is the good guy?"

"I would say so. Hartmut is decent and honest. Luckily he is also brilliant, otherwise he'd be completely doomed as a lawyer."

They both laughed.

"Where does Harry Gumpert fit in?" asked Ben.

"Sort of like pre-War Belgium between Germany and France. He's a useful buffer that can in theory swing with one or the other. Neither as devious as Casterway, nor as decent as Glick. However, getting close to Hartmut is virtually impossible, whereas Casterway always requires allies and people he can control or at least count on. I'd say he is definitely in the Casterway camp."

"How do you know all of this, Kelly?"

"Nicholas Casterway is not the only devious lawyer with a network of informants."

Kelly grinned as she saw Ben's nonplussed face.

"Come on, Ben. You should be able to guess the first one. It's pretty obvious. Monique has been worming information out of Harry for me. There's got to be some payback for me having to listen to all her sob stories about how Harry uses her and will never commit."

"Is Monique really in love with Harry, then?" Ben was surprised.

"Depends on the day. But she seems to be less and less happy being the other woman. Selfishly, I hope it lasts a bit longer, as it is rather useful to have an informant like that. I can't believe Harry opens up so much with her – he must feel really guilty. Or perhaps he's just another emotionally stunted wreck. Law breeds them."

"Tell me of another informant, Fraulein Danvers."

"Believe it or not, my next one is in fact largely a soul of discretion. Unexpectedly, our very own office manager, Cornisha Burrows, can be somewhat more open when generously lubricated with Harvey's Bristol Cream."

"Oh? Heavens. I really like Cornisha. I'd like to adopt her as my British mother. She reassures me."

"Not that it has any bearing on her ability to mother you, or anything else really, but you do know that Cornisha started life as Conrad Burrows, don't you?"

Ben had been pouring himself another glass of water. By the time he had recovered his senses the water was flowing over the table and off on to his lap. Kelly grabbed the bottle and threw him her napkin.

"I would offer to help clean you up, but I seem to remember only Rubens gets near your groin these days."

"OK, funny. But... Cornisha? A transsexual? I had no idea."

"She's pretty marvellous, isn't she? Anyway, she thinks that Nicholas Casterway disapproves. It does not fit with his world view, having a sex-changed office manager. Of course, Nicholas would never openly say anything at all, at least not until he was ready to make his move."

"But surely he must have known when she got the job."

"How so? *You* couldn't tell. And what difference does it make? She's not being hired for her vagina. Unlike some of the more attractive trainees. Anyway, Ben, it seems that Hartmut Glick hired Cornisha. That's another reason why Nicholas is not on the best of terms with our friend from Berlin. It's also why Cornisha will sometimes let her cloak of discretion down and feed me gossip."

"I thought that these days it was against English law to discriminate against people on grounds of sex or sexuality?"

"It is. This is why Nicholas can't do anything too obvious. It doesn't stop discrimination dead, though, does it? Don't start fretting about you and Rubens, mind. I would simply keep private life private for the moment, if I were you. Just be discreet. Nicholas apparently thinks that people with "alternative" sexual choices will also make "alternative" lifestyle choices. He may be right, for that matter – as anything I do might well count as "alternative" for him. It is those issues which may drag the partnership into disrepute, as far as he's concerned. I reckon it's simply that he doesn't like people being open and upfront about things. Or indeed enjoying themselves. That wouldn't really tie in with a scheming 1984 outlook on life."

"He sounds mediaeval or at least a throwback to Victorian times. It's bizarre. Look around at the city we live in!"

"But this is a strange place, Ben, much as I love it. Especially when it comes to sex. It seems to produce the loosest women on the planet – when they are being filmed for reality TV shows, that is – and yet part of it still tries to live to a *Daily Mail* dictated pre-1950s morality. It does make Monique and me laugh. The kind of stories that the French just shrug at have the British demanding their politicians' blood. If anyone in Britain had had an illegitimate daughter like Mitterrand did – to say nothing of Giscard d'Estaing's almost ludicrous womanising – the British press would have been foaming at the mouth. And unlike back home, none of it is based in religion. It's just the way these islanders are. Anyway, we won't solve that now – I, as a woman of average passion, found it impossible to navigate at first. But I've got far better at it over time."

Foaming at the mouth was one of the few practices that Hartmut Glick had no interest in at all. As Caroline and he had both reached highly satisfactory verdicts on the lunch a few days earlier, they had progressed to the next event. Tonight, Hartmut had followed Caroline Napier Jones into a private room at PPLAY. But they weren't alone. He wasn't ready to explore that path yet. No, Caroline had led two drooling slaves in there too, making them walk on all fours, and having them yelp when she gave their leads a particularly strong tug.

The male slave was wearing black leather Doc Martins, a green latex jockstrap and a leather mask; the female slave was in knee-length black leather boots, pink latex crotchless pants, and had a black leather bit in her mouth. The slaves were both bare-breasted. They were each kitted out with a harness to which their leads were attached.

Hartmut himself was in tight leather pants, boots and a black leather overcoat that was a cross between the Matrix and the SS. His peaked cap tipped the balance in favour of the latter. As he adjusted the cockring which kept him in a state of constant readiness, he savoured the idea of being merciless whilst at PPLAY. The only creature, in fact, that could dare to trifle with Hartmut Glick, was the vision in the scarlet catsuit and matching thigh-length boots with six-inch heels brandishing a three-tailed whip as she pulled her slaves along. Caroline looked amazing. With zips in all the right places allowing access when she decided, the catsuit had been custom-made for her in Amsterdam. Not everything Dutch was dull. Dramatic black eye make-up, scarlet lip gloss and extra volume, slightly unhinged-looking dark brown hair completed the look of the exemplary dominatrix that everyone aspired to be corrected by.

The slaves knew that they were particularly fortunate that evening, as they had risked coming to PPLAY alone but for their leads, and yet had managed to pick up the most desired mistress at the party. The male slave could hardly keep himself from whimpering constantly as he imagined the delicious humiliations to come. Hartmut gave him a gentle but firm smack across his bare buttocks to remind him that there was a master as well as a mistress to please.

"I want to sit down." Caroline said, curtly. "You. Get over here now and let your mistress rest her feet."

The male slave scuttled delightedly over to Caroline. He sighed with pleasure as the mistress sat on his back and opened up her bag of tricks. Handcuffs, nipple clamps, dildo, poppers... what was her mobile phone doing in there? Maybe she could use it to build the tension. She had to show who was in control here, even hinting to Hartmut how he might be eased into playing the role of second fiddle.

Caroline looked imperiously over at her companion.

"His boots look dirty to me. Clean them!"

The female slave eagerly started to lick Hartmut's already sparkling boots. Hartmut's cockring felt a bit more strain as the pleasure rippled up his body.

Suddenly the mobile phone rang. Caroline was momentarily furious at having ruined the scene. She quickly concluded, however, that making the others wait whilst she took a phone call might be worthwhile. She would enjoy punishing those two worthless dogs for the nuisance that they had caused by not thinking to remind her to leave her phone in the coatcheck.

"Yes?"

Although surprised by her daughter's rather stern tone, Eleanor Napier Jones was far too excited by her news to be put off.

"Darling, it's Mummy. I have some wonderful news for you. Have I caught you at a bad moment? I can hear music in the background."

"Oh, hello Mater. I am in the middle of something, but it can wait."

"Well, do you remember Felicity Pocock Green and Elsa, her beautiful Pomeranian? Elsa has popped! She had four pups a couple of weeks ago and guess who is going to get one? I am so excited I thought I would have to call my little girl and tell her about my new baby."

At that moment the male slave arched his back slightly so that he could feel the slight friction of the leather of Caroline's dress against his skin. Displeased that the slave had moved without her permission, Caroline gave him a quick crack across his buttocks with her whip. The slave had to summon up all his strength not to whimper with pleasure. Although he had only just met his mistress, he could feel that she wanted him to be quiet and after all he was there solely to serve.

"What was that noise, darling? It sounded like furniture creaking. Anyhow, I'm calling because I want you to come with me to Bond Street tomorrow. Felicity told me that Gucci do the most darling little dog collars, and my little sweetums must have the best. I've seen the most delightful dark gold crystal lamé fabric collar with a horsebit ring buckle on the internet, but I must see it in person. I think it might be a nice occasion for some mother-daughter bonding, darling, don't you?"

Although Caroline preferred bondage to bonding in Bond Street, it would be churlish of her to put her mother off. Moreover it might be amusing imagining her mother in the collar. Caroline stood up, brusquely, and leaned over the slave, placing her left stiletto heel on its back, exercising just the right amount of pressure, driving the point down. This stimulated exquisite pain and pleasure in the slave. She winked at Hartmut, and tossed him the large pink dildo, motioning him to use it on the female.

"Believe it or not, Mater, I do have rather strong opinions on collars."

Caroline glared at the female slave as she said it. The dildo had started to have an effect on the slave's vocal chords and Caroline did not remember giving permission for any noises to be made.

"The lead must be good quality and strong. Preferably you should get a harness as well. The last thing you want is for the thing to escape, or worse, to asphyxiate it when it gets too frisky."

Caroline couldn't resist giving her slave's lead a good tug as if to emphasise the point.

Eleanor Napier Jones was delighted at the input:

"Well, I haven't seen any designer harnesses yet, but if you're such an expert maybe you know where we could go?"

For a moment Caroline wondered if she should take her mother to the London Fetish Fair. Maybe not. She doubted her mother would see the "All Day Dungeon" as a particular draw. And it would be so embarrassing to be with the only person kitted out in Laura Ashley and asking if it were possible to get a scone and a dry sherry.

"I'll look into it, Mater. And have you thought about how you are going to deal with discipline? You have to show them who is boss right from the start."

Caroline directed a particularly baleful look at her borderline-disobedient male slave who seemed to be enjoying her stiletto a little too much. She removed her boot from his back. It had left a small but painful-looking red indentation. She whipped him sharply across the buttocks again, daring him to flinch, whimper or make any such unauthorised sign of pain or pleasure.

"I hadn't really thought of that Caroline. I mean, how could I possibly scold such a darling little thing?"

"You must start as you mean to go on. Lay down the rules from day one. And never forget to rub its nose in its own mess, if you want it trained. It is essential, if you are both to be happy."

The male slave knew he was seriously breaking the rules, but at that point with his pathetic little penis straining at his latex jockstrap he gave a yelp of delight. He knew that would merit some severe punishment. He couldn't wait.

Sadly for the male slave, Caroline Napier Jones was far too skilled in the dark art of domination and knew that he was desperate for a thrashing. Although she obviously believed in the "spare the whip and spoil the Pomeranian" school of discipline, she also knew that a too liberal use of the whip could also spoil the slave. Nothing disgusted her more than when they came before she did, without her permission. It could totally ruin her evening. No, this one would need to be put on ice. She deliberately didn't touch the desperate creature, and instead went and spanked the female slave, surreptitiously admiring Hartmut's fluid technique with the dildo as she did.

"Oh, Caroline, that does seem rather old-fashioned and brutal. Are you sure that's what they recommend these days? I really don't think I could do that. No. I rather think I shall reward sweetums with doggy biscuits for getting it right. I am surprised at your Neanderthal ways, darling. Anyway, how are you fixed tomorrow afternoon? Maybe we could have lunch at the Wolseley again?"

"Excellent. I'll see you there at 12:45. Listen, I really need to go. I have a few things I really must tie up. See you tomorrow for the collar."

Caroline hung up, switched the phone off and turned on her six-inch heel.

"So, it seems that everyone is having a fine time apart

from me. This will change now! No one is leaving this room until your mistress has been well and truly satisfied. Mr G, bring those two worthless specimens to me immediately."

Hartmut Glick had been struck by the telephone conversation. He was unable to work out whether Caroline had planned it as a stunt or not. She was really rather spectacular. He rather enjoyed watching the alpha female in action and thought he could get quite accustomed to being her second-in-command. He gladly acquiesced, with flashing eyes, and a swelling sense of anticipation.

In another part of the city, Harry Gumpert had just received a telephone call that would have as big an effect on Hartmut Glick as Caroline Napier Jones had. It caught him in the Castle Lofts reception, and the conversation echoed round the hall.

"Harry, it's Nicholas. How are you?"

"Nicholas, how wonderful to hear from you. Are you back in London yet?"

"I leave Cairo in a couple of days, and then I need to spend a few days in the country with my mother. I'll be back in time for the cocktail party."

"It will be splendid to have you back, Nicholas. SBK just isn't the same without you."

Harry's second sentence was truthful, even if the first wasn't. Nicholas' network and devious ability certainly contributed to the partnership's billing, but even Harry had to admit the office had been a nicer place to work in over the previous four months.

"How kind of you to say so, Harry. I have missed it, 'though of course it has been a delight to spend quality time with Britta without work getting between us."

"Of course, of course. Now, I guess you haven't called just to ask me how I am, Nicholas?"

"Always the same perspicacious Harry Gumpert. On the nail again! We have to address a rather delicate matter."

Harry's ears pricked up at the word delicate. Nicholas could be master of the silver-tongued understatement, especially when it was the prelude to a particularly ruthless action.

"Harry, it has come to my attention that certain personal behaviour at SBK, should it get into the public realm, might damage our reputation. Although naturally I am the last person who wants to pry into other partners' personal lives, it would ill behove me if I did not place the greater good of SBK ahead of individual sensibilities."

Curses! How had Nicholas Casterway found out about his affair with Monique? Harry had always tried to keep it under wraps. Who could have told him? Of course, how stupid was he? It must be that ruthless little minx from Baton Rouge! How the hell could she betray him to someone like Nicholas?

"Nicholas, I really don't know what you are talking about!"

"And how could you Harry, as I understand that you lead a steady and regular life. Not for you the disreputable perversions that it is my great sorrow to even hear talked of."

So it wasn't him that Nicholas was accusing. Harry felt a

gush of relief. But if it was not Harry, who was it? Intense curiosity ballooned in Harry. Who was Nicholas describing, and what on earth was he, or she, doing?

"And it saddens me even further to say that the person around whom such feculence is swirling is our own supposed paragon of decency, the upstanding Hartmut Glick."

Although Harry had never encountered the word feculence before it certainly didn't sound good. Everyone knew carbohydrates were out. What the hell had Hartmut done? Harry registered the scarcely hidden delight in Nicholas' voice. It was the worst kept secret in SBK that those two heavy hitters couldn't bear each other, despite the veneer of professional respect that it was incumbent upon them to maintain.

"What have you heard about Hartmut's personal life, Nicholas?"

"Harry, I don't like to go into details over the phone, but suffice to say that if particulars of Hartmut's supposedly respectable private interests came into the public domain I believe a number of our clients would consider it inappropriate to entrust their confidential business to such a sexual deviant. We must schedule a meeting as soon as possible to discuss how we are going to manage this. Can you have my secretary schedule a meeting with you the first day I am back? I want this dealt with immediately. I am sure Hartmut will agree that there is only one suitable outcome. See you soon, Harry. Godspeed."

Heavens! Harry was even more curious now. *Gott in Himmel!* When Nicholas talked of just one suitable

227

outcome Harry knew exactly what he meant. Whilst hiding behind the veil of protecting SBK's reputation and client base, Nicholas Casterway was plotting to finally get rid of his arch enemy Hartmut Glick.

13

Intoxication: the highs

Silent entreaties do work. Arabella Gumpert had invited her brother to the annual cocktail party for Bella Models. Harry arrived slightly too early. He pretended to be bored. His aim was to convey that he was merely there to support his sister as she schmoozed her way round the room. He was entirely failing to achieve the desired effect. The bright look in his eyes betrayed him, as did his alert posture. Really, who was he kidding? He looked like a bitch in season.

It was Harry's favourite social event. He always made sure that Sarah was otherwise engaged and of course it would be far too dangerous to bring Monique. As he wasn't there to look after the client base, he could concentrate on talent spotting. Harry had a pretty good eye for talent.

His sister, who would have been prettier if she did not look like Lady Cynical of Cynical Hall, wandered over. Cynically.

"Having fun, Harry? Such a shame Sarah couldn't make it. Once again, I'm starting to think she must look down on what I do for a living."

"Arabella, don't be silly. She thinks you're marvellous," said Harry smoothly, looking over Arabella's shoulder. "It just isn't easy with young children, that's all. Have I ever told you what it's like getting babysitters in SE1? And yes, I am enjoying myself. What do you expect? I do like a good Mojito."

"That's a relief. I rather thought you might be bored here without any of your intelligent lawyer friends. Our industry isn't exactly famous for its conversation."

"Conversation has its downsides, Arabella. By the way, that woman looks awfully familiar. Do I know her?"

Harry's eye had been caught by a six-foot vision in a white Versace mini dress. Her long black hair framed a near perfect Latin face. He took in the green eyes, perfect nose and lips that could suck blood from a stone.

"Now how would I know, Harry? I hope not. She's one of our top models and the last thing I want is for her to get covered in my brother's drool. That dress cost a fortune."

"Arabella, come on. Give me a little more credit than that."

"Oh, am I being unfair? I keep forgetting that it is you who has to beat them off, so to speak. How could any sane woman resist you?" She jutted her chin towards him with a pinch of contempt: "Harry, I mean, just looking at the way you ooze charisma and power. Even I feel weak at the knees. Would incest be such a sin, dear, dear brother?"

"I hope you're not so outrageous with your customers," said Harry stiffly. It was not as if Arabella could not be overheard.

He had been trying to follow the vision around the

room without Arabella noticing, but she was far too good an observer to be fooled by such an amateur attempt.

"Oh God, Harry, can you please close your mouth? You get in here and suddenly you morph from a sober lawyer into an excited Jack Russell who's just been taken to the park for the first time in its life. You don't know where to look or where to run. You're all over everything. Next time, I swear, I'm going to put you on a leash."

Harry was staring still. The girl looked more beautiful every time he glanced her way. Her face was alive. Her eyes were laughing. Harry had the look of somebody who had just been given the one thing that they had long been waiting for.

Arabella had a flashback to a sunny day when they were children. They had been taken out for ice cream. There was a particularly delicious ice cream that they used to enjoy together as children, and they had been promised some of it. It was the same damned look. She softened slightly, like a leftover sundae on a summer's day:

"Really, Harry. Predictable does not begin to describe you. Oh, I give in. Gabriela, could you come over here a moment? I want to introduce you to someone special."

Gabriela de Souza glided over, like a cheetah stalking its prey.

"Gabriela, this is my brother, Harry Gumpert. He's one of those frightfully intelligent but really rather boring City lawyers. For God's sake don't let him talk about work or you'll find your eyes closing before you can finish your drink. Or maybe that's just me he has that effect on. Harry, this is Gabriela de Souza, special even amongst our

231

enormously talented Brazilian contingent. Anyhow, I can see a very dull client on his own and without a drink. I am such a slave to my business."

Suddenly Harry was alone with the vision. Ice cream. Everywhere. He knew that he would never get a better chance than this, not in a month of sundaes. He had to get it right. Thankfully, Harry did not lack confidence. He was sure enough of himself to slip into what he considered charisma overdrive.

"Gabriela, I would normally ask a girl how she got into modelling, but with your looks, that just seems a ridiculous question."

After the compliment, Harry directed his most winning smile at Gabriela. Should he go in for the kill? Would a one-night stand be so bad? Although he didn't make a habit of cheating on Monique, it did happen occasionally when some particularly irresistible prize offered itself up. Who could possibly resist Gabriela? Hang feeling guilty tomorrow, this one was not going to get away. *Go for it, Gumpert!*

"Well, I do try to watch my figure, despite the evil intentions of Valerie and her Patisseries."

Arthur wasn't used to having tea in marble-clad salons in Mayfair, but sitting opposite Cornisha Burrows, he thought he could get used to it. He had always rather eschewed the West End. Central London seemed to him to be a slightly foreign place that he came to work in, before swiftly retreating to the comfort of West Ham, in London's East End. In West Ham you were still more likely to find a plate of jellied eels than a king prawn and pesto panini with sunblush tomatoes.

Arthur felt that the real London could now only be found outside of Zone 1. Zone 1 itself was for tourists or the more transient of workers. They would land there after college, love the buzz and "diversity" of the city and then promptly retire to somewhere in the suburbs when they hit the grand old age of thirty-five and wanted to have kids. He admitted grudgingly to himself that there were still pockets of real London in the city centre, but they were mainly council estates that nice people tried not to notice. They seemed anyway to house ever greater numbers of immigrants who would move themselves somewhere more pleasant when they got the well-earned chance.

For the last ten years, Arthur had seen no reason to challenge his perceived wisdom about the place. But now he had met Cornisha Burrows. Things could change: they just had. Suddenly that alien city centre seemed to be alive with new stimuli calling out to him, inviting him to dive in. Of course, he would experience them gladly with Cornisha at his side, guiding him through the minefield. He beamed at her, not knowing what to say, just content to be there. Christ, with her. It was amazing. He felt like a teenager.

"That was your cue to compliment me on my figure, Arthur."

Momentarily bemused, Arthur relaxed when Cornisha gave him the sweetest of smiles. She had no need of compliments. She could feel how happy he was in her company. Arthur may not have been the most talkative of men, and yet he had a strangely powerful way of communicating with her. She felt that she knew what he was saying even when he was not actually expressing himself. Although she had been single virtually all her life, she was still fairly well-tuned into the way men thought. It helped, obviously, that she too used to have a penis.

"Cornisha, I would say it is game, set and match to you. With a silhouette like yours, Valerie never stood a chance."

Pleased that he had been listening to her – not that she had much doubt, given his general disposition – Cornisha thought it was time to bring up the "F" word, and broach when to do it.

"So, Arthur, let's plan. When are we going on our day trip to Frinton-on-Sea?"

As they sat there planning their gentle day out together, a haze of well-being settled over the table. Arthur wondered whether it was, possibly, visible to others. Cornisha felt very much at ease too. In her case, however, it only lasted for a few moments at a time. In the back of her mind, she had twinges of doubt.

What would happen when she told Arthur the truth – as surely she must, inevitably? She decided to forget about it for the time being. These moments were just too good to throw away and she thought they should both enjoy them. As for Arthur, without the persecution of any of those doubts, he was feeling rather splendid. He found Cornisha Burrows intoxicating.

"Figlio mio, I'm flying Virgin Atlantic First Class – I think I deserve a little luxury. After all I will be saving so much money not taking a hotel and staying with my darling boy."

The joy of having his mother stay with him for a week in his flat was starting to concern Ben Barlettano. Was it too late to book a hotel for her? Maybe they could compromise.

"Mamma, my flat is small – well, very basic. Why don't you come over on Saturday morning when you arrive, stay for the weekend with me and then I will book you into a nice hotel for the rest of the week? We can have the whole weekend together and then when I am at work you will be living in luxury. We can still spend every evening together."

"Va bene. OK, if you think that's best. But I hope you're not just pushing me away because you've suddenly got secrets from your Mamma! Is there some girl I need to know about that you haven't told me about?"

"I've met some lovely people here, Mamma. There is a girl I like, but she is just a friend."

Ben couldn't really tell the whole truth. He imagined for a second launching into a proper explanation – *"Yes there is Kelly, but she has stayed at the "just a friend" stage because, when she finally came round to make a move on me, I was fully occupied having sex with a Brazilian gym instructor with huge biceps and a rather delightful dick."* No, his mother really would not know how to deal with that, other than to launch into the typical Italian mother's tragedy when the son wasn't doing what Mamma wanted.

"I knew it, bello della Mamma! You must introduce me when I come over!"

"Of course I will. Anyway, Mamma. Love you. I have to go now. I'll get you a lovely hotel."

"Don't worry, Ben. I have heard of Expedia, you know. Or I'm sure my friend Elizabeth will be able to recommend something suitable. She's always going to London."

"Va bene, Mamma. I love you. I'll call you. I can't wait to see you."

"Goodbye, caro figlio mio. I'm so looking forward to seeing you and meeting your new friends."

Oh God. Ben had never lied to his mother about anything really important before. What's worse, he would have to get his friends to lie to her, too. Either that, or pretend they had all gone away for the week. What a charade.

Anyhow, as he put the phone down and ran a hand over his face, he felt better. The call was over. It was a London Saturday night, and Ben had a big night ahead of him. He was going out with Rubens, Jamal and Alex to Intoxication, a new, once-a-month gay extravaganza. He was assured that all the A-List went there, whoever they were.

He smiled to himself as he got into the shower. He loved getting ready to go out. Anticipation was half of it all. He felt like a professional clubber as he sipped his Vodka Red Bull while carefully ironing the brand new Abercrombie shirt he had bought specially for the night.

The night was held at one of London's newest superclubs, Cable, near London Bridge. Rubens would be dancing there. He had to get there early, so Ben would be going with Jamal and Alex.

Ben felt a thrill of excitement as he knocked on their door. Muffled club music thumped out of it, a heartbeat of anticipated fun and sex. Ben paused before knocking again, listening to the bass line, smiling to himself. The door opened and he slipped into the flat.

The men looked pumped up. Alex was wearing combat jeans and a skin-tight Diesel singlet that showed every contour of his muscular torso. Jamal had selected a pair of loose D Squared jeans, a black studded belt with an oversize silver buckle, and an open De Puta Madre green vest top with a dog tag hanging between his pecs. The two men looked shockingly good. With his crisp shirt and baggy chinos with the crease down the side, Ben suddenly felt less like the professional clubber and more like the father who was taking the kids out for the night. Kind of humiliating, as he was over a decade younger than the other two.

Jamal looked at Ben levelly:

"Hey Ben, you do know where we are going tonight, don't you?"

Alex glanced over at Ben with kindness:

"Jamal, don't say that. Not everyone is an old trollop like we are, you know."

Ben waved a hand, embarrassed but self-aware:

"No, Alex, Jamal's right. Looking at you two I am a bit overdressed. Or dressed like Uncle Tedious. I guess I am more used to going to nice parties in the Hamptons than a club in London."

"Ben, don't worry. You look great. You have your own charm that way."

"Sure," said Ben, "My own charm. It's been quite a burden these last twenty-odd years."

Ben felt a bit hopeless. Looking round the room at the minimalist lines, designer everything, the forty-five-inch LED screen showing some kind of crazy looking Rio Carnival as backdrop to the music and of course the essential perfect lighting, Ben realised just what a babe in the woods he really was. A few minutes earlier he had been on top of the world; the ultra cool young New Yorker who was taking London by storm, going out with his new friends to one of the hottest clubs in town, all of course fuelled by a couple of those fabulous Vodka Red Bulls. Now he felt like an awkward teenager who had just found out that what had passed for hip at his local school was seriously uncool at college.

Ben decided to make up for his sartorial ineptitude by showing the guys that he was at least accomplished at negotiating London transport:

"So, we get the Northern Line two stops up to London Bridge, right, and then we can walk from there?"

"Habibie, we don't do public transport at night," asserted Jamal firmly, "unless, that is, you count taxis, of course. It's taxi, or driving."

"Absolutely," agreed Alex. ""We either jump in the Jag, or it's a quick call to Elephant Rides. Best cab firm in the area, Ben, by the way."

Ben was struck by the fact that they sometimes drove when they went out at night.

"That's impressive. So you'd consider not drinking when you go out?"

The two men gave Ben a momentary look as if to say *"What are you talking about?"* before smiling at him. As the penny dropped, Ben again felt like the naïve teenager who had left the familiarity of the schoolyard, and was having difficulties adapting to the new rules. Of course Alex and Jamal didn't drink. At least, not regularly. Alcohol plus over thirty-five years on planet Earth did not equal abs like theirs.

Ben felt a bit uneasy. Was it too late to back out? *"Oh, to hell with it"*, he thought to himself. He had to see this scene once in his life. He had plenty of cash on him so he could get his own cab home if things got too much. But he needed to see this place.

In the lift Ben felt better again. Hanging out with these two was intoxicating. They knew what they were doing. And Alex would look out for him. It was going to be alright.

There were at least two hundred people outside the club. Ben felt half-dazed. Apprehension and adrenaline pumped through him. It was a potent feeling. Ben followed Alex and Jamal past the entire snaking queue to the other side of the door where there was a line of only about ten guys.

"Guest list. Knowing one of the dancers has its benefits." said Alex confidently.

Jamal shot him an amused look:

"Alex, darling, *I* got us on this guest list. I don't need Rubens to open doors."

They had to wait for the "door whore" to process all those special people on the guest list. Looking at the queue, Ben was struck by just how ordinary it all looked. Ben had been expecting something extravagant, exceptional. He looked around for party people, those people whose mere proximity suddenly awaken senses you didn't know you had. At this moment, everyone just looked a little cold, a little bored.

Maybe such feelings lived mainly in the imagination?

Wasn't imagination great.

Ben worried for a bit. Would it actually end up just like a frat party back home? One of those urban safaris, watching young singles in their natural habitat, off their heads and making idiots of themselves in their non-stop search for sex and beer? He was starting to feel a little underwhelmed and no longer bothered about his chinos and sensible shirt. It was only a vague air of expectation that he could pick up from those at the front end of the queue that gave him any hope at all.

They finally were allowed through a door to an antechamber.

The darkened space was somewhere between a rather too long, narrow hallway and a heavily pregnant corridor. It was devoid of life. It was followed by a much larger room, but which, disappointingly, still had the air of a lonely vestibule. A few guys were hanging round the edge, texting or talking on their mobiles. Ben was losing the last hopes of this being anything other than a colossal disappointment. So much for London clubland.

Then he noticed a set of double doors on the far side. Jamal was heading purposefully in that direction. As they went through, the noise levels boomed. The loud music grabbed Ben's senses and brought all that Vodka Red Bull straight back to his head.

Even without having sunk down some alcohol, Ben would never have been able to forget this first time of viewing a room of hundreds of bare-chested men strutting their stuff in the way that only gay men could. His Abercrombie shirt had just walked into a room of Abercrombie models. The music was a sonic wall of cool. It was loud, it was urgent, it was raw. The atmosphere was thick with eroticism bursting out of the tensed abdominals, the flexed biceps, the intensity on faces and dancing in the wide eyes of the crowd. Bodies and movement. Nothing else. Like vertical sex – right there, in your face. He could see a scattering of token female friends, seemingly oblivious to the seething currents of repressed desire in that sea of glistening tanned flesh and cropped heads. The lighting swirled around the room, picking out shadows, reflections and outlines.

As Ben took in the details of the industrial-styled room, he saw the two large podiums. Spotlights illuminated them, starkly yet compellingly. He had to watch. On the right hand podium, there were two poles. Wearing the smallest pair of speedos with a leopard print pattern on them, Rubens Ribeiro was hanging upside down gripping the apparatus with one foot whilst the other stretched out towards another dancer on the next pole along. The second man wore identical speedos – and he looked similar to Rubens, but for the deep black colour of his skin. His glistening muscles tensed as he held on to the pole, and gyrated around it. The two had obviously worked hard on the routine.

The second podium vied for the crowd's attention like a competitive salesman nearing the end of the quarter. Ben's eyes were immediately drawn to a huge blond guy, standing there, immoveable. He looked like a Viking warrior, one that had probably raped and pillaged his way through all the British Isles single-handedly. It helped that he was wearing a Norse helmet, thick carved silver armbands round his arms, a fur loincloth, and huge boots of fur and leather. As he posed and stared menacingly yet somehow lasciviously at the crowd he wielded a short sword with obvious dexterity. But it was the person that he was dancing with that really took Ben's breath away. She was five foot eleven, with full flaming lips, long black hair and completely naked. Well, not completely. There was the small matter of the tiniest brown leather thong, an extravagant headdress full of white feathers and fake animal horns, a long necklace of bones hanging between her breasts and a few slashes of white body paint. To complete the look of the Voodoo priestess, and just in case there was any doubt that she meant business, she was brandishing a stick with a skull at one end and serpents carved into its length.

As she moved about the stage next to her Viking, she commanded the room with her sensual gaze, safe in the knowledge that the crowd was far more interested in the men. She was there solely to add glamour to the spectacle.

Quite suddenly, with no prior warning, the Viking leapt over the heads of the crowd below to the other podium, pretending to try to slay Rubens and the other dancer, who in their turn escaped to the safety of the girl's podium. Ben noticed how a couple of the guys on the dancefloor turned their heads up to get a closer look at the bulging speedos passing just over them. Being gay, of course, they remained mindful of appearances. There was no question whatsoever of them attempting to reach out. Studied nonchalence prevailed.

The routine was well practised. The Viking continued

to smoulder and throw out burning looks. Meanwhile, the goddess turned her attention to the wretches that had dared to invade her space. She pointed the skull theatrically at the escaped men. One after the other, they fell to the ground under the high priestess' spell, writhing on the floor rather like Shakira on acid. Just like the singer, every movement was tailored to show off a particular part of their oiled bodies.

Dry ice hissed out and enveloped the podiums. As the fog cleared, Ben saw that a trapeze and two ropes had descended from the ceiling. The high priestess was sitting on the trapeze being gently lifted out of sight, whereas the two boys had been tied by their feet to the ropes and were being hoisted upside down to the roof, somehow managing to make sure all their best bits were still on show. Not to be outdone, on the other podium, the Viking had the sword in his mouth and was swarming up one of the poles. Then they were gone. It was over. Ben was left alone with the five hundred mere mortals that had so arrested his attention when he walked in.

So much for London clubland! Ben's heart seemed to be thudding in rhythm with the music. He had walked into a den of pure hedonism. It was superb showmanship, and yet it was not a game. These people were up for grabs. He rubbed his eyes. He had been momentarily transfixed by the show. He had completely forgotten Jamal and Alex. They were watching him with an amused expression on their faces.

"So do you think you might get to like Intoxication, Ben?"

"It's *phenomenal*. But I'll need some wardrobe guidance before I come out with you boys again."

"Oh habibie, you'll learn quickly, don't worry. Once I too was a nicely dressed foreigner. My first experience in a London night club made me feel as if I had walked into a culture decades ahead of me. I felt so inadequate. Then I discovered Soho gyms and Covent Garden's shops. And of course the T3 rule – teeth, tan and tits. Now look at me. Am I not a *fabulous* specimen of Maghrebi manhood? Look and weep."

"Jamal's so wonderfully modest isn't he, Ben? Anyhow, let's go in and see your boy. Nothing like a bit of reflected glory."

Squeezing through the crowd, attempting minimum physical contact with the glistening bodies around him, Ben stuck close to Alex and Jamal. He felt somewhat invisible walking through that futuristic crowd, seemingly oblivious to his presence, all intent on their own enjoyment, their own entourage, their own charge. Ben could barely hear when Alex turned to him.

"Watch them as they change. This is still warm-up stage, Ben. The drugs haven't really kicked in yet, so they're keeping themselves to themselves in their little groups of friends. Next comes the friendly stage, then the sexual predator stage, then the closing down sale – followed by the "avoid at all costs" finale."

"The closing down sale?"

"When there's only an hour or so left in the club and the guys are getting desperate. You'll see. They start to drop their standards. Kind of an extra desperate "beer goggles" effect. Before Jamal, I went home myself with a few trolls that I had dismissed out of hand earlier in the evening."

Maybe this London tribe wasn't so different to his college crew after all. Ben could remember quite a few regrettable ends to parties. Especially the ones where he had picked up the not very pretty girl he really didn't want, gone home and ended up in a sorry yet eminently predictable state. More than once his night had ended with him being vomited all over by a drunken stranger. Ben was fairly sure that some of the girls involved could recount a similar story about him. The joy of sex, indeed. He guessed this is what Alex meant by the "avoid at all costs" finale. Different ways of getting intoxicated, different looks but the same desires, the same reactions, and sometimes the same outcomes. Maybe he could fit in here after all. Maybe anyone could.

As Jamal opened the door to the *"private – staff only"* dancers' changing room, Ben was floating on cloud nine. Not only was he here in what might be the coolest club he had been to, with cool friends and a gorgeous boyfriend – God, that word still jarred – but now he was going into "private rooms". He had really arrived.

They were greeted by the priestess he had just seen rising into the roof on a trapeze.

"Boys, come in! How did you enjoy our show?"

"Superb! Gabriela, you make the most incredible high priestess. I would have liked to see you whip Rubens, but apart from that, it was perfect."

"Thank you, Jamal. Next time maybe we can get you up there and I'll see what I can do."

After they had been introduced to the Viking, who was actually a Norwegian called Thor (and a frequent victim of typecasting), they met the black dancer, John, who told them he went by the name of Dorothy.

Dorothy wasted no time in informing them that he thought names were up for grabs. "I don't think parents know what they are doing with names, do you? I mean, look at Thora over here. He may live up to his Scandinavian God handle now, but believe me he puts the "Her" into "Hercules" once he's had a few white wine spritzers."

Thor, apparently still sober, smiled gruffly and took Dorothy into a headlock.

Ben found himself standing with Rubens and the gorgeous Gabriela, who was dabbing at her breasts with some tissues, removing the traces of bodypaint that were still on them. Ben didn't know where to look, as he just wanted to look everywhere at the same time, and was trying not to cause a stir in his perfectly ironed Chinos. There was an almighty spirit here. It was heavenly.

"Ben, Ben," tutted Rubens, "did the boys not tell you what this place was going to be like? I mean, Chinos and a shirt. What were you thinking?"

"Rubens, go easy on the boy. Ben, you look very nice. You should have seen the way this one dressed when we first arrived from Rio. He always tried to be so regular, and now look at the little puta!"

Rubens dismissed Gabriela with an airy wave:

"Really, Ben, you cannot go back out of that door wearing those clothes. The shirt is the easy part. Dorothy, can you remove that offensive piece of fabric for me, please?"

Before Ben could react Dorothy was unbuttoning him and with a flourish the shirt was off his back. Dorothy cooed appreciatively:

"Girlfriend, your Big Ben is one smokin' hot hunk underneath that middle-aged exterior."

Ben wasn't sure whether to take the compliment or be offended. He did however fancy a cigarette when he heard the smokin' reference.

"You've got sneakers on at least. All is not lost. Here, get those Chinos off now and put these on."

Rubens handed Ben a pair of what looked like loose boxing shorts. Although Ben was slightly nervous at walking out into a club dressed in just a pair of shorts, there was a part of him that looked forward to being nearly naked amongst all those men. It was all about fitting in. When in Rome. He felt more confident about his body now than he had previously. And after all, hadn't he come to London for wild experiences like this?

He undid his belt and slipped his trousers off. As he pulled the shorts on, he realised that the excitement of the club had actually given him a slight semi; yet again he was in company with an unwanted erection. He could see the bulge even with the shorts on. Surprising even himself as he did it, he very obviously reached down, adjusted himself and sighed with relief.

"That's much better. Thank you, Rubens."

At that point Gabriela started laughing approvingly. She truly was beautiful, thought Ben.

"Well, well, gostoso Americano – I wasn't expecting that. Maybe you will be able to live with this naughty ex-boyfriend of mine after all. Rubens, I think you should stick very close to this one. He's special."

Although he knew Rubens had had a girlfriend, hearing this goddess talk of him as her ex conjured up all sorts of interesting images. Remembering that he was wearing a very thin pair of shorts, Ben smiled and thought of England. He suggested they go and get a drink, and then maybe a sneaky cigarette.

"Gostoso, we've got all we need in here. But you go get yourself a drink and we'll meet you in the smoking area. I just need to help Gabby get her tits cleaned up, the dirty girl."

The club that Ben went back out to looked the same but felt totally different. He realised what had changed. As Alex had prophesied, the crowd's drugs were kicking in. It was obvious even to the neophyte. There were marked reactions to Ben's shorts and his half bared body, even as the crowd lurched in spasmogenic dancing. Ben was learning to appreciate being the object of such attention. He drank in the eyes eating him alive and the friendly, slightly flirty smiles, as he walked through the crowd to the bar. Some of the looks came from the sort of guys he had always felt inferior to. His bar presence checked out, too. The barman immediately served him his Vodka Red Bull.

Ben wound his way to the smoking area. He reached it before Rubens and the others and so he found himself standing alone in his boxing shorts with a drink and a Marlboro Light, in the middle of a sea of tanned, muscular flesh.

Maybe it was the attention or maybe it was the drink, but

Ben felt on top of the world. Those fit muscular guys that had always made him feel inadequate at school and college were now making him feel like one of their own, and, what's more, one of their informal leaders. Just when he thought it couldn't get any better he felt two arms round his waist and a kiss planted in the middle of his shoulders.

"Gostoso, aren't you just the sexiest man in London!"

The whole entourage was out of the dressing room. Thora and Dorothy stopped bickering for a moment and gave Ben warm smiles and a wink.

"Now listen, Ben. I don't want to push you, but we have all had a pill and if you want to join us, then it would be kind of cool."

Ben looked Rubens in the eyes, and thought he saw love there. As they kissed, he asked himself if there would ever be a better time to have this experience. It might be hard to beat being in the middle of a group of friends, in an amazing club. He was already feeling more uplifted than he had ever felt before. As he pulled apart from Rubens, he found Gabriela by their side. She truly was a sensual night spirit. She somehow embodied the feeling of the occasion. It sent Ben even higher. The answer would be yes.

As Ben was already feeling high, he couldn't quite tell if the pill was kicking in. But later he found himself on the dance floor. He was grinding with Gabriela, Rubens dancing on his other side. He wasn't even aware that he knew how to dance like that. He certainly wouldn't habitually have made such a show of himself in public, and he wouldn't have enjoyed it, had he not been flying. He loved everyone in the club, he loved everyone he'd met in London, he would even make an effort with that poor misunderstood Amber Bluett. Then he remembered his darling mother and he almost had tears in his eyes thinking about when she would visit and how he would just be so open with her and he knew she would understand and all would be OK. Love! It was the most blinding feeling in the world.

Arms around the two Brazilians, surrounded by the most beautiful background of cool and sexy, he also thought back to poor Rubens' family back home. He suddenly knew he had to help Rubens raise the money, by whatever means possible.

How could he have doubted it?

That guy Rubens had lined up – *what was the big deal? Kelly was right.* The guy just wanted to watch two beautiful men together. What could possibly be wrong with that? He had to help his gorgeous Rubens in whatever way he could. He felt so in love with Rubens. But then he also felt in love with Gabriela, Kelly, and everyone in London. How had he ever managed to live anywhere else?

He leant over to Rubens and spoke loudly:

"Rubens, darling, you know the other day? What you said? I want to do it with you. I had to think about it – I'm sorry I did – but I know it is the right thing to do and I am so happy to do it. For you. For who you are."

If Rubens had been Ben, he would probably have felt guilty about getting his man to agree to prostitute himself part-time, while Ben was so manifestly under the influence of ecstasy, vodka, Red Bull, compliments and his first delirious night in a London superclub. But he was Rubens

Ribeiro, and it did not occur to him in the least. He just smiled at Ben and was happy.

Days later, all Ben could recall of the next few hours in the club was a haze of friends, amazing dancing, lots of sexy new acquaintances wanting to meet him and Rubens at his side.

The next thing he remembered with any clarity was being in a taxi with Alex and Jamal, on their way to Spartacus Spa in Vauxhall. Ben had fondly said goodnight to Gabriela, promising her that they would get together soon, as they had so much in common and he just loved her. She patted his cheek with a smile that made his already hyperactive heart pound. He could not believe how lovely women were.

Harry Gumpert's next door neighbour, Caroline Napier Jones, had not thought that mixing Hartmut Glick and a weekend in Germany would necessarily lead to romance. Since arriving in Berlin on Friday evening they had not left each other's side for more than a few minutes, no handcuffs required.

Hartmut's secretary had upgraded them on the short flight to Berlin. It was, as he gravely informed her, completely pointless on such a short flight, especially for two people who enjoyed confinement and restriction. But, as Hartmut said, what the hell.

He twinkled uncharacteristically at the stewardess, securing generous rounds of champagne. Caroline felt her spirits lift. A steward took over the task of refreshing the pale gold bubbles. Hartmut took in the crew member's less than entirely attractive appearance.

"Dear me," he murmured conspiratorially to Caroline, "Less like a Greek God, more like the Greek deficit."

Caroline giggled. "A BOBFOC," she said.

"Excuse me?"

"Body off Baywatch, face off Crimewatch."

"Dear me," repeated Hartmut thoughtfully, "Still. Nothing a supple leather mask couldn't deal with." He allowed his hand to rest on Caroline's knee. She was inexplicably thrilled.

It was strange, being alone with Hartmut for so long. Their relationship seemed so exposed, fragile even, like an animal breaking cover from the woods. They were both used to walking away independently from sexual partners, as a rule.

Caroline was an excellent public relations executive, used to carrying off the most far-fetched fairytale story-telling in the name of protecting the brand. Her vision was clear – her ruthlessness and self interest finely tuned. She could be relied on to smooth over the difficulty, find the right angle, tone, and reason. She cajoled and flattered for a living – operating one step away from action, but shadowing every move, every decision. But here she was on a plane like a small square snack in a box, next to a stern looking German. She felt entirely fluttery – a butterfly, hanging onto a twig in a light breeze.

Hartmut was comfortable. This was unusual. There was something... masculine about Caroline. She had a controlled bawdiness about her. Seeing her wandering around the airport, simply but beautifully dressed in clean lines and neutral colours, but in fabrics to die for, calm and confident, he kept experiencing flashbacks to her standing over groaning men in bold leather, whipping with precise method, eyes blazing – before calmly unzipping her crotch piece to lower herself on the nearest pulsating member to take her pleasure. Caroline fascinated Hartmut. It was wonderful to be with her. He did not believe that it had ever crossed his mind that he would meet someone like her.

Berlin was a favourite destination of Hartmut's. It was a strong-willed yet laid-back city, steeped in history, carrying its battle scars with pride, decorating over bullet marked stone with colourful graffiti, the wallpaper of the urban sprawl. It was reserved yet passionate. The grey concrete opened up like a cactus flower into extraordinary clubs and bars. Hartmut was not an artist, but he respected creativity. He also appreciated the relative ease about the city, the sense that people were happy to live and let live unencumbered by moral imperatives handed down through the years, uncomprehendingly, by non-thinkers.

Ursula Himmelfarb greeted her brother with affection and Caroline felt immediately welcome. Ursula let them into her appartement in Mitte. Caroline looked around appreciatively. It was white-walled, wooden-floored and very large, with a wonderful entrance, high ceilings and a terrace on which a party of twenty could happily sit. The sun was setting. Ursula was bustling in the kitchen, checking the supplies. To Caroline's surprise, she was vacating her home for them, staying with her artist friend Gertrude. Caroline murmured to Hartmut in surprise and his eyes flashed. "It is good – we agreed this. I have some things here." He indicated a large wardrobe. His hand pressed into Caroline's crotch. "I think you will enjoy my cupboard."

Caroline could not wait for Ursula to leave.

There hadn't been a cross word all weekend, despite the threat of friction in the Grünewald on Sunday morning when they both wanted to go in front on the antique tandem that Ursula had lent to them. Caroline had graciously ceded the place to Hartmut, as he was local, and she was no longer in her ultra dominatrix outfit from the KitKat Club the night before.

She stole a glance at Hartmut. He was more than she could have hoped for. Her trust in him was one of the strongest feelings she had experienced. Hartmut was extremely distinguished-looking, it had to be said. He drew glances for his impeccably dressed, arrestingly confident manner. Caroline by his side softened the picture. They attracted a great deal of discreet attention.

On Sunday evening, they had dinner with Ursula. She had invited her best friend and hostess for the weekend, Gertrude Plassnik, to join them. Whilst Ursula was essentially Hartmut in a dress, down to her being a lawyer like him, Gertrude was an artist.

Caroline thought that the term was being used rather loosely. That afternoon, they had all been to see Gertrude's latest exhibition, featuring a collection of messy bathrooms.

Gertrude was keen to elaborate.

"You see, I believe that we have lost a lot of what makes us human by simply flushing it down the drain, or cleaning it up with the latest wonder product from soulless global corporations. A person can put on a face to show you when she sees you in the street, but the real person can be truly seen by what she leaves in her bathroom."

Caroline thought she should merely nod politely. So much of it seemed to be literally a pile of poo. Ursula and Hartmut, who even amongst Germans were renowned for being straight-talking, had no such qualms.

Ursula was frowning:

"But my dear Gertrude, I do not know bathrooms like that. I could not imagine having anything out of place. It is not logical, it is not hygienic, I simply do not see how this can be a real situation."

"Ursula, of course *your* bathroom could never look like that. I did have half a mind to have a showroom at the end and call it Badzimmer Himmelfarb, in fact."

After directing a look of utter incomprehension at Gertrude, Hartmut gently attacked.

"I have to agree with my sister, and really Gertrude, I do not see anyway that this is art. To me, it is laziness and sloth. And rather worrying, as physical sloth can often imply moral turpitude."

Ursula snorted in agreement:

"Gertrude, I understand your realism, but unflushed toilets, even with cellophane to seal in the smell, is really not something I can consider anything more than contrived scheiße."

Poor Gertrude was starting to look upset under the combined onslaught of Hartmut and his sister. Desperately trying not to laugh, Caroline thought she would play devil's advocate and ride to Frau Plassnik's rescue.

"Actually, Gertrude, I thought it was very imaginative. I liked the way you used different products to tell us about the people who owned the bathrooms. Some were quite minimalist. I also liked the green one, the one containing what looks like every product that Clinique has ever made. That was a well thought out monument to narcissism. I think you *should* have finished the show with a Badzimmer Glick. You would only need to prepare for a vase of flowers appearing in there, as I am going to make it my mission to break up the perfection when we get home to London. That is, of course, if I ever penetrate the outer defences of Herr Glick's castle in London. I should not be surprised if he has a moat, for extra protection."

"You did not tell me that you had moved from your penthouse, Hartmut."

Caroline couldn't tell if Ursula was being ironic or not. Then she remembered that she was dealing with Ursula.

"Of course, I am joking about the castle," clarified Caroline, "but, Gertrude, I promise you that I will mess up Hartmut's bathroom and send you a photo."

"Although there is no logic to this feeling, as an untidy bathroom would actually be extremely displeasing, I cannot say that I do not anticipate your influence during my morning ablutions." said Hartmut genially.

"Hartmut!" exclaimed Ursula, "Was passiert? I cannot believe that you are finally planning to invite a lady back to your home. However, now I have met you, Caroline liebchen, I can see why my brother is finally melting. He and I are two sides of the same coin. I find you utterly intoxicating, my dear."

Things were going better than Caroline could possibly have hoped for. Caroline clasped Hartmut's hand under the table. He held her hand tight for a moment. Caroline flushed with a sudden rush of happiness. She looked round at the friendly faces. Gertrude looked happier now the onslaught had stopped. Hartmut looked serene, solid, but as warm as a plate of Weißwurst with lashings of mustard, and Ursula seemed content; dear Ursula, who by her own confession was basically a second Hartmut. Caroline couldn't help wondering if she too was proficient in penetrating slaves with dildos. Life was looking up.

14

Intoxication: the comedown

"Tell me about Brazil. Which part of it makes people like you?"

Harry winced as he remembered his opening gambit with Gabriela a couple of nights earlier. Unfortunately for him, Gabriela didn't really have a thing for the powerful, older man. Truth be told, Gabriela would have liked to meet another Rubens Ribeiro, just one that didn't happen to be gay.

In the fashion industry this was something of a tall order. The problem was that it was difficult to find a beautiful man who she actually liked. When she did chance upon an attractive, young, straight male model, the bed filled up pretty quickly once his ego had climbed in. But Gabriela knew what she wanted, and it was not, and could never have been, a smug middle-aged lawyer.

As for Harry's compliments, Gabriela had heard most lines many times. She was by now pretty resistant to all but the most original and genuine of remarks. She hadn't wanted to be rude to the boss's brother, but she had had to put this man in his place. Quickly. Before escaping.

She had looked at Harry with steel in her eyes.

"Rio made me. I love that city. It's a *young* city. The beaches there are fabulous. I guess I have a thing for *young* men in speedos."

"We get better as we mature, you know. Like a fine wine."

"Funny how all older men say that to me. For a few it might be true, but the majority remind me rather more of the fruit that makes the wine. I prefer the grape when it is ripe and bursting with life, rather than wrinkled, with a future involving imminent decay. Anyway – nice meeting you, Mr Gumpert. Enjoy the party."

Gabriela had left Harry a bit too quickly, and her smile had faded so fast that it was clear she didn't care in the slightest if Harry noticed or not. In fact *"didn't care in the slightest"* was exactly how Harry interpreted her reaction to him. Correctly, as it happened. It had been a while since a woman had not pretended to be interested, not even giving him half a chance.

What sort of female confidence was this? Weren't women supposed to be faintly desperate? She had just called him old and run away. *Is this what things would come to?* Harry had looked round the room and realised just how much younger all the models were.

Harry had fallen back to earth with a thud. Perish non-needy women and all who sail in them. He had felt momentarily alarmed at what this implied for him. *What was wrong with him?* He gathered himself up. *I should be happy with what I have – a wonderful wife, two beautiful children, and a gorgeous lover. Not many have that much.* But was that all for Harry Gumpert? *Was nothing else left out there?*

He had decided, in any case, that the wrinkled grape needed another drink. Immediately.

After his beatification at the hands of all those wonderful new-found friends, Ben floated out of the club in a state of rapture. Mind, he wasn't expecting real sunshine in the sunny uplands his altered state of mind was joyously skipping through. The daylight felt blinding.

Ben was the only ill-prepared member of the party. With a sigh that seemed to say "here we go again," Alex and Jamal extracted identical RayBans from their carefully prepared cases and blocked out the offending glare from their tender eyes. Rubens also swiftly donned a pair of Diesel glasses, with a broad grin rather than a sigh. Ben wondered whether nights out with the boys usually outlasted the night itself. It could be quite a commitment.

"Minicab, mate?"

Jamal haggled the driver's fee down and they all clambered into a battered old Nissan. Ben was crammed in between Rubens and Jamal; the city passed by in a blur of bright light and shot suspension. It seemed but moments later that they were admitted to Spartacus Spa.

Ben had heard about men's bathhouses, but he had never been in one. Few straight men had, although the venues were a source of constant ribbing amongst curious boys. Ben had never had any reason to consider going there. He had been far too straight for that. However, whatever he was now, it was time to visit.

Alex and Jamal, supplying the momentum, had decided against heading over to Afterlife, an after hours club. But they were not ready to go home, either. They were still high from Intoxication and didn't want the night to end. After all the stimuli and playing around, they were feeling horny. Through many trials and much error, this state of mind had been revealed to be a proven side effect of partying. Spartacus was the ideal place to find similarly horny men making themselves available for no-strings sex.

Rubens suggested he and Ben should go too, so they could carry on partying. Whatever that meant.

Not knowing what to expect, Ben was slightly disappointed as he walked into a boxy entrance more akin to a rather nasty takeaway, albeit one with adverts for gay nightclubs and syphilis tests in lieu of the plastic menu. After paying what seemed like a lot of money for a glorified shower, Ben grabbed his towels, a little plastic bag with a condom and another metallic sachet of something called YouLube.

A door opened when the surly Eastern European guy on the till pressed a button. Narnia for nutsacks, thought Ben. He entered a different world. A male world, one where the people wore nothing but a white towel and a libidinous look. Had he been older and British, he might have felt like a semi-clad Mr Benn on one of his lesser known adventures.

Ben undressed next to the other three boys. He realised that there was a not-so-discreet crowd of men around them. These observers were making sure they got a good look at the newcomers' briefly naked bodies before they could get the towels around their modesty. Ben deliberately didn't hurry to cover himself up as he was feeling generous, and happy with the world. Who'd have thought? What a surprising night.

His confidence was sky high and his semi felt ready. After all those years of feeling second best, he knew he had arrived. He wasn't sure where he was, but it was an arrival of sorts. He had the coolest friends, the sexiest boyfriend and was basking in admiring looks from all around.

Like many a pretty foreign boy before him, he was actually enjoying being fresh meat in town. Aided and abetted by illicit substances, to say nothing of the lingering effect of Vodka Red Bull, London's gay scene had cast a spell on Big Ben. It was good to be alive, young and sexually attractive.

With his clothes safely packed into the locker, and the key on a rubber band stuck around his upper right arm, Ben followed the boys out of the changing area, through yet another door. The world changed again. The same men padded around him, but the lighting was softer and moodier. The steam in the air and the sound of showers caused an involuntary stir in his groin. Noticing that some of the guys were coming out of the showers in a full state of arousal, and no one was in the slightest perturbed, save for a lustful look, Ben was finally in a place where he needn't be embarrassed by an erection.

He followed Rubens into an area with four showers side by side. Two muscular tattooed skinheads were getting friendly with each other. People moved around in a constant stream of carnality – it was not long before one of the skins winked at the other, motioned with his head (the one on his neck) and the pair went off together, presumably to find somewhere more private. Or perhaps somewhere more public? Who could tell what proclivities they embraced? Indeed, who cared?

Ben thought how it was so much easier being horny and gay than horny and straight. *This was just wanktastically unreal-ly amazing*.

Rubens laughed softly.

"Hey, gostoso, someone's awake. But then I guess whenever I see you in the shower you always seem to have a hard on. I guarantee you this time, my Big Ben is going to have some real fun."

Before the real fun, however, the steam room called.

Ben had been in many a Turkish Bath. This was, however, his first time in one where the steam seemed utterly incidental to proceedings. He smelt the sex in the air before he saw it. A young Latin-looking man was kneeling on the floor giving head to a tall blond guy, who was leaning back against the wall and manifestly appreciating his work. A third guy sitting beside him was also being rather hands-on, whilst simultaneously being serviced by the industrious Latino. As Ben's eyes grew accustomed to the dim light and swirling clouds of steam, the hazy forms of the trio became more defined. Ben could make out every shape and every movement. Whilst the three men seemed not to even register the presence of Ben and Rubens sitting a respectful distance away, Ben couldn't take his eyes off the frenzied pursuit of climax the three were engaged in.

Ben's senses were totally overloaded. His dick felt as if it was going to explode; he had never even conceived of a place like this. How was this bathhouse even legal? Is this what the ancient Romans got up to? Did Sodom and Gomorrah boast a branch of Spartacus? Why the hell had he never had such an experience before? He never wanted it to end. But he was going to have to move Rubens along. His hand went under Rubens' towel.

"Gostoso, wait a minute. Too tacky to do it here. Besides, not everyone is as polite as us and I do not want audience participation. These men can turn into octopuses with their hands just everywhere. So rude!"

When Ben and Rubens got out of the steam room they found Alex and Jamal.

Alex grinned:

"I think we should take Ben for a tour of the corridors of pulling power."

Ben wasn't quite sure what Alex was talking about. He didn't really care, either. Arousal takes over everything. Everything seemed so exciting that he would have followed his companions anywhere. Still dripping from the steam bath, Ben was led down a dark corridor. Some passers-by seemed to be busily trying to get somewhere, but others made Ben realise that the walls really did have eyes. Lots of them. A few hands as well. A whole new meaning to a passage way. Turning a corner past a jacuzzi and a water fountain, Ben found himself in another corridor with doors on either side like some weird Alice in Wonderland set. The fourth door on the right was open. Ben peered in. The cubicle was about seven feet deep and three feet wide. It offered up a blue vinyl mattress on a raised area. That was basically it, with the frill of a small space at the front, allowing for the door to open. On this particular blue mattress a man lay with his legs open, masturbating. Although Ben had seen a lot of sexy guys in Spartacus, this one didn't really appeal. It wasn't the extremely average nature of the specimen on offer, it was more the fact that his particular ploy struck Ben as being very… well, overly… obvious. For the first time that night, Ben decided that what he was seeing was slightly unpleasant. The drugs were wearing off. He hurried after the others.

"Here's a free one. Come on."

Ben followed the other three into an empty cubicle. He wondered what was going on. He was there with three horny gorgeous guys just wearing towels, in a space three feet by seven. He wasn't sure if he was super excited or slightly uneasy. Before he could work out how he felt, Jamal produced a small bag with some white powder in it – where it came from, Ben had no idea. Jamal unwrapped the bag quickly and deftly snorted some powder from his fingernail. Rubens and Alex eagerly followed.

"Do you want some "K", Ben?"

Ben wasn't sure what "K" was. He was too embarrassed to ask and would not have known what ketamine was even if he had. For the third time in a few moments, Ben felt uneasy. He decided he would pass.

"So, what do you think of this little den of iniquity then, Ben?"

He wasn't quite sure how to answer Jamal's question. A few minutes earlier everything had been so perfect; an intense combination of love for his fantastic friends, confidence at the attention he had been receiving, the exhilaration of what his new home could offer him and of course the sheer high octane sex factor of Spartacus Spa. But now, alongside all that – and it was still there, if only because Ben was clinging to it – he also felt a harder edge creeping in. It felt as if there was a fringe of insecurity around him – as though his edifice of ecstasy was built on a rocky foundation. Sort of akin to California and the San Andreas. It looked fantastic on the outside but the unease seemed to be pointing towards some sort of horrible crash.

Ben leant back against the wall.

"I never knew places like this existed before." he said uncertainly, "I'm glad I'm here with you guys. I feel I'm in a Roman orgy or something."

"Gostoso, we haven't started yet! Boys, maybe that's your cue to leave us alone for a while."

As Jamal and Alex left the cubicle, Ben felt there was a look of complicity between Jamal and Rubens. He remembered Alex telling him about how they were partners in crime. But Rubens then turned to him. Rubens had a smile that lit up the world. It made everything right again. Rubens' touch steadied Ben's foundations, and, as Rubens did what he did best, Ben's high returned. Ben gave himself over to feeling and abandonment. As they got lost in each other's bodies he felt alive. Every pore, every neurone, every cell in his body felt directly connected to electricity. Twenty minutes later the climax came, both furious and yet sweet. There is a reason why Governors bugger off to Argentina. There is a reason why people risk it all for a lay. This is why the world fights off its sensuality and yet embraces it at every turn. It just feels really, really good.

Ben and Rubens lay side by side dripping with sweat. Rubens sat up, smiled, and expertly peeled off Ben's condom, disposing of it in the wastebin thoughtfully provided.

"Gostoso, time for a shower."

Normally after he came, Ben would enjoy the feeling of wellbeing that he was left with, for some precious minutes. But when Rubens suggested going outside the safety of the cubicle, he was disconcerted at the return of his fringe of insecurity. After probably the best sex of his life how could he not feel as if he was floating on air?

As they walked back to the showers, Ben stuck close to Rubens. He wasn't sure but it seemed as if the sexy hunks he had seen walking round earlier now looked a bit more ordinary, and that much more hungry than before. Some were definitely creepy, he thought. Even sad.

When they got back to the shower area, all four showers were occupied. Ben was slightly put off by the first man he saw. He was clearly in his fifties, or maybe older and he was certainly looking his age. After the mild disgust at the sagging skin and over-generous stomach, Ben immediately felt slightly guilty at judging someone for – effectively – just being normal. The second man was really skinny and seemed to be looking at the unattractive older man. The third guy was possibly the hairiest man Ben had ever seen. It was too much. A wave of revulsion came over Ben. He wondered how the creature had the guts to get all that fur out in public. Surely he would be more at home in a zoo. Had he never heard of shaving, waxing, electrolysis, a paper bag? Of course, Ben then felt guilty again. Where was his tolerance? Buying shares in Gillette? The fourth person seemed to fit in better with Ben's expectation of a gay Londoner. The man obviously knew what the inside of a gym looked like, was quite good-looking, tanned and with one of those short trendy haircuts that still looked cool when it was wet from the shower. Thank God at least one of them was attractive, thought Ben.

The last person evidently knew Rubens. When he turned round and looked at them, after being distracted for a good few moments by the rather sizeable bulge in Ben's towel, he suddenly let loose with what could only be described as an inappropriate shriek.

"Ciao bella! I should have known you'd be here. I tried to get into Afterlife and the fucking doorman turned me away. He said I was too high. I mean, can you fucking believe it? I was so angry! Do I look that high to you?"

Ben was struck by how camp and whiny the guy's voice was. He noted that the shrieker had been alternately looking at Rubens and staring at Ben's bulge whilst speaking. His accent reminded Ben faintly of his mother's family in Milan. As to the question about being high, Ben couldn't see the man's eyes clearly but the jerky movements did seem a bit strange.

"Ciao, Carlo. They can be bastards at times. I don't know – I'm not the judge – but, hey. You look OK to me."

Ben wondered if Rubens was looking at the same man that he was. At that moment the bear lumbered off to find some honey. Rubens hung up his towel and motioned to Ben to join him under the shower next to Carlo. Slightly uncomfortable, Ben removed his towel and hung it up next to Rubens. As he turned round there was another unpleasant shriek.

"Puttana Eva! What is that thing, big boy? Can I help you wash it? Rubens, you don't mind sharing with me, do you, darling?"

Before Ben was even properly under the shower, Carlo's hand was already firmly grasping his dick. He was giving Ben what he evidently thought was a come-to-bed look, but from that awful boy it felt more like a go-to-the-toilet-to-be-sick look. Ben felt like punching Carlo in the face and telling him to keep his damned distance. The thought of being physically close to him was revolting, but, with a huge effort, Ben controlled his disgust, smiled at Carlo and simply removed the offending hand, gently but firmly.

"Thanks, but I'm fine."

"Oh I see. I see. Too good, are you, bella? You found yourself a stuck-up queen here, Rubens. I'm off to find a real man. Huh. You look like one of those plastic guys who has no idea how to use a thing like that."

Managing to simultaneously scowl and pout at a startled Ben, Carlo grabbed his towel and stalked off. Ben couldn't believe how quickly Carlo had turned the venom on him, just because he had politely refused sex. He certainly had never been called a stuck-up queen before. It would be pretty funny if Ben didn't have a rising sense of unpleasantness at the whole scene. God help the next poor man Carlo's eye fell on.

Rubens hadn't really paid much attention to the messed-up Italian. Carlo was always a nightmare on drugs. He had enjoyed the shag with Ben, but he was already starting to feel like another bump of "K" and a talk with Jamal. He wondered if the other boys had got lucky. Rubens had noticed a couple of guys walking round that he wouldn't have minded getting closer to.

"Gostoso, let's go find Alex and Jamal, if they're not locked in a cubicle somewhere."

Ben hoped that that was the signal that they would be leaving Spartacus. Everyone seemed to be staring at him with those awful unattractive hungry eyes, and he had no idea where all the gorgeous guys he had seen earlier had gone. Then he noticed a slightly overweight guy with a devil tattoo on his shoulder. He had seen it when he walked in – but on a much sexier guy. Surely it wasn't the same guy? Ben shuddered as he realised that the guys in the sauna had probably not changed. It was Ben who was coming round.

Rubens spotted Jamal:

"Hey, Jamal. Where's Alex?"

"In the lounge, talking to this guy he knows. Do you fancy another bump, habibie?"

"Absolutely! Gostoso, you coming?"

Ben declined. He did not want to go into another cubicle and watch his two friends stuff white powder up their noses, especially as he was starting to feel that he was on a different level to Rubens altogether. The "K" would only make it more pronounced. He resolved to ask Rubens if they could leave when he came out.

Walking back to the lounge area, Ben passed by a cubicle with a door open. Even though he was getting more and more uncomfortable in there, his curiosity wouldn't let him pass by without having a look in. He wished he hadn't. Carlo was in there shaking uncontrollably, being held by another guy who was trying to keep him awake. Carlo was chattering unintelligibly and looked as if he was going to pass out.

"I told you not to have so much "G", you dickhead!"

The guy turned and saw Ben looking at them.

"Stupid little sod. It's always the same story. First, he's quiet, then he gets friendly, then flirty, then a bit too flirty, then a mess, and then this. Oh no, Carlo – fuck!"

The moment that Carlo lost control of his bowels was the moment that Ben decided he had to leave. Immediately. As he got to the lounge, Alex looked up and saw things were not right.

"Hey, Ben, are you OK?"

"Not really. I want to go home."

"OK. Where's Rubens?"

"Back there with Jamal. Talking. In a cubicle."

"Got it. Listen, babe, you sit here. I'll go get them."

Before he walked off Alex gave Ben's hand a firm squeeze and smiled at him. It was the first thing that had made Ben feel slightly better since leaving the cubicle with Rubens. Ben watched as some of the miserable-looking staff went back and forth. When one of them walked past with a mop he started to realise why they didn't look so overjoyed to be working at Spartacus Spa. A few minutes later, Alex walked back with Jamal and Rubens in tow.

"Gostoso, did you see the state of Carlo? Those amateurs that can't handle what they take, they spoil it for the rest of us."

Alex raised his eyebrows imperceptibly and gave Ben a look of tacit understanding.

"Rubens, I think Ben probably saw a bit too much of Carlo's inability to handle himself. That might be part of the reason he is ready to leave."

For the first time since he had met Ben, Rubens had to choose between what the American wanted and what Rubens Ribeiro felt like doing. There was never really going to be any contest. But at least he could present the result with a killer smile and an implicit compliment.

"Oh, gostoso. We've just had another bump. I want to stay a bit longer. In a couple of hours the guys will start coming in from Afterlife. I said I'd see them here. I wanted you to meet them."

There was no way Ben was going to stay any longer in what was rapidly becoming a hellhole for him, even if his ego had been massaged by the fact that Rubens wanted to introduce him to all his friends from Afterlife. He made up his mind. Rubens' smile had its limits.

"Listen, Rubens, I don't want to cramp your style but I am ready to go. You stay, and I'll see you later."

"Oh, gostoso, you're too good to me. I'm just a bad Brazilian boy. So. We'll see each other later, anyhow?"

"Sure."

Alex looked at Ben, reflectively.

"Actually, I'm done here as well. Jamal, you stay with Rubens – have a little *Arabrazilian* time together. OK if I leave with you, Ben?"

"Sure."

Ben wasn't really feeling like talking much, but he

appreciated Alex's gesture. Although he was desperate to leave, he didn't fancy making his way home alone. And of the three men, Alex was the one whom he was getting to trust.

"Come on, Ben. Let's go and get changed then."

On the way out, Ben noticed plenty of eyes eating him up, desperate to get a good visual imprint of him naked, just in case they had no success in the sauna and needed some new material for a little solo sexual gratification later. This time, Ben displayed none of the generosity he had showed earlier when he had got out of his clothes. He made sure that those sneaky eyes were frustrated in their quest for the money shot. He modestly pulled up his Calvins beneath the cover of his towel, as if he were at the beach with his grandmother, in Santa Margherita.

"Got everything? Let's go find us a minicab."

Standing outside the doors of Spartacus in the warm sunshine on the Albert Embankment in front of Vauxhall Cross were half a dozen men waiting for potential clients to stumble out. Ben was glad to be back in reality where strangers were more interested in the wallet in the back pocket of his trousers than the package in the front.

In the cab on the way back to the Lofts, Alex could see that Ben's ectasy high was well and truly over. He had looked really rather lost just before they had left Spartacus. Alex also realised that Rubens had taken the sauna shag with Ben as more of a particularly tasty appetiser, rather than the main event. That Brazilian had his eyes on a session today, as he suspected did Jamal. After all the years they had spent together, the things they had been through together, Alex and Jamal had a strong relationship which permitted the very useful arrangement which allowed either one of them to go home alone without a drama.

They had an understanding. They knew the scene and its significance intimately. They knew each other and accepted each other. It made everything simple. Alex had a book on microlending in Bangladesh that he wanted to finish and he was perfectly at ease with the thought of Jamal staying with Rubens, taking more "K" and probably shagging at least one guy during the morning.

But this would not be the case with Ben. That much was obvious. *Ben was way out of his depth*. Alex felt a twinge of compassion. Ben had only just met the Brazilian. He did not have seven years of love, nor even fifteen years' experience of the gay scene to help his feelings through such a minefield.

"How are you doing, Ben?"

"I'm cool, Alex. Sorry. I'm a bit quiet. Thanks for coming home with me, though. I didn't want to leave alone. Now I just want to go to bed though. See if I can sleep."

The cab drew up and disgorged them at Elephant & Castle. Alex guided Ben in and told him they would speak soon. His strong arm reached around Ben's shoulders and gave him a reassuring hug. It felt like a siren call back to reality. Ben was entirely at odds and ends as to what to feel, and why.

Moments later, Ben was lying alone on his bed in his sweat pants and a T-shirt. He would normally have been naked, but he needed the comforting feel of towelling on his skin.

He felt rudderless. He manifestly had a foot in each of two worlds. He'd had a similar sensation once, in quite different circumstances, after riding the Coney Island rollercoaster. After a couple of amazing highs, his imagination had got the better of him. It had suddenly and weirdly felt as if he had come off the rails. Somehow, in his mind, he had left the ride – perhaps even been thrown off – and had landed in the cold Atlantic ocean, disorientated, sick and wondering what the hell had just happened.

Ben had felt on top of the world, in love with his life and everything and everyone around him. That was gone. Now he felt empty and doubting of everything he had felt and experienced earlier. Did any of those people really give a damn about him? How had he gone from being popular and surrounded by people, to lying alone on his bed feeling like nobody cared at all? Worst of all, the guy he thought he had fallen in love with was still in a gay sauna doing drugs, and probably having sex with other men. Ben felt deeply depressed. All the highs he had dreamt of really seemed to mean nothing. He was left without anything to hang on to. Was this really the kind of relationship he wanted?

There was a knock on his door. It was good timing. Ben did not want to face anyone – but he also felt desperate to see someone. He got up and went to open the door.

It was Kelly. She looked lovely. She was calm and strong and real. He drank in her strength and her presence. He had rarely been so glad to see someone.

"Hello, Ben. I heard some news and I wanted to tell you about it. Geez, you look tired. Are you OK? You look a bit strange."

Ben felt a rush of warmth. He gave Kelly the biggest smile and hugged her before he could stop himself. Then he pulled her by the hand into the flat.

"Yes, I'm fine. I just had a long night out with the boys and haven't been to sleep yet."

Kelly held him with affection. It still felt very natural to be close to him. She felt dangerously at ease with Ben.

"Oh my God, they're already leading you astray. I'm not interrupting anything, am I? Should I stay out of the bedroom? I'm not going to walk into Rubens waving an erection at me, am I?"

"Don't worry. I'm not as much of a party boy as the others. I came home but Rubens stayed out with Jamal."

Something in Ben's voice gave away the fact he was not as OK as he was pretending to be. Kelly had heard lots of stories from Rubens and knew what he and his flings were like. She hoped that Ben hadn't already been burnt by him. Or maybe… just maybe, she wished he had.

"Don't tell me. You went out, had a fantastic time, did things you shouldn't and then when you were ready to leave, he wanted to stay out."

"You got it, Kelly. Obviously I'm not the superstud I briefly thought I was last night."

Ben's wry smile was confirmation that, although he wouldn't admit it, something was not quite right with him and the Brazilian. He passed a hand through his hair, and looked down.

"By the way, Kelly, I have decided to help Rubens out, with you know what. I said I would in the club last night and I can't go back on my word."

"Oh, Ben are you sure? Many a word said under the influence... well, you know what I mean. Don't feel you have to do it if you are having second thoughts. No one would judge you. You need to do what's right for you."

Kelly was making Ben feel a lot better, but he did not want to go back on his word. He wasn't sure it was the right thing to do. In fact, it almost definitely wasn't. However, he had given his word and he would not let Rubens down. It may be either the end or the beginning of the end – but it would finish things off with a bang rather than a whimper. In for a penny, in for a pound. After all, even though he had been feeling a bit lonely until Kelly had arrived, Rubens had shown him the most amazing night. And after what he had been through, it no longer registered as quite so unusual or extreme.

"I'm sure, Kelly. It's very little, in reality, from where I stand. Anyway, I'm fine. Now, what news?"

"I bumped into Amber in the health café and she apologised to me! Not very warmly, but it's still a shock. She admitted that we didn't exactly get on, but she said she wanted to treat it as water under the bridge."

Kelly sat down and looked at Ben:

"Ben, do you think she means it? I mean, how can anyone go from so angry to resigned, like that?"

Ben reflected a moment. He didn't trust Amber, but then what sort of a character judge was he? He considered the question:

"My first thought is: don't trust the woman. But, given my track record, that probably means she has become a saint and you'll be best friends with her by Christmas."

"Ben, what an awful thought. Monique would disown me! And she would clash with all my outfits."

Kelly stayed for another half an hour. Ben would have liked her to stay longer, but he was falling asleep on her – so she guided him gently to bed before taking her leave. His hold on her tingled. She wondered if she was imagining it. How was it possible that she was still getting those signals from Ben even after he had fallen for Rubens? Kelly felt as if she was wired wrong. How was it possible that she still felt something for that New Yorker? Was he really sending her messages?

Ben lay in his darkened bedroom wondering about the situation. Kelly couldn't have done anything more to show that she was different to the Brazilian. Rubens had swept Ben off his feet and left him lying down alone on a Sunday morning. Kelly was there for him, concerned for him, and, frankly, attractive. He had so nearly attempted to drag her down onto the bed, softly, insistently. He had been too tired to muster the energy. He didn't want to risk any more debacles with the girl.

Ben was, to put it mildly, a tad confused. He could only follow his natural tendency not to budge from a chosen path until kicked off of it by a horde of stampeding buffaloes. It was his own fault if he had let his dick push him down a path that maybe wasn't the right one after all for him. What seemed clear is that he couldn't play around with a girl like Kelly. She was rather too special to be treated as anything other than, well, a princess, or something akin to that.

Kelly certainly could not be the other lover, decided

Ben. No, Ben would have to suffer in silence and think of what might have been if he hadn't decided to try to make the relationship work with Rubens.

Hartmut and Caroline took the Heathrow Express together following the flight back from their most memorable weekend chez Ursula Himmelfarb. Paddington Station felt cold and grey and a little sad. Parting was as poignant as it should be; the sweet sorrow that promised more pleasure down the way. Caroline stole looks at Hartmut and resisted the urge to wrap herself around him like an expensive and well-loved jumper. Hartmut was just about in control of his feelings. They felt as if they could deliver the kick of a powerful horse. Feelings, thought Hartmut grimly, could run amok like manic ponies at the first glint of glass on the ground.

He put Caroline in a cab and bade her farewell, a little stiffly, but with a genuine regret that she could read. Warmth flowed between them. She recognised – or at least hoped she did – a lover's look in his eyes.

Although Caroline would be receiving an invitation to the Glick residence in due course, Hartmut considered that all things should happen when they should happen, and not a moment sooner. He felt that there were a couple of hurdles still to get over.

In fact, Hartmut was thinking. He needed to work out how he would deal with the feelings of present happiness, yet simultaneous sadness that he was experiencing at the thought of another week at work, without seeing Caroline Napier Jones. Hartmut was concerned to find his equilibrium disturbed. It wasn't, however, a big enough problem to think about terminating the relationship before any further damage could be done. He would live with the sense of unease at being less able to control his formerly subservient emotions.

A rather tinny rendition of Beethoven's Fifth alerted him to the fact that someone was trying to contact him on his mobile telephone. He answered crisply:

"Glick!"

"Mr Glick, it's Cornisha Burrows. I am terribly sorry to disturb you on a Sunday evening. Do you have a few minutes for me?"

"Certainly, Cornisha. I do hope nothing is wrong. How may I be of assistance?"

Hartmut could sense that Cornisha was struggling for words. This was highly irregular for Cornisha Burrows, and betrayed an acute sense of embarrassment. Hartmut's already disobedient emotions were now on full alert.

Cornisha was indeed most upset. Arthur Bilks had overheard Harry Gumpert on the telephone and, as there was mention of SBK, Arthur had immediately called Cornisha.

"Mr Glick. I don't even know if I should be making this call. I have been struggling with this all day. You must be aware that I have always had the highest regard for you, as a true gentleman. Well, it has come to my attention, that... there are voices in SBK that may be conspiring against you."

Hartmut couldn't believe his ears. This was a pre-posterous thing to hear from anyone, but from such a stable lady as Cornisha Burrows? And on a Sunday evening to boot. This was indeed most unusual.

"Mr Glick, I know I must sound like a mad woman, but I have heard that other partners have been discussing aspects of your private life and how they may damage the firm. A friend of mine overheard a conversation quite by chance, and heard your name being mentioned in the context of a scandal that could not be allowed to hit SBK. I'm terribly sorry to be the harbinger of such news but I wanted you to know."

Hartmut Glick was utterly flabbergasted. Who had found out about his personal life? Surely Caroline had not talked? What had Cornisha heard? And did they know anything meaningful anyway?

He breathed deep:

"Cornisha, I appreciate your concern, but I have nothing to hide in my personal life and in any case I have no enemies at SBK. Please put your mind at rest and do not worry about me."

"Oh, Mr Glick, I do apologise. I feel rather stupid, but you are such an honourable man, and my conscience wouldn't allow me not to warn you, even at the risk of making myself appear foolish. I promise you that I know no details, but I just felt it was my duty to be honest with a man to whom I owe a great deal. I so hope that I am wrong, but I could not risk doing nothing."

After further reassuring Cornisha, Hartmut put the phone down, feeling most disquieted. He had been living a double life for many years and there had never been even a whiff of anyone suspecting. Although he had assured

Cornisha there was nothing to worry about, Hartmut felt that something had indeed changed. After the most wonderful weekend, Ben Barlettano wasn't the only one experiencing an unwelcome Sunday comedown.

15

Liars, sluts and obsessive gardeners

Harry Gumpert stared into the bathroom mirror. Despite soft lighting that he had had fitted especially, it was a disappointing sight.

When exactly had he started to look like this? What did others see, these days? The lighting was subdued and slightly rose-coloured – but he could still make out his "distinguished" laughter lines a little too clearly.

Would it be too much for him to consider Botox? If so, he would have to be careful. He would not want anyone to realise what passed between the needle and him. But something had to be done. He couldn't possibly risk any more Gabriela de Souza situations.

Harry winced again. The recollection of her treating him like an irrelevant annoyance and leaving him standing there had seared into his mind. It burned. It hurt. She had emphasised all too well her preference for younger men who looked good in speedos. Really good in speedos. People who would actually look good with only a sock on their penis. That would not be Harry Gumpert, these days.

Harry groaned as he recalled his body of yesteryear. *Why, oh why, have you forsaken me? I do not want to grow old.* He ran a hand through his hair. He was still in reasonable shape for his age. *For his age.* What a terrible expression. Were the glory days over? *Was he in fact no longer attractive?* Maybe he should get a little work done. Or he could hire a personal trainer. Or both.

Nonsense! He straightened up. Harry Gumpert was not going to go through a mid life crisis just because some dumb model hadn't fallen swooning at his feet. Monique had plenty of class. She was able to realise that there was more to a man than toned muscles and looking great in tiny items of clothing. Harry looked distinguished. And sexy. He didn't need to pose in order to attract the women. But just in case…

"Do you think I've aged since we first met, Sarah?"

Sarah looked up from her quickly grabbed bowl of cereal.

"Darling, we have all changed with the passing of years. But you have nothing to worry about. Some might say that you are more handsome than the day we first met."

He looked at her eagerly. This was exactly right. It had to be. At very least the clothes were better now.

Sarah sighed, as she contemplated her own sneaked appraisals of her body.

"I'll tell you what, though. It's not fair. Men are perceived to grow more attractive, whereas we women are constantly struggling to keep up with younger models."

Younger models. That was an unfortunate choice of words. But Sarah was good for Harry's ego. She could no longer excite him but it was a respectable match, and he had to admit they had had some good times together. And of course she had given him his daughters. He couldn't imagine leaving Sarah, but then neither could he imagine being without a Monique, nor giving up flirting with other women. And why should he? When a man was as attractive as Harry Gumpert, surely there was enough to go round. Gabriela had made Harry more determined than ever to show that he could still reel them in. He wondered when the next opportunity would be.

The only party he had coming up where he would hopefully be alone with the other sex was the SBK cocktail party. That brought Hartmut to mind. The impending return of Nicholas Casterway was already causing ructions and he hadn't even arrived in the UK yet.

Harry had never had any problem with Hartmut, even though they were not what could be described as friends. It clearly made sense, however, to take Nicholas' side on this matter. Ally oneself with the stronger party. But could he actually trust Nicholas Casterway? Maybe Nicholas was going to gang up on individual partners, before then turning on his erstwhile allies, after he had manoeuvred himself into an unassailable position. Like a latter-day Stalin. Was poor Hartmut supposed to play Trotsky? Would Harry end up as Zinoviev or Kamenev, forced to recant and then falling on his own sword? It needed careful consideration. *Bloody partnership! Bloody lawyers!*

Harry wondered exactly what kind of dirt Nicholas had picked up on Hartmut Glick. From the phone call, it had certainly sounded juicy. Harry would have to be even more discreet than usual himself. He didn't want to give that wolf Nicholas any bones.

It was the first time in ages that Ben had woken up and not thought straight away of dealing with his morning wood. As soon as he opened his eyes and realised that not only was he alone, but it was also Monday morning, that empty feeling returned.

As he was showering, still feeling miserable, he wondered if it would be too needy to text Kelly and ask if they could travel into work together. He really was in a bad state. Thinking about Kelly in the shower and still not the slightest sign from him down below, the bishop that would not be beaten, the monkey that would not be spanked, the suspect that would not be roughed up. He decided something had to be done.

"Tube 2 work 2gether 2day? Ben x"

There. It was sent. A few anxious moments later his iPhone barked at him. Even on a day like today the barking noise for a text message made him smile.

"Sure. C U in lobby 8.15. Kelly x"

Although he felt desperately in need of a big hug, Ben contented himself with just giving Kelly a quick kiss on the cheek and a smile. She looked amazing.

"Is that a new dress, Kelly? You look beautiful. I actually feel like it was worth getting out of bed now."

Being gay did have the advantage that he could say the things he had always been too fearful of saying to girls because he was worried they might think he was coming on to them. Anyway, she did look properly beautiful. The dress covered just enough of her voluptuous breasts for her to appear appropriately dressed – but no one could fail to notice that there was a lot going on under there, a lot for another occasion, when she wasn't a serious woman going to work. Did he feel the clergyman call out to him? *Yes. He did*.

Kelly registered the compliment. Was she just imagining something in Ben's eyes indicating that this was more than just one of those typical comments from gay men, overly sensitive to glamour and prone to exaggeration as they were? She decided to play it cool. But not too cool.

"So, how are you this morning, Ben? Did Rubens call last night?"

Kelly knew that her question would probably meet with a negative answer and that it might not be what Ben wanted to hear, but she couldn't help herself. She cared for Ben. She didn't want to see him hurt by the Brazilian flibbertigibbet – however fabulous a friend he was. She told herself defensively that her question was *only* to protect Ben. Who was she kidding? Ben was tall, handsome and sexy. She knew in her heart that she hadn't completely given up on him. Hope really could spring eternal. Lust springs inconveniently too – always catching you by urgent surprise. On a Monday morning, hope was really quite important. Lust was unexpected, but it was a very welcome feeling.

"No, he didn't call, but I'm fine. It's nice to see you."

Ben really was happy to see Kelly. She radiated warmth and it reassured him. The fact that she looked so hot didn't hurt either. He never thought that he would feel guilty about liking a beautiful, respectable American girl because he was supposed to be faithful to a Brazilian male prostitute.

"Anyway, when are you going to tell me about what goes on in Spartacus Spa?"

"Dear me, Kelly, I'm not sure I can face that on a Monday morning. It was a parallel universe. Don't remind me in fact. I'm actually much happier just being here with you."

They looked at each other, both rather surprised at what Ben had said. Kelly rarely felt awkward with men. She was normally in control. But with Ben Barlettano she felt at a disadvantage. She felt vulnerable. She knew this was a game that she had lost so far and yet she was becoming increasingly keen to win *something*. At the same time she couldn't bring herself to risk getting another slap in the face.

She would resolutely refuse to make any move. It would all have to come from Ben, if it came at all. Kelly hated not being able to take the initiative, but her fear of that second rejection, that second humiliation ensured that she did nothing that could be construed as wanting him. She also needed to change the subject before she started to blush.

"So you are going to do the Rubens thing, then?"

"I gave my word. The last thing I want to become is one of those superficial people who say one thing on a night out when everything is fine and then go back on it in the cold light of day. I'll do it. It's only sex, and it finishes the Rubens cash crisis once and for all. I'll get through it. Call it my lightning porn-star phase. It'll be a one-off."

Ben dropped his head. Kelly was stuck for words. The

boy wasn't at all sure about doing this. Although she wanted to make him feel better, Kelly couldn't. She wanted to ask him if he was *really* sure about any of this; if he really thought Rubens was right for him; if he shouldn't just reassess what he was doing. But she didn't want to seem as if she cared one way or the other. She forced out a smile.

"You're right, Ben. *"In for a penny, in for a pound"* as they say round here. As long as you don't decide to bring Rubens to SBK so he can experience what our working life is like. Mind you, I for one would like to see how some of our starchier colleagues would react if he came in wearing his disco kit. Anyhow. We can deal with it all. Give me a call if you want to grab a sandwich at lunch."

Ben's day passed off fairly uneventfully. He noticed that Cornisha Burrows didn't quite seem herself. Ben saw her having a meeting with Hartmut. Hartmut was speaking seriously to her. It looked as if he were giving her advice. It was all most out of character.

After another sweetly enjoyable but slightly awkward journey with Kelly, Ben found himself back home, wondering whether he should call Rubens or not. Rather than feeling sorry for himself, he decided that what he needed after work was to work out. His body felt delicate after the excesses of the weekend. But a gentle gym session would put things back on track – and Rubens was likely to be there.

As soon as he walked into the health café he bumped into the Brazilian.

"Gostoso, it's so good to see you. I was just going to call you!"

So men lied to men just like they lied to women. Ben couldn't help but feel a bit cynical. He hadn't heard from Rubens for a day and a half, and the last time he had seen him was in the sauna. But then Rubens flashed him that smile and looked at Ben with those deep brown eyes of his, as if he wanted Ben to fall into his soul and stay with him forever.

"I'm so sorry about not calling you last night, Ben. I just got so wasted and then I remembered I had to dance again on Sunday night. So I had to keep taking more coke to keep going. I was a bit of a mess and I didn't want to put you through that. I guess I'm not ready for you to see the worst part of bad boy Rubens yet. After that," he waved his arms "I have been asleep all day. Just got here twenty minutes, or three espressos ago."

Damn, he was good! Ben had to admit that it almost passed muster, as pathetic excuses went. He felt it would seem insecure to ask where Rubens had been working. Yes, that would seem really tacky. And he wanted to believe him.

"You could have texted me, Rubens." said Ben, as casually as he could. "I don't want to cramp your style. I certainly don't want to change you. I would just have appreciated a sign."

"Oh gostoso, you're right. I promise I will not do that again. Can I make it up to you tonight? I've only got one client here tonight. I can leave in an hour. I'll cook you dinner. Bring your things for tomorrow so you can stay the night."

It was effortless. Rubens managed to say exactly what Ben wanted to hear. But then Rubens was a master at charming the birds down from the trees. It helped that this was exactly what Rubens wanted too. At that moment. Such a shame it was impossible to predict how he would feel the next day, never mind the next week or year. Ben was only just beginning to realise that, although Rubens did indeed like him now, like most of the others, Ben would probably end up as background twittering. And Rubens would drift away. Smiling.

It was a shame Rubens usually got bored of men so quickly.

"OK, Rubens it's a date. Er – thanks. I guess I had better go and use the equipment rather than stare at it. See you in a bit."

"I'll be staring at your equipment, gostoso. Mine, all mine!" said Rubens cheerfully.

Halfway through the workout, Ben saw Alex O'Connell come into the gym. They waved at each other and Alex came straight over. Ben reflected on how he had misjudged the Englishman at first.

"Hey, Alex. No Jamal today?"

"No Jamal. I think he deserves a medal just for getting through work today after the antics of the weekend. I've left him upstairs collapsed on the sofa watching Grand Designs Revisited."

Ben looked at Alex. What made Alex tick? Emotionally, he seemed on another planet. Alex was very strong.

"Tell me Alex – how long have you two been together?"

"Seven years."

"You're so lucky."

"It's a lucky number. We are. He is my life. I wouldn't know what to do without him."

As soon as he said it, Alex realised that he might have been a touch insensitive. Ben was trying to give Alex a happy smile, saying how fantastic Alex and Jamal's relationship was, but Alex could see disquiet in the American's eyes.

After a moment Ben sighed:

"Can I ask you something, Alex?"

"Sure." Alex leaned on the treadmill bars, feeling strangely paternal. At least he didn't feel avuncular. That would have been deeply depressing.

"As you can guess, this whole gay thing is pretty new to me. Yesterday, I wasn't exactly happy to be leaving Rubens alone in the sauna. I wanted him to come home with me. I think you knew how I felt. After such a wonderful night out, I ended up hugging my pillow in bed yesterday. It felt pretty awful. I wondered what the point of it all was."

Ben stopped, and looked straight at Alex:

"Are gay relationships *like* this? No offence, and forgive the indiscretion, but is this what it is *like* with you and Jamal?"

Alex looked at Ben.

"Every relationship is different, Ben. You don't need me to tell you that everyone is an individual. Rubens is a party boy and that's part of his charm. You'll never get bored with him, and he is sincere, giving, loving. But he is also used to looking after Rubens. When he's with you, at least you'll know that that is exactly where he wants to be."

"So, if I am going to make it work with Rubens then I need to get used to being alone a lot of the time?"

"People can change. Rubens might change. But at the moment you have just met. You cannot expect him to give up the life that has kept him going, both financially and emotionally, for the past few years. Even for a guy like you."

Alex put a friendly hand on Ben's shoulder as he spoke.

"You seem to be in a good place with Jamal." mused Ben, "To me, as a rank outsider, you two seem to have an understanding, the nature of which seems foreign – ha ha – to me. You don't seem to be at all upset about leaving him in the sauna, or him going out clubbing without you. I can't imagine not being jealous, Alex."

"I suppose that I have never been a physically jealous person, Ben. But it's not quite as straightforward as that, either. I am insanely jealous of my partner's heart and mind. It has always seemed to me that men are complex but also fairly simple creatures. They are occasionally powerless to prevent their groins from ruling their minds, despite all their best efforts. I, for one, don't believe that there is a man, or for that matter woman, who doesn't have – er – urges. It's just a question of how you handle them."

Ben looked at Alex expectantly, waiting for him to continue. Alex smiled reflectively:

"I do believe fairytale couples might exist. Some people may very well be so much in love that they don't even notice anyone else for the rest of their lives. Such people are incredibly rare, in my opinion. So rare that I have never met an example of this happy state myself. I like the ideal. I think we all do. But for my own part, I only know people who've got away with it."

Alex looked at Ben to see if he was with him, before

continuing, warming to his theme:

"The vast majority of couples – not just gay ones – simply get tired of having sex with the same person after five, ten, twenty years or so. Even where they aren't tired as such, every so often their eyes are caught by an attractive third party. The forbidden fruit. So, given that you are going to have urges, you have three choices. You can have an open and honest relationship like Jamal and I do, where sex is just sex, and if you are lucky the emotional attachment is strong enough to make it a liberating and satisfying experience. Loving a person so much that you can imagine them having a physical escapade with a third party, and not only not be jealous, but actually be happy for them, because they have had fun, is a rather pure and altruistic emotion. Of course it only works if you have an unshakeable confidence that, no matter what the sex is like, he is going to always come back to you. Why? Because that's where he wants to be. That's where his heart is, and his libido is just his libido. In my view that really does put sex where it belongs. On an animalistic level. It is comparable to hunger. You don't have to eat when your partner does – but eating together still is an important thing."

"And that describes you and Jamal?"

"Yes, it does, Ben. I have had a fair bit of anonymous sex since I've known Jamal – some good, some bad, some ugly and one or two pretty amazing, but I have never even had the slightest glimmer of interest in pursuing anything more concrete with another, because it is Jamal that matters to me. He has the power to make me happy or sad. He makes me want to get out of bed every day. I can swear on all I hold dear that I wouldn't want to live without him. What is sex compared to that?"

Ben wondered if it were at all right to feel moved by someone justifying living his life as a bit of a whore, albeit an honest one. But he followed Alex's reasoning, and having seen the boys together he had no reason to doubt his words.

"You said there were three choices. So what are the other two?"

"Well, the second choice is to lie. You profess blissful monogamy whilst all the time carrying on with affairs on the side. Sometimes, there is balance, when both parties are at it; occasionally one partner is still so in love he or she is faithful whilst the other partner is philandering to his or her heart's content. This seems to be the basis of most films, TV programmes and celebrity scandals."

Ben couldn't argue with that. Alex moved on:

"Now the last option is the one I personally believe is most common in real life. The scenario here is that sex is pretty much over, apart from maybe the occasional half attempt when a lot of alcohol has been consumed. In some cases the two partners don't even fancy each other any more. Or they have fallen out, and all that remains is a power struggle. At worst, they don't even like each other. In extreme cases, they might not even be able to bear touching each other any more, their repressed sexual energy feeding a growing sense of resentment at how their partner has theoretically ruined their life – or is at least standing squarely between them and a good shag. But they almost invariably remain too decent, too respectable or too scared to opt for sex with anyone else, or, terror of terrors, face life alone. So they bottle up their libido, try not to become too bitter or masturbate too much – and they turn to gardening, for example. Or charity dinners with the other ladies. Or anything to take their minds off the old urges."

"So," Ben summed up, "people are sluts, liars or obsessive gardeners?"

Ben blocked out the thought of his mother's endless round of charity dinners whilst resisting the charms of her plastic tennis instructor.

"In a nutshell, yup. Now Ben, tell me – do you think I am a cynic?"

Ben smiled at Alex by way of reply to the question. Obsessive gardeners, eh. Ben thought that it was ironic that flowers are in fact a plant's sexual organs, shamelessly put on display to the world, and given as gifts at dinner parties. A rose was just a cock by another name. Ben got on with his workout. He would need to think this one through.

Alex made some interesting points and Ben could conjure up an abundance of relationships fitting Alex's descriptions. Yet Ben also found Alex's world view too harsh. Did that make Alex a cynic? If he was, he was a cynic who seemed happy and deeply in love.

Was it cynical to give up on youthful ideals and just accept, embrace even, the ugly truths of human weakness? It might be. There was always another way. It would be good to live according to ideals, even if one fell off the higher plane occasionally. Surely the point was to climb back onto it with fierce, stubborn determination. Alex had clearly given up on the ideals. Or maybe he had formed his own ideals and was living a life true to himself.

Ben felt open to Alex's arguments. He'd clearly given it some thought. Ben's own strong belief in his own youthful ideals made him wonder whether Alex's analysis might not just be a convenient way of justifying a gay lifestyle choice? Ben wanted to believe in a happily-ever-after. He was not prepared to give that up. At least, not yet.

On the other hand, the stark truth remained. Out there, amongst the outwardly happy, one would find, without looking too hard, a fair proportion of people who disapproved of sex, didn't like young people having fun, and were rather obsessed by the state of their herbaceous borders.

Crystal Smith's own herbaceous border had undergone the full Brazilian treatment at the Sleek and Beautiful Beauty Salon in Camberwell. She was looking forward to showing it to Kerwin later. Before that magnificent open garden moment, she was having some girl time with Amber and Millie in the Health Café.

Millie was in full commercial expansion swing:

"I've been trying to think up some new ideas to drum up a bit more business for the café. I need to think outside the envelope. I mean, I keep trying to get my customers to try these marvellous organic vegan recipes I get from Beverley Lynn Bennett, but people around here are like lepers that never change their spots. They just don't get it. They are such ignoranuses!"

"I think you mean ignoramus, Millie."

"Actually Amber, ignoranus sounds pretty good. Kind

of an intelligent way of saying dumbass."

Crystal and Amber started giggling in front of a mystified Millie.

"Well I'm glad to see you two are getting on better again, even if you should be trying harder to figure out a way to help me improve my business here," sniffed Millie. "You tell me, ladies – how do I get people to try my curried tofu cutlets? I had to give most of the last batch I made away to the homeless."

"I'll bet they were grateful," chortled Crystal. "I mean homeless, hungry and when they finally get a nice hot meal – it's curried tofu cutlets!"

"Crystal Smith, you can be such a douchebaguette at times!"

"What are you calling me? Is that, like, from douchebag?" Crystal was fighting to keep a straight face. "Have you been talking to those Americans again?"

"I just heard baguette and thought it must be the latest thing off your menu, Millie."

Crystal and Amber laughed out loud.

"Honestly, I don't know why I bother with you two silly girls. Maybe I should ask that nice American boy over there with Alex. I'm sure he could help me."

"Girlfriend, I think he could help out a lot of girls round here. He is one fine piece of ass."

"Crystal Smith, you just speak for yourself. How dare you, when you are already getting served from your own piece of genuine British beef?"

"Amber, I am just as greedy as the next person. That's you."

"Oh, you two are getting worse. Honestly, it's like preaching to the perverted. Have you really got no ideas at all that can help me here? I thought about a party but I can't serve alcohol and if I get people to bring their own then they won't notice my food because they'll be too drunk. I feel it's a Catch 69 here."

Amber had an idea. This could well be the chance she was waiting for to get back at Kelly Danvers. She lowered her eyes and examined her long talons:

"Millie, wait up. A party, you say? What about a fancy dress party which starts out with canapés from the Health Café and a competition for the best costume? Like a catwalk, or something? That way you have a pretty good chance of people turning up at a reasonable time because there is an event, and of course they will get a chance to try a wide selection of your marvellous food. We could use the party room on the other side of the reception. Everyone bring a bottle or more. Delicious food first, get trashed on your own cheap alcohol later. Everyone's happy. I'll help you organise it."

"Amber, girl, I like it!" crowed Crystal, "We'll need dancing too. No one dances enough any more. We get ourselves a compère for the show and a DJ for later and we're sorted. I'll help you too, Millie!"

Millie was delighted.

"See girls? I knew you were more than bird brains. I just knew you would help me out. It would work really well. We'll do it. When in Rome, let them eat cake."

Crystal squealed out loud:

"Oh, wait wait wait! I went to the funniest party a

couple of years ago. It was called an "Underground Party". Everyone had to come in a costume inspired by a London Underground Station. I went as Wimbledon in a dress made of Astroturf with tramlines on it, a tennis racquet in one hand and a Womble in the other. It was *fierce*!"

Crystal Smith saw that this could be a way for her to have fun, and to do something vaguely altruistic for the community. Millie Myers saw that this could be a way for her to get something from the community. They had taken her for granted for too long. Amber Bluett saw that this could be a way to infiltrate the community with her duly disguised brothers. This was her chance to take something from that American girl who had taken her safety for granted for too long. It was a cinch. With motivation like that, the party was sure to happen.

Hartmut Glick had, in truth, been rather troubled by Cornisha's unexpected call on Sunday evening. But Harmut Glick also knew a challenge when he saw one. Being Hartmut Glick, he had decided that there was certainly nothing that could be gained from worrying about the matter. He had always managed to get where he wanted through rational behaviour, hard work and a logical approach to solving problems. Very few things resisted an onslaught from Hartmut's intellect.

As such, he had met Cornisha's worried greeting that morning with a courteous "Good Morning" and had enquired after her weekend as if nothing had happened. When she continued to look somewhat perturbed he decided that he should advise her in no uncertain terms to act as if nothing had happened.

"My dear Cornisha. I am very grateful for your call yesterday. I have pondered your words. My considered response is that we should all prepare ourselves, physically, mentally and on an ongoing basis, for whatever life may throw up. However, there is nothing to be gained by trying to second guess the nature of any highly irrational developments, or worry about the motives of those involved. If called upon, I will act. So, please do not be concerned about this and let us talk no further of it."

Although Hartmut could tell that Cornisha was still a little upset, he couldn't help but notice with a twinge of pleasure how perfectly turned out she was. As always she and her office were a picture of harmony and organisation. It settled his mind to see such order. He would be more than a match for anything that SBK might decide to throw at him.

Harry lazily stroked Monique's back. She sighed with pleasure. This was a lazy, immoral way to get her kicks, but it still felt good. She rolled over, showing off her lean, taut body. It contrasted neatly with Harry's flab. She did not mind, being lazy, and he did not either, being deluded.

"Oh Harry, I do wish we could go away for the weekend, just the two of us. I respect your situation, but I would so like to take you to Paris."

How could he possibly have had any doubt as to his attractiveness to women? Harry wished that *irritating* model could see how women desired him. Monique was in his thrall. Harry loved it. This felt so sweet after the rudeness of the night at his sister's party. He could feel his ego swelling like a bruise, as it had done many, many times before in Harry's notoriously charmed life.

"Monique, I think we must put our thinking caps on. There must be some utterly boring legal conference that I need to attend coming up. Darling, there is nothing I would like more than to spend a weekend in Paris with you."

It was almost true. Harry could already envisage making love to Monique Mottin in a five-star hotel in Paris with champagne on tap. She had a way of making love that poor Sarah had never mastered. He wondered how that irksome Brazilian model made love. He was sure he could show her how a woman really reached orgasm. And he would. Some day. A temporary setback. That was all. He would have his victory, and she would be so upset that she had wasted so much time in not falling for Harry Gumpert on the first night. Harry took a moment to savour his imaginary sweet revenge. In the meantime there were surely plenty of other women just queuing up for the Gumpert treatment. And just like that, Harry's irrepressible lust for life was back in control.

He left Monique's flat to sneak back up to life with Sarah. There was a noticeable spring in his step. What was all that nonsense about not being able to have it all? What Harry had, in spades, was buckets of delusion.

16

Two's company, three's a bit pervy

"I always think that an ample supply of public toilets is one of the marks of a civilised society, Arthur."

Cornisha Burrows was spending the day in a very civilised place. She was running no risk whatsoever of having to run into the nearest McDonalds just to spend a penny, for Frinton-on-Sea had public conveniences galore located at regular intervals along the seafront – and this in addition, of course, to the new toilet block at the top of the cliff, on the Greensward near Connaught Avenue. Nothing so vulgar as a hamburger restaurant with those frightful plastic seats and menus with photographs on them graced a town which so prided itself on the preservation of the best of England's traditions. The Big Mac and the Cadbury Crunchie McFlurry were kept well away, away in Clacton-on-Sea, Frinton's brasher big sister down the coast.

"Oh look, Cornisha, there's a free bench. Phyllis always used to love sitting on the Greensward looking at the sea."

"I think we should re-live those happy memories, Arthur. I'm sure she is here with us in spirit."

As Cornisha gave Arthur a warm smile, Arthur thought

how lucky he was, and how strange it was, to have met a lady who didn't feel threatened by the mention of his wife. He had been nervous at making the trip to Frinton. He worried that it might make him sad, or that he might feel as if he were betraying Phyllis' memory. Or even, Lord forbid, that Cornisha might get jealous of his memories.

But Cornisha wasn't like that. Indeed, Cornisha wasn't like any of the other ladies that Arthur had known in his life.

"I rather fancy Peggy's Place for lunch. What do you say, Arthur?"

"A fine idea. We'd better get there for twelve o'clock sharp, though, if we want to get a table. You know how Frintonians like to have their lunch early."

"Not just them, dear man. I do too. It's the same wherever there is a large retired community. Mornings are important to us oldies, and when you get up early, you're ready for lunch by twelve o'clock."

Arthur looked around, with a wistful expression.

"Phyllis often mentioned moving to Frinton. I always told her that whilst I loved coming for the day, we would need to wait a few more years before we got old enough to live in Frinton. You must have heard the old music hall joke round these parts?"

"No – do tell."

"Well, if ever you want to provoke a most un-Frintonian welcome from one of the locals, just ask if it is true that people say *Harwich for the Continent, Frinton for the incontinent.*"

"Arthur, that's awful!"

For a moment, Arthur thought he was going to get a

Frintonian look of disapproval from Cornisha, before she gave him that mischievous grin that was always so unexpected from a classy lady like her. She was irresistible when the corners of her mouth curled up like that and the dimples came out in her cheeks. She always preserved the elegance that came so naturally to her, but also, on occasion, suddenly became more sensual, more physical. Age had most certainly not withered her. She effortlessly awakened the long dormant man inside of Arthur Bilks.

Arthur had given up hope of meeting a woman about whom he would not only have feelings but also urges. He had long resigned himself to belonging to the *"that part of my life is over"* school of misery. Maybe, just maybe with Cornisha, there could be a reawakening. An upset, if you will, on a grand, incongruous but blissful scale. Viagra not necessarily required. Was it too much to hope that he would one day soon get to see just what was inside that dark green dress?

Ben couldn't help but smile at the irony of it.

When he had arrived in the UK a few weeks earlier he had been disappointed to find that his new home in SE1 had none of the history and elegance that he was expecting from London. However, in modern Elephant & Castle he had settled in rather well. He felt very much at home now, in the concrete bunker. Today, though, his destination was Belgrave Road, the very epicentre of those marvellous Georgian terraces of SW1, which epitomised the faded yet regal beauty and old-fashioned, understated sophistication of London. The views brought to mind the type of places that he had dreamed of from afar.

That being said, things had moved on rather spankingly from his previous dreams. Rather at odds with any notion of respectability, he was making his way with Rubens Ribeiro to a splendid house, alas long transformed into the Handford House Hotel, Victoria, in order to perform for a man named "Peter".

As they walked down the road from Victoria Station, Ben struggled with unexpected feelings of melancholy. It seemed to be infused in the buildings. In this part of town, almost every one was a down at heart hotel. They all seemed to promise nothing better than a bedful of crabs and some very bad sausages for breakfast. Naturally, they were undeniably convenient for Victoria Coach Station – convenient, that is, if you want to wake up covered in angry red bites from things too small to squash. Ben felt cross on behalf of the travellers of restricted means who suffered there. A budget traveller should be respected. Minimum standards should apply.

Mind you, he was being harsh. Not every hotel looked down at heel. But it still seemed strangely sad to see all those nasty little reception areas, brightly coloured cheap neon signs and AA recommendations marring the once simple beauty of the architecture. How much better was it to imagine the premises with a polished brass nameplate, announcing the name of the family to visitors, with footmen to carry the trunks, a butler to see that everyone was taken care of, and delicate features subtly adorning the house?

Those elegant days were gone, and maybe that was not so bad. There was always a chance that one would have been the footman. Reality intervened in Ben's musings. They had arrived at the Handford House Hotel.

"Are you OK to do this Ben?"

It was largely a rhetorical question from Rubens, who might have been headed to the bakery for a bun. They had been walking down the road in silence. Ben still wasn't convinced that Rubens could even come close to committing. Ben had decided to control his emotions. In a way, doing this for money made it easier. There was no anticipation of a relationship to besmirch or trust in.

"I'm fine." he said.

Peter had asked them to come in business attire and to carry briefcases. Rubens had had a thorough briefing. They would carry out every instruction as if they had an Oscar riding on it. They found the main entrance and walked straight up to the reception desk.

"Good evening, Miss. My colleague and I have a meeting with a Mr Peter Jones. I believe he is in Room 23. Could you possibly ring up and tell him that Paulo Pauzao and Dick Burns from BluePont Performance Lubricants have arrived?"

The middle-aged lady behind the counter with purple rinsed hair and horn-rimmed glasses looked rather frosty when they entered. However, her determined chilliness presented no defence against Rubens' warm, confident charm. His sensual accent and perfect skin had her at "Good evening". He dazzled her with an easy smile, and briskly flicked some dust off his suit, looking every inch the travelling salesman. She visibly melted and even assumed a slightly coquettish attitude with the handsome foreigner in a dark blue Armani suit off the back of a lorry.

"Ah yes, Mr Pauzao. Mr Jones left a message saying he was expecting two gentlemen around 7.30pm. You businessmen work all hours to keep the wheels of industry turning! The lift is over there, second floor. I believe Mr Jones already has refreshments for your meeting but please don't hesitate to call down if I can be of any assistance."

"Thank you, Miss," said Rubens.

"Don't push it," hissed Ben.

The cheery wallpaper on two of the three lift walls singularly failed to lift Ben's mood. However, he had to admit that, looking at himself and Rubens in the full-length mirror on the third wall, they made a somewhat handsome couple in their stylish suits. No wonder Miss Frosty had got a little hot and bothered behind her desk. Peter was sure to be pleased. It was just advanced masturbation all round. Maybe Ben could even get off on the fantasy himself.

The carpet in the hall matched the one in the lift. Cheap and cheerful, or cheap and nasty? Ben couldn't quite decide. Maybe he should come back and try to make up his mind when he wasn't about to go and perform sex acts for money.

On with the show.

Rubens knocked smartly on the door. The tall, bald middle-aged man in a dark grey pin-striped suit and sombre charcoal tie who opened it looked more like a lawyer that Ben might be having a real business meeting with rather than some pervert who was just playing dress up.

Ben squared his shoulders.

He would play the game.

He was there to help "Paulo" sell Performance Lubricants to Peter Jones. He wondered if Paulo had a PowerPoint presentation hidden away somewhere in his underpants. Best place for it, really.

"Good evening, gentlemen. Sorry for the late hour of the meeting, but it's been a very busy schedule and I am keen to see what you have to offer. Please come in – and take a seat."

So Peter would be playing it for real.

"Thank you, Peter. By the way this is my colleague, Dick Burns. He will be demonstrating some of the key benefits of our product today."

They had gone into a small suite. The living room area was spacious enough. It held a table with three chairs. On the table were some notepads, a couple of pens, a jug of water, and water glasses. It seemed rather hot in the room so they took off their suit jackets before sitting down.

"Would you like some water?"

Peter poured the water. Rubens hadn't told Ben the entire plan, just to do what he told him and to enjoy himself. Ben couldn't help but hope that making a sales pitch for the Performance Lubricant was part of Peter's fantasy. What a way to put his pitch training to good use.

"We were glad to get here on time, Peter, as the traffic was awful on the way down from Manchester."

Where the hell had Rubens got Manchester from?

"And then we finally got into London and the whole distance from the M25 in the north – oh no! Sorry, Dick!"

Ben hadn't seen that one coming. Presumably as part

of Rubens' cunning plan to avoid spending too long on foreplay, as he was indicating north with his hand, he had caught Ben's glass of water and managed to carefully spill it all over Ben's groin.

"Have you got a towel, Peter?'"

Peter went into the bathroom, reappeared at the door and threw Rubens a small towel. He stayed half-hidden behind the doorframe, intently watching.

"Stand up, Dick!"

Oh Lord, here we go. Did the Victorians engage in role play? Stand and deliver, like some twisted highwayman, with an appropriately loaded weapon to hand. Maybe it was because of such excruciating moments that they purported to control temptation by dressing up their table legs? *Anything to avoid this.*

Ben did as he was told, with his soggy suit trousers clinging rather unpleasantly to his groin. Rubens knelt down very affectedly in front of him and started dabbing at his trousers with the towel. All the while, he made sure that Peter had an unobstructed view from the bathroom doorway. Rubens had told him not to watch the client at all, but Ben couldn't help noticing out of the corner of his eye that Peter was touching himself, as Rubens made his pathetic attempt to dry Ben's trousers.

"I think you'd better take these off, Dick. I'm sure there must be an iron here to dry them out."

Trying not to criticise Rubens' choreography, as it would have been far more natural for him to have worked the trouser-patting scene a bit more, Ben played along. He unzipped his trousers and let them fall to the ground.

Lifting his shirt up and checking his Calvins he did his best to sound convincing.

"Oh no! My underpants are wet as well. I guess they'll have to be ironed too."

As Paulo pulled Ben's underpants down, Ben noticed that he was also managing to stick his butt out as far as possible so that his trousers looked like they were going to burst. Out of the corner of his eye he saw that Peter, too, had started to lose clothing.

"God. Dick, I can see why you are so popular with the women back in the office. Do you have a licence for that thing?"

Despite Rubens' appallingly bad script, Ben was actually starting to enjoy himself, and was even getting aroused. He had found it difficult not to laugh at the "drying by ironing" scenario as it was. All exceedingly macho, this. Still, it was going to plan. If they were good, they might even get a tip.

"Paulo, please don't mention women when I am naked. Oh, hell. Too late. What am I going to do with *that now*?"

At that point Rubens thankfully decided his mouth had done quite enough talking and would be better employed doing something else. In fairness, Ben thought Rubens was a far better prostitute than he was a thespian. For the next twenty minutes, Rubens and Ben did what they had done numerous times in the past few days, the only difference being that Rubens seemed to be very aware of how he might look from the other side of the room and to subtly adjust the positioning every so often. Their observer was now fully naked and pleasuring himself, ably assisted by what looked like a small black butt plug.

"I want to do it standing up, Dick."

As all this was still fairly new to Ben and his twenty-something libido was not tiring of it, he would have been happy hanging off the ceiling if Rubens had told him to. Positioning himself behind the Brazilian's perfect rear, he checked his rubber and got back to work.

"Spread your legs, Dick, it's sexier that way."

Ben was momentarily confused as he thought it should be him saying that to Rubens, whose legs had in any case been spread for some time already. Then he understood why. As he could feel the climax was not far off, Peter suddenly made a move from the doorway. He lay down with his back on the floor and moved underneath the boys. Peter then winked up at the Brazilian in the secret code to say that he was getting ready.

"Dick, I'm coming. Pull it out and let it flow, man," gasped Rubens. It was by far his most convincing line of the day.

As Ben certainly didn't want to be left alone with Peter, he took that as his cue to finish the job. He was careful not to look down between his legs until he was done.

It was a good thing too, as the sight that greeted him when he dropped his eyes to the floor could well have arrested him in mid-flow. It wasn't just the physical aspect of an older man naked, dappled with come, and in close physical proximity. It wasn't the fact that Peter was using that come to help him get to his destination. No, there was something in those cold screwed-up grey eyes (more come?) that made Ben feel something was deeply wrong.

Those eyes and Peter's contorted face didn't convey the usual ecstasy of pleasure, but something deeply unpleasant that made Ben shudder in the warm room. There was a tension between the obvious physical need that Peter had and the thinly veiled disgust he harboured for the boys and the whole sordid scene.

Unable to wrench his eyes away from his client's face as the climax juddered into sight, Ben experienced the same sense of prurient fascination mixed with revulsion that one gets from staring at a particularly grisly road accident. Peter's miserable couple of drops barely seemed to make it out, before he quickly extracted himself out from under the boys and slunk off into the bathroom. By now Ben's revulsion had got the upper hand. Thank God the man had not tried to touch him.

Peter reappeared in a bathrobe.

"You can use the bathroom now." he said curtly.

Leaving their clothes in the room they went to shower. Ben was now desperate to get away. He tried to forget that vision of a middle-aged man lying between his legs having too much fun with Ben's ejaculate. He doubted that he could. Rubens seemed to be completely relaxed. After drying himself he left the towel on the floor of the bathroom and walked back into the main room completely naked. Ben followed him with his towel firmly around his waist.

They dressed in silence. It was obvious that Peter no longer had any use for them. He didn't even seem to want to acknowledge their presence. In fact, he seemed rather offended by them continuing to be there, rather like the take-away curry that had been delicious only hours earlier, but after the hunger had been thoroughly sated was now just an unpleasant looking mess with an off-putting smell. His cold pale blue eyes glinted with disdain and there was a palpable feeling of impatience about him. As Rubens was picking up the papers that were extolling the virtues of Blue Pont Performance Lubricants Ben noticed that a large envelope had appeared. Rubens opened it and quickly counted thick wads of fifty-pound notes. Peter's sudden hostility propelled them out of the room in silence, which reigned until they were in the safety of the lift.

Rubens was delighted.

"Gostoso, you were amazing! He gave us an extra five hundred pounds."

Ben really didn't know what to say. Such a lot of money in such a short time. No training or real preparation required. No certificates. No endless interview process. Although, oddly enough, he had had to iron a shirt before coming out. This was extreme ironing, all round.

Normal work, however, did not leave Ben with the appalling vision of a naked older man straining to reach his putrid climax between Ben's own legs. Why does one always have to look at the car crash?

What a sad, sick man. The client's reaction when they had emerged from the shower was really rather nasty. Peter had treated them like inconsequential servants who were not even worthy of a word once their job had been done. The cold, calculating ruthlessness of the man had been wholly masked whilst the boys were still serving a purpose. Ben shuddered again, before giving Rubens what he hoped was a cheerful smile. The lift doors opened before he could get any words out.

"Goodbye gentlemen. I hope you had a fruitful meeting!"

Ben couldn't help but contrast the warm friendly smile of the lady on the reception desk with the almost malevolent air that had swept them out of Peter's room.

As he walked down Belgrave Road back towards Victoria he felt that SW1 would be forever besmirched by the memory of his first ever experience inside one of those lovely Georgian buildings. He knew it was hardly an original thought – but it struck him that you never knew what manner of things happened in the nicest of places. Maybe his gritty Elephant suited him better after all.

Felix Skink was well aware that it was often the most salubrious of exteriors that harboured the least savoury of interiors. In the right hands, scenes from those interiors could yield great profit. The rubbish of the rich was a favourite seam to mine. Turning the nineteenth-century aphorism on its head, Felix knew that where there was glamour, there was grime.

Felix had earned a steady stream of money selling all sorts of titbits to the press, but eventually the remnants of his conscience rebelled at seeing all those hatchet jobs in the Daily Mail and he decided he would have to turn to a slightly more honest career. So now he was a private investigator. He mainly dealt with spousal infidelity, and also specialised in unearthing the carefully hidden secrets of the outwardly respectable.

Although he had left the press job behind him, there

was little else that Felix Skink would draw the line at. So when he got a call from a high-flying businessman who wanted him to uncover some dirt on a business partner, Felix had absolutely no qualms.

His initial investigations merely revealed meticulous recycling, including the washing and squashing of all materials to eliminate smells and minimise space occupied. Nothing was out of place. Everything was perfectly in order.

Felix had to go to plan B. He was master of the shadow. No one ever noticed they were being followed and neither did they ever escape. Three weeks of following the man to the office, the supermarket, the theatre, the gym and even to lunch with friends on occasion had yielded precisely nothing out of the ordinary. The man was a paragon of respectability. After staking out the target's abode on a cold Saturday evening for hours with not even a sign of life, Felix was getting frustrated. He got a bonus for results and this was going nowhere.

Felix resolved to tell his customer on Monday morning that he was off the case.

Just then the main door opened and the target stepped smartly out and marched off towards the tube station. Finally, a break. Saturday evening sorties could often be interesting.

After playing hide and seek on the Northern Line, Felix watched as the victim entered what looked like a nightclub in one of the railway arches near London Bridge.

As he got closer, he could see that beside the two large doormen, there was a woman wearing a leather bra, leather miniskirt, thigh-length leather boots and a military style cap, standing under a sign with the word PPLAY emblazoned across it.

Jackpot! Felix always savoured the eureka moments. He knew exactly what PPLAY was. He also knew that if he wanted to wrap things up quickly and get his money, he had to act extremely fast.

A cab ride later, he was buying an outfit in Soho. Half an hour after that, he was struggling into it in the fitting room, carefully cutting a tiny hole in the full head mask to allow his miniature video camera to film without being visible to the outside. In under an hour he was back outside PPLAY.

Fortune was certainly smiling on him that night. Not only had he finally had a break, but chance had brought him to one of his favourite haunts. This was his home turf and he would be able to move around effortlessly. The target would be tracked, stalked and brought down.

The woman at the door opened her eyes wide as she recognised a familiar face.

"Hello, Felix. We haven't seen you here for ages. I thought you had found yourself a mistress who was cracking the whip. So to speak."

"Just been busy, Suzie, that's all. And experimenting with vanilla a bit. But you know me, I can't resist for long. Seen anyone I might like?"

"Quite a few, darling. But look out for the scarlet catsuit. She's the queen of the night, I think."

Thus it came about that, barely an hour after watching his prey enter PPLAY, Felix Skink found himself shut in a private room with his secret helmet-cam filming a naked female slave, Caroline Napier Jones and Hartmut Glick. With the double thrill of getting dirt on his victim whilst simultaneously being humiliated by his victim's dominatrix friend, it was no wonder that he was yelping with delight.

Nicholas Casterway relaxed in a Chesterfield armchair in his preferred corner of the Empire Club in Mayfair. He revelled in the feel and smell of the old leather, the refined ambience, the humility of the staff and, of course, the fact that the vast majority of humanity were simply excluded from its hallowed interior. He waited a moment for Jacques to finish topping up his Scotch, before continuing his conversation with Harry Gumpert.

"Harry, thank you for bringing me up to speed with everything in the office. Now, how are the preparations for the cocktail party shaping up?"

"Nicholas, everything is under control. Cornisha has been exceptional."

"Yes, she certainly is... exceptional." Nicholas failed to hide his grimace. "Now, to the matter with our Teutonic problem."

Harry's ears pricked up. He had been burning to know what exactly Nicholas had found out about Hartmut.

"Nicholas, what exactly is the nature of the... misdemeanour?"

"It pains me to discuss it. But it is sadly unavoidable. It seems that Hartmut has been attending certain events where – shall we say – regular people would not care to be seen, never mind videotaped. And now we have a blackmailer on our hands."

"We're being blackmailed?"

Harry couldn't believe his ears. No wonder Nicholas was keen to address the issue.

"Have you spoken to Hartmut yet?"

"I didn't think it was appropriate to discuss these matters in detail over the telephone. That's why I am keen to discuss it face to face as soon as possible. The first occasion will be the cocktail party. I feel I would prefer to speak to Hartmut in an informal setting. I'm sure you understand me."

Harry wasn't sure he would choose to bring up such a subject at a party. However, given the history between Nicholas and Hartmut, maybe Nicholas would actually enjoy spoiling Hartmut's party in that way. Maybe he thought he could catch him with his defences down and gain a certain advantage. Of course he would. The sly old fox. For a moment Harry wondered whether he should suggest choosing a different moment to break the news to Hartmut. He immediately thought better of it.

This could only go one way. There would be only one outcome. Better to show utter support to the person who would emerge more powerful than before.

"Absolutely, Nicholas. I think you are being most sensitive about this. You have my absolute support."

"Excellent. I am delighted, as I want you to be present when I take Hartmut aside. It is of course reassuring to know that I will have someone who fully understands the import of a case like this, and the damage that could be done to the partnership."

"So, what are you going to ask Hartmut to do?"

"By that time, I will have seen the incriminating video. It's on its way. When Hartmut is presented with evidence of what has happened then I am confident that he will see that, regrettably, there is only one possible outcome for the good of the partnership. Scandal must be avoided at all costs."

"I don't see how this will stop the blackmailer, Nicholas."

"I feel this is such a tragedy for poor Hartmut that we shall meet the blackmailer halfway. He shall have his pound of flesh, or at least a few ounces. That much we can afford. However, we cannot let this be a continuing millstone around our necks. Hartmut must unfortunately take his chances outside of SBK. It is the only solution."

They had had a perfect day in Frinton-on-Sea. As they sped back to London in Arthur's comfortable old Citroën, Cornisha realised she was starting to feel something for the calm gentleman sitting by her side. Would it be possible to keep her past a secret forever?

Cornisha discounted the idea. She was proud of who she was, who she had been, and how the two were linked. She would not live a lie – not even for the promise of happiness with a man like Arthur Bilks, not if it meant hiding the truth from him. And the longer she kept quiet, the worse it would be when she did tell him.

"What is it with bloody penises?" she thought ruefully. "Decades after consigning mine to the medical wastebin, it is still popping up and trying to run my life. Damn control freaks."

Yet she was starting to fall in love and she could see that Arthur was too.

If she just carried on all Pollyanna-esque there was the potential for a horrible situation. Yet she yearned for an easy outcome. Could Arthur prove her wrong? Might he be a man that could accept who she was and love her anyway?

Arthur sensed her disquiet.

"Penny for your thoughts?"

Cornisha dragged herself back from brooding on the ghost of her penis past.

"I really enjoyed our day out today. But more than that I am starting to fall for you, Arthur Bilks. I would miss you awfully if you weren't in my life."

Arthur couldn't stop his face from breaking out into a broad smile. But then he wondered why such a message was delivered with that air of foreboding.

"Why would I ever not want to be in your life, Cornisha?"

As Arthur glanced at Cornisha he saw that she looked uncomfortable. His smile vanished as quickly as it had appeared.

"You know I have never been married." she said carefully.

Arthur felt anxious. He narrowed his eyes:

"Yes, Cornisha. I know that."

"There is a reason for that. I've never found a man that I wanted to share my life with, who could love me, knowing everything there is to know about Cornisha Burrows."

"Do you have some deep dark secret? Don't tell me. Were you a pole dancer in a previous life? Or, God forbid, did you use to be a politician? Or an estate agent?"

Arthur's attempt at humour was slain by the obvious look of pain on Cornisha's face.

"Cornisha, what's wrong? Although we haven't known each other for long I can't imagine anything that could change my mind about my beautiful, beautiful lady. Tell me, my dearest. You must not worry."

Cornisha's mind was racing. Arthur was saying all the right things. They had something special. He wouldn't throw it all away for something that had no relevance to anything any more. It was the twenty-first century. It was.

She took a breath:

"Arthur. I want to be with you and I don't want to have any secrets. What I want to say to you is that I haven't always been... like I am today."

"I'm sure you were even more beautiful in the past! But do you mean that you were a different woman when you were younger? Are we talking about cosmetic surgery?"

How long was she going to go beating about her bush? She summoned up her courage and decided enough was enough.

"Different, yes. But a woman, no."

There, she had said it.

Arthur was confused. What the hell did that mean? Of course she wasn't born a fully grown woman.

"None of us is born an adult, Cornisha. I still don't understand what you mean. Were you raped?"

"Oh, for God's sake, Arthur. I'm a transsexual. I was born Conrad Burrows. A boy. I grew up as a man. I changed when I was in my twenties."

Arthur Bilks jumped so violently that he almost swerved

into the pavement where an old woman was struggling along with one of those plaid shopping baskets on wheels. She gave Arthur a panicked look as he passed her, narrowly missing the hideous basket.

"You used to be a man?"

"Yes, Arthur, I did."

"What are you now then?"

"Arthur, I am a woman. It would be a challenge to have children but apart from that I am as much of a woman as any other you could meet."

Cornisha was shaking as she tried to steady her voice and work out what Arthur was thinking.

His first thought was that he wanted her out of his car. He had no problems with fairy fellas, gays as they were called these days, but he was not one of them. It disgusted him to think that he had been imagining having sex with Cornisha. He would try hard not to treat her, if that was the right word, too badly, but he couldn't bear the thought of being close to her. He couldn't bring himself to talk or even to look at her.

"Arthur, please, say something to me!"

Cornisha's tears would have melted his heart only five minutes earlier, but now he found them pathetic. She may look like a woman but she was brought up a man. For God's sake, where was her dignity? He still couldn't speak to that person.

"Arthur. Please talk to me. I imagined that you would be like this. I tried to tell myself that you would be different, but I suppose that it is something that most men just can't cope with. It's very, very sad – but I have to respect your view and be grateful that you're gentleman enough not to call me names."

Cornisha couldn't stop crying into her handkerchief as they drove the last few miles back to her house in silence. When Arthur stopped the car outside her door, she opened the door, grabbed her bag and left him, without saying a word.

17

Mamma mia

Clubbing became a regular feature. Ben soon got used to all that bare flesh. In fact, he wondered if he would be able to keep his shirt *on* next time he went to a party back home. He better had. His take on party garb would have to be carefully monitored, as he didn't think the Vineyard was quite ready for the Muscle Mary scene.

Same old, same old. Amazing how quickly you adjust to a new scene. Rubens was right up there, again, dancing on a podium like an electrocuted snake. The club was a dancer short that night, but Ben declined the chance to earn fifty pounds. He had had enough of working with Rubens for one week.

In fact, Ben was starting to think that he had had enough of Rubens, period.

It wasn't that he didn't like him.

It was not as if Rubens had changed since they had started seeing each other.

In fact, that was the main problem: Rubens hadn't changed at all.

Before meeting Ben, Rubens went out most nights. After

meeting Ben, Rubens went out most nights. He played the field to his heart's content. When a go-go boy like Rubens decided to play the field, the field ended up being the size of Iowa. Ben wasn't even that disappointed or annoyed with Rubens. How could he be? It would hardly be fair. Rubens had never promised Ben anything other than a good time. He had delivered on that, so Ben couldn't argue.

Ben pondered what he really wanted out of his time in London. Maybe it would suit him perfectly to have a thing like this going on. It would leave him free to do what he wanted, but also guarantee him some decent sexual release. That was something to weigh up. Decent sex was a currency all of its own. That was another reason why people threw caution to the wind and embraced potentially scandalous exposure. Christ, it always felt worth it for a *proper* session. Not just the "everything must go" sale time fumbles that Ben had already had a lifetime's worth of – but the real McCoy. Good sex was so much rarer than one might think, given all the focus upon it. It was not something to throw away lightly.

But what about Kelly Danvers? Ben's body was manifestly a fan, and, although it was often dangerous to pay too much heed to his crotch, it would probably be even more foolish to ignore its general advice. Ben had no doubt that he was attracted to Rubens, but he also had no doubt that he liked women. Now there was a woman in the picture again. Maybe it was a person in the picture – maybe he liked people. Some people are sexual, and some are not. Anyway, bisexuality was not quite the same thing as being gay.

In Ben's musings, things always took a strange illogical turn. This is where the confusion about Kelly reached its climax. Ben could imagine himself settling down with Kelly, and doing all the things that he had dreamed of with a lovely girl, when he was a singularly unsuccessful straight college student. He wanted to take her to Rome, to Paris, everywhere, and lay her down on scented beds. When thinking about Kelly, Ben's view of the world took on a slightly cock-eyed lustful rose-tinted aspect. It was a cinematic take on the possibilities afforded by life. Everything always seems possible to those with active imaginations.

But even after his wilder flights of fancy, Ben was realistic. There were serious doubts sewn into the silver lining.

He faced facts. How could Kelly possibly take him seriously after she had walked in on him and Rubens? She would have to be *crazy* to consider anything, crazy to take a risk like that. Maybe Ben should just give up on Kelly. It would be a thick skull indeed that did not acknowledge that the chances were that he had blown it more thoroughly than the Manhattan project. Maybe he should just look out for another girl. Of all people, Rubens should understand. He was hardly in a position to criticise anyone.

Although Rubens Ribeiro was feeling, well, like Rubens Ribeiro, he was also feeling deeply grateful to Ben for what he had done. It was more than extra money to help his mother. It was the principle. The American really hadn't been comfortable about it, but he had done it for Rubens, he hadn't complained and he had done it well. Rubens resolved to be a good boy, at least for that night. So it was that, after Rubens finished dancing, he asked Ben what he wanted to do. And when Ben said he was ready to go home, to the American's great surprise, Rubens left with him, and they headed back to the Lofts together.

As with so many good intentions, Rubens's boyfriendish gesture did not really advance anyone's cause very far. Although Ben had all the right ingredients, somehow in bed he just didn't quite get there for Rubens. It all seemed a bit mechanical.

Rubens decided that he really, really didn't need dull sex in his life. He had never understood the concept of a mercy fuck, and here he was having dinner, giving someone a gratitude fuck, and staying the night. It would be the first and last time.

Ben thought the sex was fantastic and couldn't believe how good he had become at it. But it went no further than the sex. This was it. This was no longer right. Ben didn't feel in love any more.

Cornisha Burrows was feeling very much in love – with all its dreadful trimmings. The pain, the heartache, the longing, the intense sadness. No wonder the poets died young. This, and tuberculosis.

She started crying again as she watered her orchids. Much as she loved her floral children, she had dared to dream of having a person to spend her weekends with. Yet here she was again, on a Friday night, all alone in her little flat, with just her orchids for company. Why had she let herself pretend that Arthur would be different?

Never again would she let herself go. From now on, Cornisha Burrows would be the perfect ice queen. God help the man that tried it on with her now. They were all the damned same. It was so unfair. And hurtful.

She had dealt with unfairness all her life. It had never stopped her – but it did lap at the foundations of her confidence, like the tide at the foot of a sandcastle. She was left with very little to show for the lovely times she had spent with Arthur.

She would have to get on. Arthur Bilks was not going to get the better of her now. After a lifetime of battling she wasn't going to let a penis or its owner get the better of her now.

Her anger peaked sharply as she thought about the scene with Arthur, but it was quickly dulled, suffocated by the sadness. The inevitability of it all crushed her. She resolved to keep the melancholy feelings fresh and pure – not to let them warp into bitterness. Being alone was a curse of sorts – but it was still better than being with a *coward*.

Down the Spotted Duck in West Ham, Arthur Bilks wasn't feeling as if he had got the better of anyone.

It was a rather glum Friday night out with John and Bert.

His two friends had noticed Arthur wasn't exactly talkative, but then he never really was. Their friendship was based upon a classically British male unspoken code.

It was a simple code. Emotions did not exist – not so as to be spoken about, anyhow. *"It's difficult"* was the most anyone could ever have the need to express. No elaboration was needed. That phrase, however, was to be used sparingly, and only in appropriate circumstances – say, if terrorists had wiped out your family in a completely unprovoked and random attack.

Anything less could be dealt with adequately by a raised eyebrow, or a grunt. Unless it was to talk of football joy or devastation, the men supped their bitter in silence. It really was a fairly boring Friday night out. If Sheila hadn't come over to collect the empties, it would probably have gone on until one of them went to get the next round, went home or just fell asleep.

Sheila was not as taciturn as the men she granted a licence to:

"I didn't think we'd be seeing you tonight, Arthur. I thought you'd be up the West End with that new fancy woman of yours. I hear she's quite the lady."

Although Arthur had not told John and Bert anything at all about what had happened between Cornisha and him on the way back from Frinton, almost fifty years of friendship had informed them that something wasn't right, and also that Arthur would not want to talk about it. They were startled out of their torpor by Sheila's remarks. They barely had time to look sternly at her, communicating *more than adequately* that she should back off and shut up, before she realised that she had poured salt on a wound. There was nothing for it but to dig the hole deeper.

"Oh, have I said something out of place? Arthur Bilks, you haven't gone and ruined it with her, have you?"

Sheila folded her arms and looked accusingly at Arthur.

She was the human embodiment of a tut.

"Arthur. Arthur. Arthur. And there I was, thinking you were finally going to start getting over losing poor Phyllis. You never talk about her, or about how you're feeling. She'd have wanted you to be happy, you know."

Sheila gathered up the pint glasses with a near smashing clatter of glass, and flounced off. She had said her piece, she had lit the fuse. John and Bert wished they could just sink back and disappear into the walls of the pub. *Women! They had no bloody idea!*

Arthur was a little shaken by what Sheila had said. How dare she even bring up Phyllis' name?

Maybe she had a point, though. Maybe he should talk about what he was feeling for once. For all Arthur's hurt and embarrassement, Cornisha had made him feel as if he were alive again, for the first time since Phyllis had passed away. Did he really want to sink back into that state of just existing?

But, in practice, there was little Arthur felt that he could do. It did not seem possible to really talk about what he felt with John and Bert. He didn't want to give either of them a heart attack. So it surprised him too, when he cleared his throat:

"Trust Sheila to wade right in with her size tens. But she's not stupid. I'm not myself tonight."

"After the game on Wednesday I'm not bloody surprised. Manager wants kicking out, if you ask me."

"Bert, I'm not talking about West Ham. For once!"

Arthur stopped and breathed. He'd never talked to John and Bert about what he actually felt. Truth be told, he'd never talked to anyone other than Phyllis about his feelings – and even then it was a light, light touch. With Phyllis, he reassured himself throughout their life that she knew what he felt. That she could read him. That she... knew. He did not have to tell her anything. This had made her death obliteratingly painful, as he realised that he had never really spoken to her about what she meant to him. Arthur had always felt that this was what a man should do. But, feeling as wretched as he did right here in the Spotted Duck, he was starting to think that maybe he should try his mates out just once. *Bugger it!*

He took a long draught of beer then started gruffly:

"I had a fight with that Cornisha woman last weekend. It's over. And I still feel like I've been kicked in the balls. There, I said it."

Arthur looked at John and Bert as if to challenge them to judge him on breaking their code. John stared into his pint as if he had not heard him. Bert, on the other hand, looked him straight in the eyes.

"So, what d'you fight over then Arthur? Did she refuse to go to Upton Park with you?"

John was still trying to ignore the fact that Arthur had brought up such a subject in the pub, even with Bert's diplomatic attempt to guide matters back to a more appropriate subject. He was like a conversational sheep dog, was Bert. Arthur took another deep breath and asked himself if he could really tell them the shocking truth.

"She'd been keeping a secret from me. A big one."

"Women always have secrets, Arthur. Did she have another man on the side?"

Arthur suddenly felt an unexpected pang of guilt. Cornisha didn't have anyone else on the side at all. Arthur could tell that she was devoted to him. And he had hurt her. But he couldn't help it. How the bloody hell could he be with a woman that used to be a man? *She was a man on the side.* What the bloody hell would his friends think? *Maybe he should ask them.*

"No, she didn't have another man. She used to be a man. Cornisha told me she is a transsexual."

If Arthur Bilks couldn't quite believe what he had just said it was nothing compared to the effect it had on Bert. Bert almost swallowed his dentures with surprise. He just stared at Arthur without being able to say anything. John carried on staring into his pint.

John really didn't like talking about personal matters. However, he did care about his friends. He'd also seen programmes on men who were married to transsexuals, normal men, regular blokes like them, and he thought that Arthur might have reacted differently if he hadn't been so bloody shut off from the world. With an effort John looked up from his pint.

"Has she had the operation and everything?"

Poor Bert almost swallowed his dentures again. He thought about taking them out just in case Arthur and John came out with anything else. Maybe not. Not in the Spotted Duck. He'd only get shouted at by Sheila.

Arthur looked at John, surprised himself, before deciding that, in for a penny in for a pound. He'd answer him.

"She told me that, although it would be a challenge

to have a baby, apart from that she was all woman."

"Arthur," said John pensively, "I guess that means she has been through the operations, the hormones and everything. If you never realised she was a transsexual till last weekend, then you probably never would. No matter what you got up to."

Blooming heck! Bert really did almost lose his dentures that time. He gulped down some bitter to steady himself. John ploughed on:

"So. You're telling me it's over because the one woman who's managed to put a smile on your miserable bloody face in seven years used to be a bloke? You know I know nothing about this. But I do know you need to think about it. Where is the queue of women lining up for you? How alone does alone feel?"

John could not be serious. Arthur had expected his friends to be as shocked as he was. He looked carefully at John and Bert. Bert had no idea what was going on and was drinking his pint at twice his normal speed. John was looking into the distance, but he was waiting for Arthur's reaction to what he'd just said.

"So, you don't find it disgusting then, John, that I nearly let myself fall for... a person like that?"

"Arthur, old boy. We may be from the fifties but we're living in the twenty-first century. The world has moved on." John sounded quite passionate. It was unnerving. "I've seen programmes on Sky about transsexuals. This one, she had been married for the past five years to this truck driver from Huddersfield. Bloody huge fella he was, covered in tattoos. And he loved this woman. And the size of him, no bugger ever messed with either of them."

"But John," said Arthur plaintively, "I can't get it out of my head that if I touch her, I'm touching a bloke. I've nothing against them homosexuals but I'm not one of them."

"Neither was this bloody bloke from Huddersfield on that Sky programme. Listen mate, you ever heard that expression "It if looks like a duck and it quacks like a duck, then it's probably a duck"? As for what she used to be, well, you used to be a clumsy spotty teenager. I remember it well."

"And a Leeds United supporter. Turncoat."

Bert finally managed to contribute something to the conversation. Arthur looked from John to Bert and then thought it was his turn to have a gulp of his pint.

"Alright then, John, so if it came down to it, what would you do? Would *you* be able to do the deed with a transsexual?"

"Arthur, Arthur... if that woman is as much of a lovely lady as you told us she was until last weekend, then I am damn sure I would feel myself bloody lucky if she wanted to mess around with this old body of mine. We may have all been jack-the-lads when we were younger, but for Christ's sake, we're heading for our sixties now. It takes a bloody miracle for a woman to get interested in us these days."

"Steady on, John. I'm still quite popular down the bingo club you know. Ethel even gets quite jealous at times."

Arthur looked at Bert and couldn't help smiling for the first time that evening. He'd always been a good lad, trying to make peace and lighten the mood. And John had truly surprised him.

John pursued his train of thought.

"So, Arthur, a woman who loves you, who must have had a damn difficult life, tells you her deepest, most personal secret as a sign of how much she respects you, and what do you do?"

Bugger me! John was bloody good at this. Suddenly Arthur felt incredibly guilty. Cornisha must have been heartbroken. He had been thinking of himself and how it was all too much. He had not really thought about how hard it must have been for Cornisha.

John and Bert could both see the sudden look of shame on Arthur's face. He didn't know if he could live with a transsexual – maybe he needed to watch those programmes on Sky – but how could he have been so brutal with Cornisha?

"Well, John, I behaved like a right bastard. I couldn't speak to her. I just took her home and we haven't spoken since."

As Claudia Barlettano walked down the airwalk from the plane to the arrivals area of Heathrow Airport, she noticed that someone had got rid of the brightly coloured carpet. Not a moment too soon. She remembered from her last trip to London years ago that the British seemed to be *obsessed* with carpet. *So unhygienic.*

Claudia had been taught by her mother back in Milan to pride herself on the cleanliness of her floors. In New York they got a good scrubbing by the maid every other day. She would have to remember to wash more often over the next week.

Although the immigration lady had been very courteous to her, Claudia Barlettano knew she couldn't be too careful. She took her passport back, smiled politely at the officer and quickly moved on. As soon as she was out of sight, she extracted one of her Germ-X Antibacterial Hand Sanitizing Wipes from her Prada handbag and efficiently wiped her passport down. She used a second wipe to thoroughly clean her hands before carefully replacing her newly sanitised Italian passport in the Smythson of Bond Street cover that she had purchased specially for her trip to London. She then placed them in the left-hand side pocket of her bag next to the Louis Vuitton case which kept her American passport secure, elegant and clean.

With the first trial over, Claudia was now ready to face baggage reclaim. Thank goodness she had a family-sized pack of the sanitising wipes. The flight had been full and there was a mass of people already around baggage reclaim number four. Claudia moved towards an apparent gap, only to have a large red-headed woman in a tracksuit push in front of her.

Claudia visibly shrank away from the Roba di Kappa pink velour. Claudia never understood why baggage couldn't travel business class along with people and have its own business class baggage reclaim. Thankfully, it wasn't long before she saw her Prada cocoa saffiano leather suitcase appear. Her relief was punctured by the fact that her thousand dollar gem was being squashed by a vulgar lime green metallic case that was bound with black tape. Claudia prayed that the offending object hadn't harmed her beautiful case. As she endeavoured to *excuse me* through to the belt she was once more blocked by the wall of pink Kappa velour. It was reuniting itself with the metallic green box. It was obviously rather heavy as it took quite a lot of struggling on the part of the dreadful Kappa woman. By the time the poor Prada case was finally freed, it had passed Claudia by and was about to do a second tour round the belt. Just then a gentleman, seeing Claudia's distress, deftly pulled it off for her.

"Madam?"

Although Claudia was grateful to the man for helping her out, she couldn't help but notice the thin line of black underneath a couple of his fingernails. She smiled at him, thanked him, took the bag and then quickly got out of sight. A few more sanitising wipes and she was finally ready to head into town.

Like her son before her, Claudia took a taxi. Heading through the West End on a Saturday morning, Claudia mused that she must be taking largely the same route as her darling boy had on his arrival. Ben had warned her not to expect too much from the immediate area of the Castle Lofts. He had carefully disabused her of any expectation she might have built up as to the standard of his residence. Even so, when the cab driver pulled up outside a particularly drab concrete box by an *enormous* roundabout, Claudia Barlettano had more the impression of being in one of the less attractive parts of Sesto San Giovanni in Milan's *periferia* rather than in London, Zone 1. She pursed her lips, and drew her handbag protectively to her.

"Good morning. I am here to see my son, Ben Barlettano in Flat 80. I want to surprise him. Which floor is it, please?"

Arthur Bilks looked at the impeccably turned out lady in front of him. Her elegant dress, perfect hair and effortless politeness reminded him of Cornisha. Oh, Cornisha! He told Claudia which floor it was and watched as she walked over to the lift. As she got into the lift Arthur thought of that young American. That young American who had been fooling around with the marvellous Miss Danvers. And also with that Brazilian. *The Brazilian*. Arthur had had a few more than usual with John and Bert the night before and his head was still a touch fuzzy. Suddenly he realised it was only nine o'clock in the morning and he had sent Ben's mother up to his flat *as a surprise*. If he didn't ring straight up it might not be the younger Barlettano who would be in for the surprise.

Although Rubens and Ben hadn't been particularly late the night before, Ben was still asleep when the intercom started ringing repeatedly. Trying to ignore it didn't seem to work, so he hoisted himself out of bed. Naturally, Rubens somehow seemed to be able to sleep contentedly through the noise. Ben looked at him crossly. It was always so easy for some. Ben dragged himself over to the intercom phone, and dozily answered it.

As soon as he heard Arthur Bilks utter the word *mother* Ben was one hundred per cent totally awake.

"You sent her up, Arthur? Oh no. Oh no no no."

The time it took Claudia Barlettano to clean her hands once more after having touched all those door handles and lift buttons was nowhere near enough time for Ben to get Rubens dressed and out of his flat, but at least it was time for him to get some trousers on. The thought of his mother being the third woman to be greeted at Ben's door by Ben in boxer shorts and a semi was just too shameful and too wrong for words. His mind was racing to come up with a cover story. Maybe the obvious one was best.

"Mamma! Welcome to London. Come in, come in."

"Figlio mio! Give your Mamma a hug!"

"How was your journey? You must be exhausted, Mamma."

"My journey was perfect. The beds on the plane are wonderful. I slept most of the way and I am feeling fine. But I am desperate for a proper cup of coffee. Please tell me you can make proper espresso here?"

Knowing that his mother was serious about her coffee, Ben went straight over to his rather bare kitchen cupboards and produced the espresso *macchinetta* with a flourish. He then opened the fridge and got out the *Lavazza Qualità Rossa* with another flourish. After beaming with delight and relief, Claudia's critical eyes surveyed the space in front of her. Although Ben had told his mother that his flat was modest, Claudia was shocked at just how modest it really was. Her son, in a concrete bunker, with orange swirls on the inside.

"Now, where can I hang my coat up, Ben? Shall I leave it in the bedroom? Is it through there?"

"Let me do it, Mamma. I have a little confession to make. I've joined a soccer team and we had a team night out last night that I couldn't get out of and it was, well, very British, let's say. Anyway, a friend of mine crashed here. He was so drunk he fell asleep in my bed and I had to take the other room. When I got up this morning, he was still asleep. He's still asleep in there now."

Ben smiled weakly, conscious of how feeble his excuse sounded.

Rubens had been shaken wide awake only moments earlier. He giggled to himself as he listened to Ben's conversation with Claudia. Soccer team? *What balls!* However, he sympathised. Knowing how difficult he still found it to even think of having the gay conversation with his own mother, Rubens felt uncharacteristically awkward at still being there. He thought he would leave immediately and leave Ben with his Mamma. He looked round for his clothes and then hurriedly got dressed.

Fortunately for them both, Claudia Barlettano had had very little conscious experience of gay men. It is fair to suggest that otherwise the sight of a handsome muscular Brazilian man with perfectly styled short hair cropped to zero at the sides, dressed in a pair of Dolce & Gabbana jeans and a skin tight vest with *Sexy Boy* written across the chest walking out of her son's bedroom at nine o'clock on a Saturday morning might possibly have rung an alarm bell. As it was, Claudia was immediately cheered by the sight of such a stylish young man who clearly had an eye for the finer things in life.

"Mrs Barlettano, I am delighted to meet you. My name is Rubens. I play for the same team as Ben. Ben, you didn't tell me how young your mother was! And is that Chanel, Mrs Barlettano? It's beautiful and it suits you marvellously."

Claudia Barlettano visibly swelled by a couple of inches at the back-to-back compliments coming from such a charming, beautiful and clean-looking young gentleman.

"Rubens, I am so happy to meet you. And please call me Claudia! I am so happy to see Ben has a lovely friend like you here in this city."

Ben wanted Rubens out of the flat *now*, before his mother realised something was up. Claudia on the other hand seemed to be rather taken by the young Brazilian and gave him her warmest smile.

"Rubens needs to go now, Mamma, but we'll try and meet up during the week."

"Ben, where are your manners? You cannot send a man out like that, straight from bed, without even a cup of coffee in the morning? Rubens, you must stay and have some good *Lavazza* with us."

Although Rubens had had the best of intentions, Ben's mother did seem rather fabulous and that coffee did smell good. *What harm could one espresso do?*

"Oh, Claudia, I am late already, but how can I possibly say no to you?"

"Wonderful! I knew you would like to have one. Rubens, please excuse my son. He can be a little thoughtless. He is used to having his Mamma looking after his friends when they stay overnight. Ben was always bringing one of the boys from the football team to stay the weekend with us. My Ben was very popular. I never knew if it was his personality or what the boys looked forward to in the mornings."

Blissfully unaware of how that sounded to a Rubens Ribeiro who had enjoyed quite a few Barlettano breakfasts, Claudia gave Rubens an affectionate pat on the shoulder.

"Oh my goodness, you are like a rock, Rubens! Have

342

you felt his muscles, Ben? Incredible!"

Ben couldn't be sure, but through his acute embarrassment at his mother's comments, he thought he noticed her playing with her hair, adjusting her top whilst sticking her chest out to maximum advantage, and looking slightly coquettishly at Rubens. Heavens. His kitchen was rapidly becoming a temple of embarrassment. Thankfully, the coffee was ready by now.

"You're right Mamma. Rubens has got the most incredible muscles, but they are no defence against Gabriela who told me to make sure he was on time for her this morning. So I think you had better drink your coffee, pick up your jacket and go, Rubens. Otherwise we will both be in trouble."

As Ben practically pushed Rubens out of the door, he didn't know which was worse. His mother almost catching him in bed with the Brazilian, or her then starting to flirt with the go-go boy herself. Claudia on the other hand was delighted with her welcome to London.

"Figlio mio, what a lovely young friend you have. I do hope I will be seeing more of him! Now, you must sit down and tell me all about what has happened to you since you arrived in London."

It was a fact without embroidery that, since he had arrived in London many years earlier, Hartmut Glick had never invited a lady back to his apartment. As she followed her host into the entrance hall Caroline Napier Jones felt the weight of the honour and also the oddity of being the first non-related female to enter Hartmut's hallowed sanctuary.

His space. Did this make her a space oddity?

"Please, would you remove your footwear, my dear?"

Hartmut indicated a modest shoe rack with space free for two pairs of shoes. Next to that was an umbrella stand with two large umbrellas standing up and two smaller folding ones hanging down. Hartmut then opened a small wardrobe next to the umbrella rack and hung up his raincoat. He then carefully hung Caroline's coat next to the other all-weather protective garments, all positoned ready for use on appropriate days. After then placing his wallet, keys and loose change in a receptacle on a low table next to the shoe rack, Hartmut turned once again to Caroline.

"I believe we are ready to go in now."

Hartmut's lounge was not what Caroline had been expecting. She had him down as a twenty-first century ascetic monk-like figure who would pay little attention to form and swear by minimalist functionalism. Reality however spoke of two luxurious leather sofas with four opulent ruby red velvet cushions matching the floor to ceiling curtains. Her bare feet sank into a fluffy thick cream carpet which had obviously never even come close to anything approaching outside dirt. Three walls were painted in tasteful ivory, whilst the fourth was covered with what looked like antique Chinese wallpaper. It was beautiful – quite irresistible. Caroline had to make an effort not to run her hand over the gorgeous relief flowers. At one end of the huge room was an enormous old carved cherry-wood desk with an inlay of burgundy leather. An ultra-thin MacBook perched atop it as a necessary concession to modern life. The room was dominated, however, by the splendid glass and mahogany display case positioned between the two windows. It housed Hartmut's collection of Franklin Mint Fabergé eggs. Hartmut was gratified to see that Caroline headed over to it immediately, seduced by the pieces. Her green eyes lingered over his treasures.

Hartmut smiled:

"Sadly, as I am neither a museum, nor a prince, nor even just a fantastically rich commoner, they cannot be the real Fabergé pieces. Nevertheless their beauty is enough for me. To say nothing of the history. I feel as if I am in the shadow of the Winter Palace as I gaze at them."

"Do I detect a hint of Russian romance in you, Mr Glick?"

Caroline was charmed both by the room into which she had just entered, and also by Hartmut's difficulty in dealing with her comment. She did not however dare to venture to use Hartmut's first name when addressing him. She did not wish to embarrass him by making him choose whether to spoil the moment in correcting her or to just live with the somewhat imperfect mode of address.

"Romance can have many meanings, Ms Napier Jones. If you are talking of fripperies such as Valentine cards, red roses and gentlemen getting down on one knee then you would be sadly mistaken if you thought that Hartmut Glick could possibly indulge in such fancies. However, if, as I believe you intend, you are talking of the appreciation of how real beauty can improve our experience in this world, then it might be said that I am indeed a romantic. The baubles and gimmicks of today are merely man's poor attempts to ape true romance. The bouquet of flowers trying to imitate nature's beauty; the romantic photo attempting to recreate a personalised version of Botticelli's Venus; the handwritten verse unconsciously paying homage to the Bard's sonnets."

"But surely your Franklin Mints are but a tribute to the master Fabergé, Mr Glick? Can I not detect in that an attempt at recreating your own version of the romance of a lost age?"

Hartmut Glick stared hard at Caroline Napier Jones for a moment, before unexpectedly directing another generous smile in her direction.

"My dear Ms Napier Jones. I cannot challenge your logic in that regard and fear I must reassess my own human proclivity at recreating a pale shadow where the original is sadly not available. I am apparently not so different to those whose sensitivities I generally consider beneath me. However, I trust that you will not make a habit of locating my inconsistencies."

Caroline noted with pleasure how Hartmut seemed to be quite comfortable with admitting potential mistake. He really was the most delightfully rational creature. Although he was clearly a ferociously intelligent man who had achieved much in his life, Caroline noted no trace of the ego that often marred such men. For the first time since she had met Hartmut Glick, Caroline Napier Jones wanted to make love to the man without the fun stuff; just her and Hartmut trying vanilla. She feared it would not be to his taste and feared also that it was a sign she was getting herself in deeper than maybe Hartmut could cope with.

She let her toes sink into the carpet. All in good time. She was happy. They might even venture to try the missionary position tonight.

After seeing the splendour of Flat 80, The Castle Lofts, Claudia Barlettano had decided to ring her hotel. Fortunately, they were able to let her check in two days early.

All was well. Ben had just left her at the Chesterton Hotel in Mayfair and was heading into Soho to have a quick drink with Rubens before going home for an early night.

The highlight of Ben's day with his mother had been lunch with Kelly Danvers. Although she had very much approved of Kelly, his mother had shown a little more restraint than she had with Rubens. But then again, if his mother had started flirting with a woman then Ben really would have felt physically unwell.

Kelly had behaved perfectly. In fact, if Ben had not been such a fool as to follow a drunken impulse that fateful Saturday evening after the day in Victoria Park, today's lunch might not have had to be make-believe.

As he walked down Old Compton Street amongst the throngs of people all eagerly hurrying to get to their next drink, Ben imagined for a moment how it would be if Kelly were the person he was planning his future with and Rubens was just the occasional naughty flirtation causing him to idly wonder what it might be like to…

"Hey, gostoso, over here!"

Looking over at Rubens waving at him from a table

in front of Costa Coffee, Ben realised that he had just understood what the true nature of the relationship was. Ben might be thinking it was somewhat more serious, but he was just the Brazilian's plaything, the *gostoso* who had been fun to flirt with, the American who, try as he might, had never earned himself even one of those looks of complicity that Jamal regularly enjoyed. After he had got himself a caffè latte and lit himself a Marlboro Light, he sat down and looked Rubens straight in the eye.

Rubens looked back at him:

"I can't believe you still smoke. Apart from being so last century, do you know what that stuff does to your body?"

Of course Ben knew exactly what cigarettes did. Of course he would give them up, but it was harder than it looked. He also thought privately that such concerns were rich coming from someone like Rubens who seemed to put the contents of a small pharmacy down his throat or up his nose of a weekend. Ben told himself that it wasn't the time for that lecture.

He took a deep drag:

"So. How do you see our future then, Rubens?"

So. That was how you shocked Rubens. Rubens looked at Ben as if he had just asked the most inappropriate, tactless, *vulgar* question imaginable. He shook his head in disbelief before recovering his composure.

"Well, yours would be a lot better if you would give up those damn cigarettes!"

It was what Ben had needed to hear, or, rather, needed to observe. The crashing sound of reality checking in. The thought of a future with Ben was clearly a concept that hadn't even entered the Brazilian's head. Ben suddenly relaxed, leaned over and gave Rubens a big kiss on the lips.

Such a public display of affection was a little too much for a rather conservative looking man and woman who happened to be passing right by the boys' table at that point. The man shot a highly disapproving look at the boys. The woman simply looked uncomfortable.

Rubens noticed immediately, his eyes flashing with irritation.

"Never seen two men kiss before? You're in Soho, darlings. We do much worse when we're in private, you know."

Rubens seemed delighted with the couple's horrified reaction as they hurried off.

"Get used to it!" he called after them, and chuckled.

Ben sighed.

"Oh Rubens, you are perfect. In so many ways. But you are not perfect for *me*. I know. I understand that you hadn't probably even thought of me in those terms. I think we should go back to just being friends again."

"Are you dumping me, Ben?"

"Oh come on, Rubens. You would have to be *with* me before I could dump you. Sure, you have spent a few nights in my flat, but are you *honestly* telling me that in your heart you consider yourself my boyfriend?"

Maybe it was the relaxed, almost amused expression on Ben's face that made Rubens decide that this was all fine, on balance. Rubens had been wondering how to play this one out. Should he pretend to be hurt, nay, devastated, and about to throw himself under the number 38 bus in Shaftesbury Avenue? He decided that the telenovela performance should be put on hold.

Ben had a point, after all. Rubens shrugged, not uncaringly:

"I have really enjoyed being with you, Ben, but I reckon you have understood that I am just not ready to settle down."

Rubens paused for a moment, before deciding it was definitely not a good idea to mention Ben's rather lacklustre performances in bed. He continued with something more diplomatic.

"Also, I think I am a far more faithful friend than I am a boyfriend."

Ben thought that was manifestly right. It would be somewhat hard to believe if he pretended to be surprised or offended that Rubens had gone off with other men. Ben had after all left Rubens himself, free for the hungry and lustful, in Spartacus Spa. So he just laughed and rubbed Rubens shoulder affectionately.

"So, friends from now on?"

"Friends. I will miss some parts of our relationship, you know. At least I can tell you all my secrets now, gostoso. I need someone else to talk to, not just Jamal. But you must promise me that you will come out with us sometimes – you stop traffic when I dress you up."

"Sure thing, Rubens. I like dancing. Maybe I can learn a thing or two from you about how to boogie."

Ben made his way home alone, strangely happy. Rubens

had seemed almost relieved, after a moment's feigning hurt at being *dumped*.

Ben realised that the relationship had, in fact, been weighing on him for some time. It hadn't been right. In a weird way, he felt closer to Rubens now than he had in weeks. They understood each other perfectly.

18

Cupid and Psychos

"Have you heard about the trouble in paradise, girls?"

Kelly and Monique had decided to go for a Sunday afternoon swim. A quick dip had swiftly led to the Health Café for the after-swim smoothie. Although Millie Myers' scoops weren't usually that earth-shattering, she was nevertheless a good source of local gossip. Kelly decided to take the bait.

"What's up, Millie? Don't tell me your cousin Kylie has got into another catfight over the sunbeds in *The Bronzed Elephant*?"

"Oh no, Kelly. Even more serious than that. And anyway Kylie doesn't go down there any more. She's upgraded. She's now using *Fake Bake at Home*. Do you know it? You should. It's one of those spray tans that Paris Hilton and Jordan use too much of. Gives you that perfect non-streak look, she tells me. Actually, she's planning a Spray Tan Party just before Christmas if you fancy it? You should always look your best for the festive season, I say. Think of the mistletoe, Monique!"

More than mistletoe, Paris Hilton and Jordan put

Monique in mind of camel toe. Why would she possibly wish to look like Paris or Jordan? She smiled gingerly at Millie:

"I think Kelly and I might pass on that, Millie. It would be so disappointing if we didn't in fact look like an A-List celebrity after a *Fake Bake* party. I suspect we would fail entirely in that endeavour. It could ruin my Christmas, chérie."

Kelly reverted to Millie's news.

"So, what has happened, then Millie? Come on! Spill the organic fair trade beans."

"Well, ladies, this is it. Rubens came here about an hour ago to pick up some stuff he'd left here. And what would you know? It seems that he and Ben are no longer an item!"

She watched the girls closely to see if their faces registered the appropriate levels of surprise. Bingo! They had manifestly *not* heard the news from anyone else. Millie relaxed and gave them a satisfied, beaming smile. Inexplicably, there was something of a silent *I told you so* about her delighted expression.

Kelly was momentarily stunned. Yes, that was news indeed. Why did it hit her as much as it did? Why would she even care? She managed to hide her confusion. She was far too proud to let Millie Myers know that she was troubled one way or another about Ben Barlettano's status.

Monique Mottin wasn't really in the least bit surprised. That Brazilian was too much of a party boy to be tied down. She could also see straight through Kelly's "Am I bothered?"

expression. It was a very thin and very poor mask. Action was required, yet again. Monique thought that she should immediately convene an impromptu session of boyfriend clinic. She needed to drag Kelly away from Millie.

So she sipped her smoothie as fast as the first glass of champagne at a reception where bubbles were running out and you wanted to get your paws on a second one. Then, for Kelly's benefit, she flicked her eyes over to the door.

"I cannot believe it, Millie. I thought they were so in love? It just shows you how these gay boys are sluts really. I'll bet one of them was sleeping around. Probably that Brazilian go-go boy. We know he's beautiful. He knows he's beautiful. Oh, he is beautiful, lovely – but would you trust him, chérie? My French peachy bottom, you would. Anyway, Kelly, I'm sorry to drag you away but you said you would help me with that project I have for work? We'd best get on with it if we are to have any chance of getting things moving. See you tomorrow, Millie. Sorry to rush off… "

Back in the safety of the flat, Kelly turned to Monique with a wholly different expression on her face:

"I can't say I'm surprised, Monique, but it is quite unsettling to think that Ben is single again."

Monique faced her friend, hands on hips, surveying her severely:

"Whatever you do, please don't take a bottle of wine up to his flat tonight. It was just about forgiveable the first time, given that you are only a simple country girl from Baton Rouge. A second time, however, would be shockingly desperate and thoroughly embarrassing."

Kelly agreed:

"Yes, absolutely. No way, Monique. Quite apart from the fact that he's taken his mother to Cambridge today and he won't be back till late, I am not that much of a fool. Neither am I drunk this time."

"Well, not yet, you aren't. Still, good for you, chérie! That's the spirit. It's taken me so long to build up the little bit of respect I have for you. I wouldn't want to lose it so quickly."

Monique's straight-talking teasing dressed with a smile always managed to make Kelly feel better. Kelly determined to win through over dangerous and foolhardy impulses. She had been very grateful to Monique for having dragged her away from Millie, before Kelly could say anything she might regret.

That probability had loomed large.

As soon as she had heard the news, Kelly's mind had gone back to Saturday lunchtime, when she had been passed off as Ben's girlfriend for Claudia's benefit. The fake kisses had made her tingle. Imagining that Ben might have been planning to split up with Rubens as he was kissing her made her feel dizzy. She hated the symptoms of another silly schoolgirl crush and needed Monique to shake her out of it.

"No, Monique, I think Ben is great and he'a a good friend. But I've got to be realistic. He is *just* a friend. I am not that much of a masochist as to want to compete with every attractive woman *and* every attractive gay man in London."

"I agree utterly. I just hope you can stay strong. You have the SBK cocktail party this week. We all know what happens when feelings and drinks mix. I think that is why the cocktail was invented, in fact. Anyway you don't need me to remind you what happens when you have a few drinks inside you."

"Well, darling Monique, that is why you are coming with me. You can forget about Harry for the night. You will be my chaperone."

"Yes, it's funny about Harry. I think we might be making progress, you know. He has promised that he is going to take me away for a romantic weekend in Paris. We will have a conference or something as cover. He has never said this to me before. I think Cupid might have finally got Harry with one of those arrows. It would be a step, at least."

Boyfriend clinic was truly the graveyard of common sense at times. However, Kelly felt stronger and more relaxed, and Monique felt happier and hopeful. Fully aware of the irony, they decided it was the right night to start the *Desperate Housewives* marathon they had been planning ever since Monique had bought the box set months ago.

Amber Bluett usually found the forty-minute trip to Basildon to be something between boring and depressing. It reminded her, grimly, of the life she had stepped up from. But today was different, and purposeful. The sight of the seventies station, with the kind of façade that only an architect could love, made Amber smile, albeit a little maliciously.

She was going to spend the day with the family. Her mother was always happy when she came back for Sunday dinner. That was good. It was nice to make her mother happy. However, today Amber was really there to see her brother Darren. After the meal, she suggested they go for. a walk together.

"So how's it going with that problem of yours then, sis?"

"Yes, that's why I'm here. I think we've got a chance to get her without being caught."

As Amber told Darren, and also Nathan, who had tagged along with them, about the plan for the fancy dress party in the Lofts, Darren started to wear that half-smile, half-smirk which meant he was feeling very good or planning something very bad. Or both.

"So I reckon," analysed Amber, "that with me helping out there, I can get something in the bitch's drink, which makes her lose it, and then you two in the fancy dress can take advantage when she leaves. You wear masks so no one knows who you are. She gets done over and nobody suspects Amber Bluett of nothing. Like you told me. Subtle."

Although he had been fool enough to manage to get himself caught and spend time inside, Darren was by far the sharpest member of the Bluett family. His mother always told him that if he had applied that brain of his to his studies instead of getting up to no good, then he might have been a doctor or a professor or something by now. But he'd always preferred to walk on the wrong side of the road and he had no intention of changing now. He just didn't want to get caught again.

"This needs careful preparation. Planning. You get some feeling going against the target, so she may not want to linger at the party."

Amber smiled. That would do it perfectly.

"You spike the drink. That's easy. Nathan and me are going to be wearing the disguise. But we still need a reason to be there. Who are we going to be?"

Darren wasn't expecting an answer from his siblings. Amber could be crafty, but she didn't think that straight, especially not when revenge was on her mind. As for Nathan, the baby of the family, he just got by on his boyish good looks. He appealed to most women, not least because of his misleadingly vulnerable expression, and the toned taut body that came of spending many of his waking hours playing football. However, when it came to using his head... well, that's why Nathan had a brother like Darren.

"OK, got it. We've just moved into one of them new flats there. There's like hundreds of them, right, so nobody knows everybody. We heard some people talking about the party in the café, and we thought it sounded cool. Now we just need to work out how me and loverboy here are going to get close to Kelly."

Nathan grinned lasciviously:

"When she sees what's going on here, she'll fall at my feet just like all women do!"

"You're going to be wearing a mask and costume, Nathan. She isn't going to be able to see your face. Jesus H Christ, do you ever think about using that head of yours for something other than looking pretty?"

Nathan loved his women, and thought of himself as something really special in the looks department, but he hero-worshipped his big brother and this deflated him badly. His swagger wilted. He looked at Darren like a poodle caught mid-bath.

Darren was thinking:

"We'll need to seduce her. Plain and simple. We've got to work out what to talk to this girl about. What she's interested in. Where she's from. We've got to get the chat right. We'll keep them guns of yours as backup, right, Nathan?"

"I know where she's from. We were talking about that TV show with the vampires and the guy who can turn into a dog. She said she's from the same place."

"You mean, Louisiana, sis? Cool, well, that's a start. Now if you are good you find out about her hobbies, her music, what she watches on TV, what she hates about London, everything. Then when Nathan and me accidentally start chatting to her at that party, it'll be as if we are soulmates. Why, we've just been waiting to meet each other all these years. When I ask her what the best part of the building is to get a good view of the city she'll probably volunteer to take me up. Those drugs make you dumb, and reckless. We end up in her flat, Nathan joins me and we do the deed. My only worry is that with my charm and loverboy's looks there, she might actually enjoy what's going to happen to her."

Half-hidden behind a copy of the Racing Post in the front seat of his old Citroen, Arthur Bilks felt like a stalker as he watched Cornisha Burrows open her front door. John was right. Arthur had been appallingly wrong. He could not, and should not, throw everything away.

Arthur was feeling awful about making Cornisha cry.

But he was also feeling apprehensive about the sort of reaction he would get from her. She might just slam the door in his face. And could he blame her? After promising her the world, he hadn't even been able to speak to her, or look at her, on the way back from Frinton. As he went over that journey again he could feel himself blushing in shame.

With an effort he got out of the car, picked up the orchid he had bought, breathed in deeply and walked towards the main door of Cornisha's block. The main door was open so he went in and took the lift up to her floor. His heart was beating as if he were a schoolboy on his first date or at his first match. He knocked softly on her front door.

When Cornisha saw him standing there holding a beautiful pink orchid, all her resolutions to be an ice maiden melted away. She held a hand to her cheek and started crying. They were gentle tears, but she felt completely overwhelmed. If she hadn't been so happy to see him, she would have been furious with herself.

"Can I come in, Cornisha? Even though I don't deserve to, after the abominable, unforgivable way I treated you the other day?"

"Oh. Please, Arthur. Do."

As Arthur came into her flat, Cornisha felt as if her heart were about to explode. She wanted so much to embrace him. With a painful effort, Cornisha kept her distance and instead resorted to the time-honoured British way of ameliorating awkward, difficult situations. She took refuge in the offer of a hot beverage.

"A cup of tea would be lovely. Thank you, Cornisha."

Sitting on opposite sides of the coffee table in Cornisha's lounge, neither of them knew where to begin. Arthur as usual found it difficult to approach any conversation that dealt with feelings and so just sat there looking slightly inadequate and self-conscious. Cornisha wanted to know if the orchid meant he was going to try again, or whether this was just an apology, and part of the definitive break-up. It was too much to bear for her. She could feel the tears about to start streaming down her face again. How ridiculous, for someone of her age!

"Arthur, I am so grateful that you came. But I need to know. Is this a final goodbye?"

Arthur nearly spilled his tea when he heard Cornisha's words. *How the hell could she possibly think that he had come all that way with a present, and was sitting down in her lounge, if he wanted to say goodbye to her? Women! He would never fully understand them!*

She was definitely a woman.

Arthur carefully put his tea down on the table, leaned over and took both of Cornisha's hands in his own.

"Cornisha, I did come here to apologise, yes. But I also came here to say that I want to ask for another chance. It is going to take me a little getting used to, but I know you are the same wonderful woman who I was falling in love with the day before you told me. You haven't changed and so – why should I?"

Arthur got up and pulled Cornisha to him. It was their first proper passionate embrace. It felt pretty, pretty good.

The first drink at the annual SBK cocktail party also felt

pretty good. With four hundred thrusting young lawyers and a coterie of support staff gathered in one space, alcohol was a pretty essential social lubricant. It smoothed off some of the rough edges of all that naked ambition and mutual contempt.

Cornisha Burrows was an expert at dealing with this kind of situation, being both an integral part of the organisation whilst also managing to glide serenely above it all. She had been feeling so much better since Arthur's visit the day before. She remained troubled, however, by the cloud hanging over Hartmut Glick.

She was feeling especially awkward as she was standing with Harry Gumpert, who had come without his wife, Sarah. He had no idea that Arthur Bilks had accidentally overheard his conversation with Nicholas Casterway and had told Cornisha what he had heard. The conversation tonight did seem rather stilted to him, but he put it down to Cornisha worrying about the organisation of the event.

Cornisha was relieved to see the familiar figure of Kelly Danvers making a beeline for her and Harry.

Harry looked upon Kelly with marked approval.

Kelly was looking lovely. She was wearing a silver dress which looked expensive and glamorous. The silver dappled like water upon her, flowing on the curves of her body, and stopping mid-calf for an elegant effect.

The perfect dress for the bedroom floor. Harry looked her up and down appreciatively:

"Kelly, how lovely you look. Oh, and there's Monique. Hello."

Monique Mottin had been trailing the American girl and Harry hadn't seen her as Kelly swept up to them. Cornisha's acutely honed sensibilities told her that Harry was attempting to hide the true nature of his relationship with Monique. Cornisha also noted the fact that Harry seemed every so slightly disappointed to see Monique, probably because it meant the old fox wouldn't be free to play the field that night. Passion was making a very foolish young woman of an otherwise splendid girl. Plus ça change, thought Cornisha. As always, she affected to notice nothing.

As it was, Monique was also looking good, in a bright blue silk number that fitted in all the right places. She was a dazzling young woman. Harry felt a surge of desire. Well, if you can't have 'em all…

Kelly smiled.

"Hi Cornisha. Hello, Harry. I thought we were going to be late. These French girls take so long to get ready. I told Monique it was just a boring old work party but Monique obviously thought she needed to look her best for some reason."

Kelly looked as if she were daring Harry to respond. Of course, he wouldn't disappoint.

"I wish everyone took such obvious care to look as wonderful as you do, Monique."

Harry could say that with great sincerity. The wish rang out true in an evening bulging with men in ill-fitting suits and women wearing items that drew attention principally to their brassiere straps and bingo wings.

Kelly grimaced:

"Oh, it's good to have a boss who really can charm the birds down from the trees. Speaking of someone who could do with a few lessons, there's my favourite young New Yorker over there. I'll be back in a minute. I just need to ask him about something."

Kelly had wanted to have a conversation with Ben ever since she had heard about the break-up. Ben's mother was in town, however, and Kelly herself had been away on a training course for the last couple of days. Now she saw her chance, as she ambushed Ben at the buffet.

"Ben, my darling, how are you? I feel as if we haven't spoken in days. Gosh: seared Orkney scallops in an aged Modena balsamic jus."

"That's because we haven't spoken in days. More's the pity. Try the fatigued Piedmontese artichoke hearts in an organic herb vinaigrette. I'm good – thanks, Kelly. You OK?"

"Mmm. Mini porc medallions in a curry-scented foam. I'm fine, apart from being a bit shocked to hear about you and Rubens."

As she said Rubens' name, Ben looked around nervously. He remembered the word of caution about not broadcasting his private life at work. Kelly knew she should be as offhand as possible about it. However, seeing him in what looked like a new suit, that seemed cut to perfection for his cut-to-perfection physique, she couldn't help but notice how hot he was. Pure and simple sex. She could feel all her best intentions melting away. The champagne that she had been turbo-drinking was colluding with her pent-up desire to crush any resistance offered by her weakening sensible side.

"Can we talk about that in private, Kelly? You know

what it's like at work."

"Sure, of course, sorry. It's just been so hard to get together the last few days. When are you free? Let me look in my calendar, oh, where's my phone?"

As Kelly checked her bag for her iPhone, Ben was struck by how Kelly's silver dress did just what all women aimed for their outfits to do for them. She was truly spectacular. *Why the hell had he so spectacularly blown his chances with that girl?*

"Oh, damn it! I must have left my phone in my coat. I need to go to the cloakroom and get it. Fancy coming down with me? With these heels, the champagne and those steep stairs I might just need a big strong man to keep me upright."

If Ben had had any doubt about wanting to go with her, Kelly's infectious laughter instantly took care of it. He had already had enough small talk with his colleagues about what a marvellous opportunity he had, and how he was enjoying London, without of course telling anyone anything at all. Escaping for a few minutes with one of the very few people he actually wanted to spend time with was a pretty enticing option.

Kelly was in no danger of toppling over on the stairs down to the cloakroom. She was glad to have Ben alone for a while.

They went into the cloakroom, which was a large meeting room converted for the occasion. Today it offered rail upon rail of hired coat racks, lined up smoothly, packed with expensive coats looking rather out of place in the mundane work surroundings. Kelly found her coat and with a sigh of relief pulled her iPhone out of the inside pocket.

"Thank God for that. I hate losing phones. Now, you're going to tell me about Rubens, aren't you? I've been worried about you, Ben."

Ben couldn't help but wonder if he should read anything into the sympathetic hand on his arm that seemed to linger for longer than sympathy should warrant. But then he often read things into a situation merely because he wanted to believe them, so he decided to dismiss the thought.

He shook his head.

"Well, it's quite simple. Rubens is great, but maybe I'm looking for a relationship. It's great to have fun, go out, but being alone most nights sucks. And he won't change. When it came down to it, it was actually pretty easy. I guess I have never been in love with him. I was just... dazzled."

"Can I ask you a personal question, Ben?"

Not knowing what Kelly was going to come out with, Ben just nodded.

"Given what I have seen, this is going to sound really stupid, but, do you think that you didn't completely fall for Rubens because actually you aren't totally, well, you aren't completely, well, *gay*? Oh God, it's just that you didn't and still don't give me that gay vibe that I normally get clear and strong."

Kelly was picking up on exactly what he himself was thinking. Should he tell her? Could he tell her?

"Kelly, it's an honest question. I reckon I should give you an honest answer. I definitely have an attraction for men, even though I never realised it until I came to London. One man in particular, mind you. However I still get turned on by women, too. Well, some women. One woman in particular. You, actually."

Ben looked at Kelly and put his hands on her shoulders. She was looking surprised. He leant in swiftly to kiss her. It happened quite fast and he kissed her passionately, his tongue finding what seemed to be a natural place in her mouth. His hand moved down to her breast and gently caressed it, slipping into the dress which like all evening wear provided easy access. She grabbed him and pulled him to her. Their bodies pressed together like tectonic plates, finding room, forcing connections and contacts. It felt very good indeed. They kissed hungrily, their hands and minds going everywhere, until before they knew it they were semi-naked in the meeting room, amongst all those outer garments whose respectable owners were indulging in no more than a little alcohol and rather stilted but potentially career-enhancing conversations one floor above them. As one does at such events.

One of those oblivious owners, Cornisha Burrows, was alternately amused and irritated by her own stilted conversation with Harry and Monique.

Whilst she couldn't help but enjoy seeing Harry squirm slightly as he endeavoured to give the impression that he had only met Monique Mottin once or twice before, Cornisha was also offended by the easy deceit that he was capable of. As she was getting less and less amused by the play acting around her, they were interrupted by a voice she hadn't heard for some time, a voice which was used to being obeyed in the milieu of SBK.

"Cornisha Burrows and Harry Gumpert! Well, how the devil are you both? And, Miss, pleased to meet you. My name is Nicholas Casterway."

Cornisha had never been fooled by Nicholas' fake bonhomie. She knew that he was an egotistical monster and a master of deception. He would thoroughly enjoy smiling sympathetically at the very moment that he stuck the knife into his victim. Fortunately, Cornisha was also a mistress of disguising her emotions. Nicholas Casterway had never got the slightest inkling of the deep dislike that was harboured within that elegant green dress.

"Welcome back, Mr Casterway." she said evenly, "We have missed you. How wonderful that you should make your first appearance at our cocktail party. It wouldn't have been the same without you."

As Cornisha nodded at Nicholas Casterway, it struck her that maybe she shouldn't be so harsh on Harry Gumpert. He was actually far less skilled than she in the faking department. He looked like a lost puppy. Maybe she was offended more by the fact that the dear man was just so amateurish at it, whilst all the while affecting such a worldly air. Harry, do try harder to be a complete scumbag, she thought. If a thing is worth doing, it's worth doing well.

"Cornisha, I am just delighted to be back amongst our merry band. Trips are indeed marvellous, but this is where I belong, with the people I know. Please forgive me, though, ladies, for I must steal away Harry here. Sadly I have some rather urgent but also rather dull business to take care of and I wouldn't want to impair your enjoyment of the evening."

Cornisha watched as Nicholas' smile instantly faded as he turned away from her and Monique and led Harry across the room towards the door which led to the atrium. Although Monique Mottin was actually an extremely charming young woman, with whom Cornisha would normally have gladly indulged in conversation, her attention was utterly diverted from the engaging Frenchwoman when she saw Nicholas speak to Hartmut Glick and then the three men exit the room together. *What on earth was going on?*

As Hartmut had been warned by Cornisha, he wasn't surprised when Nicholas Casterway smiled at him. Those cold grey Casterway eyes gave nothing away, but Nicholas asked Hartmut if he could have a word in private. He was slightly surprised to see Harry Gumpert in tow. *It must be important, for Harry to leave a party*. Hartmut was suddenly filled with a sense of foreboding.

Although Ben's hands were surprisingly expert and she was getting carried away by his technique far more than she would have imagined, Kelly's perennially sharp senses still managed to pick up the sounds of voices and footsteps in the corridor outside the cloakroom.

"Ben, there's someone coming!"

Not me. Not yet, thought Ben.

Kelly's urgent whisper wrenched Ben from his trance. It took a moment of staring at Kelly like a rabbit in the headlights to kick his thoughts into action.

"We have to hide. Get moving! Behind the coat rails!"

Ben felt like he was in one of those predictable early evening sitcoms as he and Kelly desperately adjusted their clothing and burrowed like frightened foxes into the coat rails. As luck would have it, there was a recess at the end of the wall behind one of the rails where they could be completely hidden. They shrank into place as the door opened.

"Let's go in here." said a familiar and authoritative voice. "For what I have to say I do not want others seeing us talking. It's not ideal, but it will do."

Peering between a faux mink stole and an elegant green coat, Kelly saw, aghast, the holy trinity of hierarchy that was Casterway, Gumpert and Glick coming into the cloakroom. From his vantage point in the recess, Ben could not see them at all.

Nicholas Casterway turned to Hartmut with a tight smile:

"I understand this must come as a bit of a shock to you, my dear Hartmut, but I hope you also see that SBK must take action over this. When I was contacted by the blackmailer, I was utterly flabbergasted and simply could not believe it. But sadly, I am afraid I have now seen the distasteful video and well, I fear this is a serious danger for the partnership."

"What exactly did you see on this videotape? Are you sure this is not a fake?"

"Hartmut, it pains me to say that it appeared to be scenes of a sado-masochistic sexual nature and I believe the… scenes are definitely genuine. However you deserve to see them yourself. Possibly you would then be able to verify if it is indeed yourself in that video and not some clever jiggery pokery. I must ask you however if you do frequent places of that nature."

Hearing sado-masochistic sex allegations in the cloakroom almost made Kelly Danvers fall into the coats and give the game away. Ben just caught her in time. They looked at each other in amazement.

The voice of the man speaking to Hartmut sounded faintly familiar to Ben. By now Ben too was peeping through the narrow gap in the coats. The man had his back to the rail. Ben had no idea who that bald head belonged to. Ben could just make out Harry Gumpert who was standing in silence next to Hartmut Glick. As the man asked Hartmut whether he went to places *of that nature* Hartmut's face took on a troubled expression.

Hartmut was not a liar. However, he was a lawyer and immediately recognised the danger of admitting anything to that shark Nicholas Casterway. The level of his trust in Casterway was accurately positioned at nil. Hartmut wouldn't have put it past him to invent the whole story just to get Hartmut to admit to something damaging. He decided that under no circumstances would he admit to anything before seeing incontrovertible evidence.

"Firstly, I am in no position to say whether or not I frequent a place when I simply do not know the nature of this place. That would seem clear to any observer. Secondly, even if I knew where you meant, I would no more talk about aspects of my personal life, whether to confirm or deny, than I would perform the Highland Fling in front of the entire partnership upstairs. Thirdly, any person in my position would be a fool to voluntarily admit to something which appears to be so damaging before seeing any evidence. So, my dear Nicholas, I am sorry to disappoint you, but I fear I must see this videotape of yours before I can possibly offer any views as to its veracity."

"I see, Hartmut, and I have to say I fully understand and agree with your wisdom on the matter. I must ask you, however, to bear in mind that if it is genuine and you are shown to be participating in such an… open-minded act, then I worry about how this will affect the partnership. Even if we were to pay the blackmailer, there would surely be copies and I would worry that the problem would simply return when the blackmailer required more money."

"So what are you saying to me, Nicholas?"

Nicholas affected a look of great sadness.

"My dear, dear, Hartmut, all I can say is that if the videotape showed myself in such an act, I fear that I would consider my position in such a high profile role at SBK to be simply untenable. And I would fully expect my dear colleagues not to stop me in my chosen solution, if they were considering the best interests of the partnership. So, painful as it is to say, I would expect a gentleman such as yourself to aid us in resolving this embarrassing and potentially damaging situation. However, I am indeed hopeful that there is some explanation that will render all of this dreadful hypothesising utterly redundant."

Nicholas' warm smile, which seemed reminiscent of Kaa from the Jungle Book, disappeared as soon as Hartmut shot his reply straight back.

"Nicholas, I see you are hoping that you have something on me so that you can force me to resign. I will certainly not expect any support from you at any point in the future. How nice to have the true meaning of partnership demonstrated so neatly. As for you, Harry Gumpert, I might have expected more from you. Or maybe not. In any case I will see you both in the office tomorrow. Kindly have this video available so that I may clear my name. Goodnight, gentlemen."

Hartmut strode out of the cloakroom leaving Nicholas and Harry alone. Or so they thought. Ben and Kelly had barely been breathing. It hadn't stopped Kelly's dress slithering down, revealing rather beautiful breasts. Although deliciously distracted, Ben was annoyed that he hadn't seen the snake's face, as he had no doubt that it would have been a study in sliminess, laced with fake concern and false respect.

"Well, Harry, that was awkward. I am afraid there is no doubt though. I have seen the disgusting tape and I would wager my entire career that it is indeed our friend Hartmut in there. I have seen more of Hartmut than I would ever have thought possible. He will not be able to deny it. And if he can't, then I will ensure that he is out of the partnership."

Just then it was Nicholas and Harry's turn to hear approaching footsteps. They immediately left the cloakroom, greeting the person who was coming in.

Once again Ben and Kelly held their breath, but as Cornisha Burrows extracted her fake fur stole from the rack she suddenly espied some bare flesh. Moving the other coats aside, she found herself staring straight at the half naked bodies of Ben and Kelly.

"Really. I thought you both looked very nice upstairs. There was no need to come down and change. Anyway, my carriage is waiting. I shall see you both in the office tomorrow."

Before Ben or Kelly could intervene, Cornisha had swept out of the cloakroom and was on her way home, wrapped up warmly in her fake fur, armed with the exhilarating expectation of seeing Arthur Bilks for a late night cup of cocoa on his way home from the Lofts.

Ben and Kelly stepped into the open. Ben zipped Kelly up, and she adjusted his bow tie.

Kelly was aghast:

"I told you Nicholas Casterway had something against Hartmut Glick, Ben. What a weasel. He seemed to actually be enjoying bullying poor Hartmut. But what the hell do you think Hartmut has done? I mean, can you see him in some S&M club? Can it be true? This is a *major* scandal!"

So the bald man was Nicholas Casterway! All this, on the man's first day back in the office. Ben could imagine that Hartmut might have secrets. Kelly could imagine Nicholas being rather happy for such a weapon to fall into his hands.

"What do we do, Kelly? Poor Hartmut. I like the man. Surely he can't be forced out of SBK because of something he does in his own private life? As long as it's not illegal, surely one's private life is just that. Why should it affect the quality of his work?"

"Since when was it about reason, Ben? It depends on what some of our stuffier clients might think. Imagine, if the video gets into the public domain, who in this mad hypocritical world would want Hartmut Glick as their legal representative? It is a delicate and difficult situation."

As more footsteps came towards the cloakroom, Ben and Kelly finally left their nest of coats and hangers and headed back upstairs.

In the excitement of what they had just overheard they had momentarily forgotten that they had just made out.

Ben decided that there was no way he was going to screw it up this time.

"Would you consider coming home with me tonight, then, Kelly? I want you, baby, and I have done since the first day I saw you."

Although his technique wasn't exactly romantic, it did have the virtue of being direct, and from Ben of all people, Kelly needed straight talking, to say nothing of the straight acting of course. She gave him a big smile as they grabbed two glasses of champagne from one of the waiters in order to celebrate together.

"Ben, I didn't recognise you at first. It's me, Sanjay!"

Kelly looked over at the person whose voice had just interrupted her *"Ben and Kelly's moment"*. It was the waiter. He was smiling over at Ben. He looked south Asian, spoke with a Northern British accent and rather disturbingly was another one of those handsome, well built guys that Ben seemed to know rather too many of.

"Sanjay, good to see you." Ben was on cloud nine after his coatcheck canoodle with Kelly. He felt as if he loved everyone.

"Oh, this is Kelly, my colleague and friend. Kelly, this is the beautiful Sanjay. Sanjay often dances with Rubens so

I know him from the clubs."

As Ben had mentioned Rubens and the clubs, Sanjay relaxed, happy to know that this Kelly girl was fully aware of Ben's private life.

"Delighted to meet you, Kelly. Ben, don't you look a heartbreaker in that suit. It hugs your body in *all* the right places. But I was so sorry to hear about you and Rubens. I think."

Sanjay then turned to Kelly, and gave her the kind of smile he would give to any one of the girls in the clubs. He saw girls in clubs as spectators rather than protagonists in the real game; there for fun, to look nice and maybe to help break the ice when boys wanted to meet other boys. Sanjay broadened his grin with a look of complicit naughtiness directed at his new found fag hag.

"But then we all know Rubens was never going to be able to keep this one all to himself. There is a bit of a fan club going on. Lucky I made myself the president of it. So, Ben, if you ever need a shoulder to cry on, give me a call. See you soon I hope, gorgeous. Nice to meet you, Kelly. You should get Ben to bring you to *Intoxication* next time. It sure could teach this party a thing or two."

Still grinning, Sanjay produced a calling card, and gave it to Ben with a surreptitious but still lascivious wink which could not possibly be understood as anything other than a call to his arms. As he turned away Kelly watched Sanjay's expression morph from gleefully sexual into respectfully professional as he began once more to offer glasses of champagne to the gathered legal luminaries.

As Kelly turned back to Ben she saw that he was still

watching Sanjay with a smile on his face. Whilst she couldn't know for sure whether that smile meant anything more than *how nice to unexpectedly bump into a friend at a slightly dull party like this* Kelly really couldn't help suspecting that it could mean *I've got his number – great!* She didn't want to be paranoid, but then neither had her friend Melisande, a thoroughly modern girl who had dated a bisexual for a couple of years before eventually having her heart broken when her boyfriend left her, and went to set up home with a handsome waiter named Andreas. Beware of Greeks working shifts, as Millie might have warned.

Or Indians with handsome smiles. Kelly had told herself she simply wouldn't place herself in competition with both other women and the gay men of London, and this was the reason why. That drop dead gorgeous champagne waiter had just invited Ben to bed right in front of her. She felt the tears rushing to her eyes as she thought *I just can't do this*.

"Shall we go and find Monique then, Kelly? I'm bursting to tell someone about what has just happened."

As he looked at Kelly's face he saw something was wrong.

"Listen. Ben. Hartmut's problems can wait till tomorrow. And what we did downstairs was a mistake. I'm just not able to deal with the fact that not only every woman but also every gay man in London seems to be after you. I'm going to find Monique and go home. Give me some space. We'll talk tomorrow."

Ben couldn't believe what he had just heard. *What was this girl going on about?* Surely she couldn't be jealous of Sanjay? Even though he was pretty sexy. *And he had really given me the nod. Hmmm, maybe she had a point after all.* As Ben watched Kelly head off towards Monique he caught sight of another gaggle of tedious lawyers who by now were drunk as skunks. Feeling frustrated over Kelly and disgusted at the machinations of the senior partner, he decided that the last thing he needed was another drink. Maybe he should just leave.

So Ben did what any slightly drunk, single, sexually frustrated twenty-something guy would do. He went home and surfed through a selection of his favourite porn web sites. *Thank God for the Internet* was his final thought as he dropped off to sleep on his bed, with his faithful laptop at his side.

19

Partner in crime?

Rubens stretched out. It was a shame things hadn't worked out with Ben. Then again, it had been fun. It was weird that the American just hadn't done it for Rubens in bed. Who would have thought? But that is sometimes what happens. Being good in bed is not a given. Remaining good in bed is even less so. Rubens Ribeiro could never fall in love with anyone he considered a crap shag.

Nonetheless, Ben was a good friend. He was certainly a committed and loyal one. And in any case maybe Rubens functioned better when he was free.

There certainly were advantages. Like being able to go out in the middle of the week, see friends in the club, pull the sexiest guy there and then bring him home for the night. Maybe he should stop feeling a little sad over losing the American. Rubens turned over and looked at Mukhtar lying on his back, still asleep, with the duvet somehow reaching up to just around his waist as if he were sleeping in some pre-watershed film. It was so much easier when guys didn't work nine to five. Or longer. It was so boring organising life around those badly fixed hours! Although Rubens did technically have the gym at the Castle Lofts to look after, he generally managed to pencil his clients into slots that suited him. And he refused to do early mornings more than once or twice a week.

As Rubens gently touched his right arm, Mukhtar stirred, opened his eyes, looked lost for a moment and then smiled at him.

"Why, hello. It has to be a good day when the first thing you see is as beautiful as you."

"Baby I don't believe a guy like you has to make do with mingers. I mean, come on, have you looked in the mirror?"

Mukhtar was another professional escort. Naturally, they thrived in club life. He was a bright man, and rather did what he did out of laziness. And neediness – a need for permanent shows of approval. Easy money, for some.

"If I'm not working, you're right, but with my job, I never know who I'm going to be waking up with. Or where. So depressing to open your eyes to the most fantastic five-star hotel room, go to the window and look at the sun shining on a shimmering sea with the beach and the boats bobbing in the water, and then see the creature from the black lagoon come out of the bathroom. When you realise that that is what you have just spent a night in paradise with, it's quite a comedown. I think I need to remove the overnight specials from the Rentboy.com ad."

Rubens had met Mukhtar Hourani through Jamal. Mukhtar insisted upon making his own way in life. He was, however, also becoming weary of the constraints of his lifestyle. He was all too aware of the less glamorous side of being an international high-class male escort. He had kissed a lot of frogs recently, and they may have paid for his lifestyle – but unlike the fairy tale version, his prince's kiss didn't improve their appearance one bit.

Although Rubens could understand the wish to be independent, he would never have chosen Mukhtar's life. Rubens only did what he did because he had to. There was a difference in there. Just.

"I still think you're crazy doing what you do, Mukhtar."

"I'm starting to think it too. I've been seeing this guy a few times and I'm thinking about starting something with him."

"Is he an escort too?"

"No, he's a doctor. An ex-client. From some place up in the north of England. Birkenhead? He's pretty open-minded but when you have something planned and then a client calls and you have to go away for the weekend, well… even an understanding friend gets a bit pissed off."

Rubens wondered if he would be able to give up what he was doing. It felt good when he had gone to Western Union and sent all that money back for his mother's operation the week before. Now he was back in the reality of looking forward to a lifetime of training other people's bodies and occasionally selling his own. It made him feel empty and sad for a moment. Like a light going out. Then his inner Brazilian took control again, he looked over at Mukhtar's beautiful form, remembered how much fun he had had the night before and smiled to himself. Life may sometimes be tough, but Rubens Ribeiro knew it was there to be lived. That is exactly what Rubens Ribeiro was doing, and would continue to do.

Millie couldn't believe that the party was actually going to happen. Crystal and Amber had been marvellous. Crystal had persuaded Kerwin to speak to a DJ he knew, and he had agreed to play. For her part, Amber had convinced half of the Castle Lofts to come along. Perhaps she had made them offers they couldn't refuse? Who cared. Millie knew that this would do her vegetarian menu the world of good. Amber had even suggested asking Ben and Monique to help out with the food; Ben to do the fetching and carrying from the bar and Monique just to supervise and check it looked all right. Ben was a dear and would be glad to help out, and to fit in, even if he was a diehard American meat-eater in Millie's book. Maybe it was time for Millie to have a quiet word with Monique about that time in the café in North London. How Monique had managed to catch Millie stuffing her face with bacon and sausage was still beyond Millie. Oh, the shame of it. The sheer, fleshy shame of it. But she couldn't let Monique keep this over her, like the... *sword of Hercules*, hanging over her for ever. No, Millie resolved to take Monique aside at the party, when she had had a few drinks, and clear the air. Anyone could make a mistake after all. Millie was sure she wasn't the only one who generally avoided meat but couldn't resist the occasional juicy sausage.

"So what are we going to go as then, babes?"

Although it was a party, Kerwin liked to be organised.

If it was fancy dress, then he and Crystal would have to do it right. He'd already sorted out the DJ for the party. That was a coup – the guy was good. He was looking forward to it. Crystal really wanted it to go well; she'd told Kerwin she thought some of the people in the Lofts looked down on her. She wanted to be accepted, this was a chance. Kerwin would show everyone just how amazing his Crystal was. The party would be fierce and they would have the best costumes.

Having decided to be mature about the events of the evening before, Ben and Kelly were also discussing the impending party on the way to the office.

"I think it's a really cool idea to dress up as a tube station, Kelly."

"Pretty amazing that this is the brainwave of Crystal, Amber and Millie. That they have a wave in their communal brain is quite something. Do you think they will be able to get it organised?"

"I think they will. Millie is determined to press as much of her wonderful socially responsible food on us, and Amber and Crystal want to have a good party. One of their friends is DJ-ing, apparently."

As Kelly thought about how many things could go wrong at the Underground party, she also reflected about what had gone wrong at the SBK party the night before. She had made it quite clear to Ben that what had happened in the cloakroom had been a mistake. It was merely the result of an alcohol-fuelled moment of surrender to lust. Kelly actually felt rather grateful to Sanjay for reminding her why she avoided bisexual men like the plague, and to Nicholas Casterway for interrupting her and Ben before things got too out of hand.

"I still can't get over what we overheard last night. Poor Hartmut! You report to him, Ben – have you ever had the idea that he was, well, a bit of a perv?"

Ben sometimes wondered if Kelly's direct approach would follow her throughout her legal career. If so, it may be doomed, although in such a good way. He was momentarily distracted from answering Kelly's question by the thought of how much he loved her directness, her sharpness and basically just her. *Damn Sanjay!*

He came back to the subject in point.

"I've never really thought about Hartmut's private life. I did catch him once looking rather annoyed at me seeing him in a café. He had company. But if I remember rightly, his companion was a very respectable-looking young woman, well-dressed and rather pretty. She wasn't in chains, or even hard-looking. He's always seemed straightforward to me, Kelly."

"I've never got the creepy feeling from him that you get from some men of his age. You would be surprised at how respectable middle aged partners can behave with younger female lawyers. Although he's never done anything specific, Nicholas Casterway really gives me the heebie-jeebies."

Although – or possibly because – Ben's only experience of Nicholas Casterway had been when he was hiding in a cloakroom with his pants unzipped, he could see what Kelly meant. Nicholas' way of trying to expel Hartmut through embarrassment was clinical and wolfish. Ben felt that, under the veneer of decent concern for SBK's reputation,

Nicholas seemed to be taking distinct pleasure in being able to participate in Hartmut's downfall. The creep.

"Do you think," wondered Ben, "that that devious snake had a hand in orchestrating the whole thing? I mean it seems a bit odd that a blackmailer should contact a partner who is not even in the country, doesn't it?"

Kelly stared at Ben for a moment. The New Yorker could be on to something.

"You might be right, Ben. But surely Harry would have asked him about it, wouldn't he?"

"Unless, of course, Harry just decided to toe the line as he was worried about his own extra-marital affair leaking out into the public domain? If he did have any suspicions regarding Nicholas' honesty in this, he may have just decided it was wiser to ride the tiger rather than side with its prey. Or, of course, our Harry isn't as smart as we think he is."

Kelly stared at Ben again. She was always more attracted to men who she could respect for both their brain and their body and this damn bisexual New York City Boy was ticking her boxes rather too well. With an effort she put her feelings for Ben out of her head and got back to the shenanigans in play.

"So you think Harry is either a bit slow, or is Nicholas' silent partner in crime? Crikey. This is getting interesting, given the skeletons knocking around in the closet here. It is getting to sound like Saint-Saëns' Danse Macabre in there. In any case, I think we need to keep a watch out today."

Ben's office was next door to Hartmut's. He was in a

prime position to keep an eye on events. Hartmut, however, was being utterly inscrutable. This led to much frustration on the part of Kelly's IM which was in constant contact with Ben. Until, that is, Hartmut returned to his office just after midday with a look of pure fury on his face. Ben's senses suddenly went into overdrive. Finally, Kelly's IM would be satisfied.

"HG back"

"Looks suicidal"

"Must have seen the tape"

"Go & ask him if he's OK, Ben!"

"As if!"

"We're talking HG here, not my mother!"

Before Kelly could get any more frustrated with Ben's unwillingness to play ball, an email flashed up on both of their screens. The entire London office was being summoned to an emergency meeting at 12:30.

"OMG! You don't think that they're making HG go today do you, Ben?"

"Fu*k knows! See you in the boardroom, then?"

An hour or so later, the couple of hundred lawyers who were free to be so summoned were packed into the SBK auditorium. Sitting next to Ben right at the back of the room Kelly could hardly keep herself from blurting out to the other trainees that she thought she knew what this was all about. With an effort she managed to just smile at Ben whilst fidgeting furiously.

Ben had immediately noticed that whilst Harry was sitting near the front of the room, there was no sign of Hartmut. But then Hartmut walked into the room. Ben couldn't see his face clearly but he could imagine how poor Hartmut must be feeling, especially as he was being shadowed by that schemer-in-chief, Nicholas Casterway. He felt an acute, cold unpleasantness emanate from SBK's senior partner as he swept by. Ben felt glad that he had had no reason so far to even cross that man's path. He would try to keep out of his way for as long as possible. Ben was watching Hartmut closely as Casterway took a seat next to Harry. Hartmut strode right to the front of the room and then turned round to face the assembled mass.

"I shall make this as brief as I can. Unfortunately, I am going to resign from SBK. Whilst my dear colleagues Nicholas and Harry urged me to do this in private, I insisted that I do it on my terms. If I am sounding somewhat melodramatic, especially for the Hartmut Glick that some of you have got to know over the years, well, suffice it to say that there is a very good reason."

He paused and looked thoughtful. The room was as quiet as a David Attenborough hide.

"I have striven for all my professional career to keep my work and my private life totally separate. Whilst I have broken no laws at all, and I am in no way ashamed of my choices, it appears that my partners view my private life as potentially embarrassing to SBK and able to cause it harm. Until today I would have been able to brush away any idle speculation. However Nicholas has just shown me video evidence that was sent to him by a blackmailer. It thus seems that I have no choice but to resign."

As Hartmut came to the end of his speech, a thousand thoughts raced round the room.

"Poor Hartmut!"

"We're being blackmailed?"

"What the hell did he do?"

"I always thought he was a bit weird!"

"How do I get to see the video?"

"I've always liked that office of his!"

"Oh My God! He wasn't supposed to tell everyone. I have to do something to put a lid on this!"

The last was from Nicholas Casterway, who realised that he should never have agreed to let Hartmut speak to the entire firm like this. Hartmut had underlined the fact that Nicholas was offering no support. He immediately jumped up and stood next to Hartmut, turning to face the room.

"Of course, Harry and I tried to persuade Hartmut to fight this. Whilst we are all well aware of the effect of a scandal on a business like ours, we also know the value of Hartmut Glick to this partnership. However, Hartmut is too much of an honourable man to ever dream of putting our partnership in any danger."

Kelly Danvers was ready to explode when she heard the words coming out of that snake's mouth. What a hypocrite. What a saltworthy slug. She had heard for herself the sympathy shown to poor Hartmut in the cloakroom the night before. She had half a mind to stand up and "out" Casterway for the heartless bastard that he was. As she turned to Ben for some moral support, she was struck by the look on his face.

Ben's jaw had dropped as far as it was humanly possible for it to go. As Nicholas had stood up, Ben caught sight of his face properly for the first time. Or at least Ben thought it would be the first time. Even without that dark grey pin-striped suit and sombre charcoal tie, Ben would have recognised those cold grey eyes anywhere. *Rubens' unpleasant client from that hotel in Belgrave Road. Pervy "Peter", whose image Ben had worked so hard to remove from his brain. "Peter" was actually Nicholas Casterway!*

Oblivious to Kelly staring at him by his side, Ben was filled with a sense of outrage against the utter, complete, heartless hypocrisy of Nicholas Casterway. Supposedly full of moral righteousness, even trying to pretend he had compassion for Hartmut, Casterway was nothing more than a cold-hearted double-crossing cheating pervert. Ben could not let this moment pass. Especially as he knew that for a moment he had a killer weapon with regard to Casterway. He had to act fast though.

As Ben stood up, Kelly Danvers nearly fell off her chair. Surely Ben wasn't going to tell the whole room about what they had overheard in the cloakroom. She couldn't believe that he would be so brave.

As Ben stood up, Hartmut Glick looked over. Even through the depths of his anger and sadness at what had happened, he recognised his new young trainee. Ben standing up for him sent a flicker of warmth into his heart.

As Ben stood up, Nicholas Casterway looked immediately to see who was breaking with the unwritten policy of the rank and file lawyers not to dwell on painful matters such as these and just let them pass by with the least embarrassment. Suddenly a look of puzzlement crossed Nicholas' face. He didn't recognise the young man's face as one of his staff. It nevertheless looked familiar, as if it might have belonged to one of the baristas who he used at Starbucks. That look was followed by a thinly disguised look of utter horror as he finally recognised *Dick Burns* from that hotel in Belgrave Road. Nicholas fought to regain his composure.

Ben stared hard for a moment at Nicholas Casterway as if daring him to deny him the chance to speak. No one said a word. Ben took it as tacit permission to make his point.

"My name is Ben Barlettano and I have only been working in SBK since the summer. However I have learnt so much in this short time from my mentor, Hartmut Glick. Not only have I been in the presence of an incredible legal brain, but Hartmut is also one of the most honest and honourable, straightforward, decent people that I have ever met in my life. Whilst I fully understand that embarrassment can cost a firm like ours in terms of certain clients disapproving of certain practices, I cannot believe that a man such as Hartmut is being allowed to leave our practice for something which is not illegal, but merely... embarrassing."

Ben then looked at Harry Gumpert who, like all in the room was listening intently to him, before fixing his gaze on the icy Nicholas Casterway.

"Moreover, I am certain that if we filmed everyone in this room in their private lives, we would for sure uncover a number of events which might lead to resignations due to that supposed bête noire of ours – embarrassment. I am positive we will have the philanderers who profess blissful monogamy to their wives, the illegal drug takers, the addicted downloaders of extreme pornography, and of course the men who have a penchant for prostitutes before going home to play the family man with their wives and children. If we allow Hartmut to hang himself out to dry and we capitulate to the blackmailers now, then who will it be next? For this reason, Nicholas Casterway, as our most senior and respected partner, I beseech you to beg Hartmut to re-think his actions. Nicholas, I urge you to fight for the greater good of this firm. Who knows how many of us might have cause to be grateful for this stance."

Ben suddenly sat down, amazed at what he had just done and completely flabbergasted at where all the words had come from. Kelly, who of course had no idea about "Peter" didn't know whether to throw her arms around Ben or to sink into the chair with embarrassment. As she was once again just staring at Ben, Cornisha Burrows suddenly stood up and started applauding Ben's unexpected speech. Kelly knew immediately what she had to do. She was quickly followed by all those who felt for Hartmut, and those who were worried about their own skeletons in the cupboard.

Faced with almost his entire firm standing up and applauding, Nicholas Casterway realised that he had little choice. However, before he could act, Harry Gumpert decided that he should abandon the sinking ship first and let the captain go down with it whilst he bounded aboard the lifeboat.

"Thank you, colleagues for this amazing show of support. Hartmut, I will speak for the partners when I say that we want you to stay, please. Young Ben may be somewhat idealistic, but he has a point. Let him without sin and all that. Hartmut, we will fight this blasted blackmailer. He will not steal away one of our best brains in such an underhand and disgusting way."

As Cornisha Burrows wiped away a discreet tear at the Disney-esque outcome to the meeting, Nicholas Casterway felt as though he had suddenly landed in a Stephen King film. Even his superb brain was having difficulty in processing all the thoughts and questions racing through his mind. He had been outmanoeuvred and then threatened by a trainee from New York who was moonlighting as a male prostitute. He felt a cold sweat as he suddenly realised just how much power that young rat had over him. In the space of two minutes he had gone from hunter to prey. At that moment he had no idea how he was going to get revenge on Ben Barlettano, but he was determined that he would. One day. When the young swine was least expecting it.

Hartmut Glick was still uncertain that he had heard right. His tormentor Casterway had been turned into a shivering wreck by Hartmut's own trainee, and his sidekick Gumpert had then championed Hartmut's own cause and practically begged him to reverse the decision that was not his in the first place. After mumbling something about whether Harry was sure that this blackmailer could be fought, and hearing Harry assure him that they would try, Hartmut quietly said that he would stay.

Hartmut had formed a positive opinion of the New Yorker as he was diligent, didn't waste too many words and seemed to instinctively understand what Hartmut wanted. But today had been a revelation. To be defended so bravely by one he hardly knew was remarkable. Hartmut felt a deep sense of gratitude to the young man. He would repay it. He hoped he'd be in a position to do so when Ben was least expecting it. Although Hartmut couldn't really understand why Ben had done this, he suspected it had something to do with emotions. Hartmut had spent a lifetime trying to keep them at arm's length. Yet he couldn't help but wonder whether this was to be the year when emotions were finally to get the better of him.

So just how was Caroline going to tell her mother that she was falling in love with an older German gentlemen with whom she liked to indulge in orgiastic sado-masochistic sex?

She had decided that she should take her mother up on the offer to go and buy some little doggie treats in Mayfair. After breakfast at the beloved Wolseley and a fruitless search round some of the finer shops of Old Bond Street, they had popped into Bolognesi to see an old family friend, Tarquin Henderson-Smythe.

Tarquin was unfortunately rather busy, but he came out to greet them, elegantly attired, his manners impeccable as ever, and embraced them warmly before heading back to work. Caroline watched him go back to his office. She admired his lithe greyhound looks. She decided to take full advantage of Tarquin's offer to let them browse the gallery. Caroline could see how much her mother enjoyed being there.

Eleanor Napier Jones was clearly at home in the elegant gallery interior, among the still lifes, portraits and a rather explicit scene of multiple naked bodies, best described as the gods having a bit too much fun with their mortals. Caroline was surprised to see how her mother actually seemed to be examining it rather closely.

"Darling, you know Bacchanalia always remind me somewhat of the sixties. Although of course we had joints rather than pipes and goblets of wine in our day."

Caroline wasn't sure how to respond to her mother's unexpected observation, other than to say that she distinctly preferred the statuesque physiques of the Romans to the skinny rather too hirsute examples that cavorted to Bob Dylan. Before Caroline had a chance to think of an appropriate response, Eleanor continued, almost as if she were musing to herself.

"It was a magical time. Your generation think you are being so avant-garde with those frightful *Ibiza Uncovered* exposés but they are merely a rather common extension of what has always gone on in the local public house."

"I didn't know you watched *Ibiza Uncovered*, Mother."

"Well, one has to keep up with what the working class are up to. Otherwise how does one know where to avoid? They think they are being so terribly shocking with all that lewd drunkenness. Dear things. The only thing that is truly shocking is their frightful grammar and those ugly regional accents."

"Why have you never mentioned the sixties to me before, Mother?"

"Dear girl, the chance never seemed to present itself. I mean one does not broach the subject of youthful drug-fuelled orgies à propos of nothing, does one? Especially with one's respectable daughter. I almost mentioned it when we were watching that splendid show about those vampires in Louisiana. One rather relates to the idea of a party where a spell is cast, and all the townsfolk probably have more fun in one night than in the rest of their entire miserable little lives."

Caroline noted with amusement how effortlessly Eleanor blended her ingrained snobbishness into her stories.

"The sixties were all about letting go and exploring yourself and others. It was magical. Happy memories."

As she stared at the heavily muscled naked body of Pan inciting the men and women around him to indulge all their carnal desires, Caroline tried to imagine how her mother must have felt when she had some dude with a guitar and a spliff trying to create a sixties Bacchanal. Maybe not so different to how she herself felt in her accoutrements and with her accessories, being urged on by modern Pan, the DJ, down at PPLAY.

Maybe Eleanor wouldn't be that taken aback after all if Caroline told her about her personal preferences. Moreover, Hartmut was a high-flying lawyer with status and breeding. Her mother would certainly appreciate that. Caroline decided that she would gently open the door to her private life and let her mother through step-by-step. She would be as careful with her mother, as she would be with a new slave.

"Art certainly does broaden the mind, doesn't it, Mother? And I need to tell you that the Bacchanal is still alive and well in certain circles. Of course, fortunately, those awfully conservative lower classes tend to self select and keep well away. The long and short of it is: thank goodness for Ibiza, Mother."

Mother and daughter held each other's gaze, and then returned to the painting which had sparked their unexpected conversation.

Was he really considering settling down with a doctor from Birkenhead? Mukhtar loved his freedom. He knew he could never even hint at the "g" word with his family. Further down the line, he might need to select a lesbian to marry, preferably one who wanted children and had a UK passport so that he could satisfy her, his family and the British Government all in one neat package. Hopefully Bob wouldn't get jealous.

There he was again, sneaking into his thoughts. Although a part of Mukhtar lived for his glittering London stage where he never knew what prize he might win, there was the other side that wanted the more banal things that everyone wanted. He'd like to have his Saturday mornings with the person that he had got to know over time; the breakfasts out at the weekend; the Saturday afternoons shopping for those perfect items from Tottenham Court Road or Chelsea; the Saturday nights preparing for the night out and then of course the nights out having fun, knowing exactly who he would be waking up with on the Sunday morning.

"How do you like your coffee?"

Mukhtar turned over in bed to see Rubens Ribeiro at the bedroom door, looking like one of those Calvin Klein models. You needed beautifully tanned skin to show off the white of the underwear to perfection. Life today was still pretty cool. However, if even a vision from Brazil making him breakfast could not dislodge Bob Boyle from Mukhtar's thoughts, then maybe it was time for Mukhtar Hourani to hang up his escorting boots and work something out with that doctor.

"Rubens, do you think it would be OK if I invited Bob to the tube station party this weekend?"

"No problem! Always great to have another sexy person at parties. Actually, we were missing one person from our group. So, let's say he is invited as long as he dresses up with us."

"He'll do it. If he comes. I've got a proposition I think I am ready to make to him."

Rubens guessed immediately:

"No way! That's so cool, Mukhtar. And how lucky am I, getting you here for the night just before you decide to go all serious on us!"

As Rubens went back laughing into the kitchen to make the breakfast, Mukhtar stared up at the ceiling of Rubens' bedroom happily thinking of his life with Bob. He was looking forward to attending a party with his boyfriend. *Boyfriend.* It sounded so good. Little did he know that the party in the Castle Lofts would be remembered for far more than the fact that another attractive young immigrant had tired of the freedom of London's magical A-List gay scene, and had convinced himself that all he wanted was love and stability in the arms of a doctor from Birkenhead.

20

Beware of the Elephant & Castle

Ben couldn't quite believe that, of all people, he had ended up getting ready to go the tube station party with Pansy Ho.

He had been in the gym the day before feeling rather sorry for himself, thinking that he had, ultimately, failed with both Rubens and Kelly. He was now destined to be the saddest single at the party.

Worse, Ben had let Alex O'Connell persuade him a few days earlier that he should go as the statue of Eros from Piccadilly Circus, just to remind Rubens what he was missing. Apart from the fact that this entailed Ben wearing nothing but a helmet, wings and a carefully draped piece of grey material round his midriff for the night, he also needed to be covered in silver body paint. And now he was going to have to apply it all alone. He debated whether he should not just give the whole thing a miss. Pansy had caught sight of his glum expression.

"Mr. Ben Barlettano, why so sad? Still feeling guilty about not getting any shopping tips for me?"

Ben closed his eyes briefly, preparing mentally for the

inevitable shriek of shrill laughter. But it didn't come.

"You think I don't notice, but I can see what's wrong. You like the girl, you like the boy, he gets in first, you end up his toy. I watch people in this block, Mr. Ben. But now you no longer with him but she not sure of you either. Not rocket science to see you feel like you have messed it all up."

A gentle smile in place of the raucous guffaw. What was happening to Pansy?

She patted his arm:

"But she still likes you a lot. I see way she looks at you. She just worried that you too unreliable. You're too successful with girls and boys. Don't understand how you think opposite about yourself."

OK, this was now getting really weird. How did Pansy know this? She had summed up the situation in under a minute and he had never even talked to her about it.

He smiled at her.

"First off, Pansy, please call me Ben. Just Ben. Thank you. You have just described exactly what I am going through. I have indeed messed things up quite royally. I have ended up with neither of the people I like. And, just to underscore my failure, tomorrow I have to get dressed up as the statue of Eros and paint myself metallic grey on my own, as I have no one to go to the ball with. I am Cinderella."

"Ah, Mr. Ben, I too am alone. Mildred is not around. I can do it for you. How much you pay me to paint body?"

Ben did a double-take before he realized that Pansy was making fun of him. Before she could screech, he decided he would play along. He may as well. She was starting to interest him, beyond his earlier vision of her popping ping pong balls in Patpong. That he accepted was a *bad* thought, coming from a deeply bad place. But those thoughts popped up as readily as any ping pong ball. One had to admit it. In any case, maybe it wouldn't do any harm to make friends with the woman who would be doing his inventory. It would also deal with the guilt he was feeling at having written her off as a banshee to be avoided at all costs. And – you try painting your own shoulder blades, alone. He had no choice.

"How about as much Vodka Red Bull as you like before we go down to the party, followed by being able to boast that you went to a party with the God of Love himself? Would that be wages enough?"

Pansy agreed that it would.

And so it happened that Pansy Ho had turned up at Ben's door at 6.30pm on that fateful Saturday night, wearing a dress made up of red carpet with a large camera hung around her neck.

"Make up artist here to drink Vodka Red Bull and get you set for big party! Are you ready, Mr Ben Barlettano? I mean Mr Ben. I mean Ben! Oh, so difficult to change old habits."

"Pansy, welcome. I am so pleased to see you. Oh I see, you're Leicester Square. Cool."

"Well, English think we Asians take photos all the time, so tonight I let them enjoy their joke. Now where's the paint?"

Just as had happened on the first morning that he had spent in London, he found himself nearly naked in his flat in the company of Pansy Ho. This time however, the woman from Hong Kong brought a real smile to his face. Ben enjoyed getting ready. Two swift drinks and a lot of rubbing later, and they were ready to go.

Pansy had helped him strap on his wings, he had donned his helmet and loincloth and with bow and arrows in his hand he marched with his new friend to the lift.

"I have a feeling this party is going to be pretty memorable, Pansy."

When Ben and Pansy reached the party room, they realised they had arrived a little early. They were greeted at the door by Millie Myers wearing what resembled a pile of grass and leaves, with a small paper deck chair coquettishly positioned on her back.

"Welcome to the party!" said Millie breezily, "Now we don't want to waste the paper cups, do we, so write your name and your tube station on the side and you can keep it all evening. There are some marker pens by the cups. The drinks are on that table. Let's keep them moving – empties in the silver bins, and hope you've brought more than you'll drink!"

"Thanks Millie, ever the conscience of The Lofts. What are you dressed as, by the way?"

"Mr Ben, she is *obviously* Green Park! Americans so slow sometimes."

The characteristic Ho shriek of laughter made a brief appearance. After the time Ben had spent with her carefully covering him in grey gunge, Ben felt strangely glad to hear it again. It was like a long-lost friend, back from a journey overseas, albeit in a slightly unhinged state.

A rustling sound intruded. Crystal Smith walked up to them, dressed from head to toe in perfectly shaped squares of white paper. After saying hello, Ben gave Pansy another puzzled look.

"The clue's in the noise, Ben. Hello, hello? Russell Square?"

As Ben had neither been in England nor even on planet earth when Paddington Bear was on British TV he had no chance of even guessing what Kerwin James was supposed to be when he walked up in a giant teddy bear costume complete with hat and a mini jar of Tiptree marmalade stuck to his chest. Yet somehow Pansy got all the jokes immediately. The clever girl was even managing to use her outfit to take photos of all the costumes.

The final member of the hosting committee walked in wearing an undone straitjacket, adorned with photos of some pretty vicious-looking dogs. Other than her bizarre dress, Amber looked quite normal until she came up to Ben and closed her eyes. On her eyelids she had drawn large, glittery, *crazy eyes*. This was nothing short of freakish. Ben thought that it was a pretty appropriate look for Amber Bluett, but of course he had no idea what she was supposed to be until Crystal filled him in.

"Barking!"

Just then, as arrivals were steadily trickling in, Cornisha Burrows walked in. She was spectacular and a few gasps of admiration greeted her. She wore a very regal-looking gown, a headdress and crown, and she carried a sceptre in her left hand. She was accompanied by Arthur Bilks who looked fantastic, dressed as Napoleon Bonaparte save for the substitution of his military badge on his chest for a photograph of Abba with the word *Eurovision* emblazoned across them. This time Ben got it.

"Cornisha, you look amazing! I'm sure Victoria herself never looked grander. And Arthur, well, you are more emperor than a penguin. No one will be giving you the Elba tonight. Ha ha ha. I will never be able to go through Waterloo again, without thinking of you."

After helping themselves to some of the now copiously available drinks, Cornisha took Ben aside and looked at him in the way that mothers look at their sons when they are filled with the pride which comes when their child has achieved even more than their hopes had allowed them to think possible.

"My dear, dear Ben. Allow me to tell you something. From the moment I met you, I suspected that there may be something special about you. But when you stood up in that meeting and defended Hartmut in that way, I was dumbfounded. Very few people ever stand up to Nicholas Casterway, you know. The way you did it was breathtaking. And you have my personal gratitude for saving the position and reputation of a man I respect greatly, and to whom I owe much."

Ben didn't know how to respond. What he had done had been purely instinctive, born of a sense of injustice at the unfairness of the treatment being meted out to Hartmut, and compounded by the disgust that he felt for Casterway's hypocrisy. At moments like that, Ben found it hard to be rational.

He had merely acted to be true to himself. It hadn't really crossed his mind that it was a risky stance to take. He simply had had no option at the time.

Before he could respond, they were interrupted by a familiar voice. A voice that now made him react deeply. The immediately instinctive reaction might be rather awkward, given what Ben was wearing.

"I need a drink. Now. These high heeled clogs are not the most comfortable things I have ever worn in my life."

Kelly Danvers was wearing a long flowing skirt, a little tunic top and what looked like a white smurf hat on her head. It was, in fact, a bonnet. She was also covered in plastic tulips.

"Holland Park! Kelly Danvers, that is superb!"

"I feel a bit clogged up."

Cornisha beamed at Kelly, visibly content at seeing her favourite should-be couple together again.

"Let me go and get you a glass of wine whilst you admire our young God of Love here. No popping off to the cloakroom whilst I am gone, please."

Blissfully unaware of how fast things had moved around here, the Empress of India swept off to fetch Kelly something to help her forget her troublesome footwear.

"You do look phenomenally sexy, Ben. Maybe I should have gone with my first plan. There was talk by Monique – manifestly not serious, I should add – of a skin tone body suit and a neatly shaped patch of wool over my groin. Shepherd's Bush. But look at you. I'm going to have to prise Sanjay and the other boys off you when they get here."

Ben couldn't honestly say that Kelly's outfit was the most flattering that he had ever seen her in, even though the tight tunic did her chest justice, in a rather Oktoberfest sort of way. But it didn't matter. Looking at her he remembered those stolen moments behind Cornisha's stole and how for a few minutes he thought that everything was going to turn out well after all. Then it had been ruined by Sanjay. In fairness to Sanjay, Kelly did seem to have a bit of a hang-up about bisexuals. Perhaps, Ben thought sadly, it would have happened sooner or later, but nevertheless he thought fate had been rather cruel to not let him have even one night with his girl.

After thrusting a very full paper cup of red wine, with her name on it, into Kelly's hand, Cornisha gave them a knowing smile and headed back to her Napoleon.

"I still can't believe you did what you did at the meeting, Ben! You have got balls, you know. Unfortunately I can almost see them in that costume of yours."

An advantage of being covered in silver body paint was that Kelly Danvers had no idea that he was blushing under the paint. Ben wondered if he had overdone it.

She waved away his concerns, catching the look in his eye.

"I'm only kidding. You look truly amazing. It is such a bummer that you like boys as much as girls, otherwise you would have been just the sort of hero I have been holding out for all this time."

Even cheesy lines sounded somehow good, coming from Kelly. Was it really too late to pull things round with her? Or pull things off her? Ben decided that he should tell her the secret he had been keeping about Peter. Not to curry favour, but just because, after all, she was the person he felt closest to in all of London.

"Kelly, I need to tell you something really, really important but you must promise to keep it to yourself."

"Please don't tell me that you want to be a lesbian now!"

"Kelly, I mean it. You have to promise."

The New Yorker looked awfully serious. Kelly nodded.

"When Nicholas Casterway stood up in the meeting, I suddenly realised something. Something pretty incredible. *I had already met him.* You remember I told you about that awful guy in Belgravia?"

"Not really, Ben."

"The job with Rubens?"

"Oh, yes. Although I had tried to blot out as many details as possible. Well?"

"Oh, come on Kelly. Nicholas Casterway is creepy Peter! *I have spunked all over him!*"

Kelly took a moment to remember how Peter fitted in. Then it was like a wave breaking over her. She nearly spat her mouthful of red wine all over Eros' perfect silver chest.

"No... way! No way! Are you sure? But he's married. With children!"

She shook her head in disbelief:

"That is possibly the most revolting thing I have ever heard!"

"Kelly, I'm not disagreeing with you there. I'll *never* forget those mental images from that hotel room. I am scarred for life. But, frankly, whatever. The point is, Nicholas is Peter. And what's more, did you notice the look on his face when I started speaking? He looked like he had just seen a ghost. He knows who I am."

"My God, Ben, that is some serious dirt. That man is such a hypocrite. Now I understand why you just had to speak out for poor old Hartmut. And why Casterway backed down. Mercy me. Great balls of fire. Has he spoken to you yet?"

"He has avoided me like the plague. But you know it wasn't just the unfairness of the whole situation. Other than that *obscene* image of him lying underneath me in that room, the other acute memory from that session was the icy way he ejected us from the hotel. The disdain for us was palpable. He's a man who has no concept of people's feelings. They are just there to be used by him to satisfy his requirements. And then they can be disposed of. Almost literally. Nasty. Really nasty! A textbook psychopath. Obviously for Rubens and me, I didn't even realise or care much at the time – but imagine if you were someone he had seduced? Someone who counted on him to be fair?"

"Yes, that may approximate the definition of a psychopath, Ben. They lack ordinary responses and feelings, I gather. Some say many so-called successful people may well qualify as such. Where would it come from, I wonder? Could be genetic, I suppose."

"Anyhow, it'll make for an interesting time at SBK henceforth. I think it would be enormously surprising if I ever became a partner there – but with Hartmut looking out for me and a fair wind, I suppose I can get a job elsewhere at the right time. Meanwhile, it's good that Hartmut is staying. More than good – essential."

"I am still having trouble processing, Ben. I really don't know how I am going to be able to look at that awful man any more. How are we supposed to look up to him now? Especially now I have that mental image of Knicker-less Casterway, coated in trainee spunk."

As Ben and Kelly talked, laughed and winced about what might come next with Casterway, the rest of the room faded away into insignificance. Ben had almost forgotten he was at a party until there was a break in the music and a man in a tuxedo holding a plastic revolver and a microphone stepped up on to the small catwalk in the middle of the room.

Ben and Kelly looked around, taken aback. The room was suddenly packed, and it was buzzing.

The DJ grabbed the microphone and purred into it:

"The name's Bond. Bond Street. Welcome to the Castle Lofts Fancy Dress Party. I have the honour of being your compère for the evening, especially for our costume defilée which will pay homage to the glorious London Underground. So this is how it's going to work. I will call you out from the crowd, either by name or just distinguishing feature. For example, the silver stripper over there."

The last thing Ben wanted Kelly to be reminded of was how neither men nor women could resist looking at him, nor how he somehow always managed to court attention. Oblivious to Ben's awkwardness, the compère continued.

"Our contestants will sweep along the catwalk, give us a

twirl and then shall reveal the name of their station. Quite simply the station with the loudest cheer shall be deemed the winner. I am asked to mention the sumptuous buffet immediately after the show, which of course is being laid on specially by the marvellous Millie Myers of the Lofts' very own Health Café. Millie also has a new motto this evening which goes to the heart of everything she tries to do. It is "Healthy food, Healthy you, Healthy planet!" I say, yes ma'am to that. I do. I think we really must start our show. And who better to start us off, than our Queen of Green herself, Mistress Millicent Myers. DJ, take it away, please."

As Millie Myers attempted to work her way down the catwalk without losing her model deck chair, Ben felt as he had come back to earth. He regretted it, as now that he had found Planet Kelly, he rather wanted to orbit it for longer. Nonetheless, it was quite a sight to see the costumes. People had really made an effort.

"Ben, look, Hartmut's here. He came!"

Kelly had spotted the German. He stepped onto the catwalk with as much assurance as he stepped onto a lecture podium. Or the main stage at the Kit Kat Club. He was escorting Caroline Napier Jones.

Caroline looked as if she had just walked off the set of an X-rated beer festival. She was wearing a pair of extremely small, tight red leather Lederhosen, long white stockings with some irregular black marks on them, and a white vest which pushed her breasts up and out like enormous portions of buffalo mozzarella. The whole look was finished off with a pair of red leather braces. On her trilby type hat, she had perched a miniature cuckoo clock. In contrast, Hartmut was dressed quite normally in jeans and a shirt, although he admittedly sported an interesting toolbelt with a can of lager on one hip, and what looked like a large metallic dildo in the other.

It was, in fact, a large metallic dildo.

The DJ approved mightily of Caroline: "There we have it, ladies and gentlemen. That was – er – Swiss Cottage, and Cockfosters!"

Before Ben could even begin to wonder how that made sense, Kelly grabbed his silver half glove and dragged him to the stage. As Ben prepared himself to sashay down the catwalk with Queen Kelly he cursed his costume; if he did somehow get another chance with her tonight, allying with his friend alcohol, he wouldn't be able to touch her because of all that damned body paint! That reminded him of Pansy. He searched the room frantically.

"Pansy! Quick! We're on. Come on! Now! Together!"

Ben turned back to Kelly:

"She cheered me up earlier when I was feeling all miserable because I was alone and not with you!"

Before they could move, Pansy was upon them with a beaming smile. All three stepped up into the spotlight. Ben felt on top of the world. He knew he looked mighty fine. He stood straight and looked ahead. Ben knew Pansy was on his side. She would not have forgotten that Ben was in "*I want to be with Kelly*" mode. She was rooting for him. And then of course there was his wonderful, wonderful Holland Park. He felt by the way Kelly was looking at him that just maybe she was coming round again. How could she possibly resist, when Ben looked every inch the Greek god?

Kelly was playing it cool. She pretended not to notice Ben's statuesque physique overmuch. The same could not be said for the seven towering figures dressed in matching pink and white checked country dresses and blond wigs that suddenly marched into the room like a gingham army.

"Oh Mary Jane, will you look at that young man up there. I need to get myself a piece of that and bake myself a man pie!"

"Lizzie Sue, there is more prime beef on that man than on my Daddy's ranch!"

"Carrie Ann, I do declare that I have died and gone to heaven, and the God of Love himself is pointing his arrow right at me!"

"Oh, Ellie May, mercy me, I think I can see the tip of that arrow just pointing itself out from under that itty-bitty silly little piece of rag there."

"Sisters, I think it needs checking out!"

"Oh hush your mouth, Shelley Marie! Mama always said you were the sluttiest!"

"Me, slutty? Miss Pammy? To quote my hero RuPaul, if your skirt were any shorter, I'd have to arrest you for dealing crack."

The Seven Sisters consisted of Rubens, Alex, Jamal, Sanjay, Mukhtar, Bob and Dorothy. After getting over the initial moment of panic that indeed his costume had slipped – it hadn't – Ben realised that Kelly Danvers' expression had changed. Although she was laughing heartily at the

Seven Sisters' jokes, her face had set in that stubborn way that Kelly's face did. There was no trace of the tenderness that Ben had thought he had detected moments earlier.

She could not have made it clearer if she had pushed Ben off the podium, there and then.

Ben knew that gay had come right in and dug the trench between them, laying that sword right there on that pillow. Kelly had been reminded that, no matter how much she liked the New York City Boy, there would always be other boys who would like him just as much, and that she would never know, or trust, which way he would swing.

It was time to make room for other costumes. Kelly led Ben and Pansy off the stage, making way for the show in itself that was Rubens and company.

Ben took it in his stride.

"No touching, girls. If I feel a hand I'll know exactly who it was. You'll have guilty little silvery fingers if you touch this body."

He was just so comfortable and natural with all the gay banter these days. Kelly wished that he could just be a normal straight guy who she could consider planning a future with. How could she think about children with a man who might borrow her clothes to go out partying with "the boys" and then spend all night on drugs in a men's bath house? *Had she just thought about children?* Kelly decided she needed to avoid spending all evening getting her brain screwed up by Ben Barlettano. There were plenty of other people to have fun with.

The last people to get on stage looked as if they could have been extras from an old Monty Python show. Theirs was the easiest costume of all to guess as one was dressed in an elephant costume and the other was a mediaeval castle, complete with neat turrets and a St George's flag. Ben had no idea who they were as he couldn't see their faces, but then there were still lots of people he didn't know here tonight. It was a perfect, topical way to finish the show.

Kelly Danvers was more curious.

"Who are those two, Pansy?"

Pansy was usually the best person to ask as she knew most things that were going on in The Lofts.

"No inventory yet, but Millie told me they two new boys moving in to a flat here next week. Came to see place, went to café and Millie invited them."

"Really?" Kelly squared her shoulders, "Well, I think I should go and welcome them properly to the Lofts. After all, Ben, we threw a party for you when you arrived. I'll see you later."

Pansy could see the look of surprise, almost hurt on Ben's face, as Kelly wobbled off on those high-heeled clogs. Just as she was about to say that it was strange that there was no inventory booked for the Elephant & Castle boys' new flat, she was interrupted by Hartmut and Caroline walking up.

"Ben, you look amazing. Hartmut never told me that he had such a hunk working for him."

"Firstly, Caroline, it is because as a heterosexual male I have not been, and am still not particularly, aware of the fact that Ben Barlettano may or may not be a hunk. And, secondly, we do tend to wear suits rather than loincloths and body paint to the office." Hartmut twinkled, before turning to Ben with more than a hint of seriousness: "Anyhow, my dear Ben, I wanted to say once again how courageous and upstanding I found your speech two days ago. It altered the course of events, you know. Be in no doubt about that. Not that I will be able to show you any preferential treatment in the office environment, but you will have the eternal gratitude of Hartmut Glick, and if ever there is something I can do for you, then you must merely name it."

Ben had always found full-frontal compliments rather difficult to deal with. He grinned somewhat idiotically. Once again, Pansy came to his rescue.

"Mr Glick, my name is Pansy Ho, seeing as no introduction from Ben or Caroline! Ben tongue-tied, but maybe you can do something for me. Please explain again those stations you two have come as!"

"Sorry Pansy," smiled Caroline, "I thought you knew Hartmut. Costumes it is, then. Have a close look at the stockings."

Ben awkwardly knelt down and saw that the black marks on Caroline's stockings were actually words. *George. Big willy. Looking for tight butt. 06879 213876.* In larger type another word simply said *GENTLEMEN*. Ben was more confused than ever. Caroline saw that neither he nor Pansy were getting the connection.

"Swiss Cottage. Get it? *Cottage*. Never mind. I knew I should have had a postcard of the Alps with "*Grüße von Interlaken*" on it. Anyway, never mind me. Hartmut has two items which plainly give it away. Think about what the dildo might represent and look at the brand of lager."

This time Pansy was quicker off the mark.

"Cockfosters! That's so funny! I think I will like you, Mr Glick!"

She giggled excitedly:

"And, Caroline, I don't know whether to say *Wunderbar* or *Wunderbra*!"

"So how are we going to get talking to her anyway?"

Amber had pointed Kelly Danvers out to her brothers when she was on the catwalk.

"Leave it to me, little brother. This is the sort of party where you can talk to anyone. You just watch the master in action. Should be pretty easy as she is well worth boning so I won't even have to pretend to be interested."

The Bluett brothers swigged carefully from their bottles of Stella as they watched Kelly leave Ben and Pansy. After stopping to talk to a guy in a bear suit and a black girl covered in paper – it looked like Crystal Smith – they were surprised to see her come straight up to them.

"Hi there, I'm Kelly. I hear you two boys are going to be moving in to The Lofts."

Darren was glad they were wearing what they were as even beneath his elephant costume he could tell that Nathan's jaw had dropped to the floor. Close up, Kelly Danvers was a total babe. He couldn't believe his luck and thought to himself how he was going to enjoy every second of his task that night.

"Hi Kelly. You're right and this looks like an amazing place to live in. I'm Daniel by the way and this is my brother, Neil."

Before Kelly could respond, she was interrupted by Amber, who looked frankly insane, as well she ought to. She was accompanied by a walking garden carrying paper plates. Millie looked mad, too.

"Dinner is served, friends. To make sure you all get a chance to try every bit of the scrumptious food we have, we've prepared individual plates with a taster of everything. It is time to concentrate on some delicious healthy food."

Kelly Danvers was used to Millie by now. Amber was being very efficient – she coolly took Kelly's glass to refill it, swapping it for a plate of what looked like seventeen different types of tofu with a couple of carrot slices for decoration. Darren Bluett had never met Millie before. But her food was welcome – it kept his wits sharp. It still was quite a challenge getting those delicious nibbles into his mouth with just a cocktail stick to help them through the rather small slit in his elephant head costume.

"This is really tasty!"

He had to make a fuss of the food to distract Kelly, so that Amber had a chance to slip the GHB into her wine.

Amber couldn't believe the moment had finally come. She was spiking Kelly's drink at last. Millie couldn't believe so many people were devouring her food.

Entirely oblivious to what Amber was doing to her drink, Kelly gingerly tried some of the food on her plate. She chanced upon some curried yam. It was really rather tasty. She tried some grilled squid which had a delicate sweet chilli flavour, also delicious. Kelly turned round to face Millie who was still at the drinks table.

"Millie, this is absolutely lovely. The flavours are divine.

416

I hope this will be on your regular menu."

At first Millie thought Kelly Danvers was teasing her. Until she saw her eat another piece of food and seem to relish every bite. She couldn't believe that so many people were being so apparently nice. Maybe Kelly could yet be fully converted. Maybe she would be a militant fan of Millie's vegetarian food.

Amber moved back into view:

"A little sip of wine to wash it down?"

Kelly reached over for the paper cup with *Kelly – Holland Park* helpfully written on it. She was feeling reckless and daring. So unusually for her, she drank most of the cupful in one go.

Fortune had smiled on Harry Gumpert again. Sarah had arranged to go out for drinks with some friends who lived near her parents. She would be staying away that night. Their daughters were also safely ensconced with their grandparents. Harry was free – free to come to the party, free to pretend to be free, free as he half-aspired to be, when he was not benefitting from the advantages of coupledom. He was at the party, he was alone. He could spend some time with Monique.

Fortune had also had a bit of fun with him, though. Sarah had organised his costume. He was dressed as a Mountie in full uniform, astride a rather elaborate pantomime horse. Sarah had said that since they had first lived together in a flat in Canada Water she would be there in spirit with him. He wasn't exactly thrilled about her choice but he could hardly refuse to wear anything so ridiculous on the grounds that it might impair his ability to attract women.

He consoled himself with the thought that Monique was already attracted, and that there were sufficient stallion jokes that he could make to compensate for resembling a bad pantomime character.

On arriving at the party, Harry had trotted straight over to the drinks area to fix himself a Scotch, which obviously he had brought himself. He debated for a second and then tucked the half-bottle of Johnnie Walker back into his saddlebag. Before the inevitable pairing-off to stuff his horse-like member into Monique's tube entrance, he wanted to talk to Ben. After his performance in the meeting the other day, it would do Harry no harm to make sure he was positioning himself alongside the young hero. Harry smirked to himself as he remembered how he had outflanked Nicholas and said the right thing in the nick of time.

As he was about to turn away he was distracted by an angel walking towards him. He was taken aback. In a sea of ridiculous outfits, this one stood out a mile. The angel was wearing nothing bar a golden bikini, wings and a shimmering halo. She was the most beautiful vision that Harry had seen for quite some time – not since Monique had stepped away naked to get into the shower.

Harry had been in exactly the same situation at his sister's party just a few weeks earlier. He suddenly froze in recognition as Gabriela de Souza walked right up to him, grabbed a paper cup and lazily wrote *GABRIELA – ANGEL* on the side.

She caught him staring at her foolishly:

"Don't I know you from somewhere?"

Gabriela's easy manner and dazzling white smile made Harry feel even less at ease than last time he had met her. Did she really not remember where they had met? The meeting was seared on Harry's memory! Maybe she was just playing a game. However, in the event, she did remember him, even wearing the ridiculous horse legs. He wished he had not come as Canada Water.

Ah well. Harry deliberately took another sip of his Black Label before replying. The warming feeling down his throat helped his confidence return. He was going to show the girl who was boss.

"I believe you work for my sister's agency."

"Oh of course, Harry Gumpert. Nice to meet you again. I love the costume by the way."

Harry was heartened by the fact she seemed friendlier than the last time they had met. Gabriela had of course not forgotten Harry's presumption. She thought she would see how this occasion went. She would relish an opportunity to put this creepy older man in his place. If he did get a bit fresh with her she knew she was more than capable of crushing him. In fact she hoped he did try it on, as she would really, really enjoy knocking him back.

"Neil, eat the triangular one. Cajun. Frigging tasty! Just like that food we used to eat when we went to Louisiana last year."

Although Amber had been pretty rubbish at gleaning much information about Kelly other than the fact she liked going to 80s club nights in London, at least they knew where she was from. Mentioning their fabricated holiday to New Orleans achieved the desired effect. Kelly perked up as she heard her home state mentioned by the Elephant.

"You've been to Louisiana?"

"Yeah, but don't tell anyone, please. It's a bit embarrassing."

Kelly had liked the two boys so far, but what could they be insinuating? Emboldened by the wine, she could feel the pressure of the birth of an animated argument building inside her. How dare he call her home embarrassing!

"What do you mean?"

"Well, although you can't see our faces, me and Neil here are like fully grown men, yet last year we went on a family holiday to New Orleans. My Mum really wanted to go, and my Dad ain't so mobile these days, so me and Neil offered to take them there. You know, do the driving and stuff, wheel my Dad about, make sure they were safe."

Kelly visibly relaxed. No offence to Louisiana detected.

"Oh that is just so sweet! Sorry, I know guys don't like being called sweet, but Daniel, Neil that is just such a nice thing to do. I'm from Louisiana, by the way. Not New Orleans, but near there."

"No way! I loved Louisiana. We went on this Mississippi cruise to Baton Rouge because my Mum wanted to go on the river and my Dad wanted to see that warship museum thing there. People were so friendly in that place. We felt like we were at home. Amazing!"

Darren's research and delivery were working wonders. Kelly beamed.

"Daniel, that's exactly where I was born and brought up.

That's my home town. You are the first person I have met in Europe who has ever been to Baton Rouge. Most people haven't even heard of it. And you visited the USS Kidd! And you liked it. That calls for another drink. I need to toast the only people in this whole damned city who have been to my home town."

As they chatted about Louisiana, Kelly felt one of her extremely rare pangs of homesickness. Daniel brought up Brunet's Restaurant where they had had their special Cajun feast. It was a Danvers family favourite. When she had escaped from Ben to go and talk to an Elephant and a Castle, the last thing Kelly was expecting was to have a wonderful, nostalgic talk about Baton Rouge and her family with two complete strangers. The red wine was helping. Kelly felt abuzz tonight. Maybe it was the fact she was wearing a costume, or maybe it was the non-event with Ben, but she felt strangely free from her usual inhibitions. She really liked Daniel and was looking forward to seeing what he looked like underneath the Elephant head costume. And – *what the heck, it had been far, far too long* – under his clothes. Both he and his brother were well-built guys. As she listened to Daniel telling her about another episode from the holiday she wondered if it was trashy to fancy a guy whose face she hadn't even seen yet. She thought it was definitely trashy to fancy him and his brother. Together, too. Why not? Why on earth not? Tonight she was playing a tramp from Holland Park and she would do whatever her mind and body told her to. At that moment her mind was telling her she needed more wine.

"Bottle's empty, sorry Kelly."

"Daniel, Neil, I don't normally do this, but would you accompany a poor young Dutch girl up to her flat where she knows where her flatmate has hidden a very nice bottle of French red wine? I don't want to go alone. Who knows, I might get attacked."

Nathan Bluett had been watching his brother, aided by the GHB in the drink, play Kelly Danvers like a violin. Although he had felt confident beforehand, Darren could not believe how easy she had been. He hadn't even had to ask to go upstairs. He could tell by the body language the girl was already getting fresh but once upstairs she was going to get so much more than she bargained for.

Amber's revenge was working its nasty way through to its appalling conclusion.

Monique Mottin had been out all day and so even rushing had arrived fashionably late. She couldn't wait to see Harry, especially wearing that funny Canadian Mountie costume. He would look so cute. Millie caught her at the door.

"Oh, Monique, my goodness, I love your outfit!"

Monique was wearing a flowing Folies Bergères blue dress, with white fishnet stockings, stilettos and a long thick red feather boa. The outfit was topped off by a hat fashioned from a little plastic Eiffel Tower and a handbag covered in cardboard Eurostar wallets. Her make-up was somewhere between showgirl and call girl.

"Thank you, Millie. St Pancras may be famous for the Eurostar to Paris these days, but King's Cross belonged to the hookers way before then. You too look fabulous, and I think Green Park is just so in keeping with the reason that you are on this earth. But anyway, chérie, I must get a drink. See you later."

As Monique flounced exaggeratedly through the crowd, she suddenly espied Harry Gumpert right at the drinks table.

Excellent!

But – who was that amazing woman he was talking to?

Monique wasn't normally prone to jealousy. Jealousy was an onlooker, and it would usually rather admire her sang froid and confidence. Equally, however, sometimes it can't help itself or others. It rushes in like a late and unwelcome guest. Monique felt the unexpected clutch at her insides, the sudden twist in the gut that hurts. Even from the back, there was something about Harry's stance that told her he was paying too much attention to that perfect angel. She remembered how he used to look that way at her.

There was only one thing for it. She was suddenly desperate to find out more. She snaked her way through the crowd, sneaked right up to Harry's back and pretended to busy herself finding a paper cup, pen and drink.

He did not notice.

Eavesdroppers rarely hear anything they would really like to.

Harry was in full flow:

"Talking of costumes, I can't imagine anybody else doing justice to the concept of an angel as you do, Gabriela."

"Harry, you are so sweet. I was worried you might have been a little angry at me after the time at the agency party."

"What do you mean? Just because you didn't fall at

my feet the first time that I paid you a compliment? I understand all too well that a woman with class likes to pretend to show some resistance."

"Harry, you obviously can read me like a book."

Harry's head spun. *So he was right!* With his desire kindled by that inch of encouragement, Harry decided it was time to seal the deal before Monique arrived.

"So when can I take you for dinner, Gabriela? How about some time this week?"

Gabriela raised an eyebrow.

"Oh Harry, I would love to, but there's just one problem. No, two. No… three, actually."

She looked at the ceiling and ticked off her thoughts on her fingers.

"Firstly, I find you entirely unattractive – and so *inflated* with your own sense of invincibility that it makes me feel slightly nauseous."

She paused.

"Secondly, dating a dirty old man who has a wife and young children is so very tacky and desperate. And – let me see – what was the third reason? Oh yes. Yes. It's your French mistress, who happens to be standing behind you carefully listening to our conversation. Hello Monique! I love your outfit by the way! Anyway, toodle pip, as they say here in England. I should leave you two lovebirds together."

With the falsest of warm, heartfelt smiles that you would need to be a supermodel to carry off, Gabriela strode off to find Rubens, leaving Monique not sure whether to cry, punch Harry or run away to find Kelly. Uncertainty made

Monique look slightly wild for a second, like a demented Marie-Antoinette. She chose the last option.

By that time, Kelly had already exited the party with Darren and Nathan, with a last crack about whether Darren knew how to use that trunk of his or if it was just for show. Not wishing to cause a scene by bursting into tears or hitting Harry, Monique went over to Ben to ask him if he had seen her flatmate.

Initially Ben couldn't keep his eyes off Kelly with those two guys. He had noticed that she seemed to be getting very friendly with those strangers. But after Hartmut and Caroline caught up with him, he had been sorely distracted by a combination of Hartmut's wits and Caroline's tits. And red leather shorts. And whole general temptress costume. *Was this Hartmut's way of saying to him and Kelly that yes, he was into some kinky stuff?*

Pansy Ho, however, had been far more sharp-eyed than the young American. She had been suspicious of the two men in Elephant and Castle costumes ever since she heard they were moving into the Lofts – *yet had no inventory booked*. She decided it was time to voice her suspicions. She tugged at Ben's arm urgently:

"Ben? Ben. Kelly getting very friendly, quite flirty with those two boys, Elephant and Castle. Then I saw her finish wine, look for more but none there. She left room with two boys a few minutes ago. I thought she went to ladies or to get more food but starting to seem a bit strange. Those boys will be living here, but no inventory booked."

Monique was still shaking, but she zeroed in on the problem.

"That is very odd. My flatmate never usually gets flirty with boys so soon. That could be explained by the wine and the boys around these parts. Still… oh, I think I know where she has gone. I have half a case of very nice red wine that Kelly loves, up in the flat."

"Monique, you don't think Kelly would have taken two strangers up with her, do you?"

"I hope not, Ben. Think of my lovely things. They might steal something. And also… well… is she safe?"

Ben looked alarmed.

"The night I arrived in London poor Crystal was attacked just outside this place – and now Kelly might have taken two guys who nobody knows back up to her flat. This does not feel right. We need to check. Monique, please can you take me up there just to make sure she's OK?"

Ben's mind was suddenly racing. He didn't want to be a drama queen, but his heart told him something was wrong. And that he had to run to Kelly immediately.

Hartmut looked at Ben:

"Ben, I will accompany you. It will be better to have two men just in case there is something suspicious. Monique, kindly lend us your keys if you please. I think you should stay here with Caroline and Pansy. Let us not make a scene. It is not necessary. At least – not yet."

As Monique gave Ben her keys, he felt very grateful to Hartmut for offering to come with him. In a tight spot, Ben felt his German boss would be a good person to have at his side. Not least because he must be good at beatings and knots. Ben smiled nervously at Pansy, and privately uttered thanks that she had noticed what had happened, and almost ran off towards the lifts with Hartmut right behind him. As he got to the end of the corridor, he heard a familiar voice shout out at him. Sanjay had arrived.

"You're in a hurry, Ben! Never would have had *him* down as your type. This is some party."

"Alone in a lift with two sexy young men. Huh. I don't know which one of you to start with."

Kelly felt on top of the world as the lift took her up towards her flat and more wine. Daniel was such a great guy to talk to, and now she was looking at Neil's T-shirt; not too tight like all those gay bisexual whatever disco boys, but she could see there was one hunk of a man underneath. Maybe Neil was more the strong silent type. And they both seemed to be such *gentlemen*. Did she have the balls to make out with two brothers?

Darren had to almost physically restrain Nathan from jumping Kelly in the lift. He knew they had to get in the flat and then everything could take place fine. As they walked down towards her door, he thought how he was going to enjoy screwing that American girl. And then giving her a good slapping. He'd use part of her costume to stuff her mouth with so that she couldn't scream! Stupid bitch had swallowed all his lines about Louisiana right along with the GHB. Serves her right for crossing his sister.

"Have a look at the view when you come in. You're going to love it in this place, boys!"

Darren smiled as Kelly closed the door behind them.

"We keep our wine in our wardrobes. Don't ask. I'm sure the wine we want is in Monique's bedroom. You boys make yourself comfortable. Please take those masks off. And whatever else you want."

As Kelly opened the door of Monique's wardrobe, she heard the boys come into the room behind her. Suddenly the main light went off. Before she could react she felt four hands on her pulling her towards the bed. As Darren and Nathan started to pull and rip her clothes off, Kelly's sense of exhilaration and excitement became tinged with a touch of anxiety. As the boys became rougher with her, the GHB was no longer enough to convert it into an enjoyable experience.

Panic set in. Kelly realised that she had made a horrible mistake. When Darren stuffed her mouth full of her Dutch lacy top and then put what felt like a hood over her head she realised how horrible her mistake really was.

"Did you see Ben rush out of here with that older guy? He's getting a bit weird, that American."

Amber looked at Crystal Smith and then around the room.

"He is a bit strange you know, Crystal. Anyway, I'm just going to the loo."

The boys hadn't been gone long enough to do all that they needed to before that bloody American had rushed after her like a knight in shining armour. Amber needed to try and stop Ben from getting wherever he thought he was going. Amber Bluett simply didn't care that she should remain incognito.

Pansy Ho noticed Amber's sudden movement and the brief look of fury on her face.

"Very strange. Now Amber has just run out of the room."

Pansy, Caroline and Monique looked at each other. Things were getting weirder and weirder.

"OK. Caroline, Pansy, you two wait here. I have your number, Pansy; I'll call if I need you. I bet that crazy pute is going to my flat too!"

Before either of them could object, Monique was the next to flee the scene of the party, which was carrying merrily along. Happy as she could possibly be next to her Arthur, not even the normally observant Cornisha Burrows had noticed all the sudden exits.

"What is it tonight with everyone rushing around here?"

Monique stopped for a second and looked at Sanjay.

"Who did you see?"

"First Ben and that older guy, and then I heard some woman rushing along swearing in an Essex accent saying she was going to fucking get someone."

Monique looked at Sanjay again and took a quick decision.

"I need you to come with me. Quick. I'll explain on the way."

"Wow. Just as well I love a mystery. This party just gets better and better! And can I just say that I love your costume. I'm Sanjay, by the way."

Ben opened the door to Kelly's flat as silently as possible and crept inside. He could hear noises in the bedroom and they didn't sound good. When he and Hartmut got to the bedroom door and switched on the lights his worst fears were realised.

"Get off her now, you bastard!"

Ben rushed in and dragged a startled Darren off the bed. Nathan took a frantic look around and decided that attack was the best form of defence. He rushed at Hartmut Glick. In her dazed, terrified state Kelly could hear Darren and Ben struggling beside her. Nathan had got Hartmut in a headlock. The boy was so strong that Hartmut could hardly breathe. Hartmut realised he only had one chance; gasping for breath he reached and pulled off the metallic dildo from his costume, managed to reach up and brought it crashing down on Nathan's head. He hit him again and again. Nathan yelled out and stumbled away, falling over. Hartmut twisted out of his grip and retrieved his ever ready handcuffs from his pocket. He had been saving these for later, or for an unexpected moment of passion with the beautiful Caroline. Lord Baden-Powell would no doubt have wholly approved, in many ways, about the German's state of preparedness. Hartmut expertly locked Nathan's wrists together behind his back. The little *scheiße* wouldn't be going anywhere now.

Ben meanwhile was coming off second best with Darren. Ben may have been stronger than the Bluett boy, but Darren had learnt a thing or two about fighting in jail and was raining punches down on Ben, who could feel the blood flowing from his nose and lower lip. With a huge effort he launched himself at Darren and shoved him into the wall. Darren just managed to push him away and then pulled out a small flick-knife from his jeans.

430

"Just you try it, Americano. You so going down, then I'm going to make you watch what I do to her."

"Ben, catch!"

Just before Darren lunged at Ben with the knife, whilst still fighting to breathe properly Hartmut tossed his trusty metallic dildo at Ben who caught it and in one smooth movement brought it down hard on Darren's outstretched wrist. With a yelp of pain, Darren dropped the knife on the floor. With adrenaline rushing through him, Ben dropped the dildo and started punching Darren as hard as he could. The second punch landed right on Darren's chin. Ben felt a stab of pain as he realised that he wasn't exactly an expert boxer and he had probably just broken a bone in his hand. Fortunately, the pain seemed worse for the boy from Essex. Ben's inexpert punch had landed so hard that it was the last thing Darren was conscious of as he fell to the floor.

With pain searing through his head and right hand, Ben looked over at Kelly lying almost naked on the bed, gagged, bleeding, and with a hood over her head. Hartmut was kneeling on the far side of the bed, still panting for breath.

"You fucking bastard! What have you done to my brothers?"

Amber Bluett had not been far behind Ben and Hartmut. She had found the door open, rushed in and immediately grabbed a large carving knife from the rack in the kitchen. Ben turned around to see the crazy woman dressed up as a crazy woman with a huge knife in her hand, rushing at him. She was not six feet away from him. Ben felt fear. He thought that this time he really was going to get stabbed. He could hardly defend himself in his state, with a broken hand to boot. But just then a black high heel shoe flew through the bedroom door. With almost uncanny precision, it hit Amber on the back of the head with the point of the stiletto. It unbalanced her crazy rush. It was followed by a vase that crashed on her like the plates at a Greek wedding. And so the third member of the Bluett family collapsed on the floor. Sanjay lept on top of her and pinned her down.

"Howzat?" he asked cheerily, "I may not have made it as a professional, but I had the best bowling figures in my local cricket team three years running, you know."

And so the Bluett family were all out for a duck.

It was not the most typical crime scene.

Firstly, the reception area of the Castle Lofts looked like something Lewis Carroll might have pictured in his more acceptable imaginings – the whole party had flooded into the area upon hearing of the happening. Cuthbert Green, who had been sent to lead the investigation, was particularly struck by six heavily made-up large men in identical pink check dresses, high heels and blond wigs.

The first person he saw upstairs was a very pretty woman in a Moulin Rouge outfit wearing an Eiffel Tower model on her head. On the sofa was a girl, sobbing, wearing a dressing gown and a rather incongruous pair of high-heeled clogs. She was being comforted by a nearly naked man covered in silver body paint, who seemed to be nursing an injured hand and who had an impressive spread of dried blood over most of his face. Others milling around included a lady who did a passable impression of a young-ish Queen Victoria, placing a large elephant's head down in the middle of the room.

The three aggressors had been neatly assembled side by side on the floor of the living room, on the instruction of Queen Victoria, who introduced herself in a business-like manner as Cornisha Burrows. She had arrived shortly after the attack had taken place.

Cuthbert had been surprised to find that the first suspect, Nathan Bluett, was already handcuffed.

"I thought we were the first police on the scene?"

"You were, officer. Those belong to me. Hartmut Glick, at your service. If I may have them back when this is done? I rather like that pair. Very well made."

The second suspect, Darren Bluett, who was still rather dazed, had his wrists tied somewhat inexpertly with the pigtails of a long blonde wig which seemed to match the six others that he had just seen in the foyer a few moments earlier.

"Hi, the wig's mine officer. Sanjay Patel, at your service. You can see it matches the rest of my costume. You may keep it though. It's not real hair."

The third suspect, Amber Bluett, was tied up in a straitjacket. Staring malevolently at the room, Cuthbert wondered whether she was in fancy dress or not.

In front of the three suspects, also very neatly laid out were the elephant's head, a small rubber castle, a flick-knife, a large carving knife, a metallic sex toy and a black woman's stiletto shoe.

"Officer, I do apologise for not leaving all the objects in the place that they fell. It was in a fit of absent-mindedness trying to return to some semblance of normality that I wanted to organise the offensive items. Hartmut scolded me for tampering with the evidence. At least I was wearing gloves."

Cuthbert had never received a confession from Queen Victoria before. It actually made a rather refreshing change from most of the grim scenes which he investigated. Surveying the items arranged in front of the alleged suspects he thought he would call the scene *Phallus in Wonderland*.

EPILOGUE

Christmas presence

It was a most beautiful Christmas Day.

Ben wondered if he had ever imagined passing the traditional feast day like this – sitting next to a beautiful girlfriend like Kelly on the sofa in Hartmut Glick's luxurious London penthouse. He looked round at all the people he had met over the past few months in Britain. After the dramatic happenings of the past few weeks they had decided that this Christmas they would all stay together rather than running off to a more conventional family gathering elsewhere.

Cornisha Burrows and Arthur Bilks were living proof that older people in love could actually be rather endearing. Ben still preferred not to think about what might happen when they were alone.

Kerwin Bold was still a new friend, but he indisputably brought essential London cool to any party. Ben had got to know him over time, and he was impressed by Kerwin's quiet air of assurance. He certainly brought a smile to the face of Crystal Smith. Ben liked him. He had already made a note to ask Kerwin for some tips, as Ben had never quite got the cool thing right.

Rubens Ribeiro had come along with Sanjay Patel. Rubens had opened a door to an entirely new world for Ben. It may not be one Ben wanted to explore any further, but he knew that he had been fortunate to meet Rubens. He had had some of the strangest and most exciting moments of his life with the irrepressible Brazilian. Sanjay, of course, who Ben had cursed for his ill-judged comments in front of Kelly at SBK's cocktail party, had more than redeemed himself with his cricketer's stiletto bowl, straight at the knife-wielding Amber. Sanjay had quite possibly saved Ben's life.

Monique Mottin was deep in conversation with Alex and Jamal. After the scene with Gabriela de Souza at the party, she had finally seen that Harry Gumpert was not worth it. In time honoured fashion, she had told him to get lost. In time-honoured fashion, she was building her confidence up again.

Millie Myers' business had benefited most from the party. It had a new lease of life, and she was grateful. She was sitting next to Hartmut Glick and Caroline Napier Jones. Ben wondered what they could possibly be discussing. Vegetarian bondage? Leather-free harnesses? Actually, Millie had been musing that she was relieved that everyone had had a chance to eat her canapés before all the unpleasantness had happened.

Another curious couple in seemingly deep conversation were Pansy Ho and Gabriela de Souza. Maybe they were organising an inventory at the Lofts? Gabriela moving in would be a bonus. A person of beauty brings at least as much joy as a thing might. Gabriela had it all.

Each of those present had touched Ben in some way.

But the person who was filling his heart to the brim was the girl from Baton Rouge sitting next to him.

Even with all the alcohol and drugs inside her, Kelly had been aware that it was Ben who had rushed in to save her. Her very own knight in shining body paint. He had stopped something dreadful from happening and had fearlessly got injured in the process. She had decided that she didn't care any more if Ben might have been partial to a little cock every so often. He had proved beyond doubt that he would be there for her. She had finally allowed herself to fall in love with him.

As they toasted the day, with Jamal politely raising a glass to the Christian festival, Ben wondered what adventures his next year would bring and what further delights the city would gift him. He loved London. It seemed as if right now it loved him back.

Amber Bluett was having a rather less good Christmas in Holloway Prison. Sharing a cell with an evil-smelling lump of a woman who had never heard of either make-up or soap was a woe she placed directly at the door of that bitch Kelly Danvers and her bastard boyfriend Ben Barlettano. However, the experience was giving Amber plenty of time for her hatred to simmer and mature. As she thought of how she was missing out on a family Christmas – and especially missing the turkey with all the trimmings that doubtless the two Americans would now be tucking into – she consoled herself with the thought that, unlike turkey, revenge was a dish best served cold.

It was not over just yet.

Contact us:

melandtimbooks.com